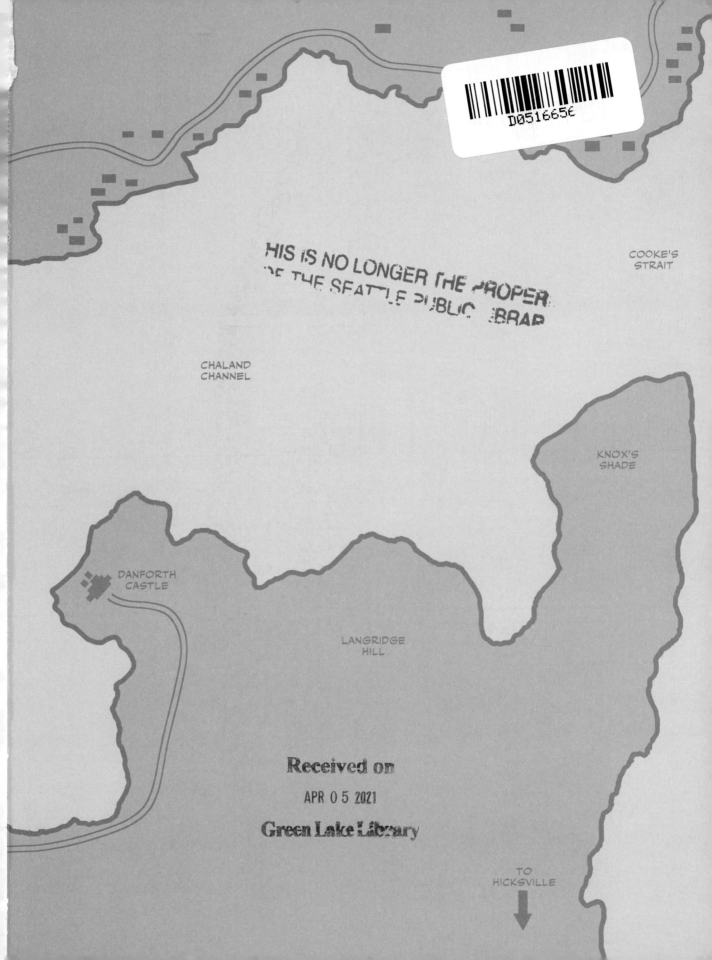

COOKE'S
STRAIT

CHALAND
CHANNEL

KNOX'S
SHADE

DANFORTH
CASTLE

LANGRIDGE
HILL

TO
HICKSVILLE

The Inkberg Enigma

FOR PIPPI, HAZEL AND HUCK

This edition first published in 2020 by Gecko Press
PO Box 9335, Wellington 6141, New Zealand
info@geckopress.com

© Jonathan King 2020
© Gecko Press Ltd 2020

Distributed in the United States and Canada by Lerner Publishing Group, lernerbooks.com
Distributed in the United Kingdom by Bounce Sales and Marketing, bouncemarketing.co.uk
Distributed in Australia and New Zealand by Walker Books Australia, walkerbooks.com.au

Jonathan King acknowledges the generous support of Creative New Zealand for this book
Gecko Press acknowledges the generous support of Creative New Zealand

Printed in China by Everbest Printing Co. Ltd, an accredited ISO 14001 & FSC-certified printer

ISBN: 978-1-776572-66-3

For more curiously good books, visit geckopress.com

The Inkberg Enigma

JONATHAN KING

GECKO PRESS

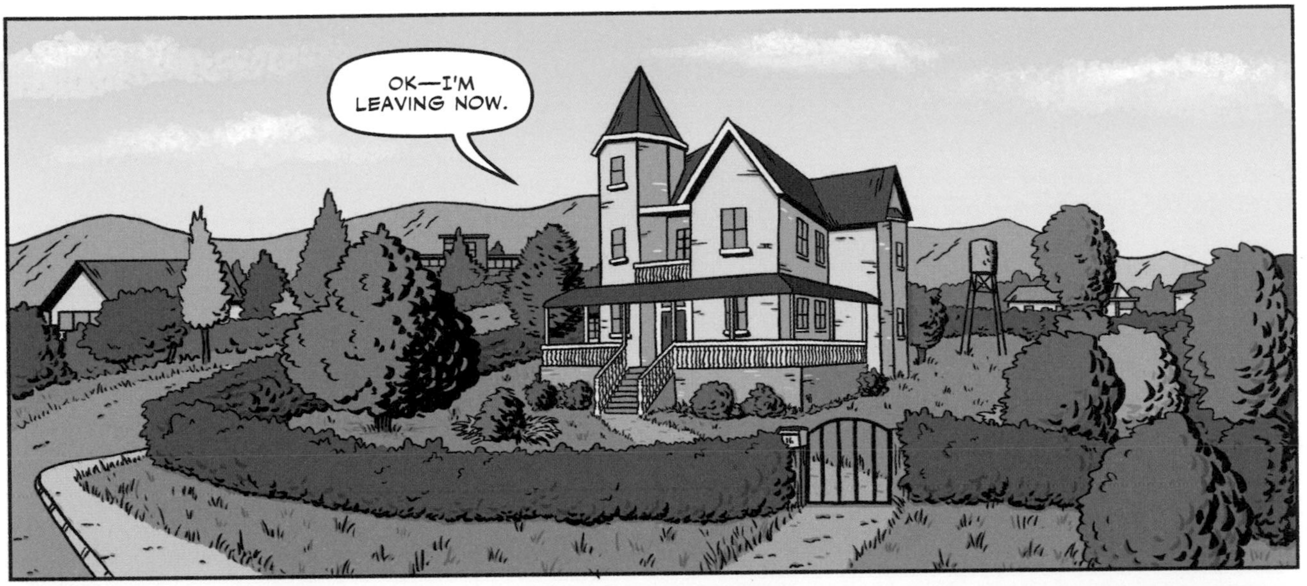
OK—I'M LEAVING NOW.

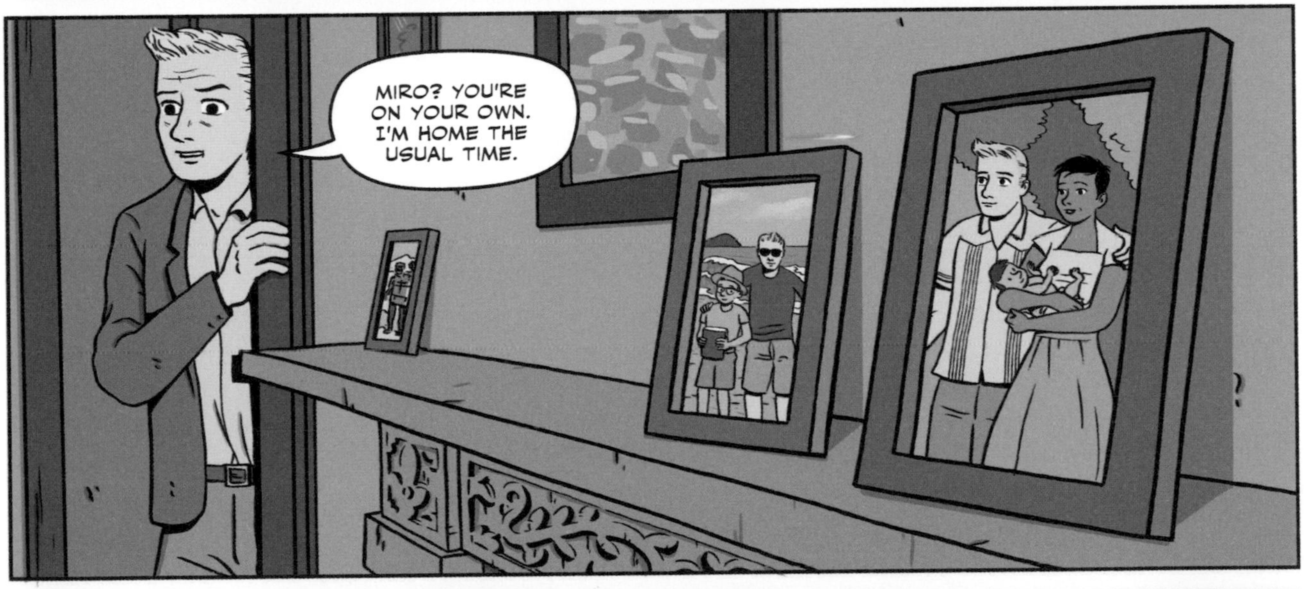
MIRO? YOU'RE ON YOUR OWN. I'M HOME THE USUAL TIME.

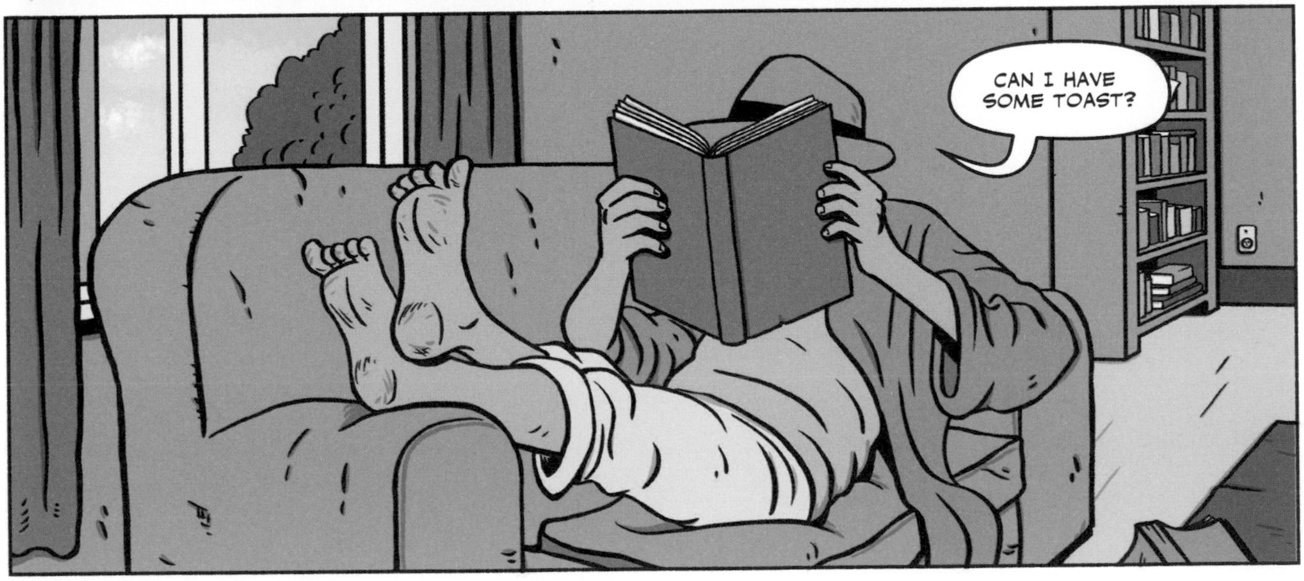
CAN I HAVE SOME TOAST?

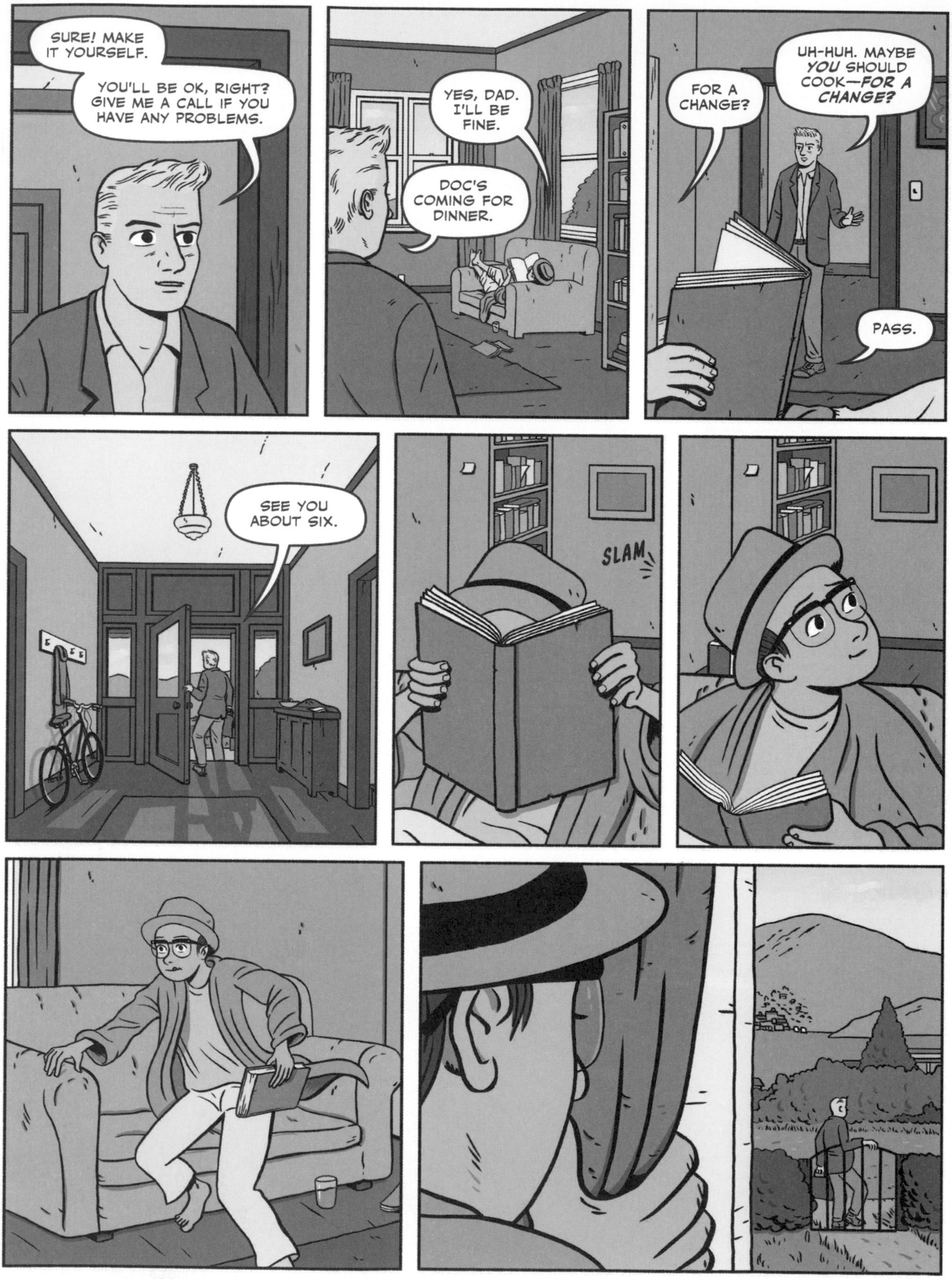
SURE! MAKE IT YOURSELF.
YOU'LL BE OK, RIGHT? GIVE ME A CALL IF YOU HAVE ANY PROBLEMS.
YES, DAD. I'LL BE FINE.
DOC'S COMING FOR DINNER.
FOR A CHANGE?
UH-HUH. MAYBE YOU SHOULD COOK—FOR A CHANGE?
PASS.
SEE YOU ABOUT SIX.
SLAM

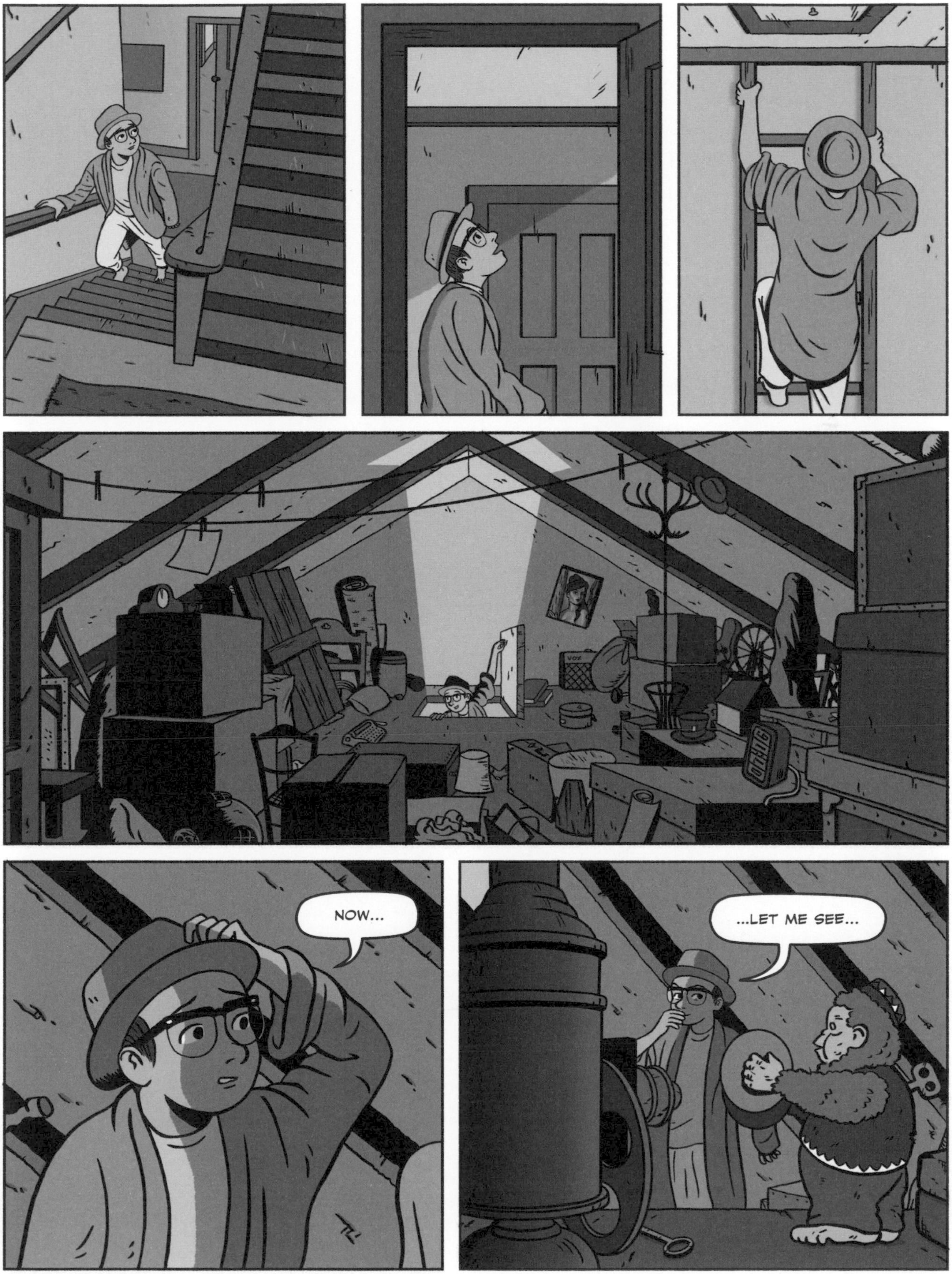
NOW...
...LET ME SEE...

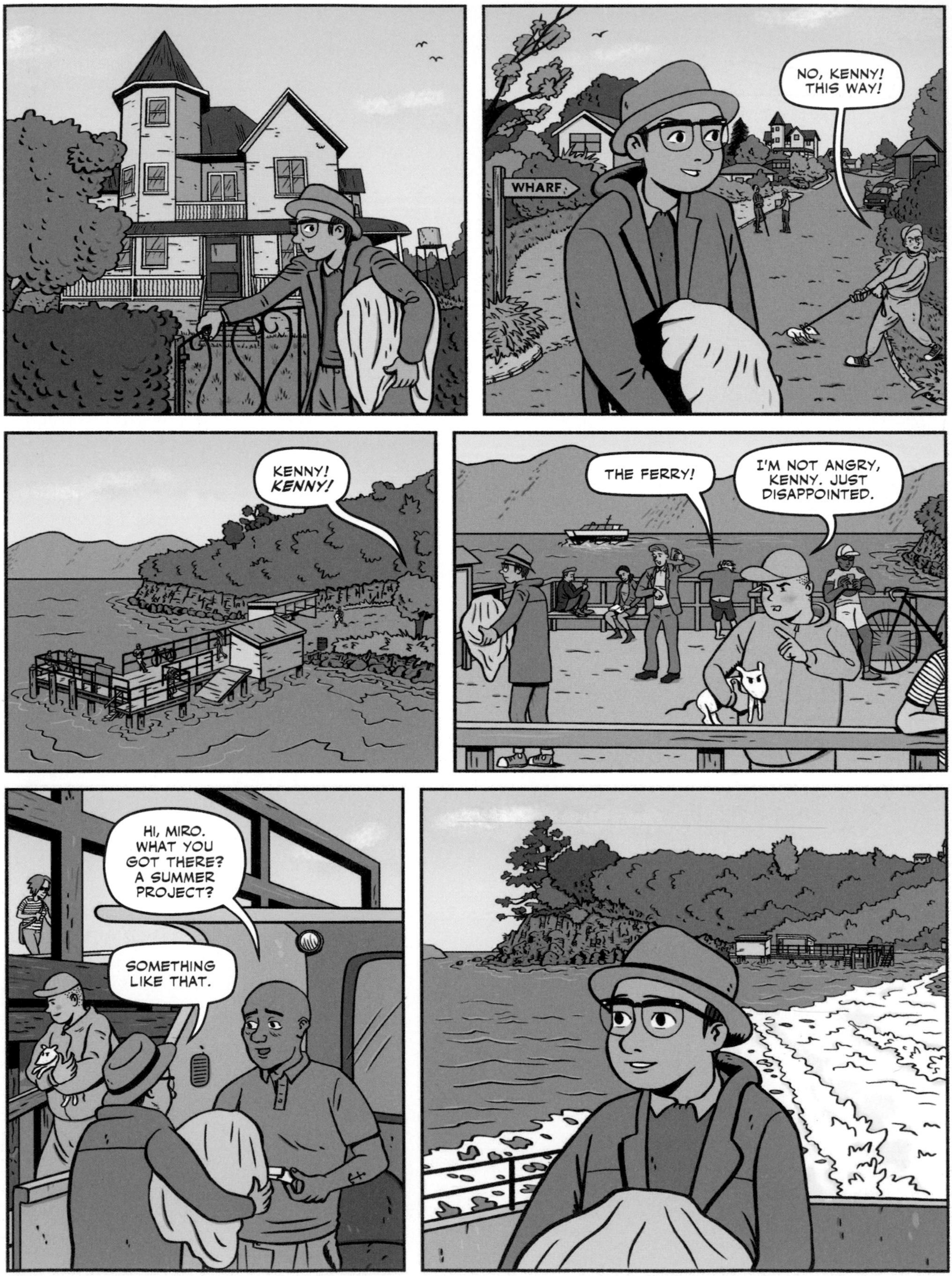
WHARF
NO, KENNY! THIS WAY!
KENNY! KENNY!
THE FERRY!
I'M NOT ANGRY, KENNY. JUST DISAPPOINTED.
HI, MIRO. WHAT YOU GOT THERE? A SUMMER PROJECT?
SOMETHING LIKE THAT.

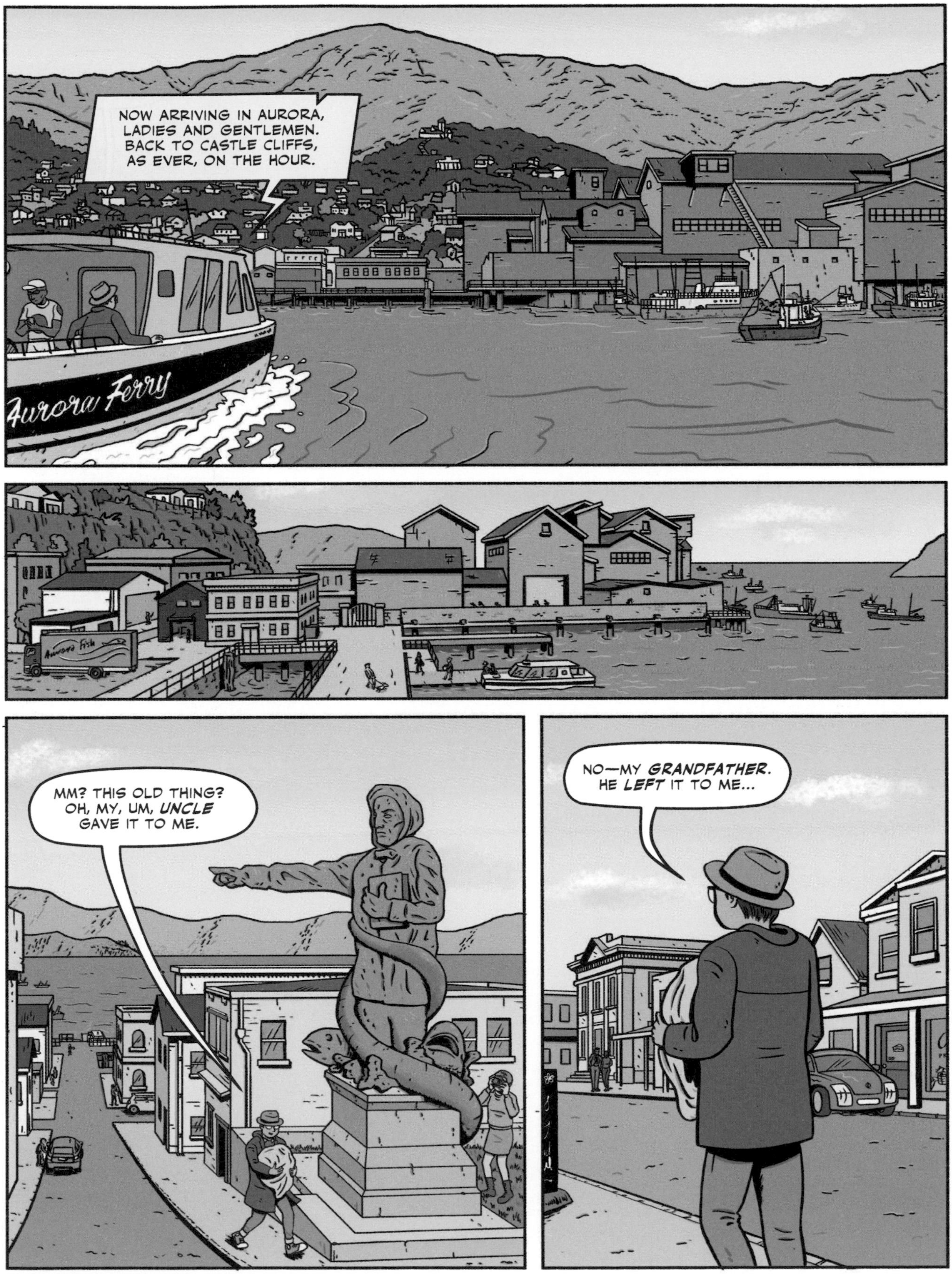
NOW ARRIVING IN AURORA, LADIES AND GENTLEMEN. BACK TO CASTLE CLIFFS, AS EVER, ON THE HOUR.
Aurora Ferry
MM? THIS OLD THING? OH, MY, UM, *UNCLE* GAVE IT TO ME.
NO—MY *GRANDFATHER*. HE *LEFT* IT TO ME...

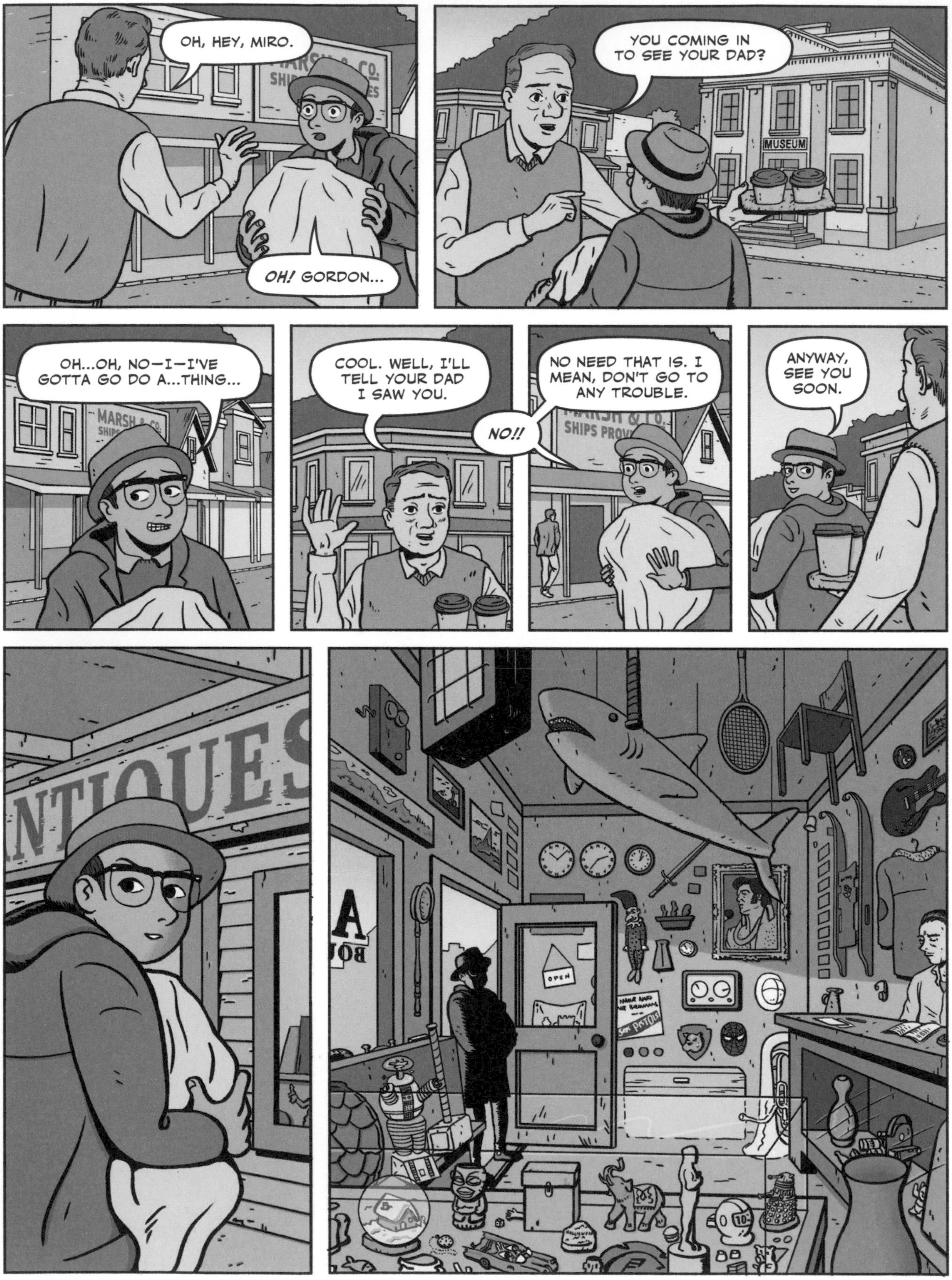

OH, HEY, MIRO.
OH! GORDON...
YOU COMING IN TO SEE YOUR DAD?
MUSEUM
OH...OH, NO—I—I'VE GOTTA GO DO A...THING...
COOL. WELL, I'LL TELL YOUR DAD I SAW YOU.
NO!!
NO NEED THAT IS. I MEAN, DON'T GO TO ANY TROUBLE.
ANYWAY, SEE YOU SOON.
OPEN

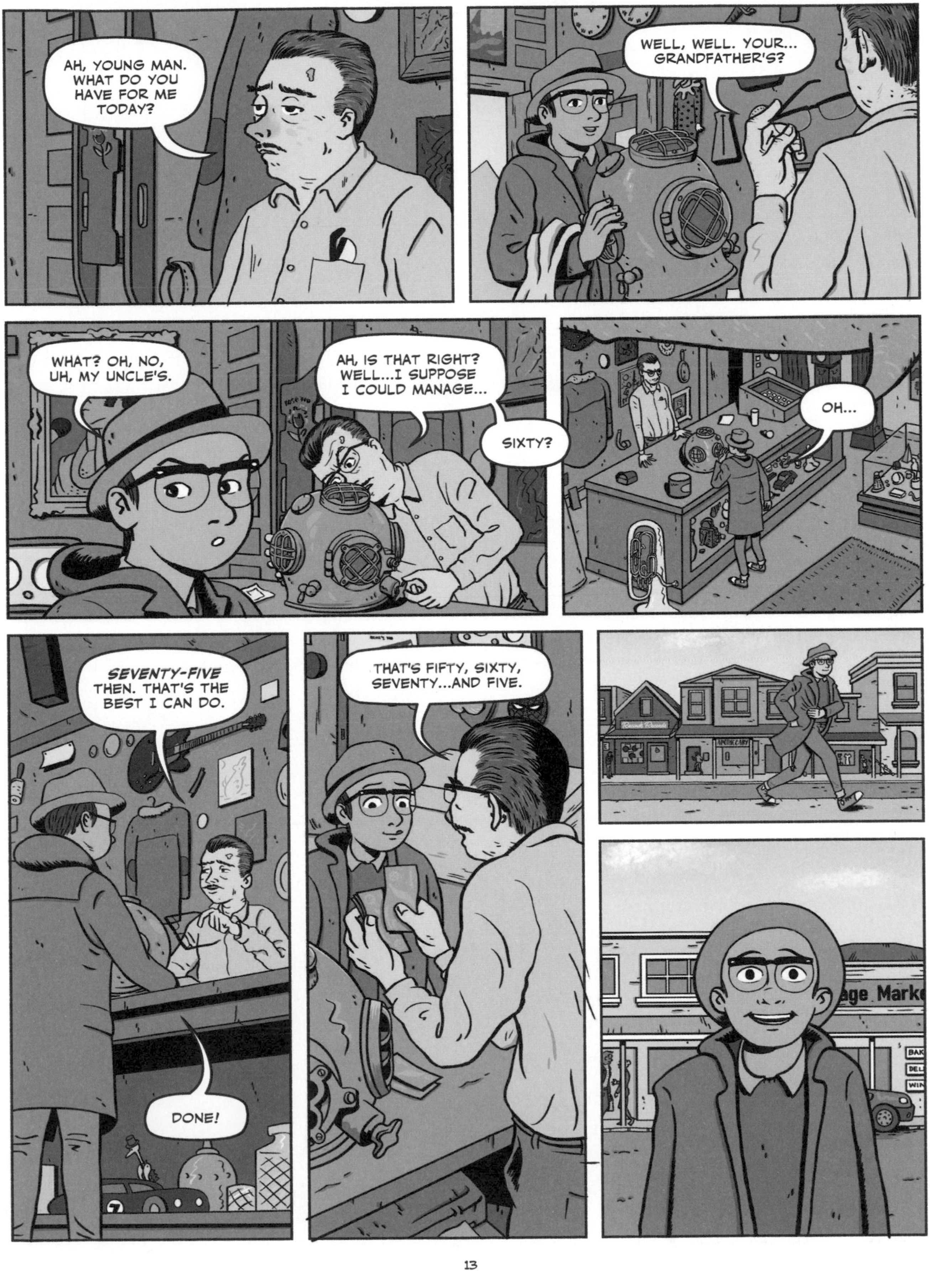
AH, YOUNG MAN. WHAT DO YOU HAVE FOR ME TODAY?
WELL, WELL. YOUR... GRANDFATHER'S?
WHAT? OH, NO, UH, MY UNCLE'S.
AH, IS THAT RIGHT? WELL...I SUPPOSE I COULD MANAGE...
SIXTY?
OH...
SEVENTY-FIVE THEN. THAT'S THE BEST I CAN DO.
DONE!
THAT'S FIFTY, SIXTY, SEVENTY...AND FIVE.
APOTHECARY

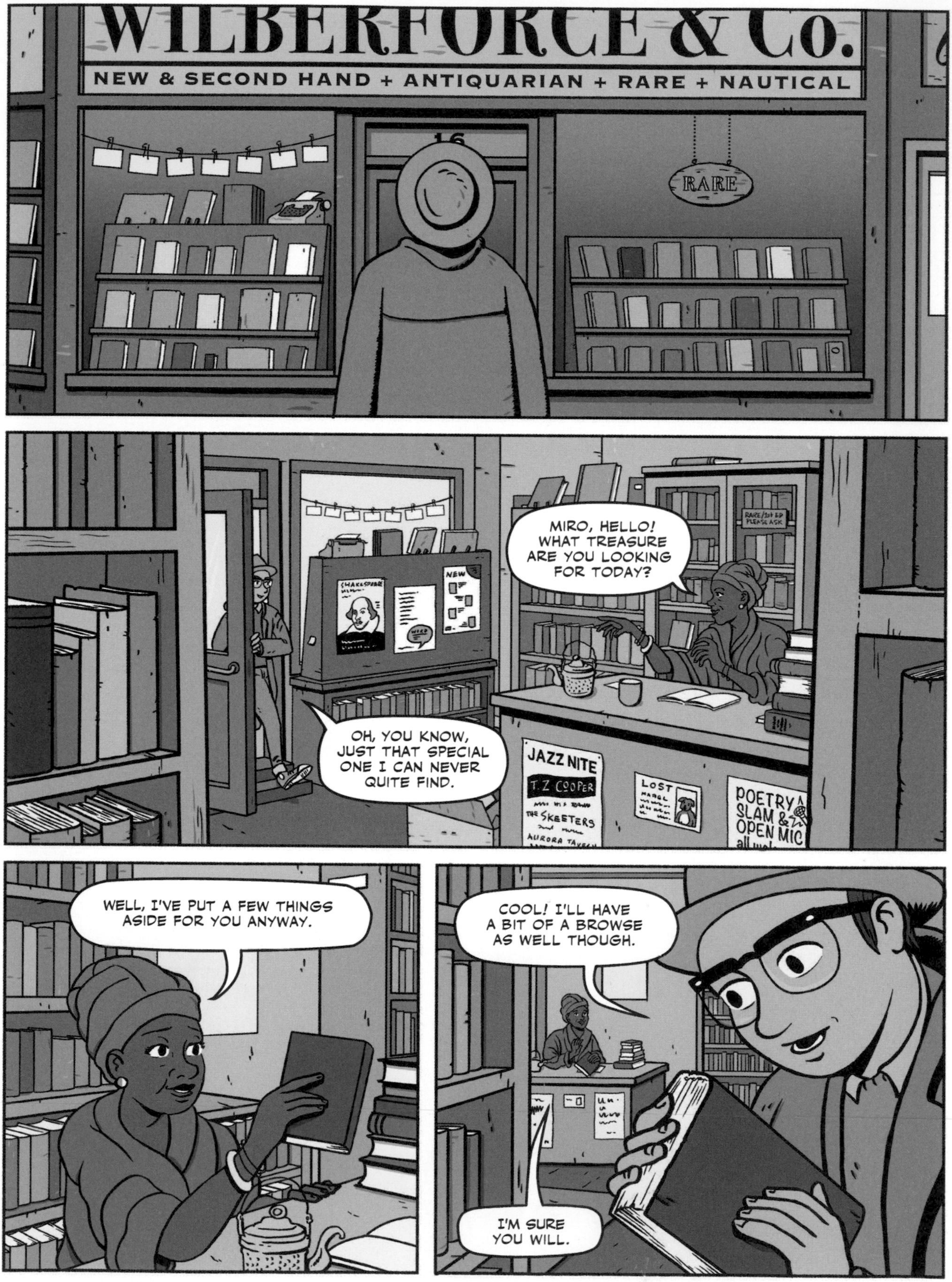
WILBERFORCE & Co.
NEW & SECOND HAND + ANTIQUARIAN + RARE + NAUTICAL
16
RARE
MIRO, HELLO! WHAT TREASURE ARE YOU LOOKING FOR TODAY?
OH, YOU KNOW, JUST THAT SPECIAL ONE I CAN NEVER QUITE FIND.
SHAKESPEARE
NEW
JAZZ NITE
T.Z COOPER
THE SKEETERS
LOST
POETRY SLAM & OPEN MIC
WELL, I'VE PUT A FEW THINGS ASIDE FOR YOU ANYWAY.
COOL! I'LL HAVE A BIT OF A BROWSE AS WELL THOUGH.
I'M SURE YOU WILL.

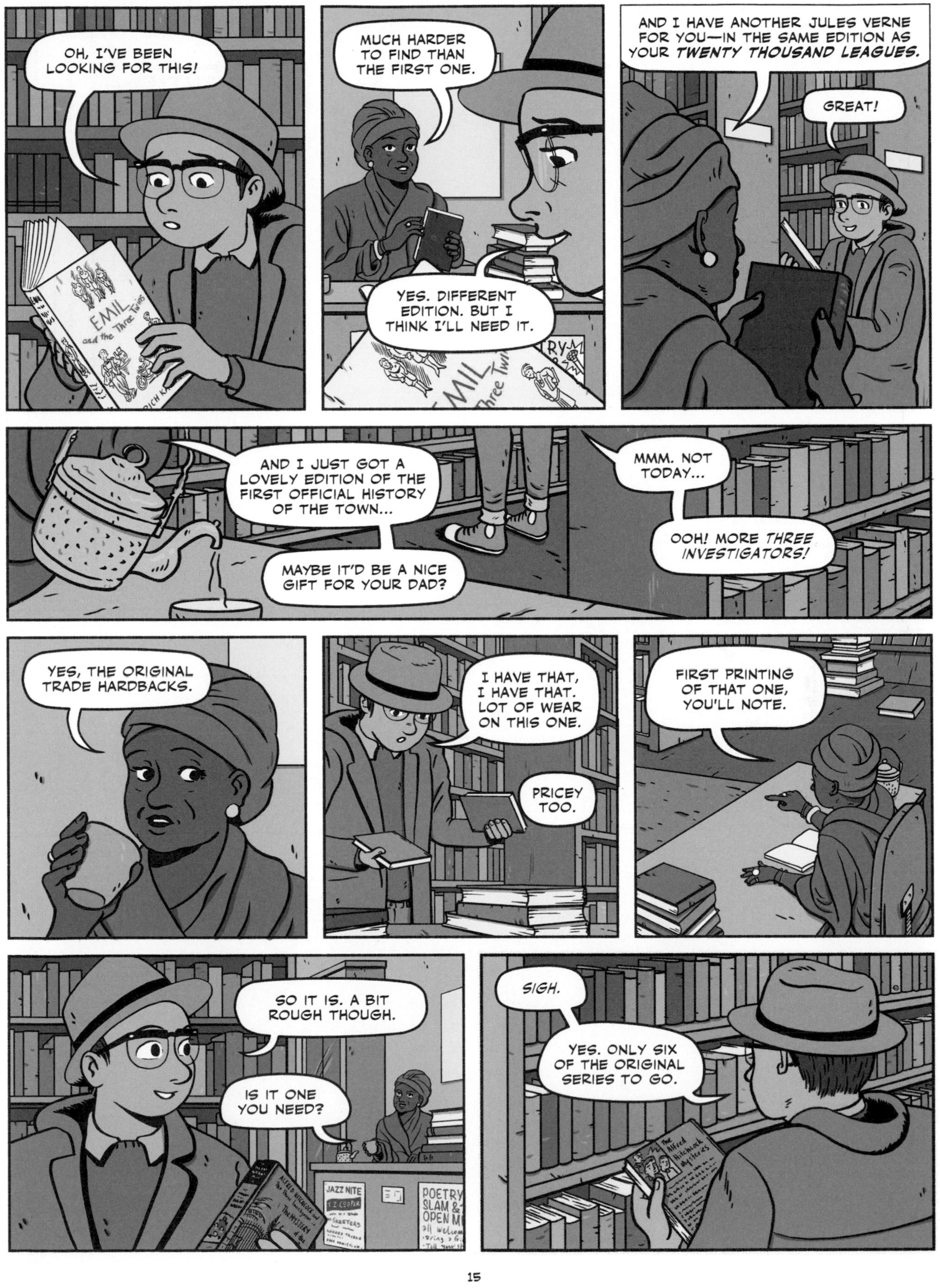

OH, I'VE BEEN LOOKING FOR THIS!
EMIL and the Three Twins
MUCH HARDER TO FIND THAN THE FIRST ONE.
YES. DIFFERENT EDITION. BUT I THINK I'LL NEED IT.
AND I HAVE ANOTHER JULES VERNE FOR YOU—IN THE SAME EDITION AS YOUR *TWENTY THOUSAND LEAGUES.*
GREAT!
AND I JUST GOT A LOVELY EDITION OF THE FIRST OFFICIAL HISTORY OF THE TOWN...
MAYBE IT'D BE A NICE GIFT FOR YOUR DAD?
MMM. NOT TODAY...
OOH! MORE *THREE INVESTIGATORS!*
YES, THE ORIGINAL TRADE HARDBACKS.
I HAVE THAT, I HAVE THAT. LOT OF WEAR ON THIS ONE.
PRICEY TOO.
FIRST PRINTING OF THAT ONE, YOU'LL NOTE.
SO IT IS. A BIT ROUGH THOUGH.
IS IT ONE YOU NEED?
JAZZ NITE
POETRY SLAM & OPEN MI
SIGH.
YES. ONLY SIX OF THE ORIGINAL SERIES TO GO.
The Alfred Hitchcock Mysteries

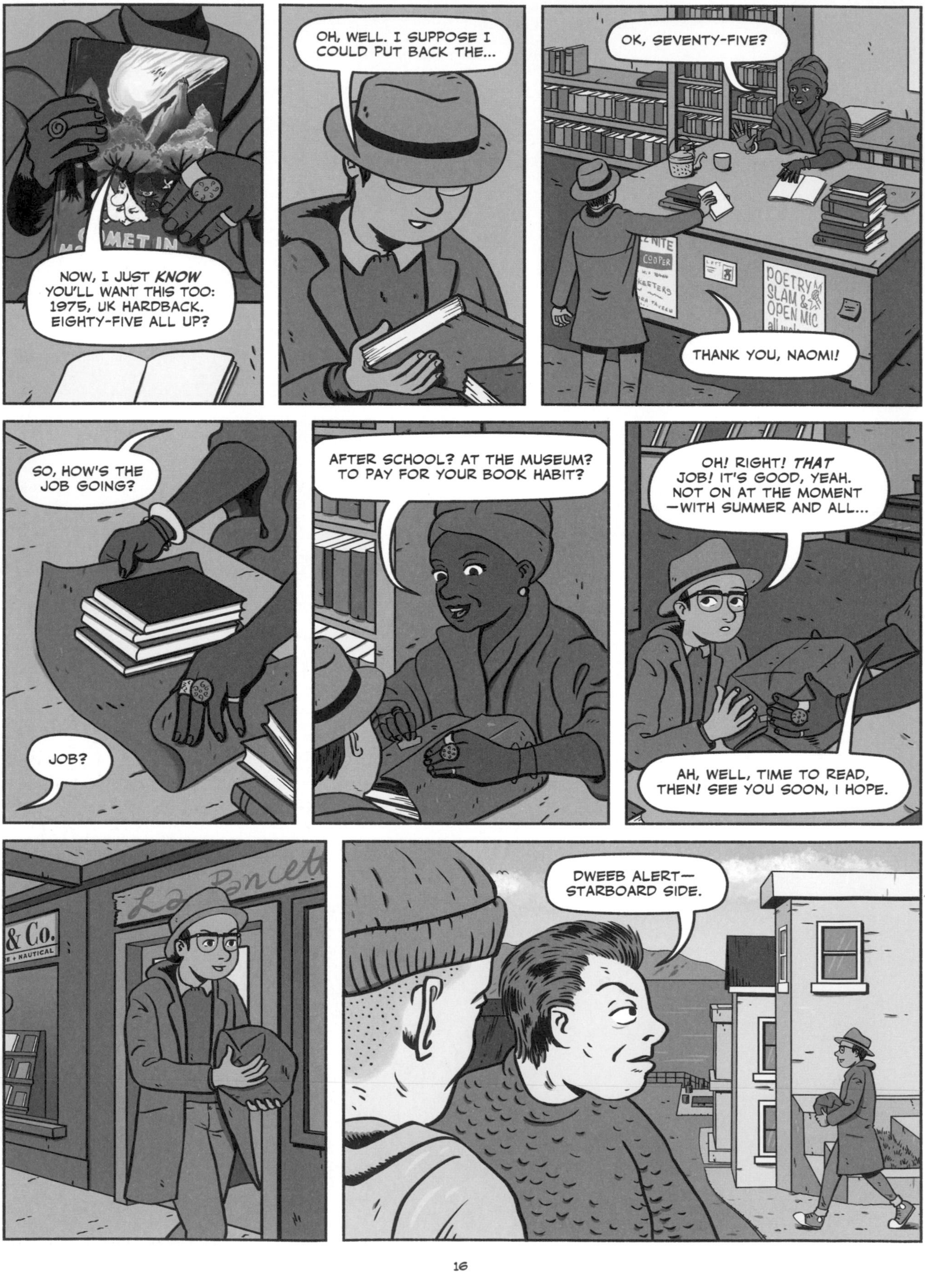

NOW, I JUST *KNOW* YOU'LL WANT THIS TOO: 1975, UK HARDBACK. EIGHTY-FIVE ALL UP?
OH, WELL. I SUPPOSE I COULD PUT BACK THE...
OK, SEVENTY-FIVE?
POETRY SLAM & OPEN MIC
THANK YOU, NAOMI!
SO, HOW'S THE JOB GOING?
JOB?
AFTER SCHOOL? AT THE MUSEUM? TO PAY FOR YOUR BOOK HABIT?
OH! RIGHT! *THAT* JOB! IT'S GOOD, YEAH. NOT ON AT THE MOMENT —WITH SUMMER AND ALL...
AH, WELL, TIME TO READ, THEN! SEE YOU SOON, I HOPE.
& Co.
DWEEB ALERT— STARBOARD SIDE.

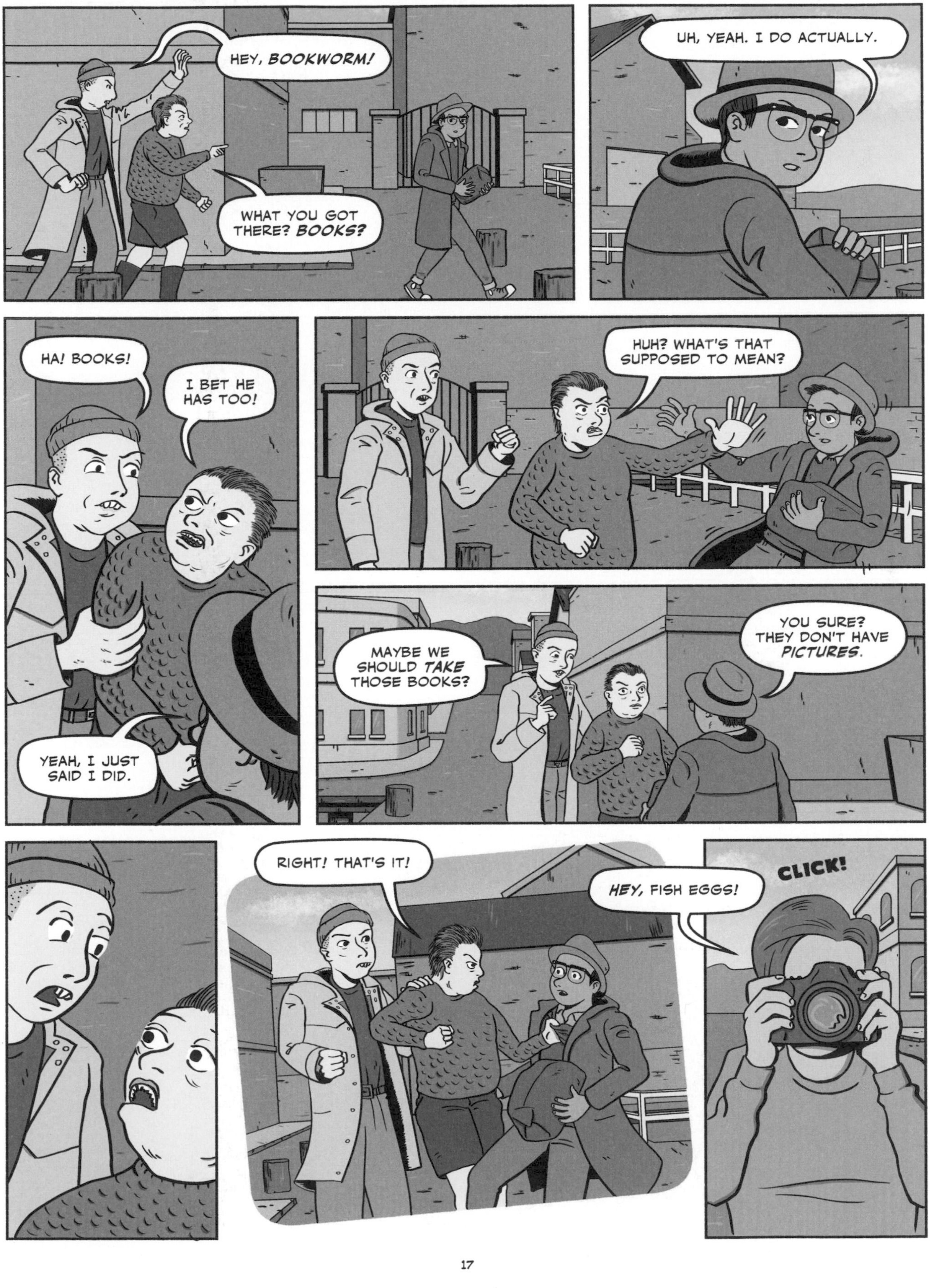
HEY, BOOKWORM!
WHAT YOU GOT THERE? BOOKS?
UH, YEAH. I DO ACTUALLY.
HA! BOOKS!
I BET HE HAS TOO!
YEAH, I JUST SAID I DID.
HUH? WHAT'S THAT SUPPOSED TO MEAN?
MAYBE WE SHOULD TAKE THOSE BOOKS?
YOU SURE? THEY DON'T HAVE PICTURES.
RIGHT! THAT'S IT!
HEY, FISH EGGS!
CLICK!

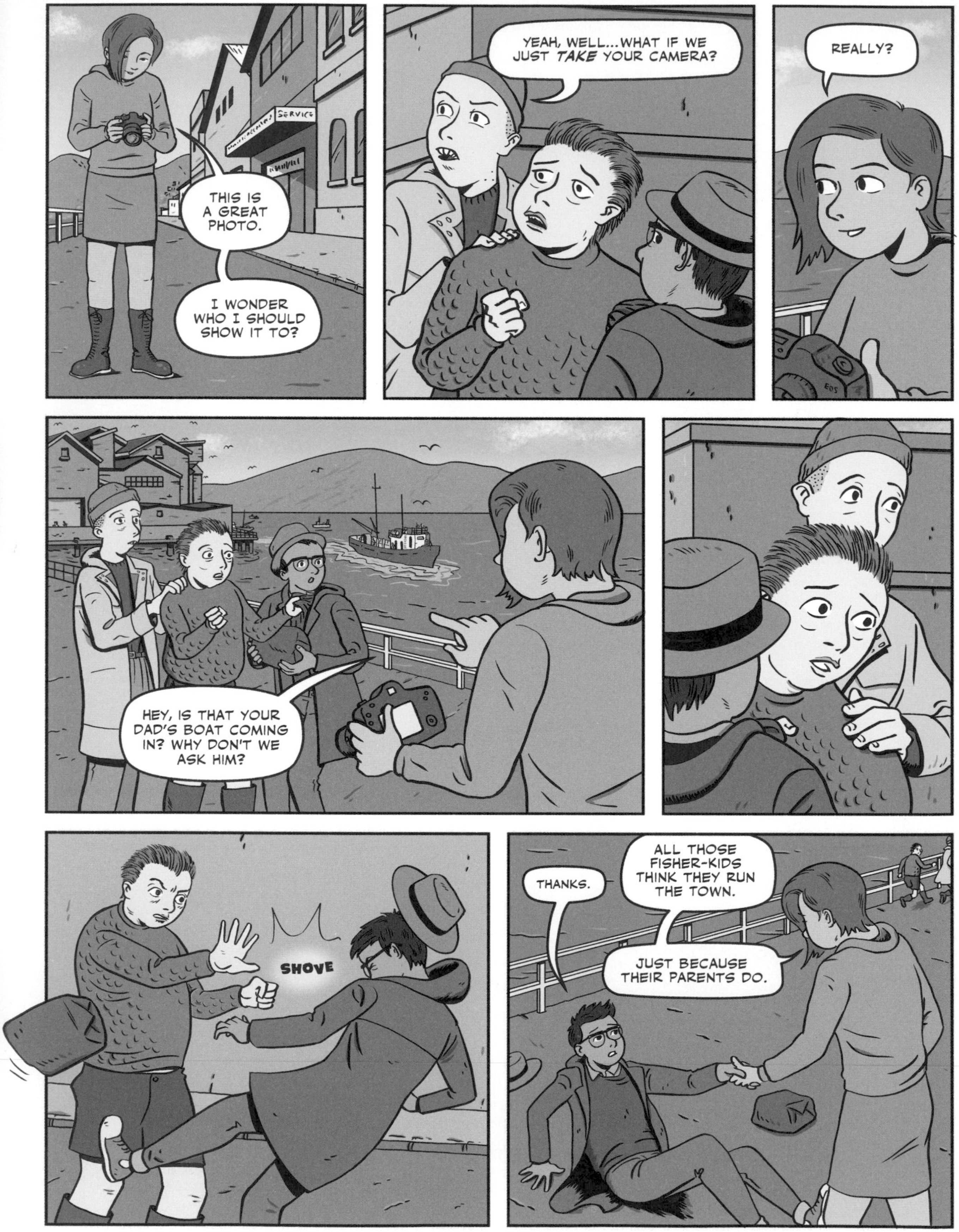
THIS IS A GREAT PHOTO.
I WONDER WHO I SHOULD SHOW IT TO?
YEAH, WELL...WHAT IF WE JUST *TAKE* YOUR CAMERA?
REALLY?
HEY, IS THAT YOUR DAD'S BOAT COMING IN? WHY DON'T WE ASK HIM?
SHOVE
THANKS.
ALL THOSE FISHER-KIDS THINK THEY RUN THE TOWN.
JUST BECAUSE THEIR PARENTS DO.

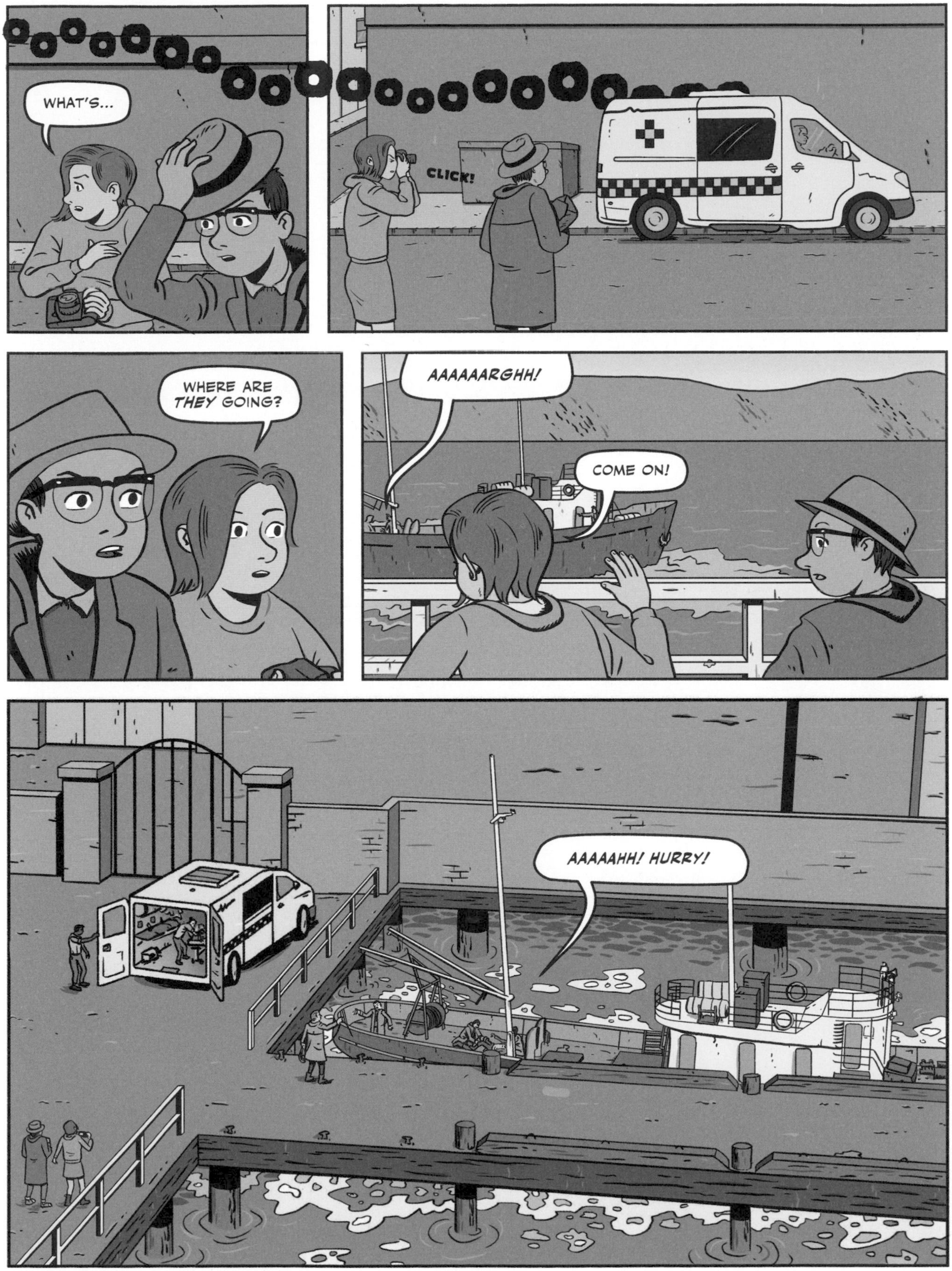
WHAT'S...
CLICK!
WHERE ARE *THEY* GOING?
AAAAAARGHH!
COME ON!
AAAAAHH! HURRY!

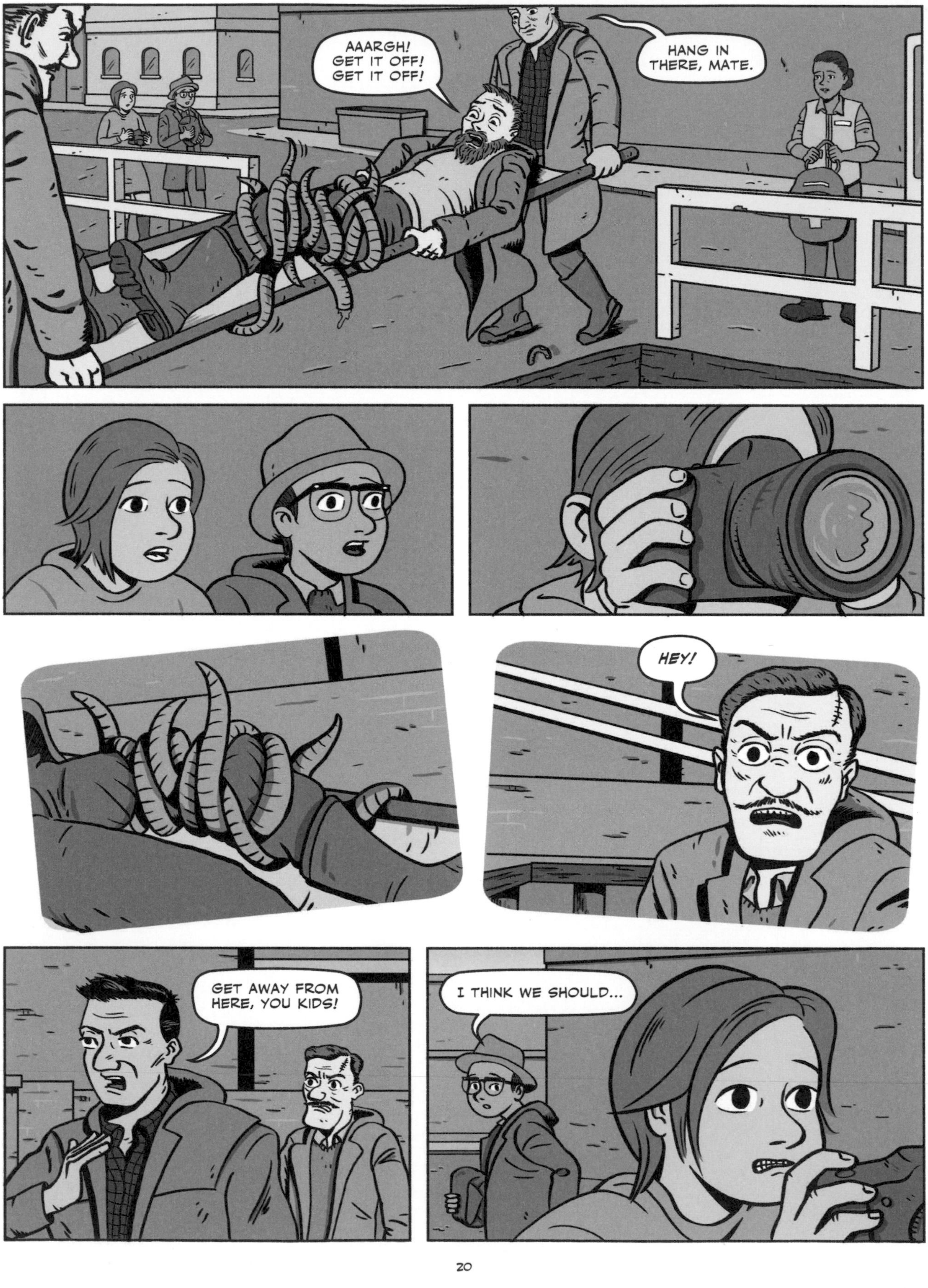
AAARGH!
GET IT OFF!
GET IT OFF!
HANG IN THERE, MATE.
HEY!
GET AWAY FROM HERE, YOU KIDS!
I THINK WE SHOULD...

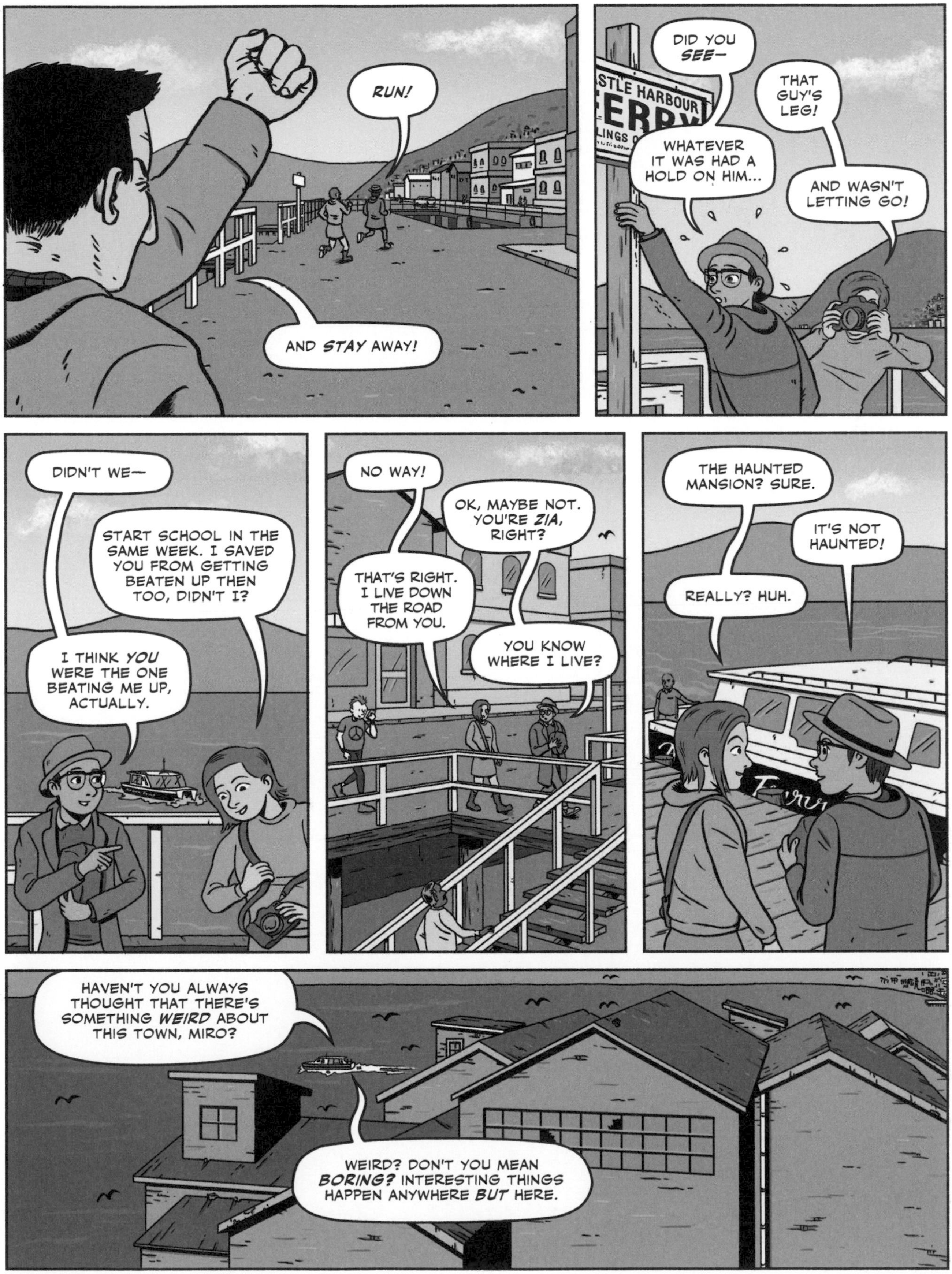
RUN!
AND STAY AWAY!
STLE HARBOUR
FERRY
DID YOU SEE—
THAT GUY'S LEG!
WHATEVER IT WAS HAD A HOLD ON HIM...
AND WASN'T LETTING GO!
DIDN'T WE—
START SCHOOL IN THE SAME WEEK. I SAVED YOU FROM GETTING BEATEN UP THEN TOO, DIDN'T I?
I THINK YOU WERE THE ONE BEATING ME UP, ACTUALLY.
NO WAY!
OK, MAYBE NOT. YOU'RE ZIA, RIGHT?
THAT'S RIGHT. I LIVE DOWN THE ROAD FROM YOU.
YOU KNOW WHERE I LIVE?
THE HAUNTED MANSION? SURE.
IT'S NOT HAUNTED!
REALLY? HUH.
HAVEN'T YOU ALWAYS THOUGHT THAT THERE'S SOMETHING WEIRD ABOUT THIS TOWN, MIRO?
WEIRD? DON'T YOU MEAN BORING? INTERESTING THINGS HAPPEN ANYWHERE BUT HERE.

INTERESTING IS ALL ABOUT WHERE YOU LOOK.

AND THERE'S LOTS TO LOOK AT AROUND HERE.

I GUESS...

HAVE YOU SEEN THAT PLACE?

THE CASTLE? ONLY FROM THE TOP WINDOW AT MY HOUSE.

THAT'S GOT TO BE PART OF IT: THE WAY IT LOOKS OUT OVER THE CLIFFS.

EVEN THIS GUY, DRIVING THE FERRY—

PILOTING?

WHATEVER. I BET THEY'RE ALL RELATED. OR PART OF SOME SECRET CLUB TOGETHER.

EXIT

THERE'S A WOMAN WHO LIVES IN THOSE BOATSHEDS— SHE'S ALWAYS TESTING THE WATER AND THINGS...

HA, OK, WELL, I KNOW YOU'RE ON THE WRONG TRACK THERE...

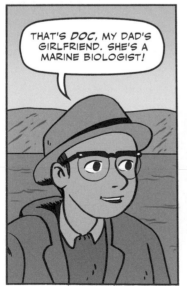

THAT'S DOC, MY DAD'S GIRLFRIEND. SHE'S A MARINE BIOLOGIST!

HUH. WELL, LOOK AT WHAT WE SAW OUTSIDE THE WORKS BACK THERE.

THERE'S MORE THAN MEETS THE EYE IN AURORA, I'M SURE.

OR DO YOU JUST PREFER STORIES IN BOOKS?

YOU SOUND LIKE THOSE GUYS IN TOWN. WHAT'S WRONG WITH BOOKS?

I'M SORRY. I DIDN'T MEAN THAT.

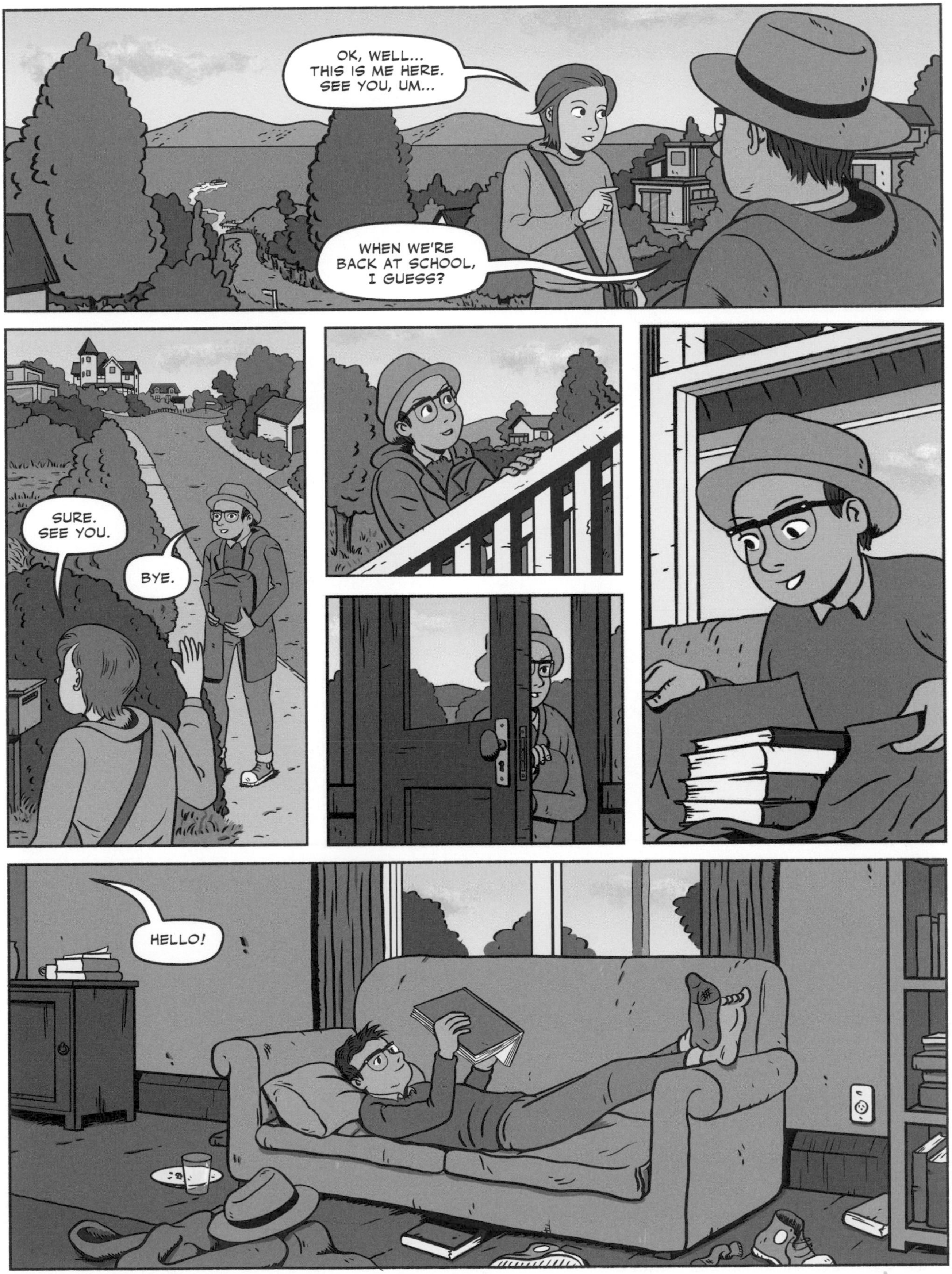

OK, WELL... THIS IS ME HERE. SEE YOU, UM...
WHEN WE'RE BACK AT SCHOOL, I GUESS?
SURE. SEE YOU.
BYE.
HELLO!

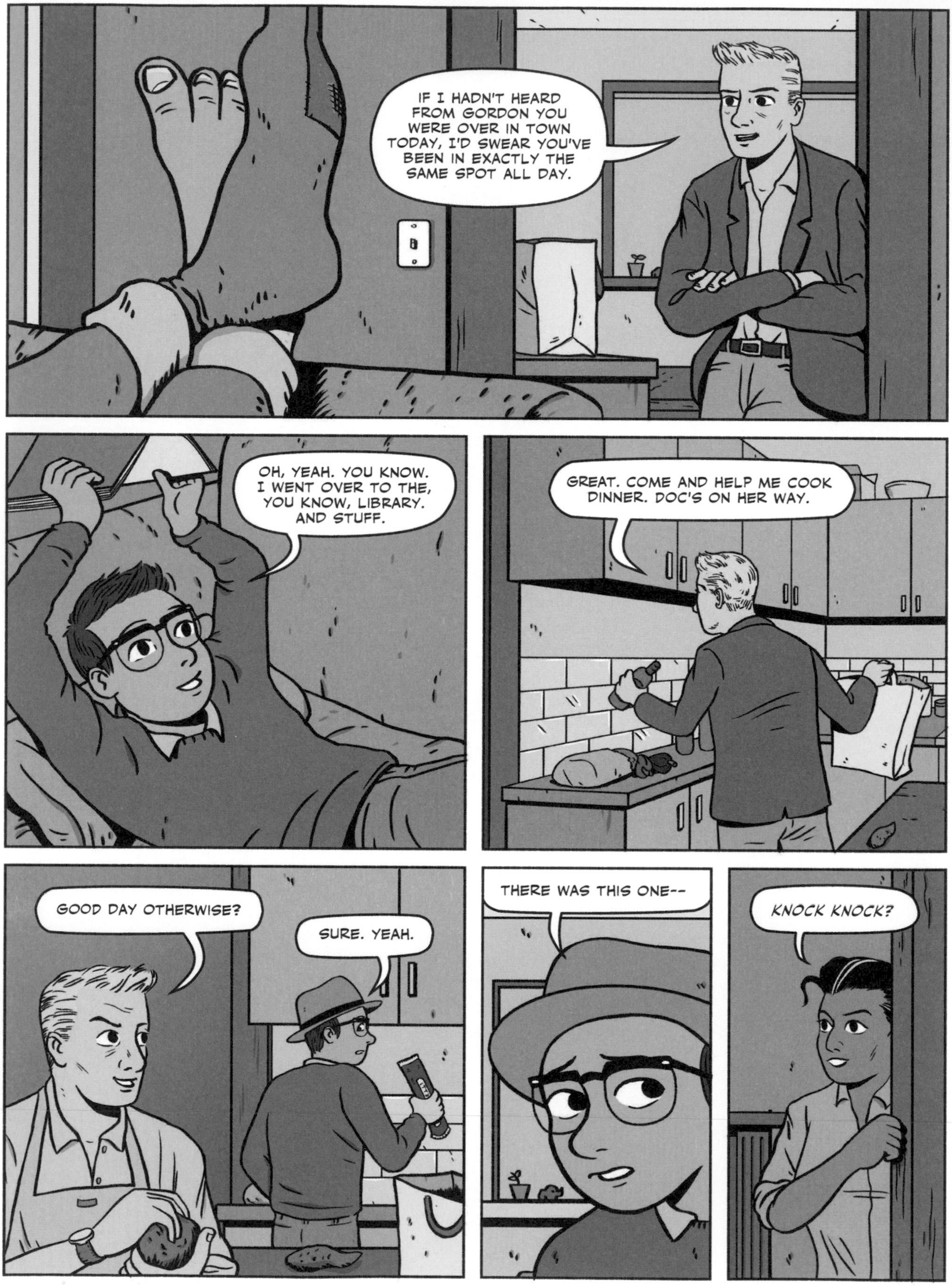
IF I HADN'T HEARD FROM GORDON YOU WERE OVER IN TOWN TODAY, I'D SWEAR YOU'VE BEEN IN EXACTLY THE SAME SPOT ALL DAY.
OH, YEAH. YOU KNOW. I WENT OVER TO THE, YOU KNOW, LIBRARY. AND STUFF.
GREAT. COME AND HELP ME COOK DINNER. DOC'S ON HER WAY.
GOOD DAY OTHERWISE?
SURE. YEAH.
THERE WAS THIS ONE--
KNOCK KNOCK?

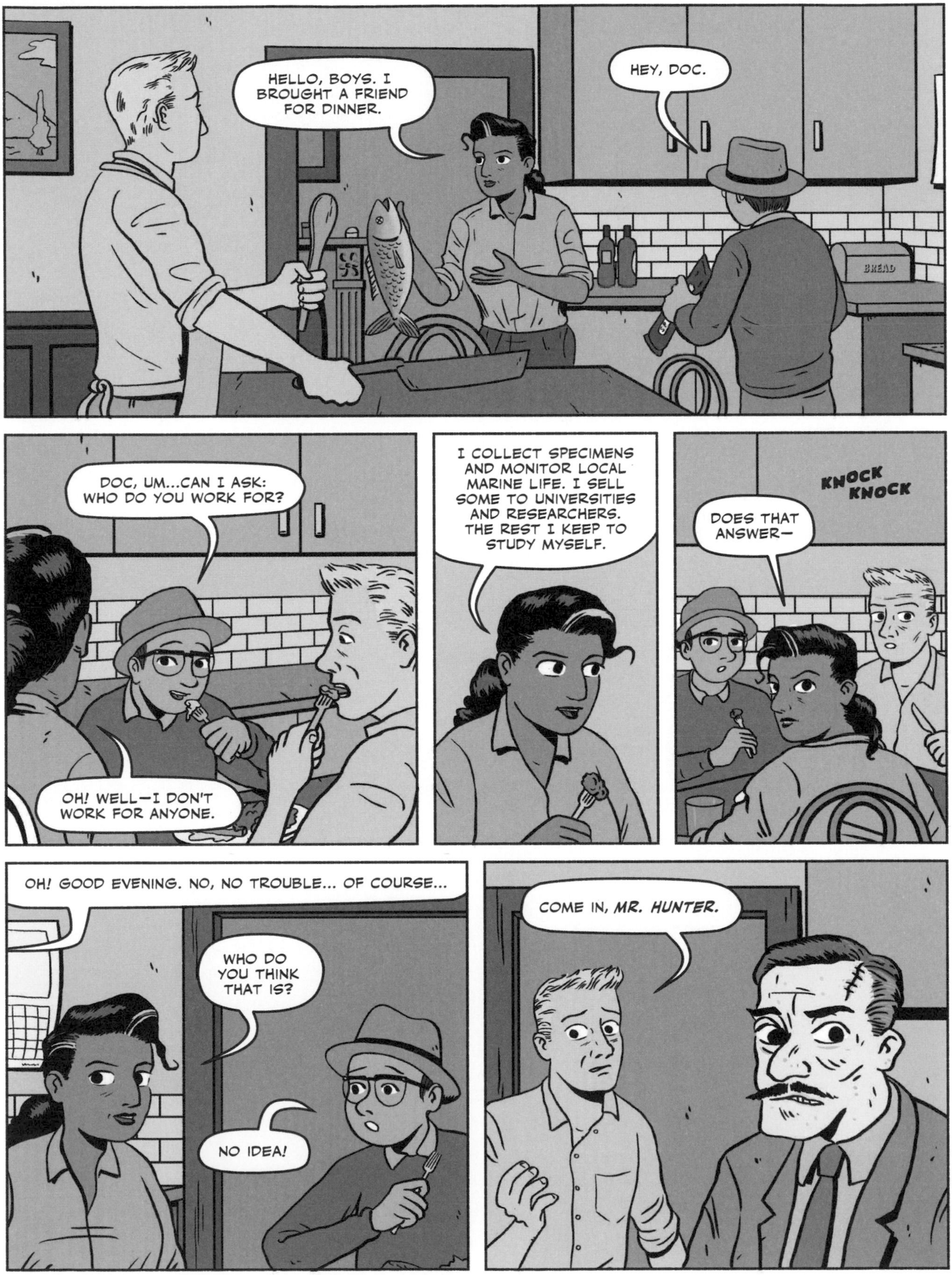
HELLO, BOYS. I BROUGHT A FRIEND FOR DINNER.
HEY, DOC.
BREAD
DOC, UM...CAN I ASK: WHO DO YOU WORK FOR?
OH! WELL—I DON'T WORK FOR ANYONE.
I COLLECT SPECIMENS AND MONITOR LOCAL MARINE LIFE. I SELL SOME TO UNIVERSITIES AND RESEARCHERS. THE REST I KEEP TO STUDY MYSELF.
KNOCK KNOCK
DOES THAT ANSWER—
OH! GOOD EVENING. NO, NO TROUBLE... OF COURSE...
WHO DO YOU THINK THAT IS?
NO IDEA!
COME IN, *MR. HUNTER.*

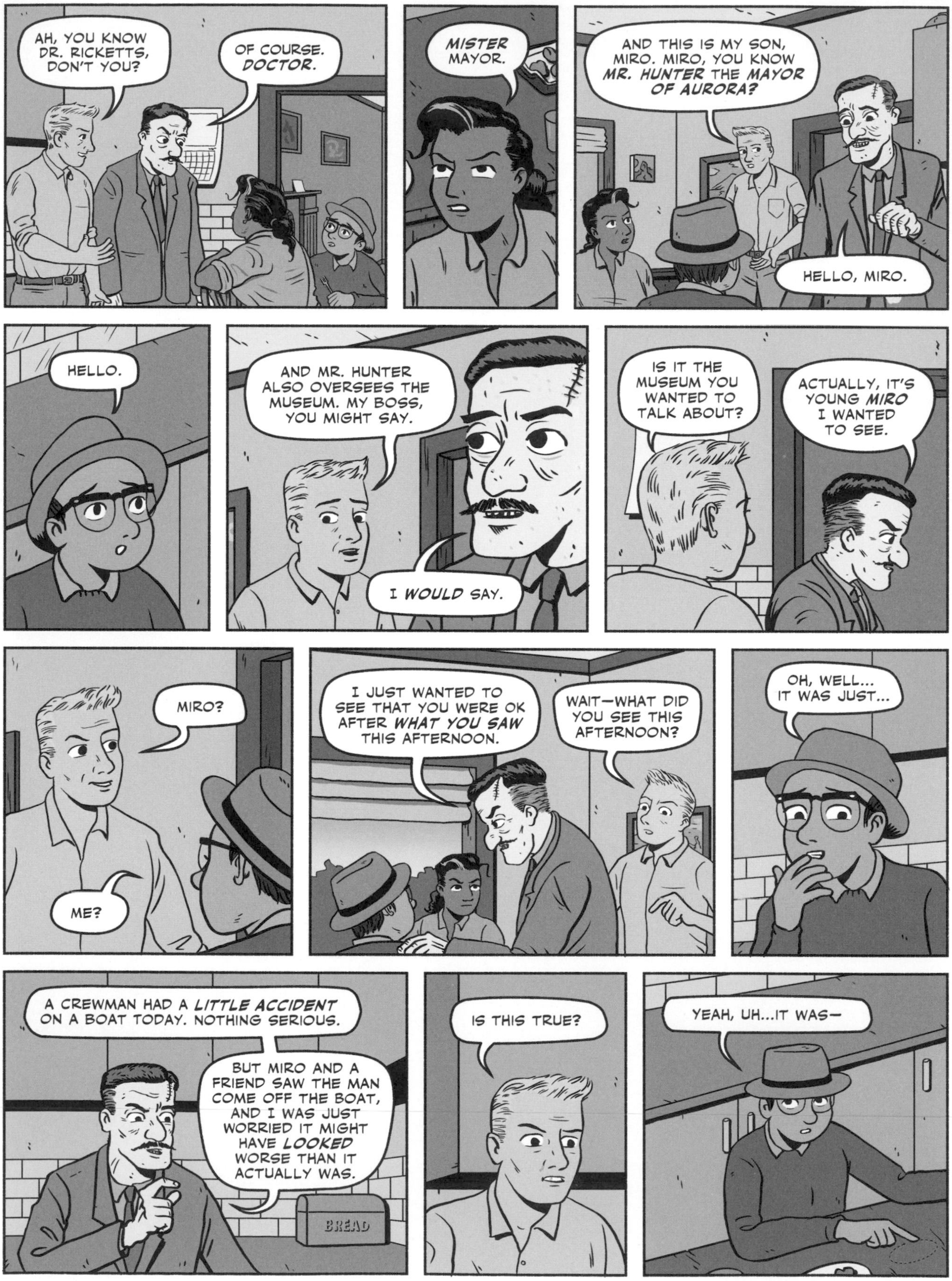
AH, YOU KNOW DR. RICKETTS, DON'T YOU?
OF COURSE. *DOCTOR.*
MISTER MAYOR.
AND THIS IS MY SON, MIRO. MIRO, YOU KNOW ***MR. HUNTER*** THE ***MAYOR OF AURORA?***
HELLO, MIRO.
HELLO.
AND MR. HUNTER ALSO OVERSEES THE MUSEUM. MY BOSS, YOU MIGHT SAY.
I ***WOULD*** SAY.
IS IT THE MUSEUM YOU WANTED TO TALK ABOUT?
ACTUALLY, IT'S YOUNG *MIRO* I WANTED TO SEE.
MIRO?
ME?
I JUST WANTED TO SEE THAT YOU WERE OK AFTER *WHAT YOU SAW* THIS AFTERNOON.
WAIT—WHAT DID YOU SEE THIS AFTERNOON?
OH, WELL... IT WAS JUST...
A CREWMAN HAD A *LITTLE ACCIDENT* ON A BOAT TODAY. NOTHING SERIOUS.
BUT MIRO AND A FRIEND SAW THE MAN COME OFF THE BOAT, AND I WAS JUST WORRIED IT MIGHT HAVE *LOOKED* WORSE THAN IT ACTUALLY WAS.
BREAD
IS THIS TRUE?
YEAH, UH...IT WAS—

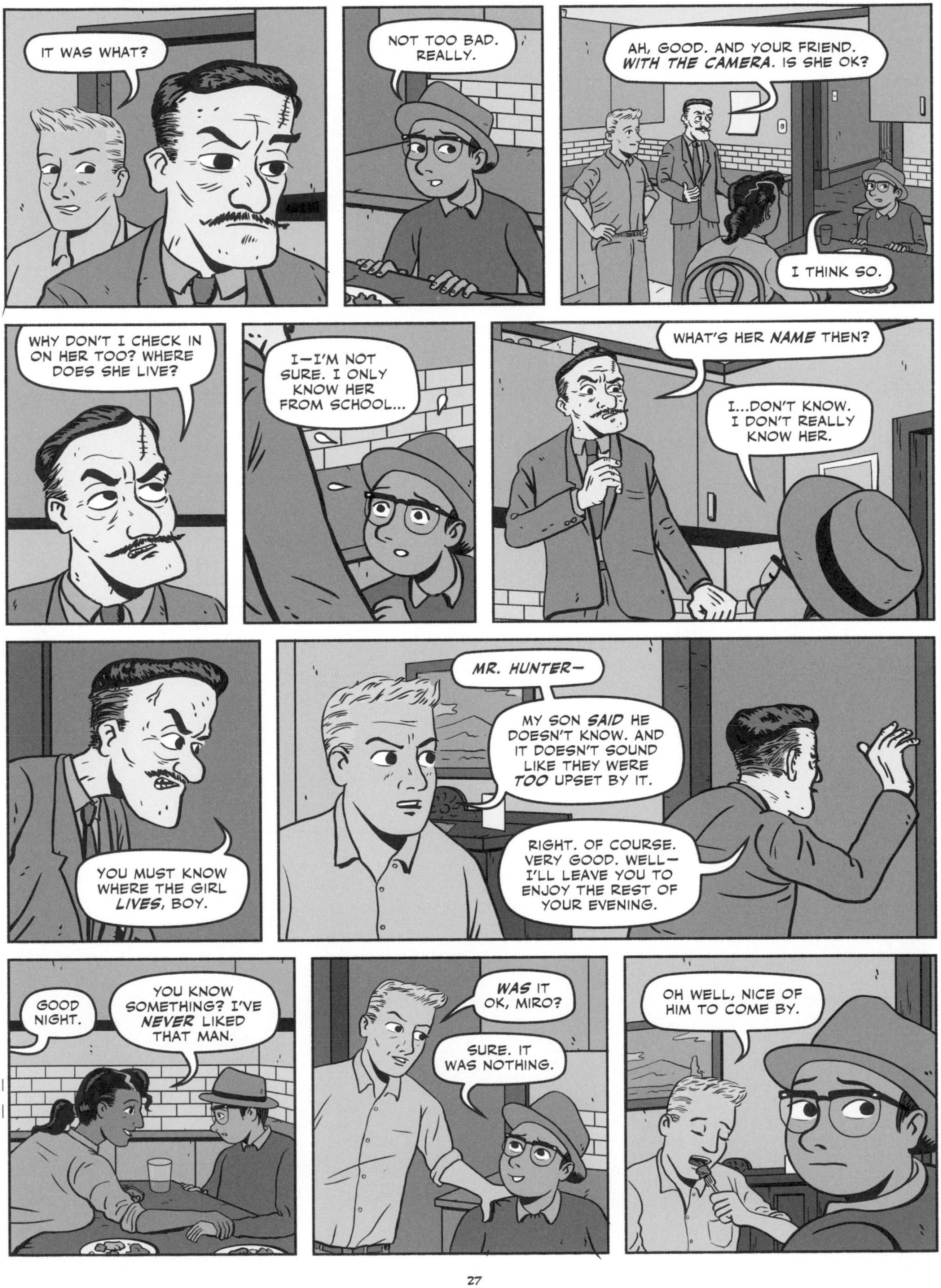
IT WAS WHAT?
NOT TOO BAD. REALLY.
AH, GOOD. AND YOUR FRIEND. *WITH THE CAMERA.* IS SHE OK?
I THINK SO.
WHY DON'T I CHECK IN ON HER TOO? WHERE DOES SHE LIVE?
I—I'M NOT SURE. I ONLY KNOW HER FROM SCHOOL...
WHAT'S HER *NAME* THEN?
I...DON'T KNOW. I DON'T REALLY KNOW HER.
YOU MUST KNOW WHERE THE GIRL *LIVES*, BOY.
MR. HUNTER—
MY SON *SAID* HE DOESN'T KNOW. AND IT DOESN'T SOUND LIKE THEY WERE *TOO* UPSET BY IT.
RIGHT. OF COURSE. VERY GOOD. WELL— I'LL LEAVE YOU TO ENJOY THE REST OF YOUR EVENING.
GOOD NIGHT.
YOU KNOW SOMETHING? I'VE *NEVER* LIKED THAT MAN.
WAS IT OK, MIRO?
SURE. IT WAS NOTHING.
OH WELL, NICE OF HIM TO COME BY.

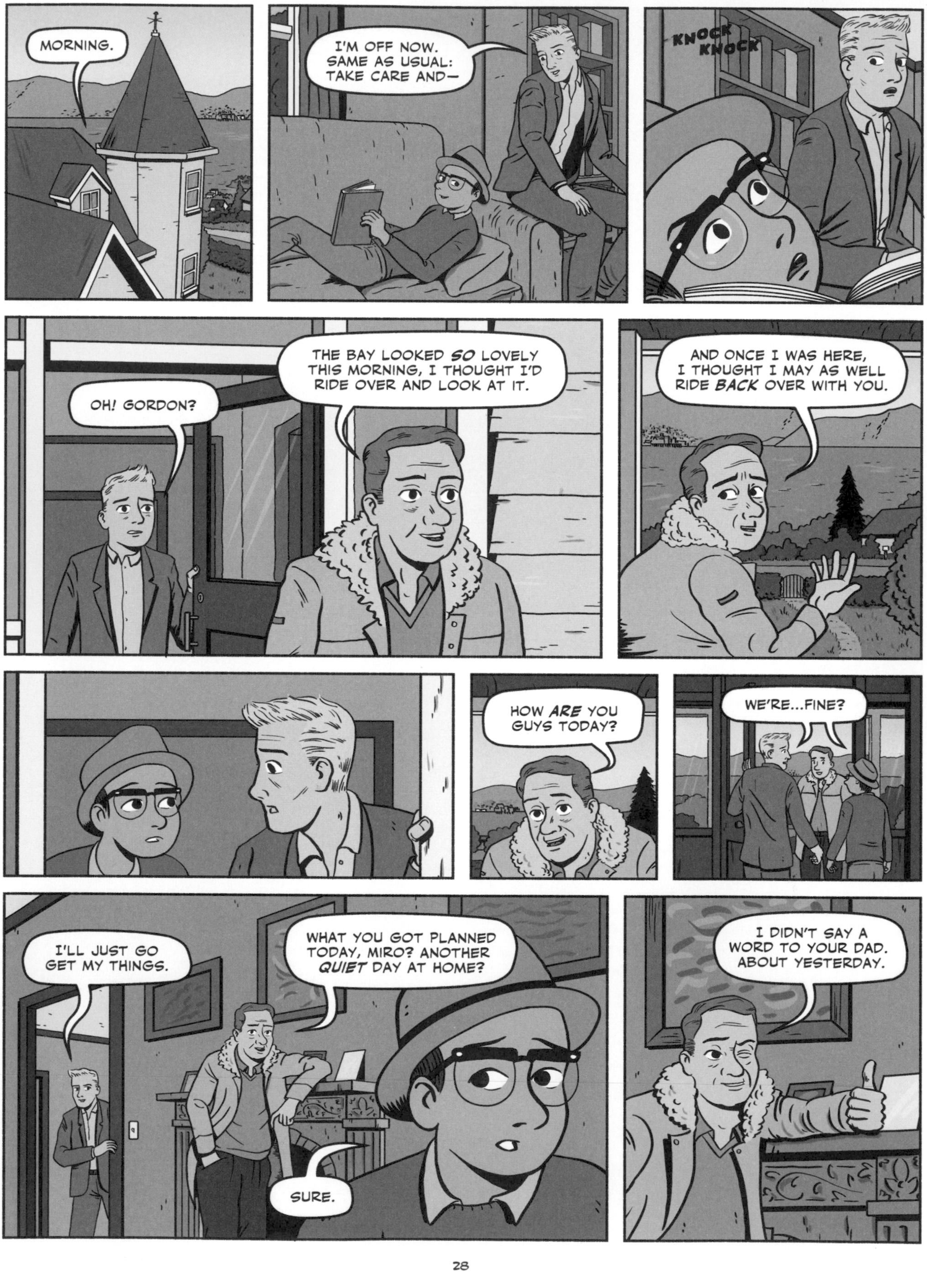
MORNING.
I'M OFF NOW. SAME AS USUAL: TAKE CARE AND—
KNOCK KNOCK
OH! GORDON?
THE BAY LOOKED SO LOVELY THIS MORNING, I THOUGHT I'D RIDE OVER AND LOOK AT IT.
AND ONCE I WAS HERE, I THOUGHT I MAY AS WELL RIDE BACK OVER WITH YOU.
HOW ARE YOU GUYS TODAY?
WE'RE...FINE?
I'LL JUST GO GET MY THINGS.
WHAT YOU GOT PLANNED TODAY, MIRO? ANOTHER QUIET DAY AT HOME?
SURE.
I DIDN'T SAY A WORD TO YOUR DAD. ABOUT YESTERDAY.

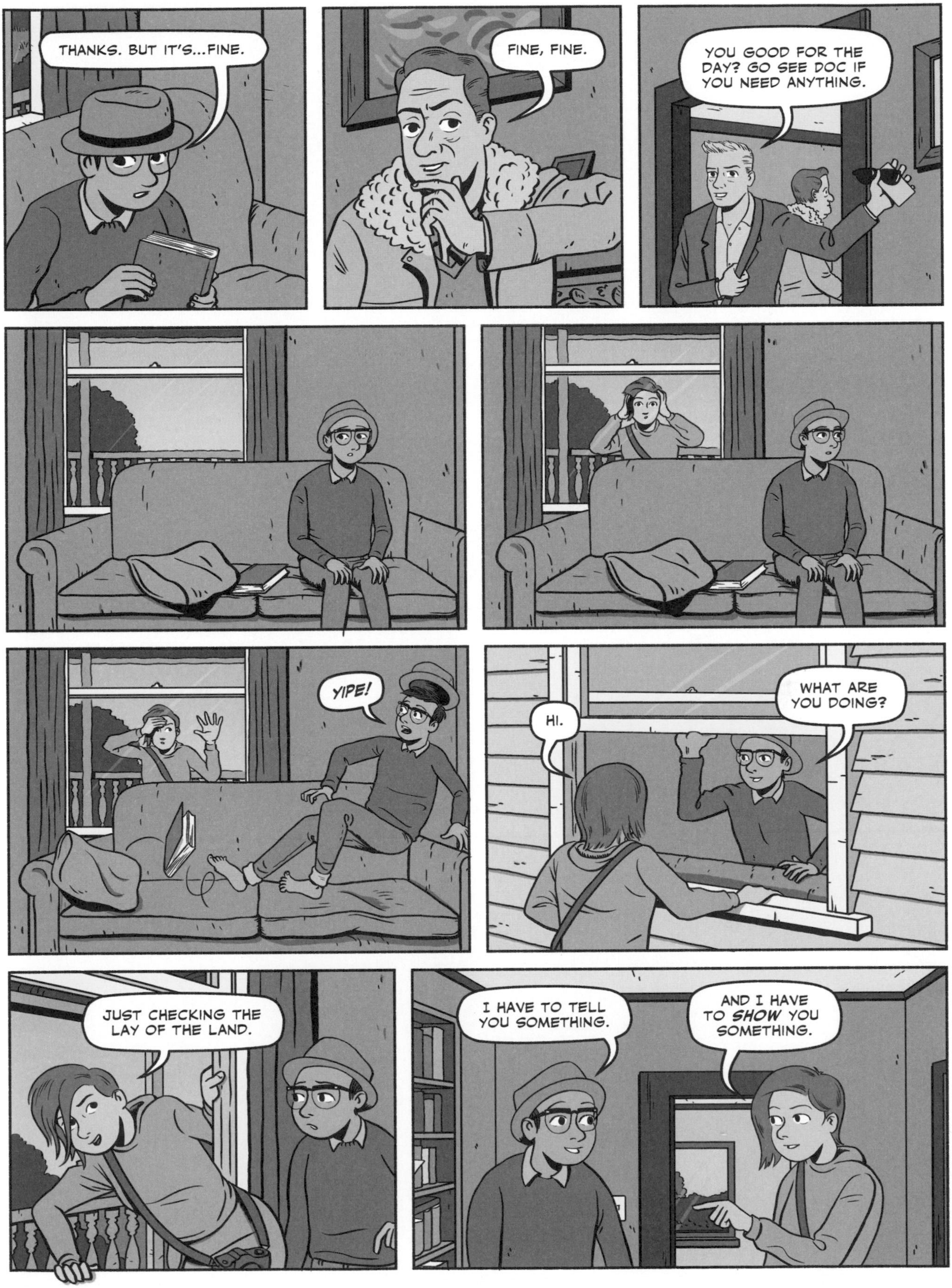
THANKS. BUT IT'S...FINE.
FINE, FINE.
YOU GOOD FOR THE DAY? GO SEE DOC IF YOU NEED ANYTHING.
YIPE!
HI.
WHAT ARE YOU DOING?
JUST CHECKING THE LAY OF THE LAND.
I HAVE TO TELL YOU SOMETHING.
AND I HAVE TO *SHOW* YOU SOMETHING.

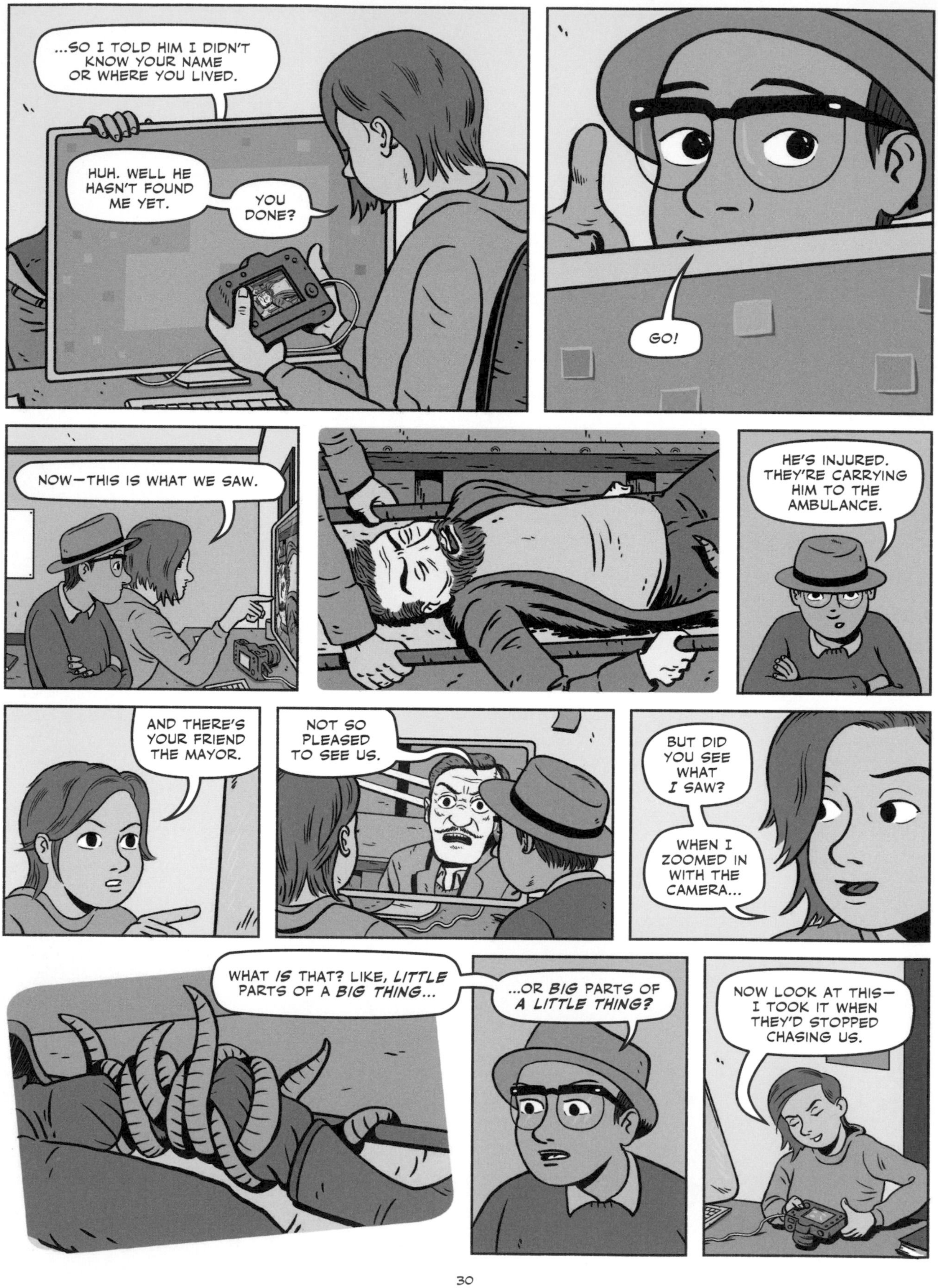
...SO I TOLD HIM I DIDN'T KNOW YOUR NAME OR WHERE YOU LIVED.
HUH. WELL HE HASN'T FOUND ME YET.
YOU DONE?
GO!
NOW—THIS IS WHAT WE SAW.
HE'S INJURED. THEY'RE CARRYING HIM TO THE AMBULANCE.
AND THERE'S YOUR FRIEND THE MAYOR.
NOT SO PLEASED TO SEE US.
BUT DID YOU SEE WHAT *I* SAW?
WHEN I ZOOMED IN WITH THE CAMERA...
WHAT *IS* THAT? LIKE, *LITTLE* PARTS OF A *BIG THING*...
...OR *BIG* PARTS OF *A LITTLE THING?*
NOW LOOK AT THIS— I TOOK IT WHEN THEY'D STOPPED CHASING US.

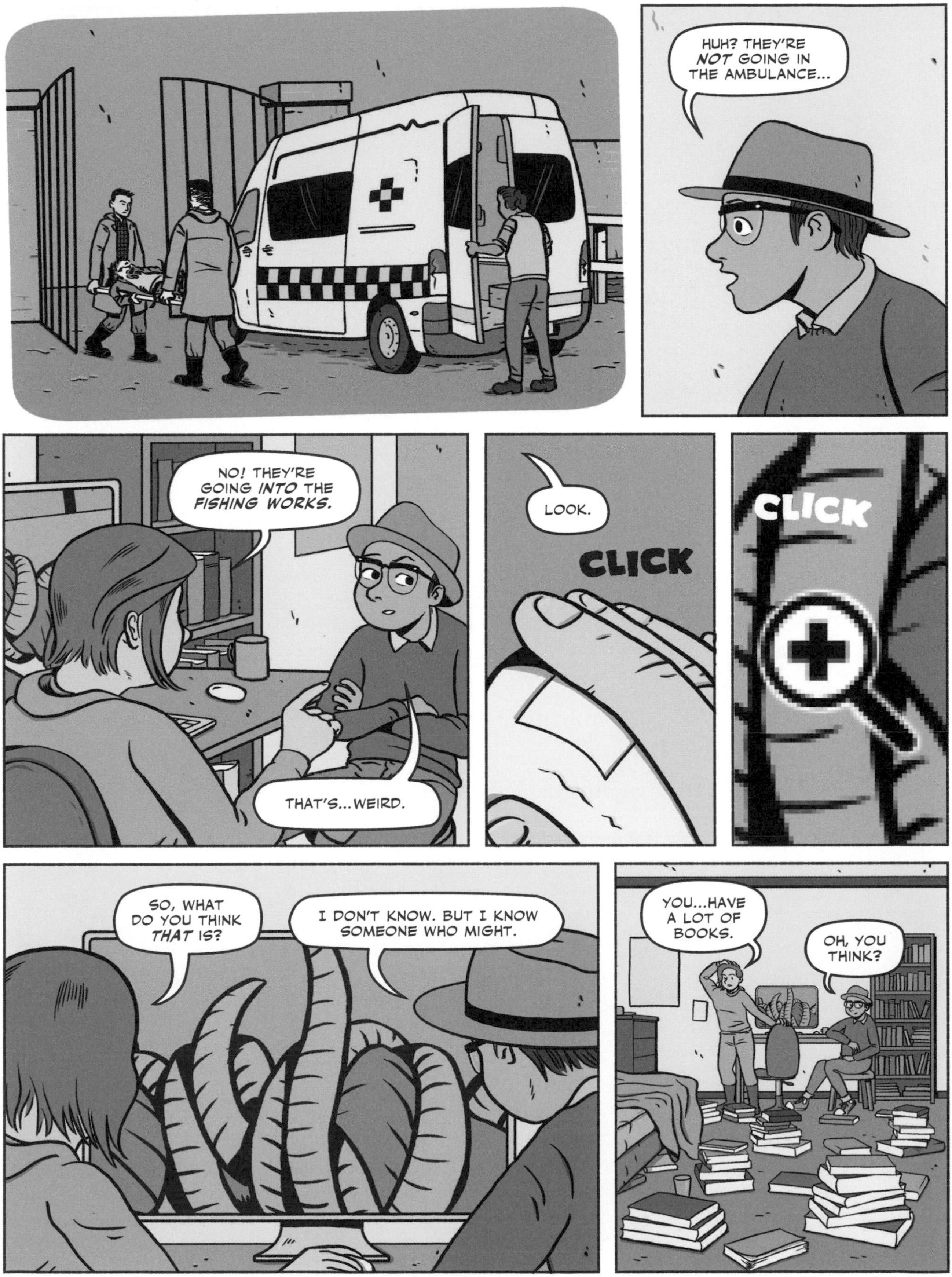
HUH? THEY'RE *NOT* GOING IN THE AMBULANCE...
NO! THEY'RE GOING *INTO* THE *FISHING WORKS.*
THAT'S...WEIRD.
LOOK.
CLICK
CLICK
SO, WHAT DO YOU THINK *THAT* IS?
I DON'T KNOW. BUT I KNOW SOMEONE WHO MIGHT.
YOU...HAVE A LOT OF BOOKS.
OH, YOU THINK?

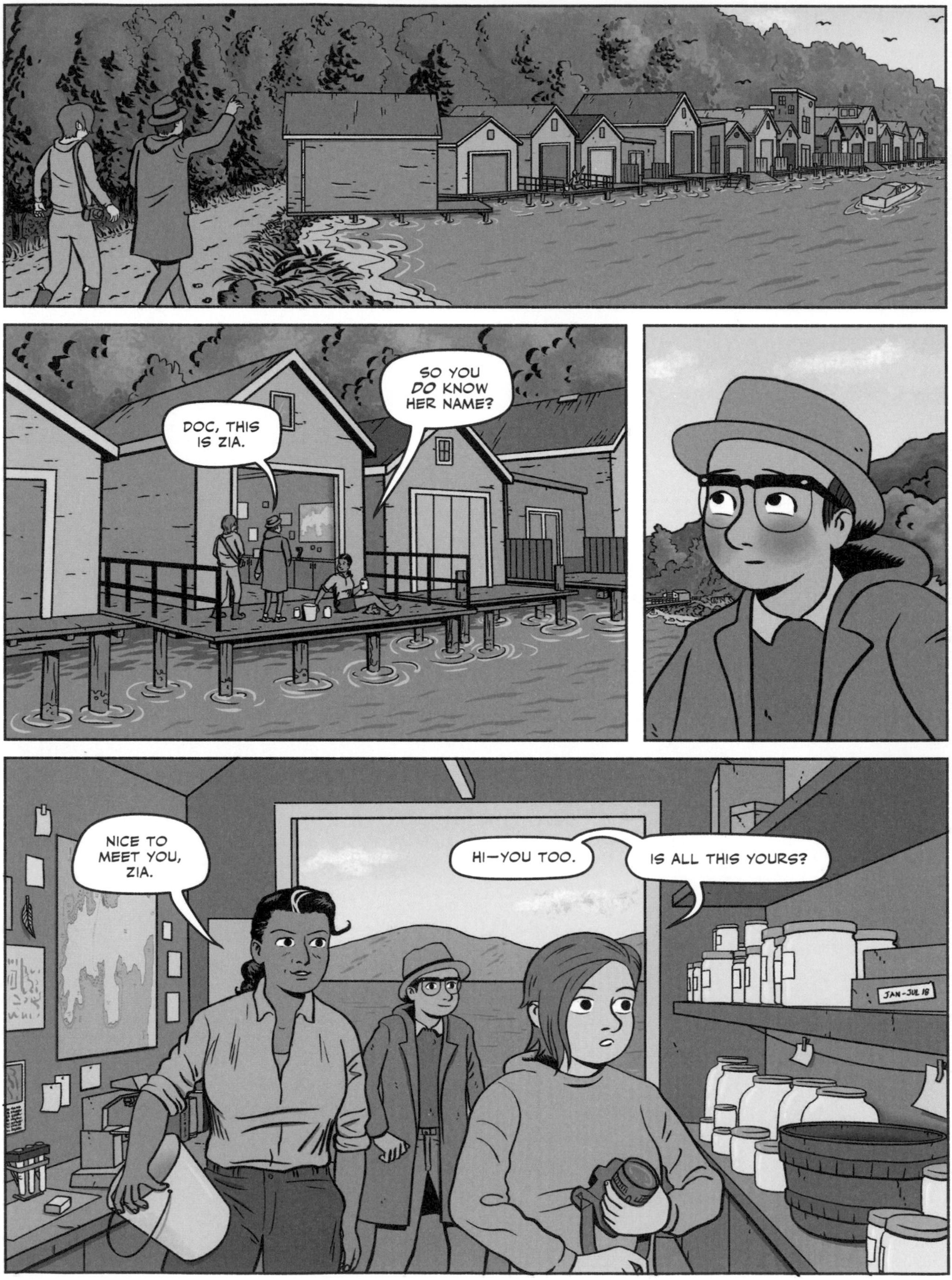
DOC, THIS IS ZIA.
SO YOU *DO* KNOW HER NAME?
NICE TO MEET YOU, ZIA.
HI—YOU TOO.
IS ALL THIS YOURS?
JAN-JUL 18

IT IS INDEED.

SHOW HER.

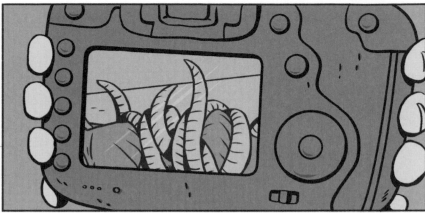

THAT'S...

IS THAT WHAT YOU SAW YESTERDAY?

YES.

BUT MR. HUNTER DIDN'T WANT US TO.

WHAT?

AURORA IS UNIQUE. THE FISHING IN THESE WATERS IS...UNLIKE ANYWHERE IN THE WORLD.

BUT THERE'S OTHER THINGS TOO... THINGS WE JUST DON'T SEE *ANYWHERE*. OR AT LEAST—

THINGS THAT HAVEN'T BEEN SEEN FOR A *VERY* LONG TIME.

THAT'S NOT WHAT WE SAW, IS IT?

I DON'T THINK SO...

THAT'S WHY MR. HUNTER LIKES TO KEEP A PRETTY TIGHT GRIP ON WHAT GOES AROUND HERE.

HE'S NOT VERY FOND OF ME—OR MY WORK. I THINK IT'S IN CASE I DRAW THE *WRONG KIND* OF ATTENTION TO THE WORKS OR SOMETHING.

SO MR. HUNTER OWNS THE WORKS?

OH NO, *MARGARET DANFORTH* OWNS THE WORKS.

WAIT—SHE LIVES IN THE CASTLE!

THAT'S RIGHT.

I *KNEW* THAT WAS PART OF IT.

IT WAS HER FATHER *WILLIAM DANFORTH* WHO FOUNDED THE WORKS—IN 1932.

HE TURNED AURORA FROM A LITTLE VILLAGE INTO A THRIVING FISHING TOWN.

AND HE BUILT THE CASTLE FOR HIS FAMILY TO LIVE IN. SINCE HE DIED, SHE'S BEEN HIDDEN AWAY THERE. SO NOW *SHE* OWNS THE WORKS, AND MOST OF THE TOWN.

AND THE MUSEUM?

THAT TOO. THE FISHING GIVES HUNTER AND HIS CRONIES CONTROL OF EVERYTHING. THEY DON'T WANT *ANYTHING* MESSING THAT UP.

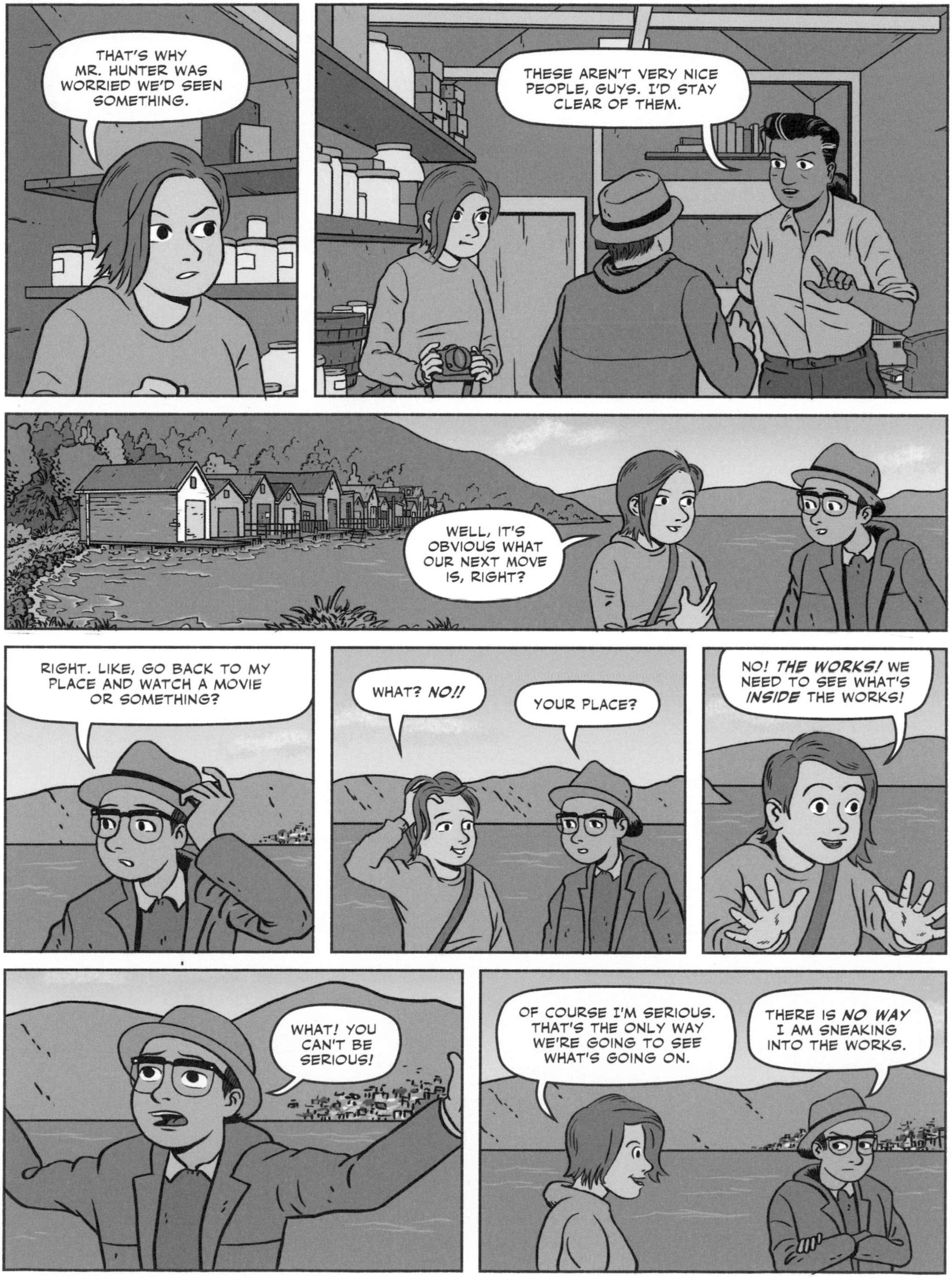
THAT'S WHY MR. HUNTER WAS WORRIED WE'D SEEN SOMETHING.
THESE AREN'T VERY NICE PEOPLE, GUYS. I'D STAY CLEAR OF THEM.
WELL, IT'S OBVIOUS WHAT OUR NEXT MOVE IS, RIGHT?
RIGHT. LIKE, GO BACK TO MY PLACE AND WATCH A MOVIE OR SOMETHING?
WHAT? NO!!
YOUR PLACE?
NO! THE WORKS! WE NEED TO SEE WHAT'S INSIDE THE WORKS!
WHAT! YOU CAN'T BE SERIOUS!
OF COURSE I'M SERIOUS. THAT'S THE ONLY WAY WE'RE GOING TO SEE WHAT'S GOING ON.
THERE IS NO WAY I AM SNEAKING INTO THE WORKS.

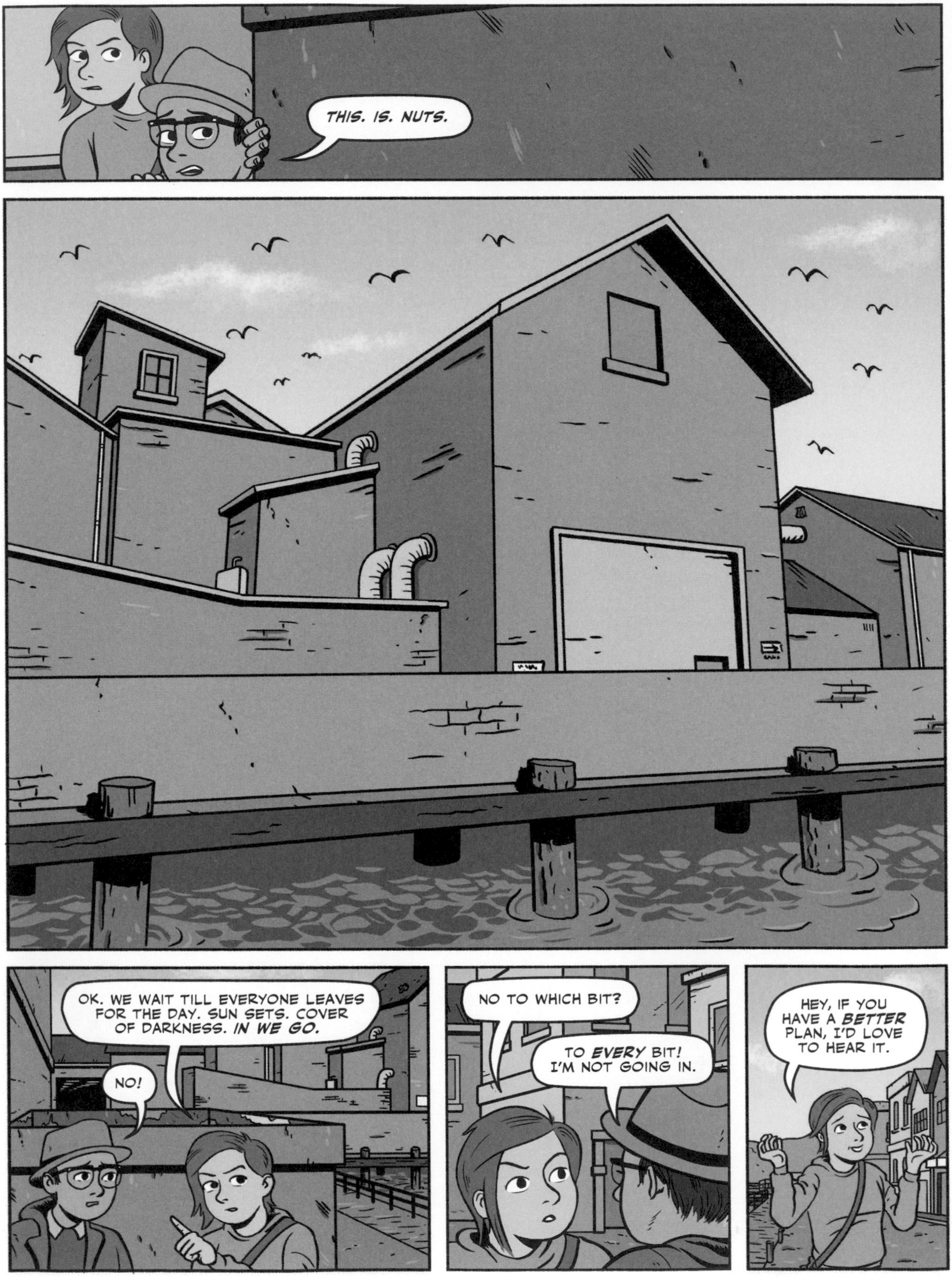
THIS. IS. NUTS.
OK. WE WAIT TILL EVERYONE LEAVES FOR THE DAY. SUN SETS. COVER OF DARKNESS. IN WE GO.
NO!
NO TO WHICH BIT?
TO EVERY BIT! I'M NOT GOING IN.
HEY, IF YOU HAVE A BETTER PLAN, I'D LOVE TO HEAR IT.

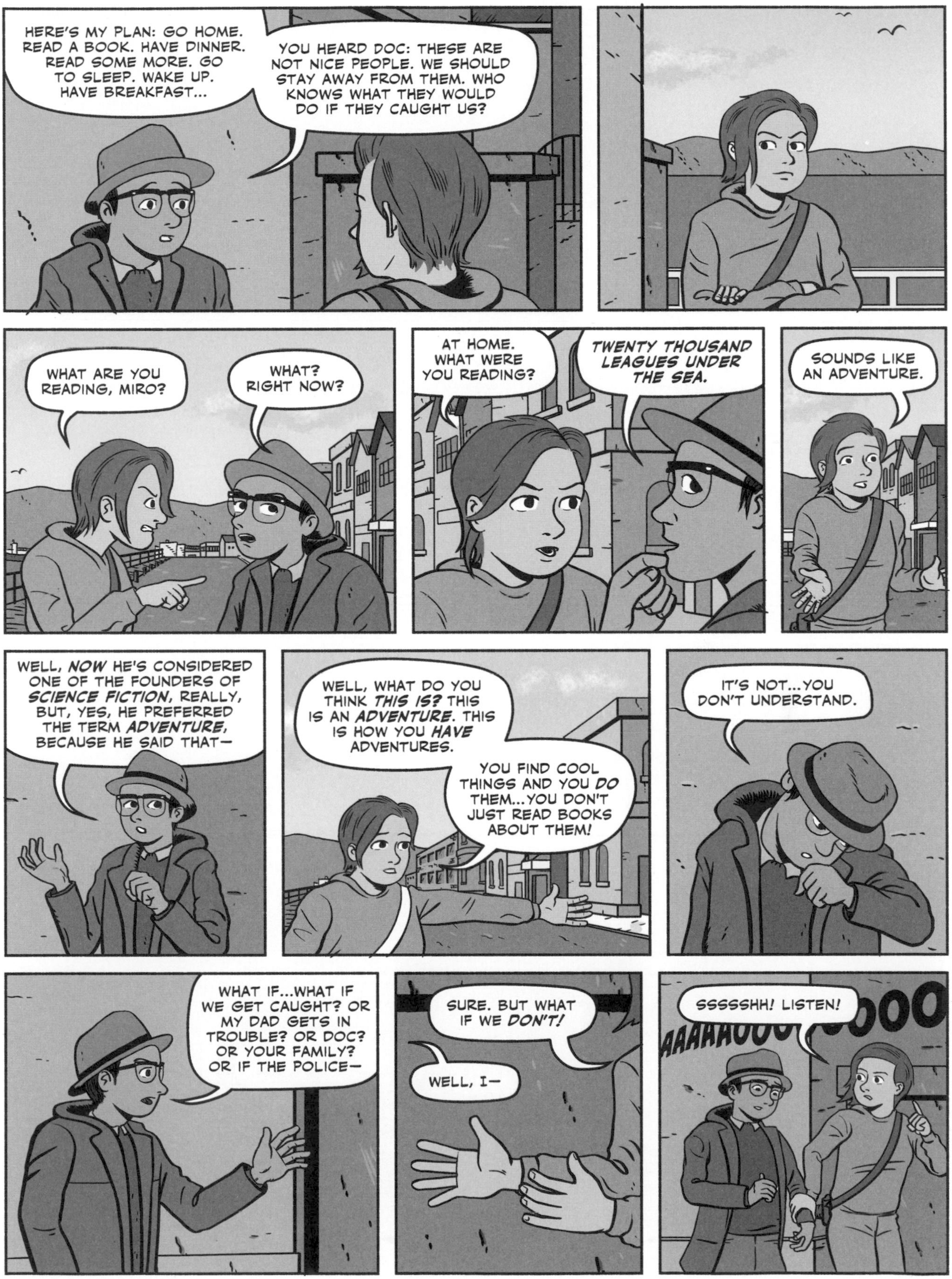
HERE'S MY PLAN: GO HOME. READ A BOOK. HAVE DINNER. READ SOME MORE. GO TO SLEEP. WAKE UP. HAVE BREAKFAST...
YOU HEARD DOC: THESE ARE NOT NICE PEOPLE. WE SHOULD STAY AWAY FROM THEM. WHO KNOWS WHAT THEY WOULD DO IF THEY CAUGHT US?
WHAT ARE YOU READING, MIRO?
WHAT? RIGHT NOW?
AT HOME. WHAT WERE YOU READING?
TWENTY THOUSAND LEAGUES UNDER THE SEA.
SOUNDS LIKE AN ADVENTURE.
WELL, NOW HE'S CONSIDERED ONE OF THE FOUNDERS OF SCIENCE FICTION, REALLY, BUT, YES, HE PREFERRED THE TERM ADVENTURE, BECAUSE HE SAID THAT—
WELL, WHAT DO YOU THINK THIS IS? THIS IS AN ADVENTURE. THIS IS HOW YOU HAVE ADVENTURES.
YOU FIND COOL THINGS AND YOU DO THEM...YOU DON'T JUST READ BOOKS ABOUT THEM!
IT'S NOT...YOU DON'T UNDERSTAND.
WHAT IF...WHAT IF WE GET CAUGHT? OR MY DAD GETS IN TROUBLE? OR DOC? OR YOUR FAMILY? OR IF THE POLICE—
SURE. BUT WHAT IF WE DON'T!
WELL, I—
SSSSSHH! LISTEN!

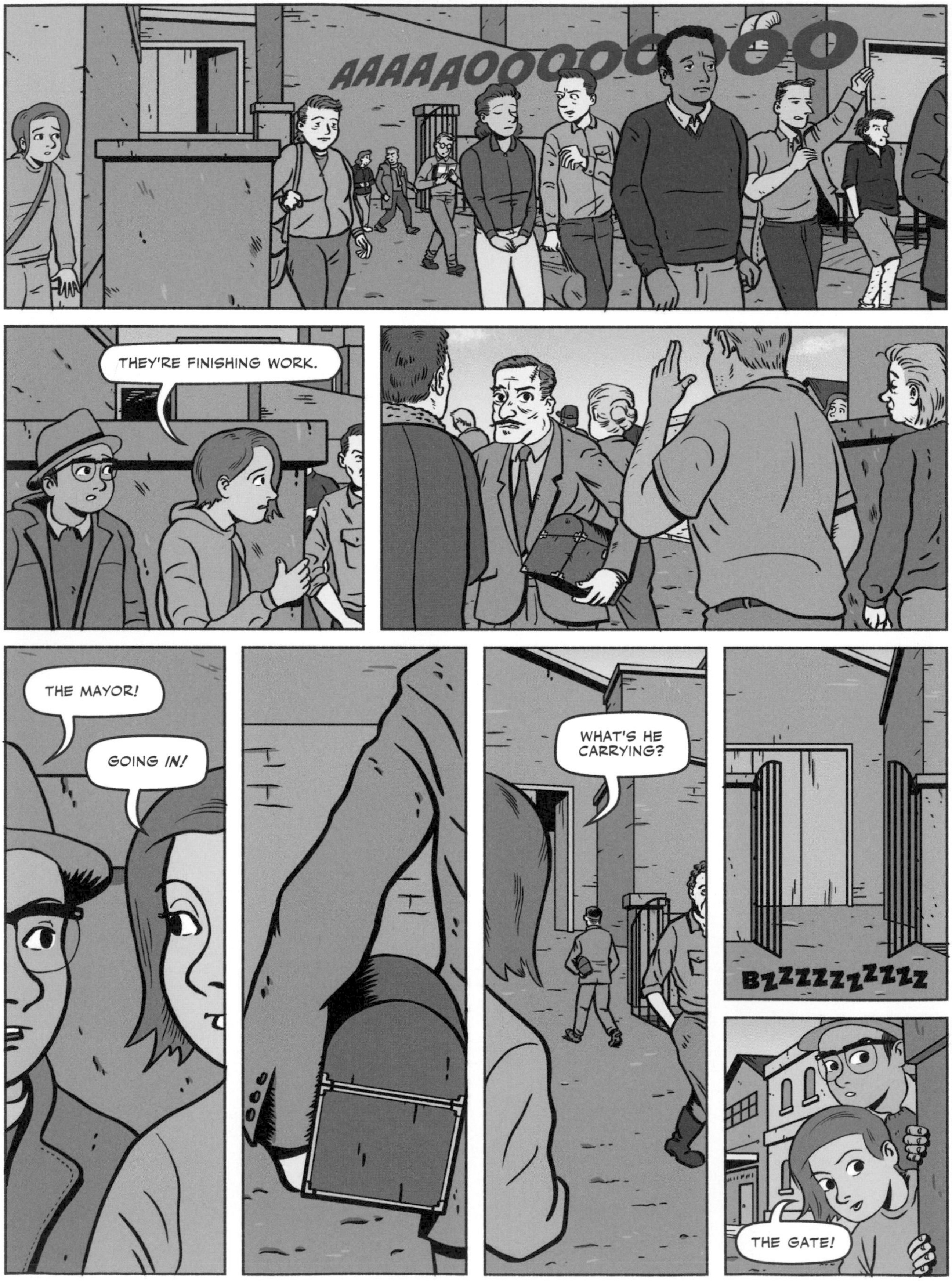
AAAAAOOOOOOOOO
THEY'RE FINISHING WORK.
THE MAYOR!
GOING *IN!*
WHAT'S HE CARRYING?
BZZZZZZZZZZZ
THE GATE!

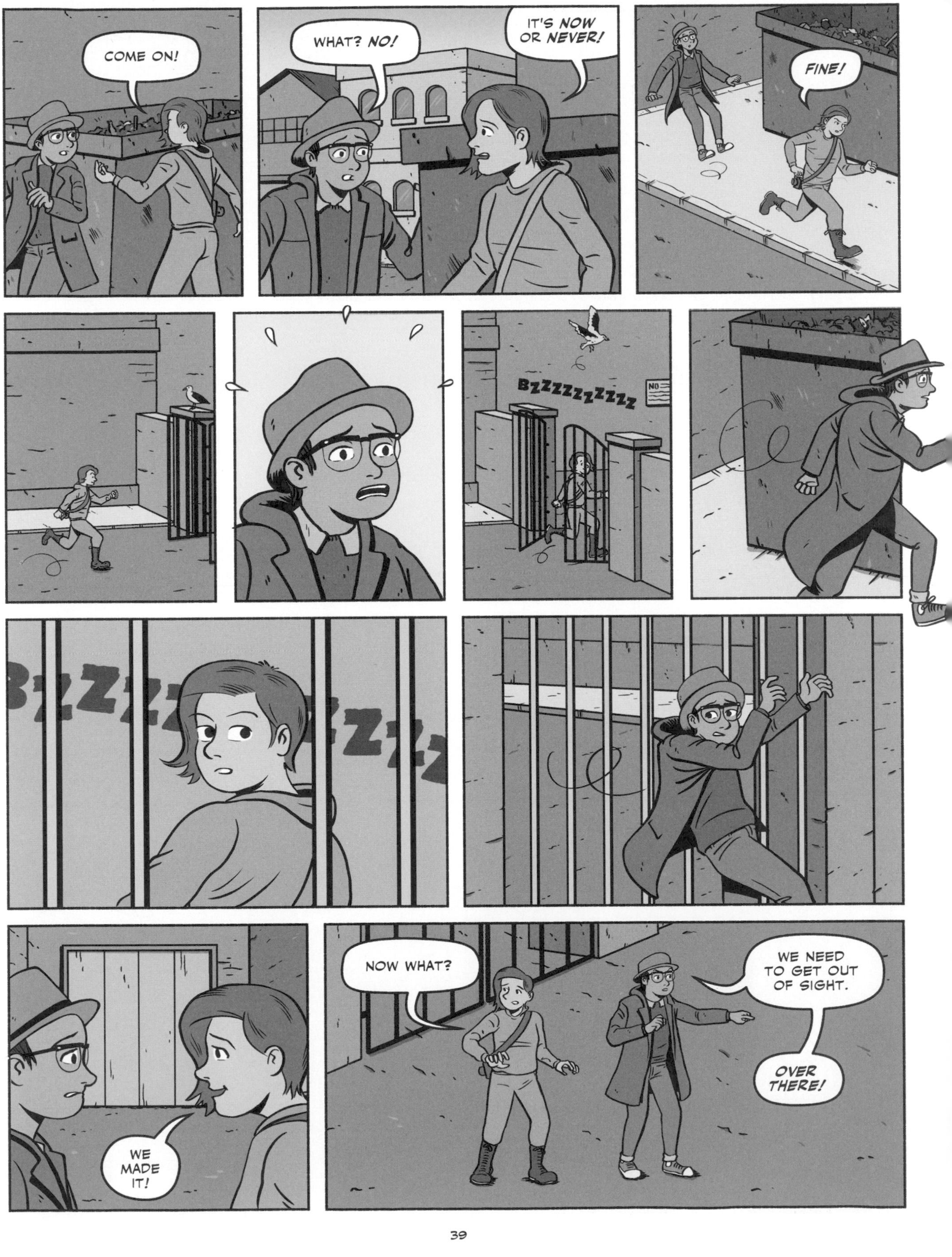
COME ON!
WHAT? NO!
IT'S NOW OR NEVER!
FINE!
NO
BZZZZZZZZZZ
BZZZ
ZZZZ
NOW WHAT?
WE NEED TO GET OUT OF SIGHT.
OVER THERE!
WE MADE IT!

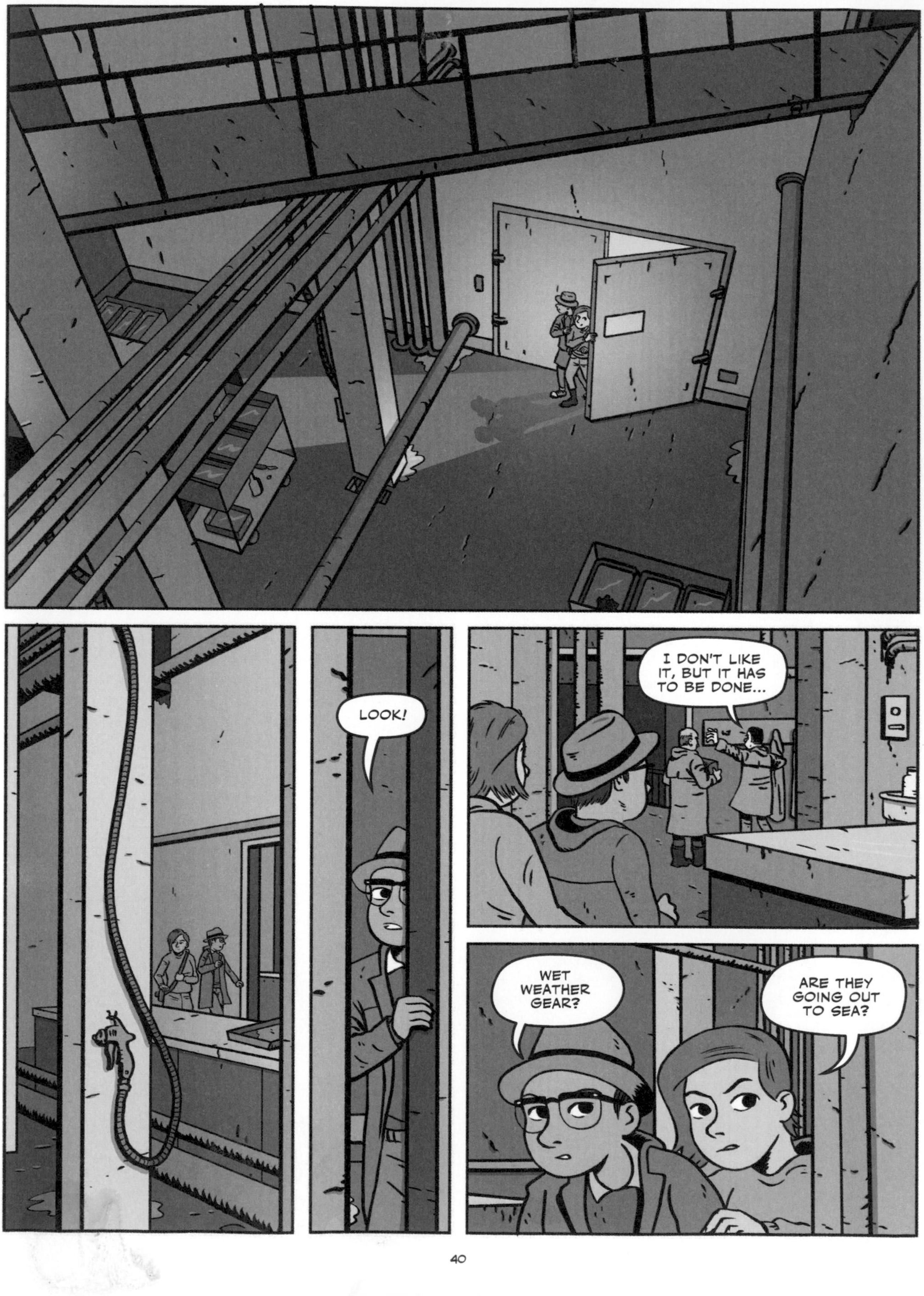
LOOK!
I DON'T LIKE IT, BUT IT HAS TO BE DONE...
WET WEATHER GEAR?
ARE THEY GOING OUT TO SEA?

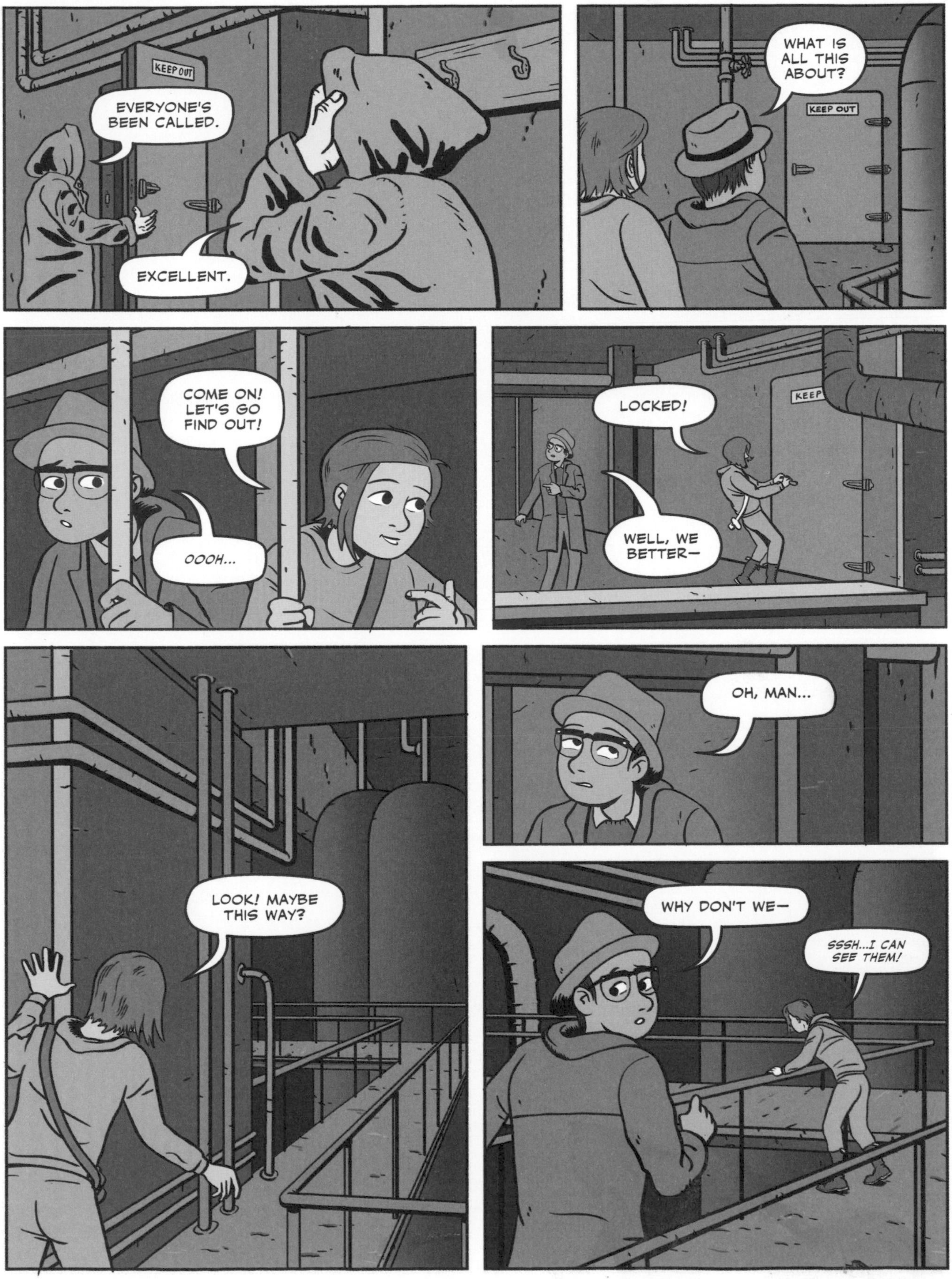
KEEP OUT
EVERYONE'S BEEN CALLED.
EXCELLENT.
WHAT IS ALL THIS ABOUT?
KEEP OUT
COME ON! LET'S GO FIND OUT!
OOOH...
KEEP
LOCKED!
WELL, WE BETTER—
OH, MAN...
LOOK! MAYBE THIS WAY?
WHY DON'T WE—
SSSH...I CAN SEE THEM!

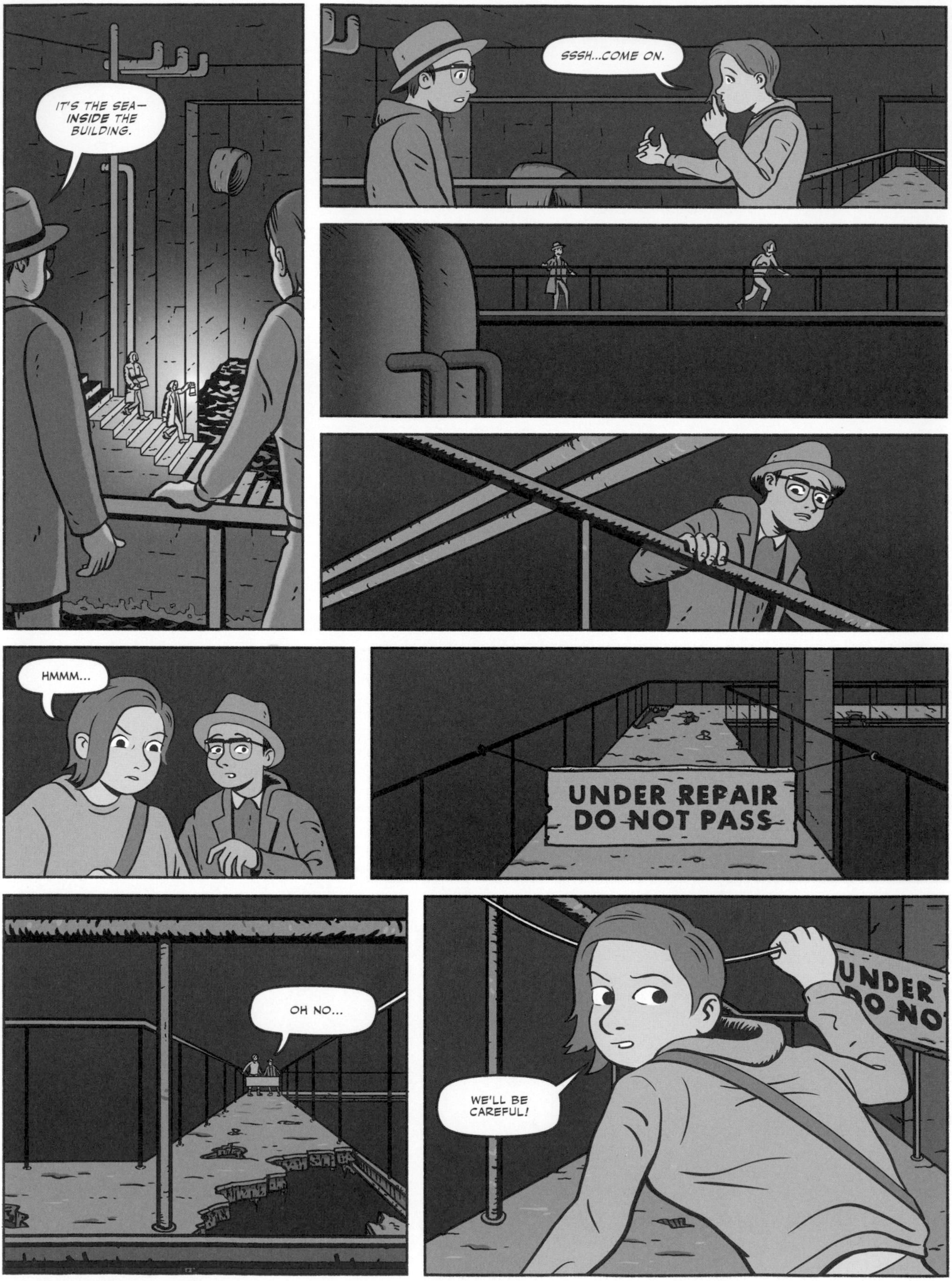
IT'S THE SEA—
INSIDE THE BUILDING.
SSSH...COME ON.
HMMM...
UNDER REPAIR
DO NOT PASS
OH NO...
WE'LL BE CAREFUL!

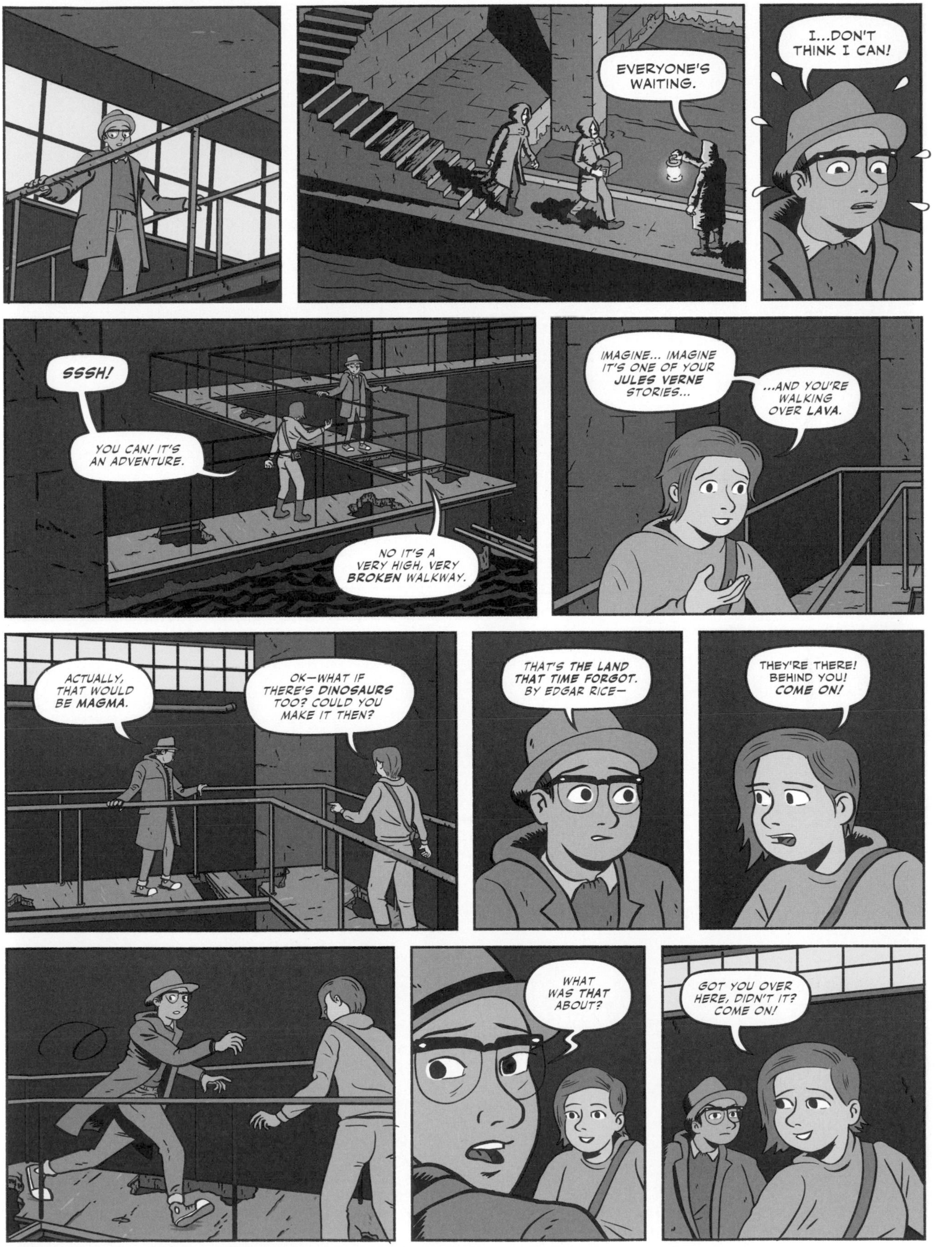
EVERYONE'S WAITING.
I...DON'T THINK I CAN!
SSSH!
YOU CAN! IT'S AN ADVENTURE.
NO IT'S A VERY HIGH, VERY BROKEN WALKWAY.
IMAGINE... IMAGINE IT'S ONE OF YOUR JULES VERNE STORIES...
...AND YOU'RE WALKING OVER LAVA.
ACTUALLY, THAT WOULD BE MAGMA.
OK—WHAT IF THERE'S DINOSAURS TOO? COULD YOU MAKE IT THEN?
THAT'S THE LAND THAT TIME FORGOT. BY EDGAR RICE—
THEY'RE THERE! BEHIND YOU! COME ON!
WHAT WAS THAT ABOUT?
GOT YOU OVER HERE, DIDN'T IT? COME ON!

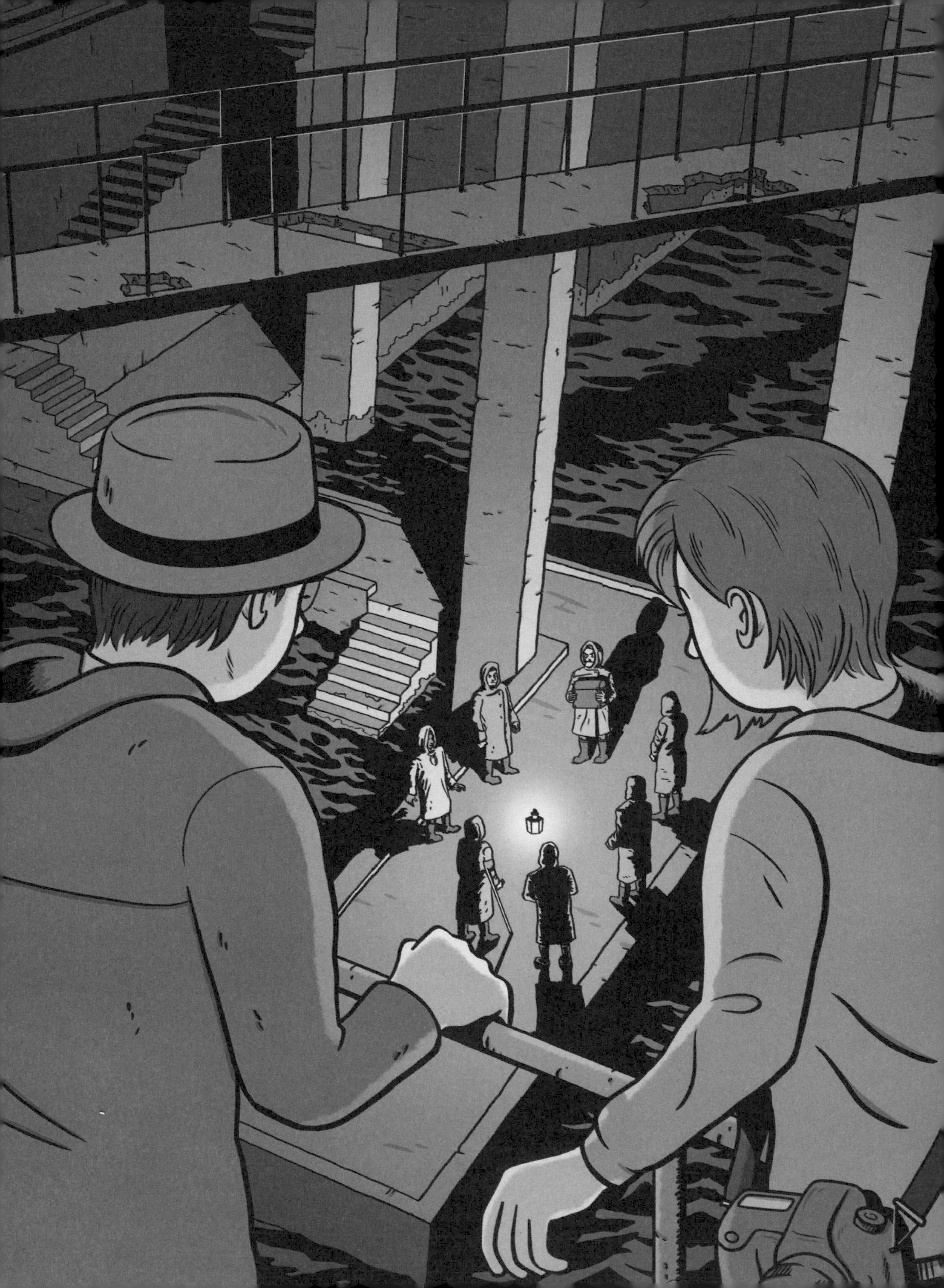

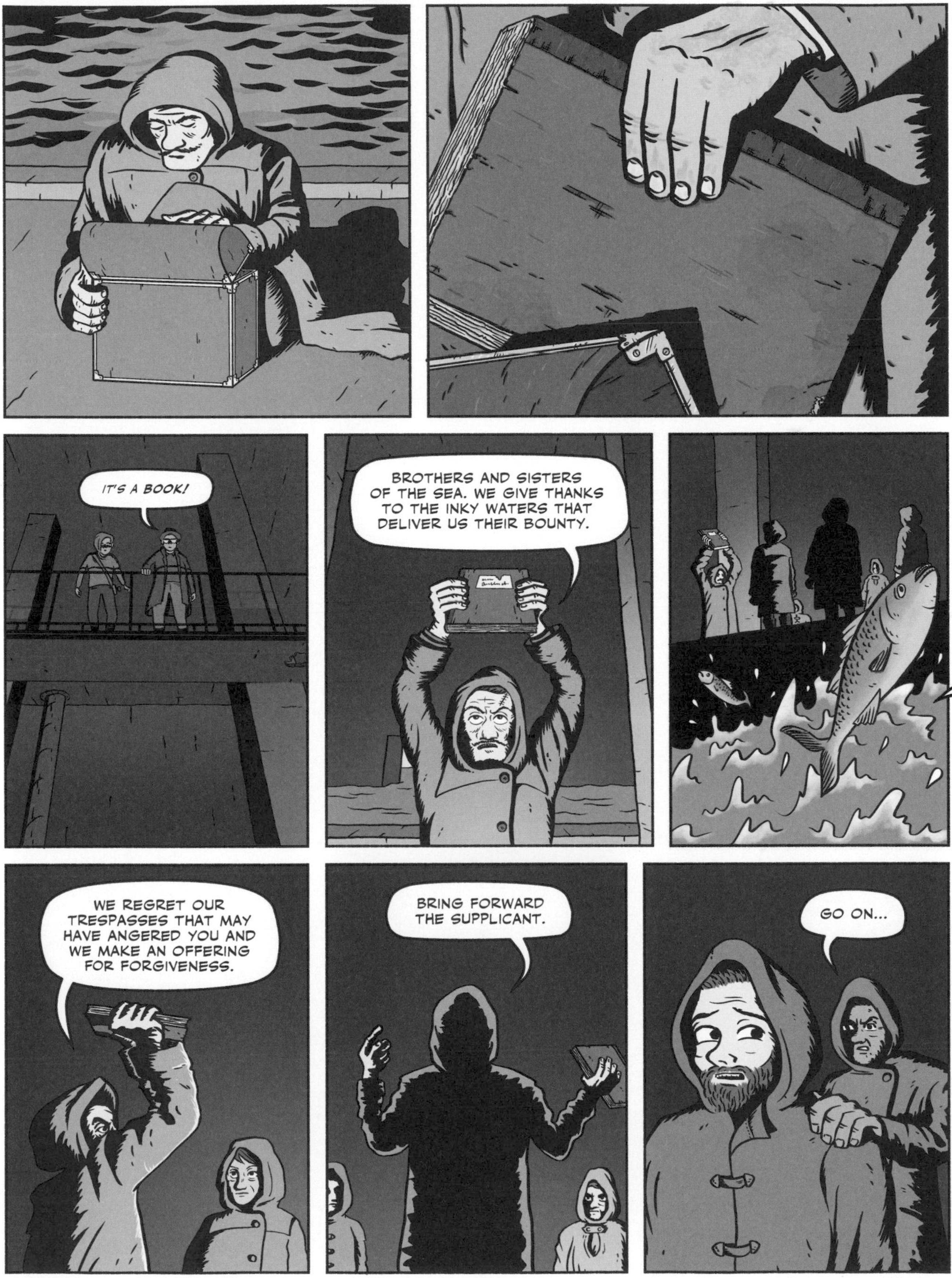
IT'S A BOOK!
BROTHERS AND SISTERS OF THE SEA. WE GIVE THANKS TO THE INKY WATERS THAT DELIVER US THEIR BOUNTY.
WE REGRET OUR TRESPASSES THAT MAY HAVE ANGERED YOU AND WE MAKE AN OFFERING FOR FORGIVENESS.
BRING FORWARD THE SUPPLICANT.
GO ON...

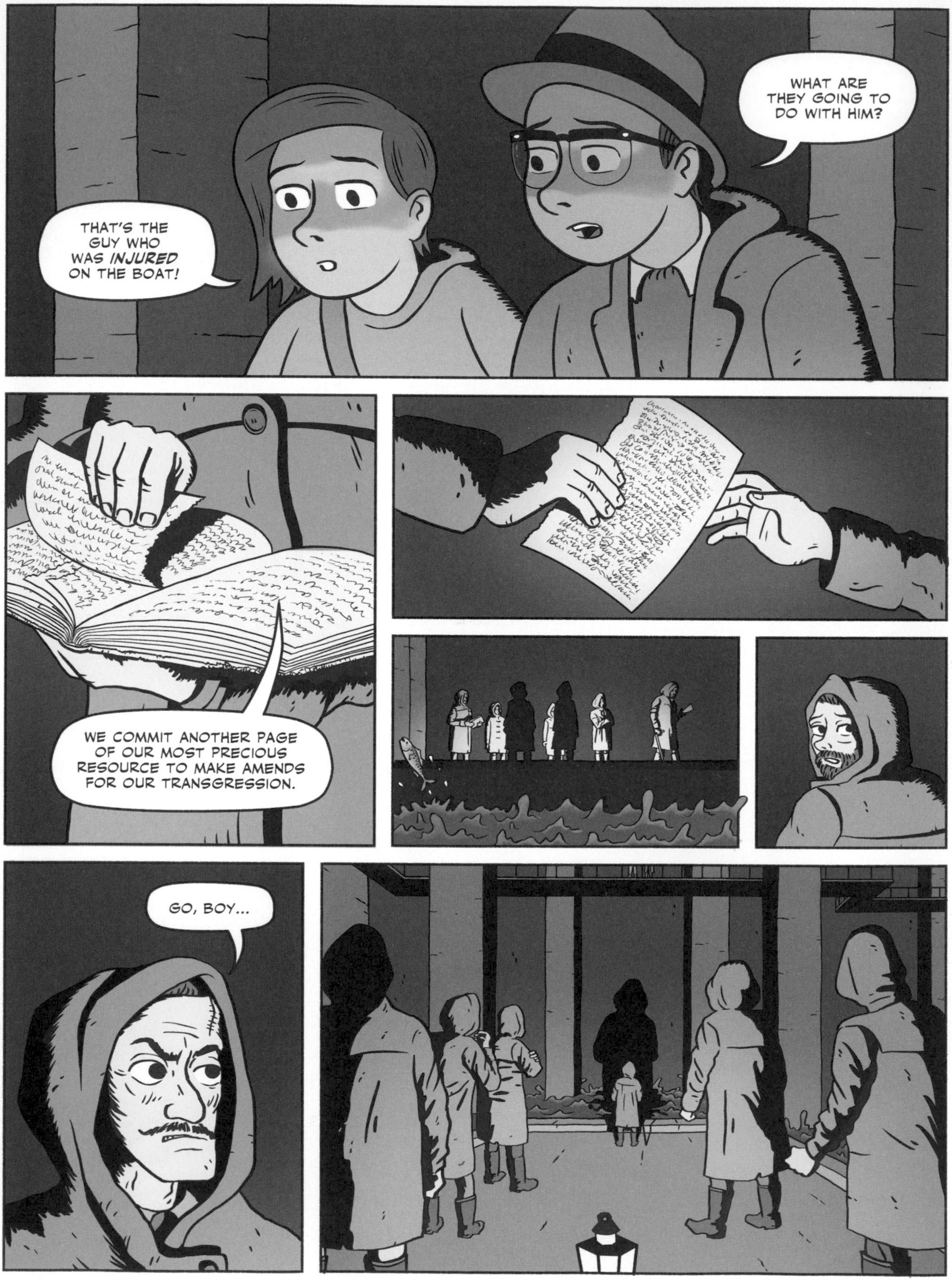
WHAT ARE THEY GOING TO DO WITH HIM?
THAT'S THE GUY WHO WAS *INJURED* ON THE BOAT!
WE COMMIT ANOTHER PAGE OF OUR MOST PRECIOUS RESOURCE TO MAKE AMENDS FOR OUR TRANSGRESSION.
GO, BOY...

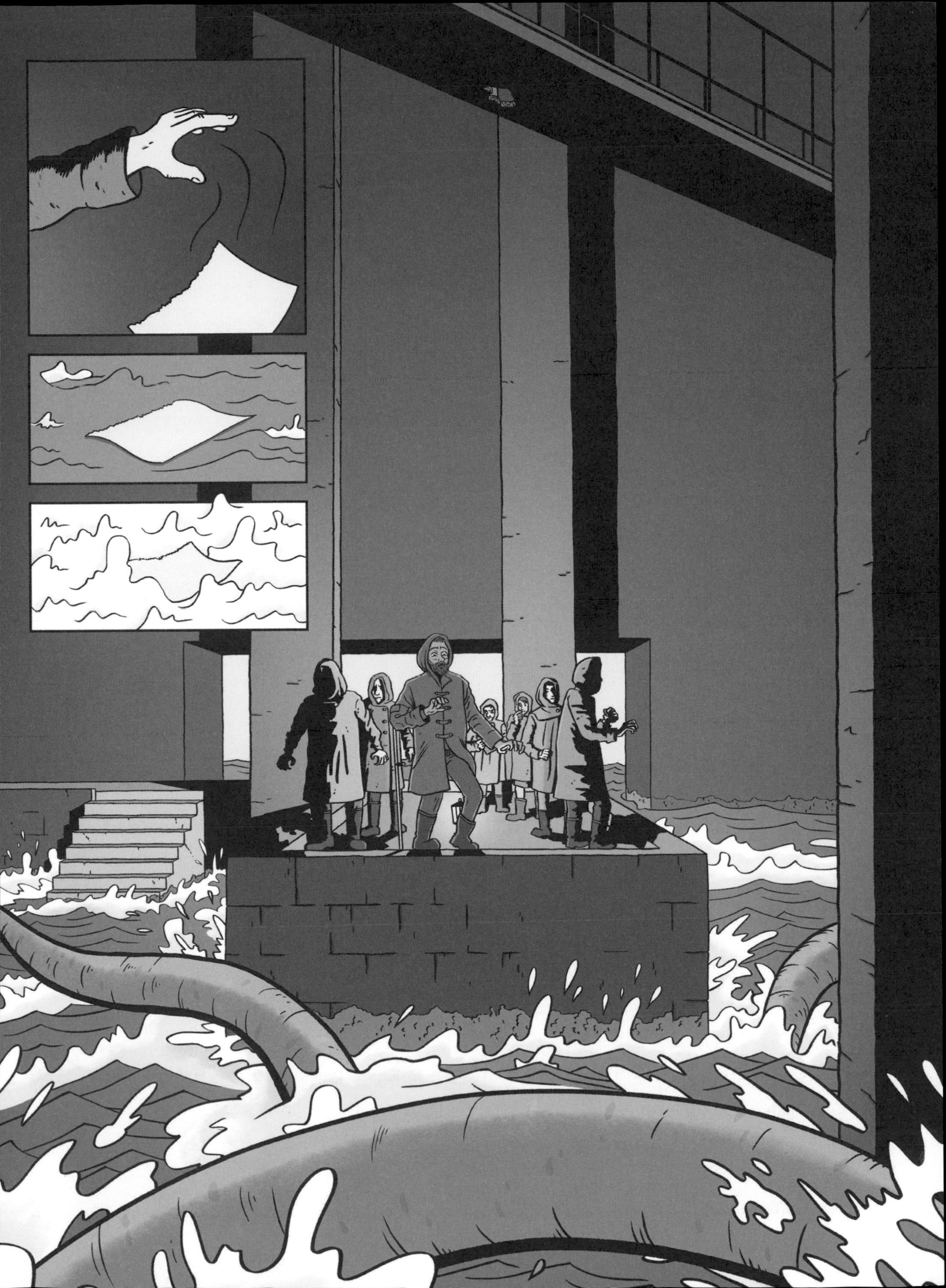

T-T-TAKE A PICTURE!

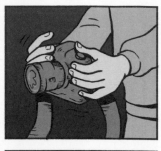

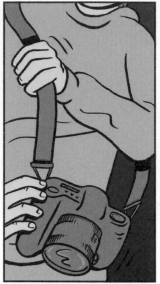

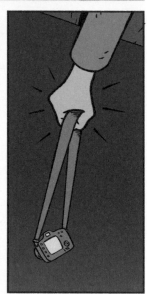

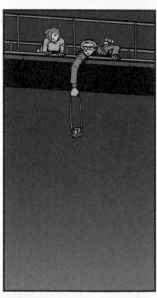

SOMEONE'S THERE!

GET THEM!

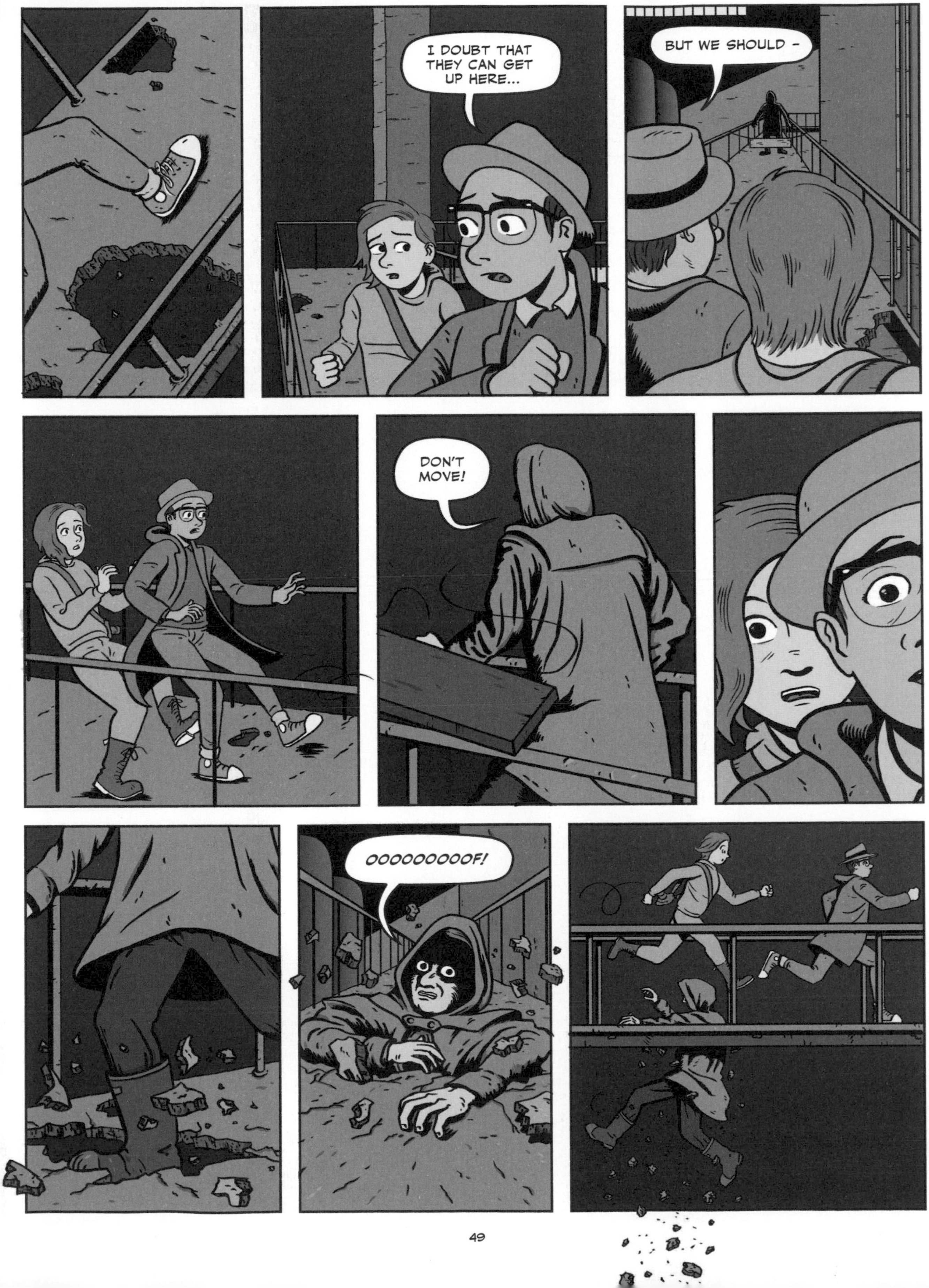
I DOUBT THAT THEY CAN GET UP HERE...
BUT WE SHOULD -
DON'T MOVE!
OOOOOOOOOF!

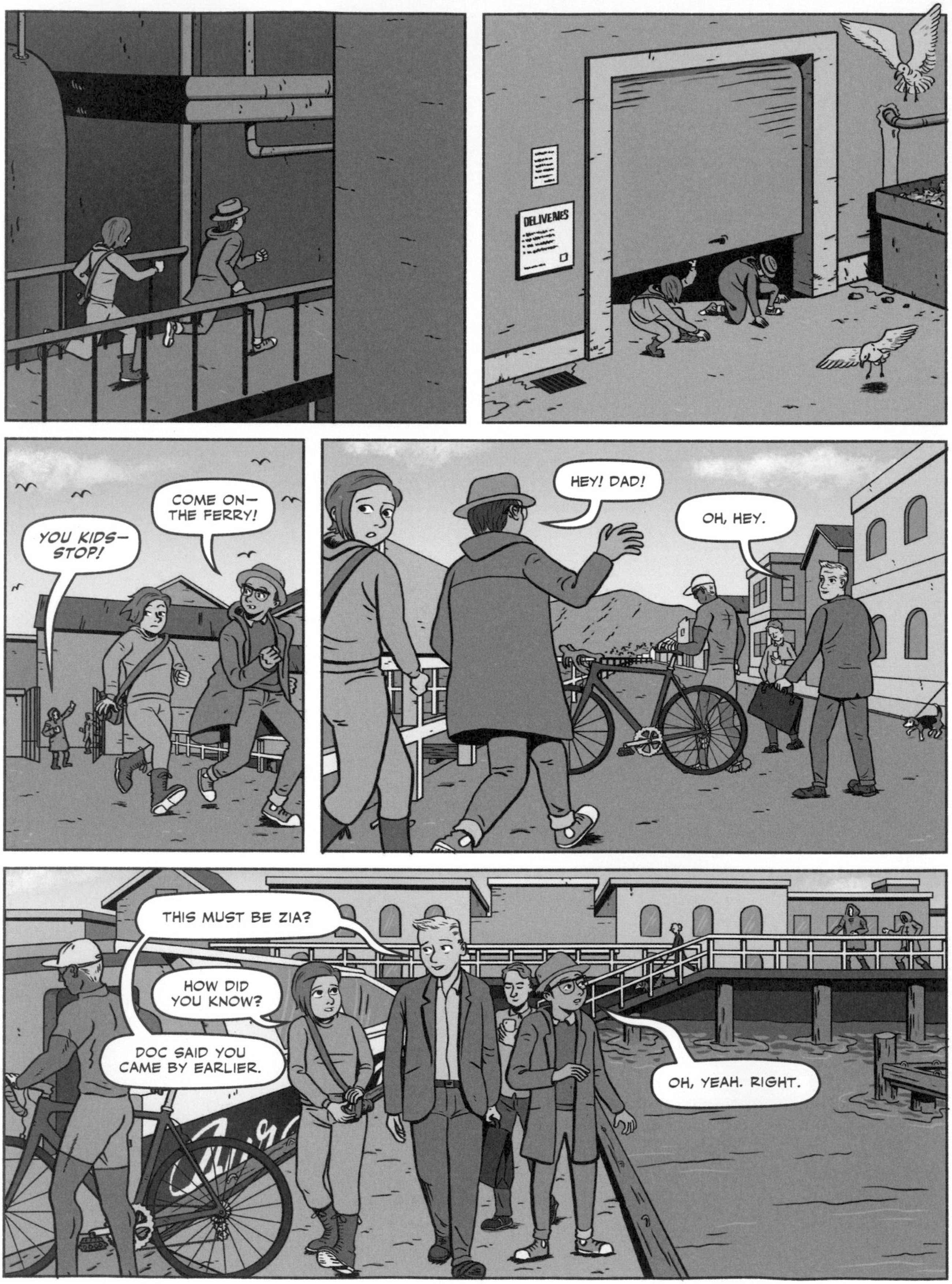
DELIVERIES
YOU KIDS—
STOP!
COME ON—
THE FERRY!
HEY! DAD!
OH, HEY.
THIS MUST BE ZIA?
HOW DID
YOU KNOW?
DOC SAID YOU
CAME BY EARLIER.
OH, YEAH. RIGHT.

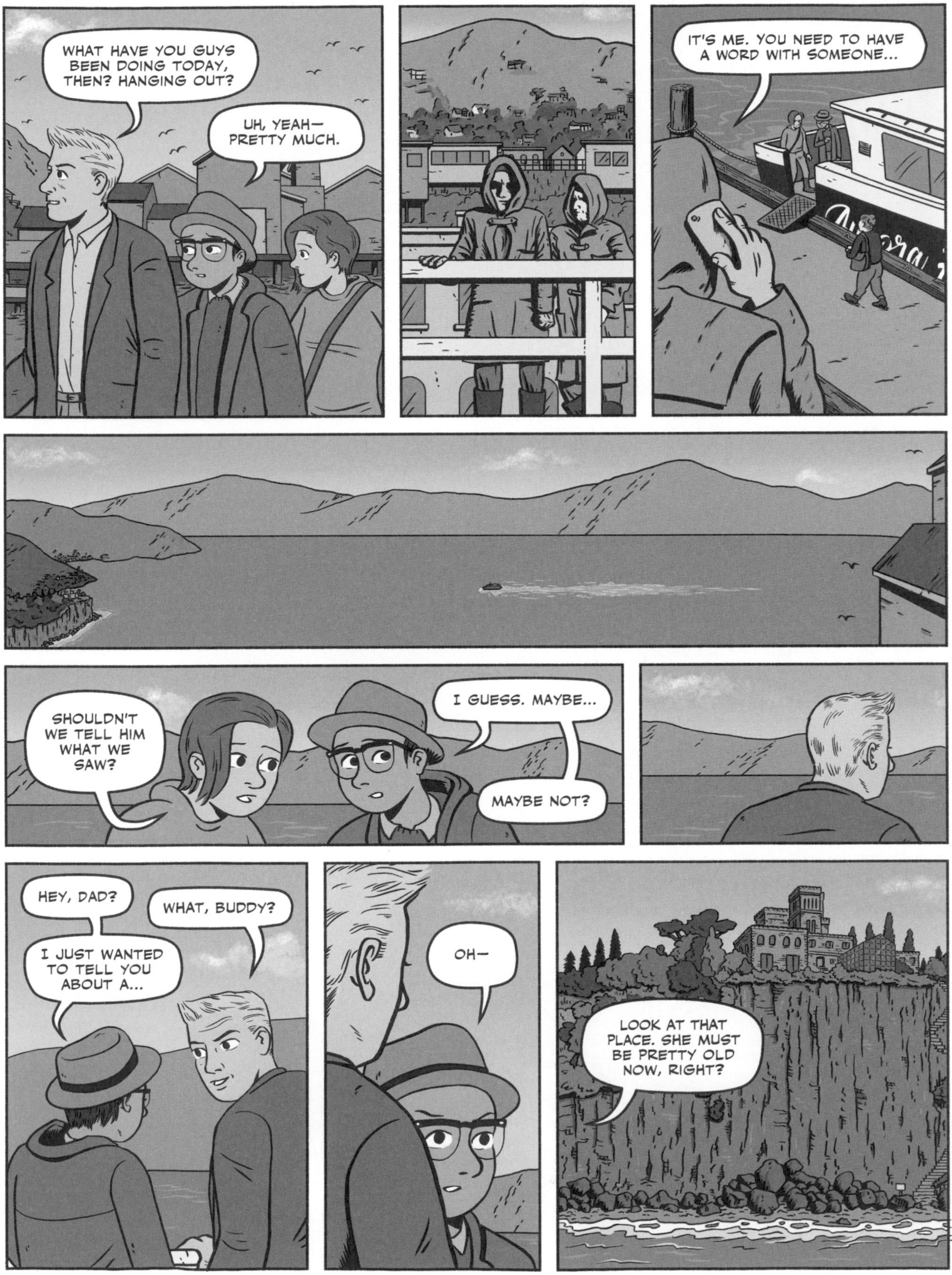
WHAT HAVE YOU GUYS BEEN DOING TODAY, THEN? HANGING OUT?
UH, YEAH— PRETTY MUCH.
IT'S ME. YOU NEED TO HAVE A WORD WITH SOMEONE...
SHOULDN'T WE TELL HIM WHAT WE SAW?
I GUESS. MAYBE...
MAYBE NOT?
HEY, DAD?
WHAT, BUDDY?
I JUST WANTED TO TELL YOU ABOUT A...
OH—
LOOK AT THAT PLACE. SHE MUST BE PRETTY OLD NOW, RIGHT?

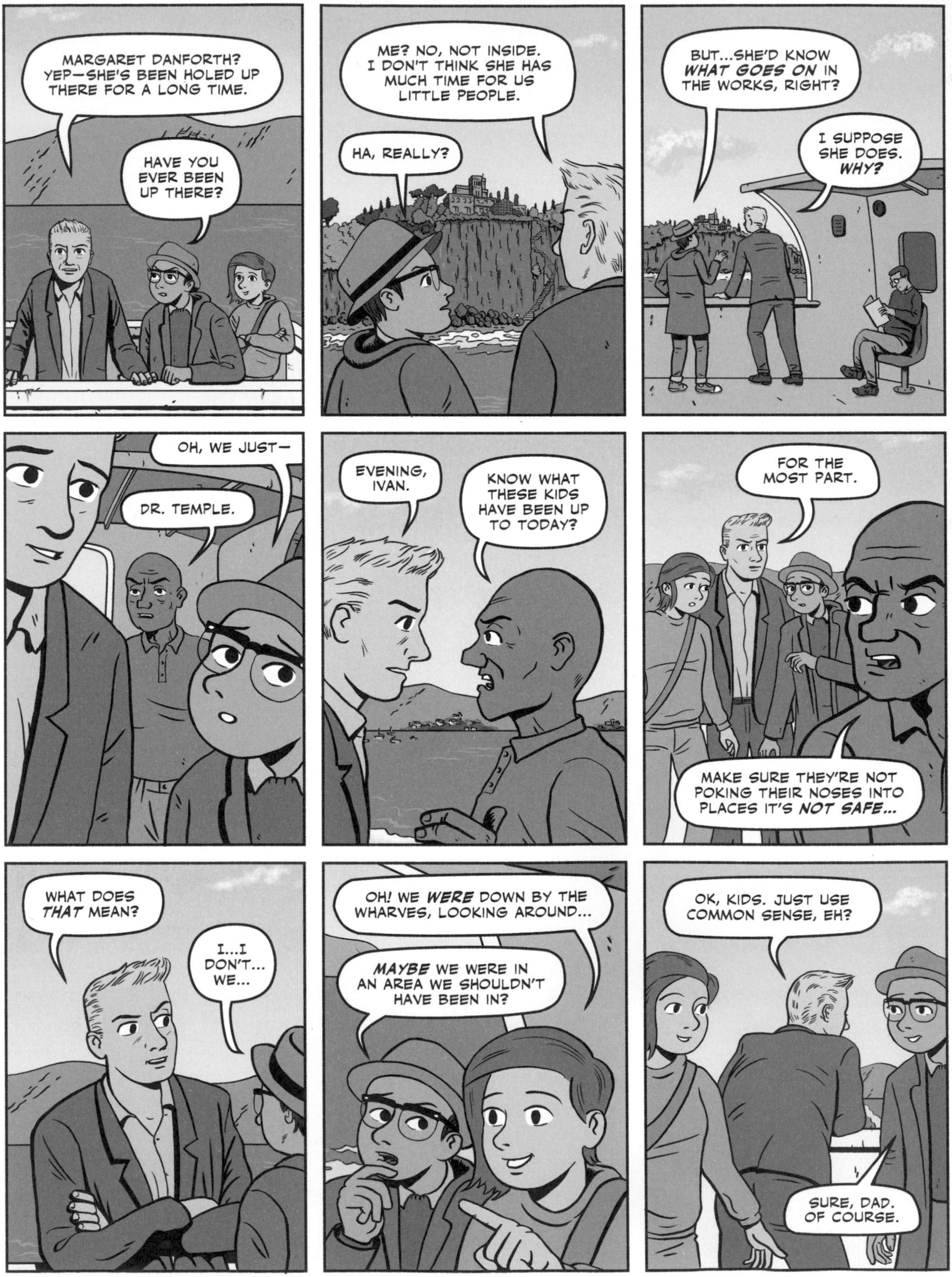
MARGARET DANFORTH? YEP—SHE'S BEEN HOLED UP THERE FOR A LONG TIME.
HAVE YOU EVER BEEN UP THERE?
ME? NO, NOT INSIDE. I DON'T THINK SHE HAS MUCH TIME FOR US LITTLE PEOPLE.
HA, REALLY?
BUT...SHE'D KNOW *WHAT GOES ON* IN THE WORKS, RIGHT?
I SUPPOSE SHE DOES. *WHY?*
OH, WE JUST—
DR. TEMPLE.
EVENING, IVAN.
KNOW WHAT THESE KIDS HAVE BEEN UP TO TODAY?
FOR THE MOST PART.
MAKE SURE THEY'RE NOT POKING THEIR NOSES INTO PLACES IT'S *NOT SAFE...*
WHAT DOES *THAT* MEAN?
I...I DON'T... WE...
OH! WE *WERE* DOWN BY THE WHARVES, LOOKING AROUND...
MAYBE WE WERE IN AN AREA WE SHOULDN'T HAVE BEEN IN?
OK, KIDS. JUST USE COMMON SENSE, EH?
SURE, DAD. OF COURSE.

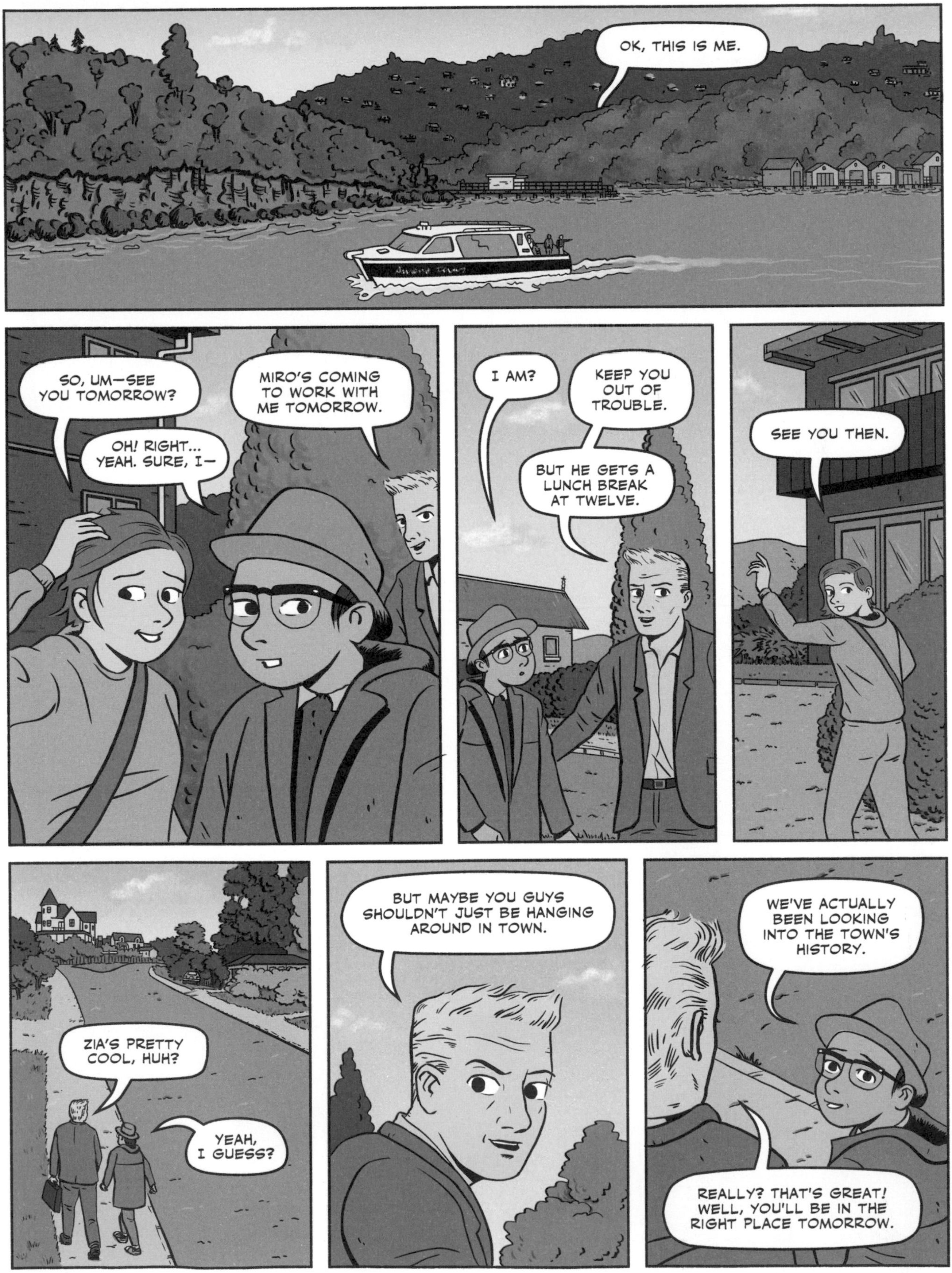
OK, THIS IS ME.
SO, UM—SEE YOU TOMORROW?
MIRO'S COMING TO WORK WITH ME TOMORROW.
OH! RIGHT... YEAH. SURE, I—
I AM?
KEEP YOU OUT OF TROUBLE.
BUT HE GETS A LUNCH BREAK AT TWELVE.
SEE YOU THEN.
ZIA'S PRETTY COOL, HUH?
YEAH, I GUESS?
BUT MAYBE YOU GUYS SHOULDN'T JUST BE HANGING AROUND IN TOWN.
WE'VE ACTUALLY BEEN LOOKING INTO THE TOWN'S HISTORY.
REALLY? THAT'S GREAT! WELL, YOU'LL BE IN THE RIGHT PLACE TOMORROW.

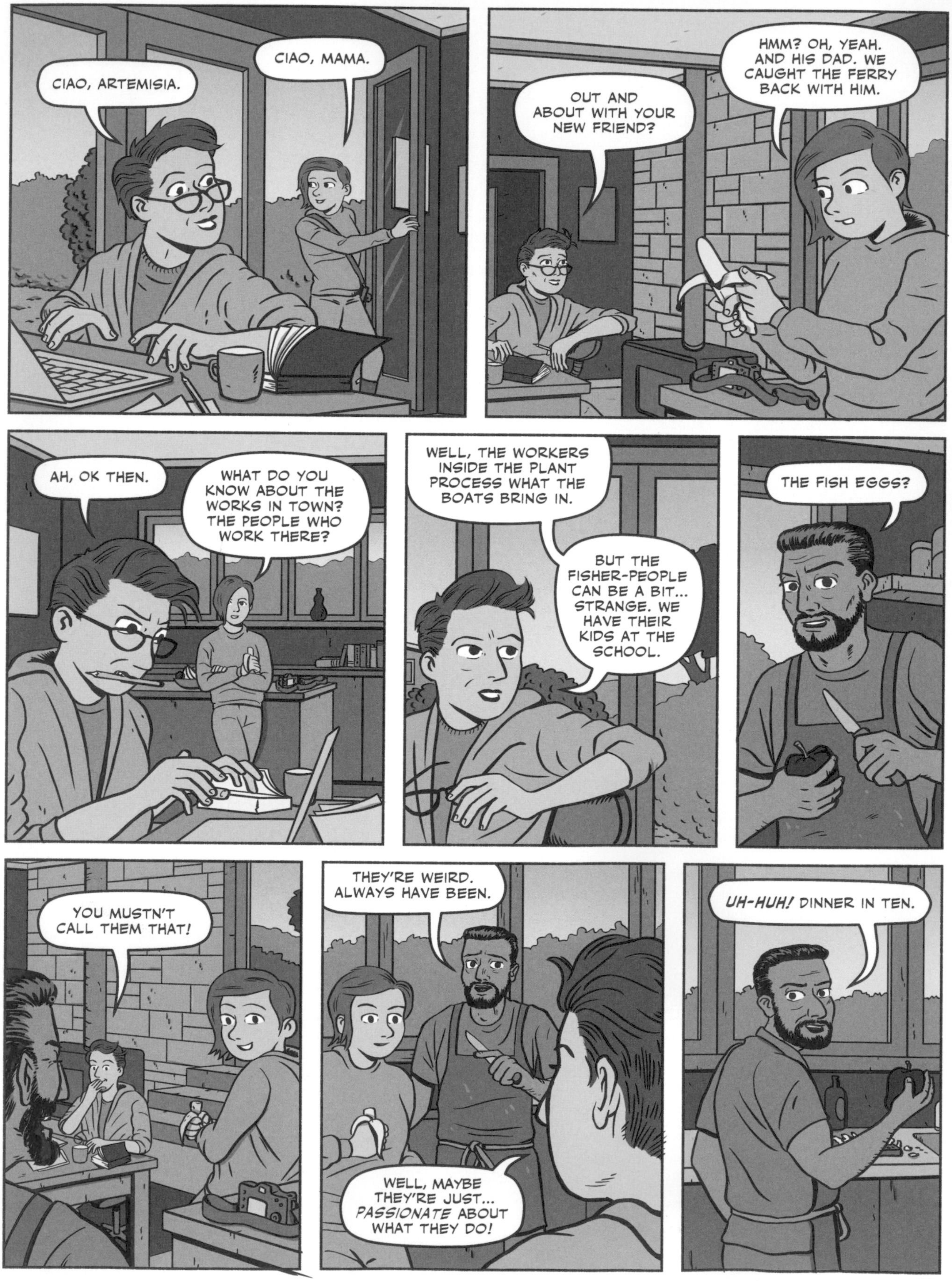
CIAO, ARTEMISIA.
CIAO, MAMA.
OUT AND ABOUT WITH YOUR NEW FRIEND?
HMM? OH, YEAH. AND HIS DAD. WE CAUGHT THE FERRY BACK WITH HIM.
AH, OK THEN.
WHAT DO YOU KNOW ABOUT THE WORKS IN TOWN? THE PEOPLE WHO WORK THERE?
WELL, THE WORKERS INSIDE THE PLANT PROCESS WHAT THE BOATS BRING IN.
BUT THE FISHER-PEOPLE CAN BE A BIT... STRANGE. WE HAVE THEIR KIDS AT THE SCHOOL.
THE FISH EGGS?
YOU MUSTN'T CALL THEM THAT!
THEY'RE WEIRD. ALWAYS HAVE BEEN.
WELL, MAYBE THEY'RE JUST... *PASSIONATE* ABOUT WHAT THEY DO!
UH-HUH! DINNER IN TEN.

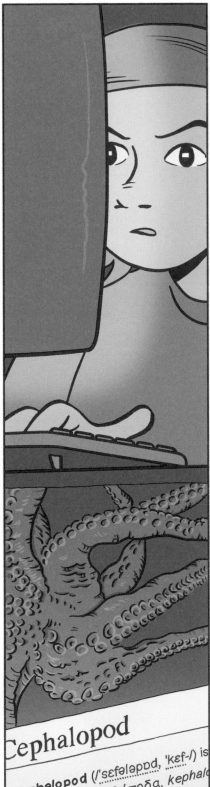

TWENTY THOUSAND LEAGUES UNDER SE
Cephalopod
cephalopod (/ˈsɛfələpɒd, ˈkɛf-/) is
Greek plural κεφαλόποδα, kephalo
These exclusively marine animals a
head, and a set of arms or tentacles
head, and a set of arms or tentacles
foot. Fishermen sometim
ephalopods

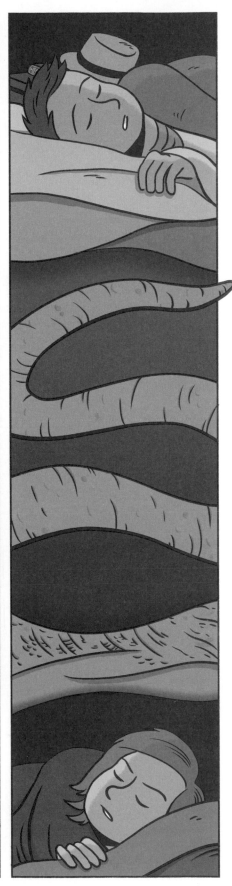

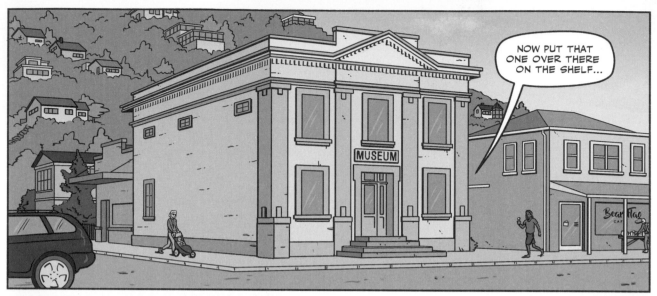

NOW PUT THAT ONE OVER THERE ON THE SHELF...

MUSEUM

...WITH THE OTHER MUSTELIDS.

UH-HUH.

YOU GOT THAT?

SURE.

THAT'S LIKE FERRETS AND STOATS, RIGHT?

BINGO!

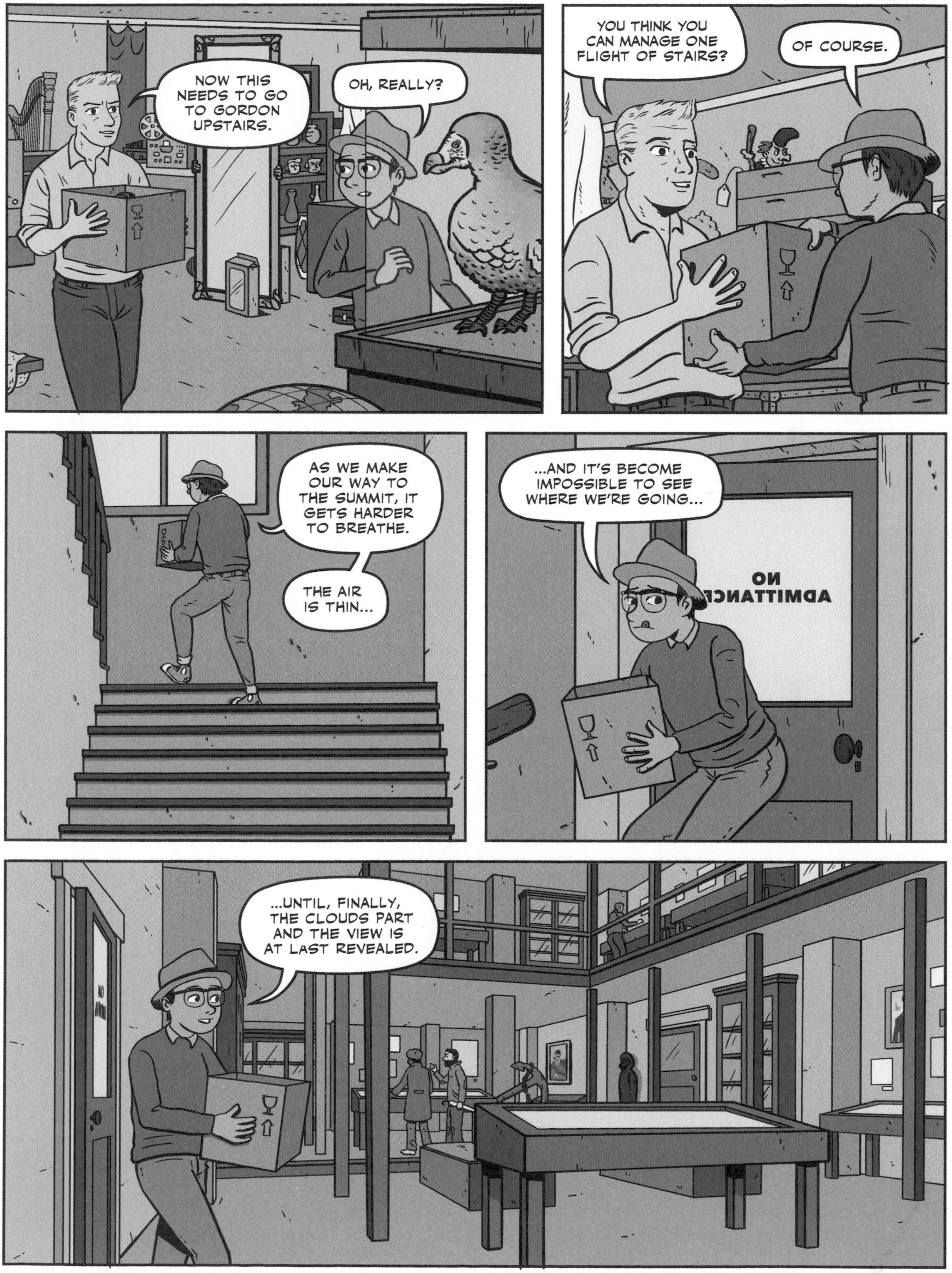
NOW THIS NEEDS TO GO TO GORDON UPSTAIRS.
OH, REALLY?
YOU THINK YOU CAN MANAGE ONE FLIGHT OF STAIRS?
OF COURSE.
AS WE MAKE OUR WAY TO THE SUMMIT, IT GETS HARDER TO BREATHE.
THE AIR IS THIN...
...AND IT'S BECOME IMPOSSIBLE TO SEE WHERE WE'RE GOING...
...UNTIL, FINALLY, THE CLOUDS PART AND THE VIEW IS AT LAST REVEALED.

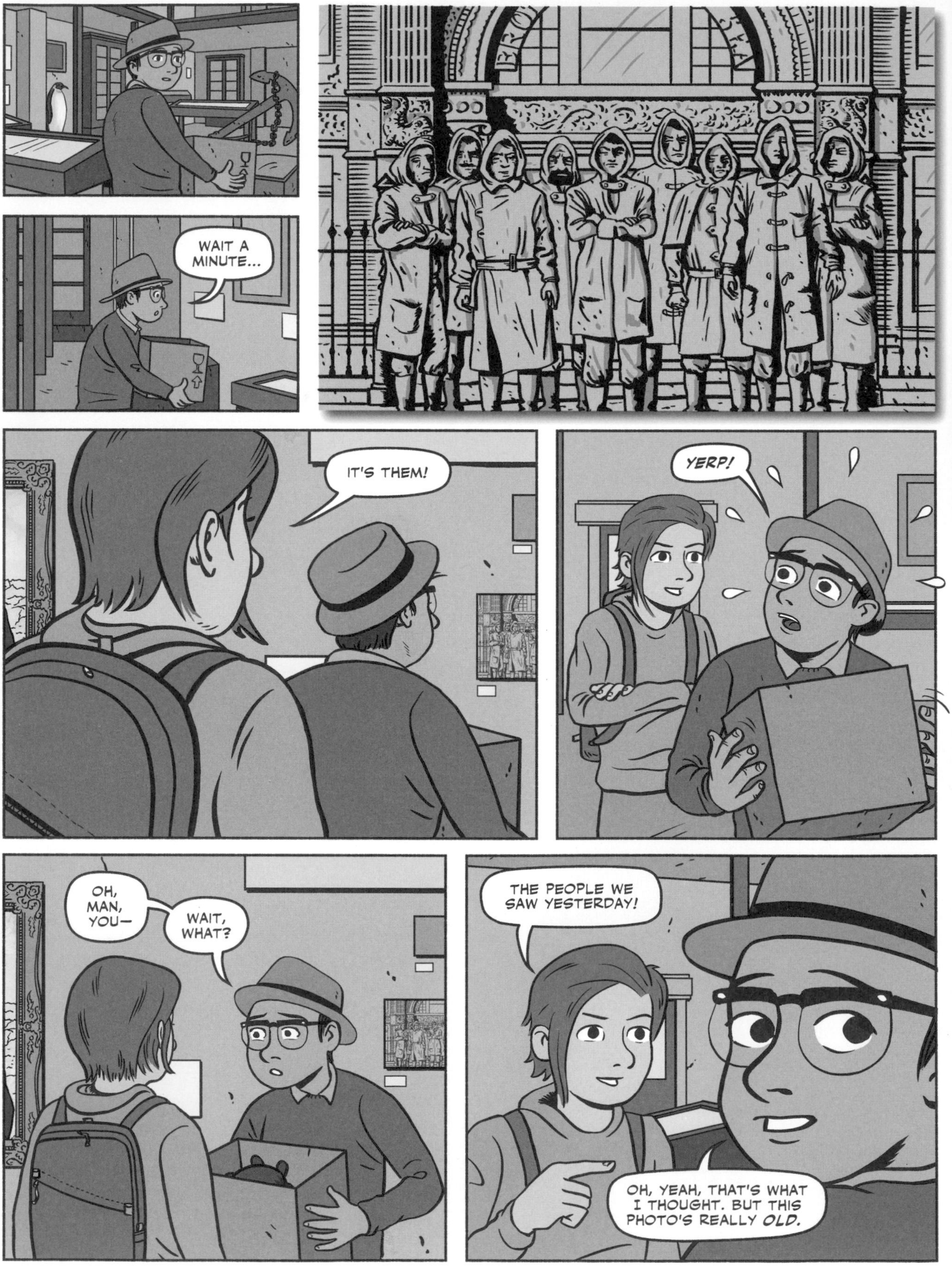
WAIT A MINUTE...
IT'S THEM!
YERP!
OH, MAN, YOU—
WAIT, WHAT?
THE PEOPLE WE SAW YESTERDAY!
OH, YEAH, THAT'S WHAT I THOUGHT. BUT THIS PHOTO'S REALLY *OLD.*

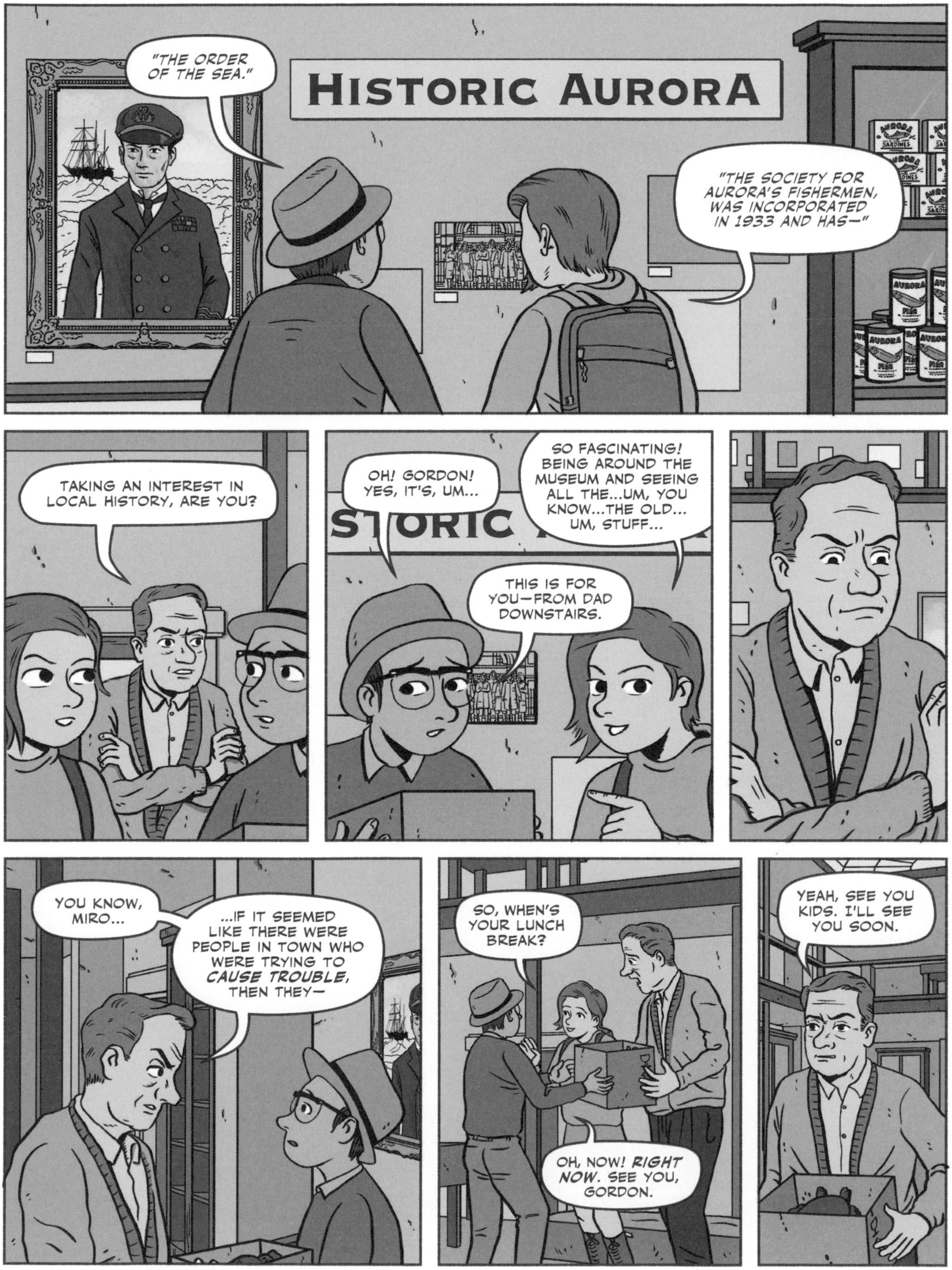
"THE ORDER OF THE SEA."
HISTORIC AURORA
"THE SOCIETY FOR AURORA'S FISHERMEN, WAS INCORPORATED IN 1933 AND HAS—"
TAKING AN INTEREST IN LOCAL HISTORY, ARE YOU?
OH! GORDON! YES, IT'S, UM...
SO FASCINATING! BEING AROUND THE MUSEUM AND SEEING ALL THE...UM, YOU KNOW...THE OLD... UM, STUFF...
THIS IS FOR YOU—FROM DAD DOWNSTAIRS.
YOU KNOW, MIRO...
...IF IT SEEMED LIKE THERE WERE PEOPLE IN TOWN WHO WERE TRYING TO *CAUSE TROUBLE*, THEN THEY—
SO, WHEN'S YOUR LUNCH BREAK?
OH, NOW! *RIGHT NOW*. SEE YOU, GORDON.
YEAH, SEE YOU KIDS. I'LL SEE YOU SOON.

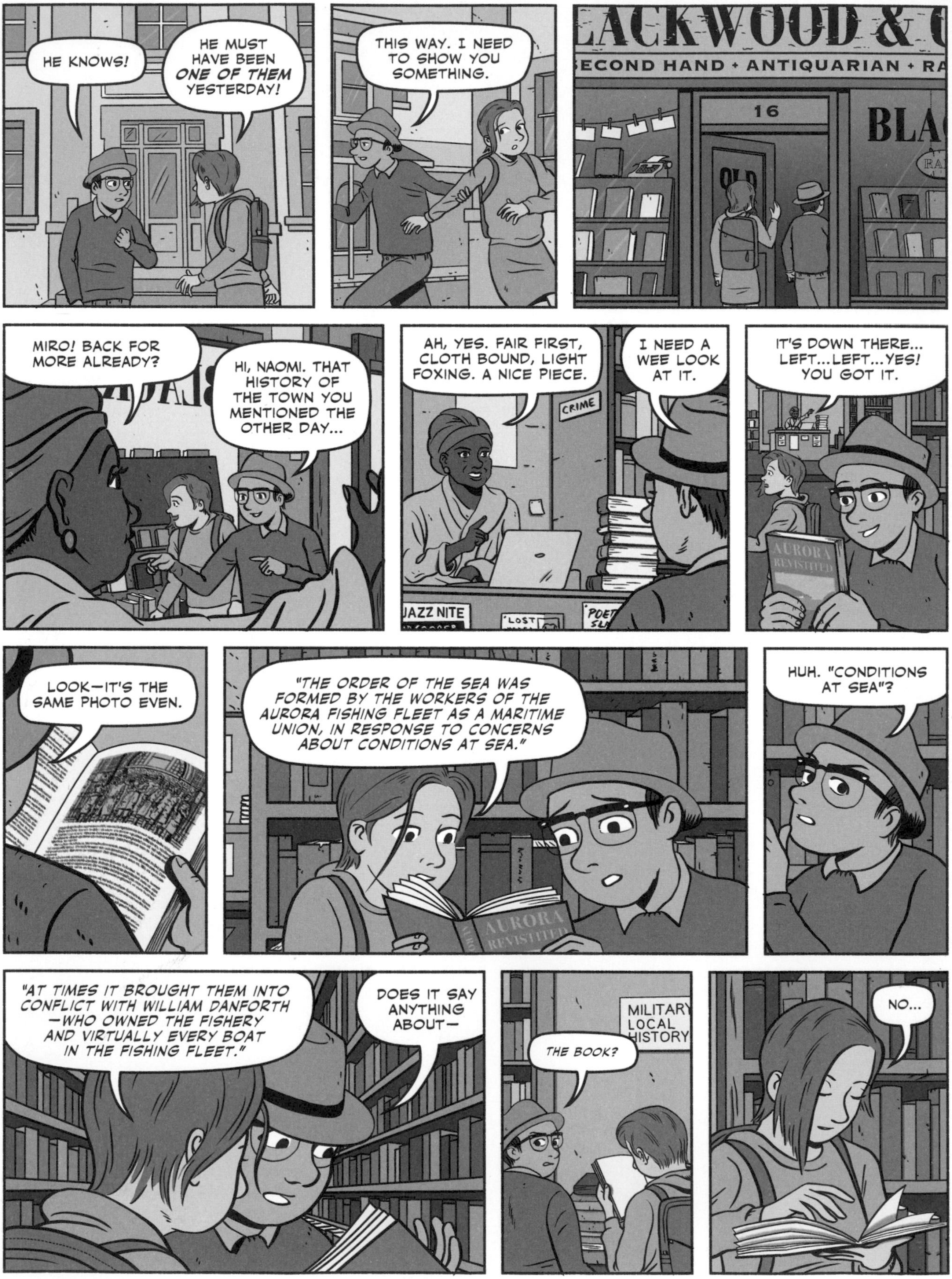
HE KNOWS!
HE MUST HAVE BEEN *ONE OF THEM* YESTERDAY!
THIS WAY. I NEED TO SHOW YOU SOMETHING.
LACKWOOD & C
SECOND HAND + ANTIQUARIAN + RA
16
BLA
MIRO! BACK FOR MORE ALREADY?
HI, NAOMI. THAT HISTORY OF THE TOWN YOU MENTIONED THE OTHER DAY...
AH, YES. FAIR FIRST, CLOTH BOUND, LIGHT FOXING. A NICE PIECE.
CRIME
JAZZ NITE
I NEED A WEE LOOK AT IT.
IT'S DOWN THERE... LEFT...LEFT...YES! YOU GOT IT.
AURORA REVISITED
LOOK—IT'S THE SAME PHOTO EVEN.
"THE ORDER OF THE SEA WAS FORMED BY THE WORKERS OF THE AURORA FISHING FLEET AS A MARITIME UNION, IN RESPONSE TO CONCERNS ABOUT CONDITIONS AT SEA."
AURORA REVISITED
HUH. "CONDITIONS AT SEA"?
"AT TIMES IT BROUGHT THEM INTO CONFLICT WITH WILLIAM DANFORTH —WHO OWNED THE FISHERY AND VIRTUALLY EVERY BOAT IN THE FISHING FLEET."
DOES IT SAY ANYTHING ABOUT—
MILITARY
LOCAL HISTORY
THE BOOK?
NO...

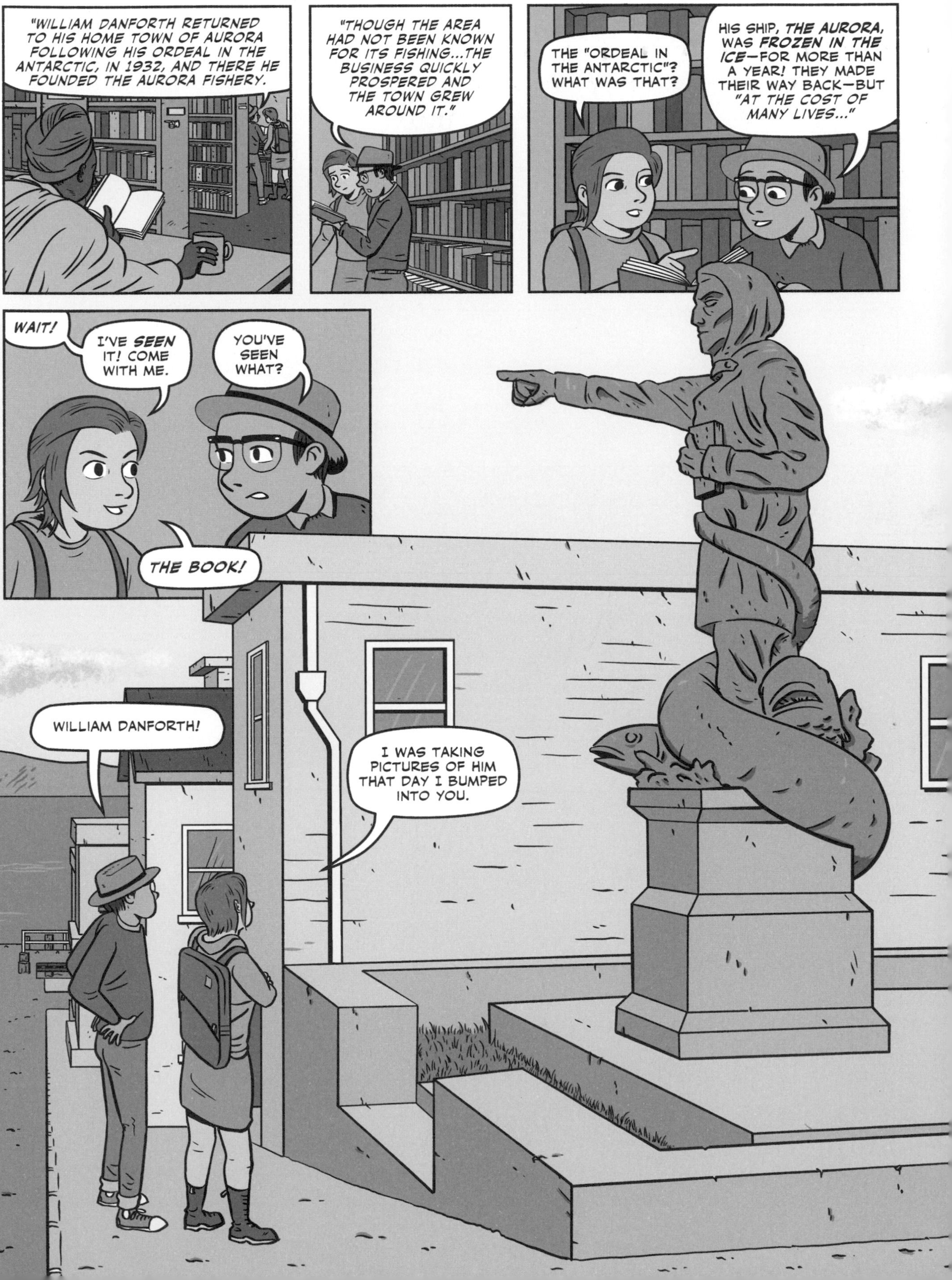
"WILLIAM DANFORTH RETURNED TO HIS HOME TOWN OF AURORA FOLLOWING HIS ORDEAL IN THE ANTARCTIC, IN 1932, AND THERE HE FOUNDED THE AURORA FISHERY.
"THOUGH THE AREA HAD NOT BEEN KNOWN FOR ITS FISHING...THE BUSINESS QUICKLY PROSPERED AND THE TOWN GREW AROUND IT."
THE "ORDEAL IN THE ANTARCTIC"? WHAT WAS THAT?
HIS SHIP, THE AURORA, WAS FROZEN IN THE ICE—FOR MORE THAN A YEAR! THEY MADE THEIR WAY BACK—BUT "AT THE COST OF MANY LIVES..."
WAIT!
I'VE SEEN IT! COME WITH ME.
YOU'VE SEEN WHAT?
THE BOOK!
WILLIAM DANFORTH!
I WAS TAKING PICTURES OF HIM THAT DAY I BUMPED INTO YOU.

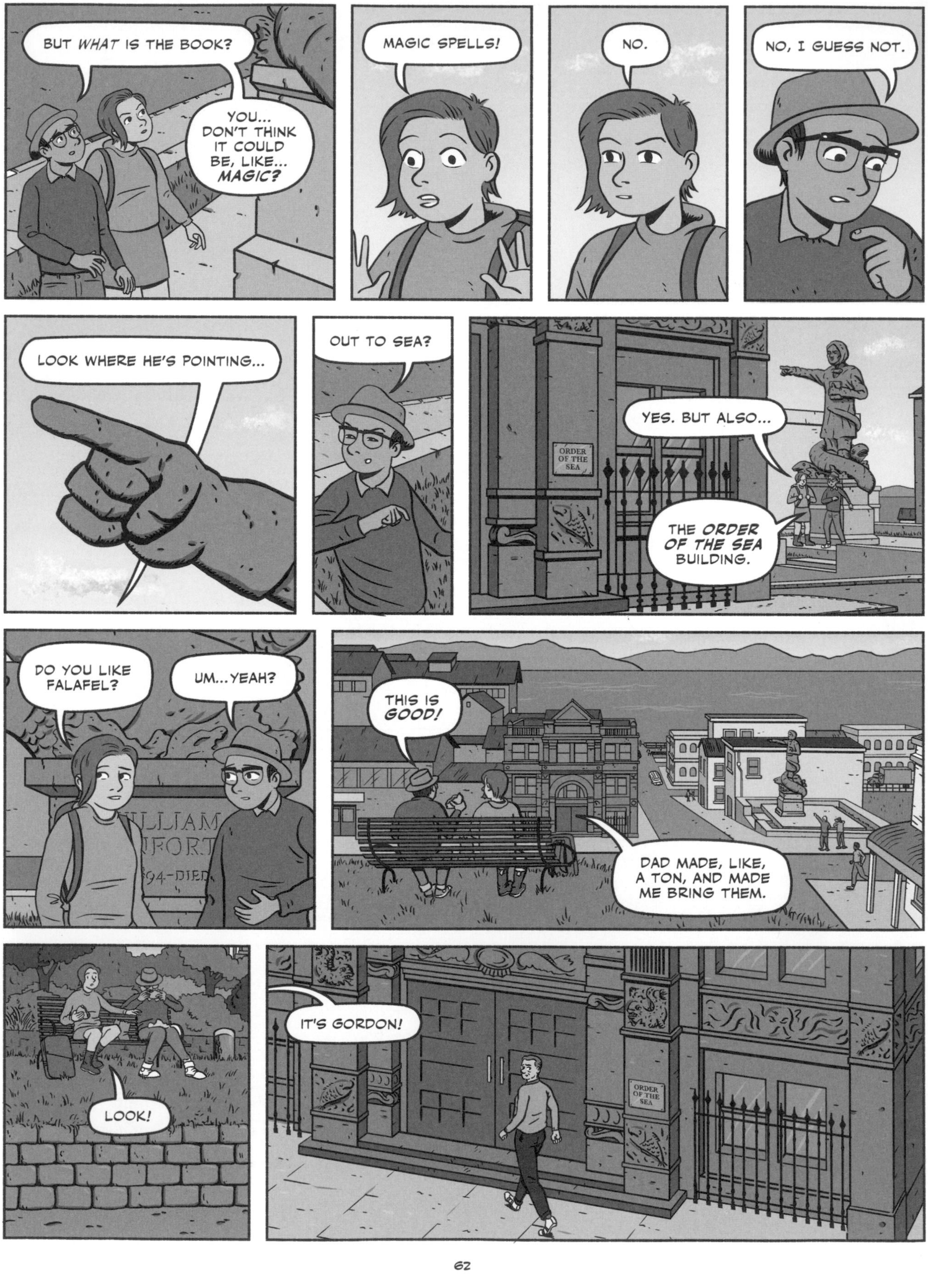
BUT WHAT IS THE BOOK?
YOU... DON'T THINK IT COULD BE, LIKE... MAGIC?
MAGIC SPELLS!
NO.
NO, I GUESS NOT.
LOOK WHERE HE'S POINTING...
OUT TO SEA?
ORDER OF THE SEA
YES. BUT ALSO...
THE ORDER OF THE SEA BUILDING.
DO YOU LIKE FALAFEL?
UM...YEAH?
THIS IS GOOD!
DAD MADE, LIKE, A TON, AND MADE ME BRING THEM.
LOOK!
IT'S GORDON!
ORDER OF THE SEA

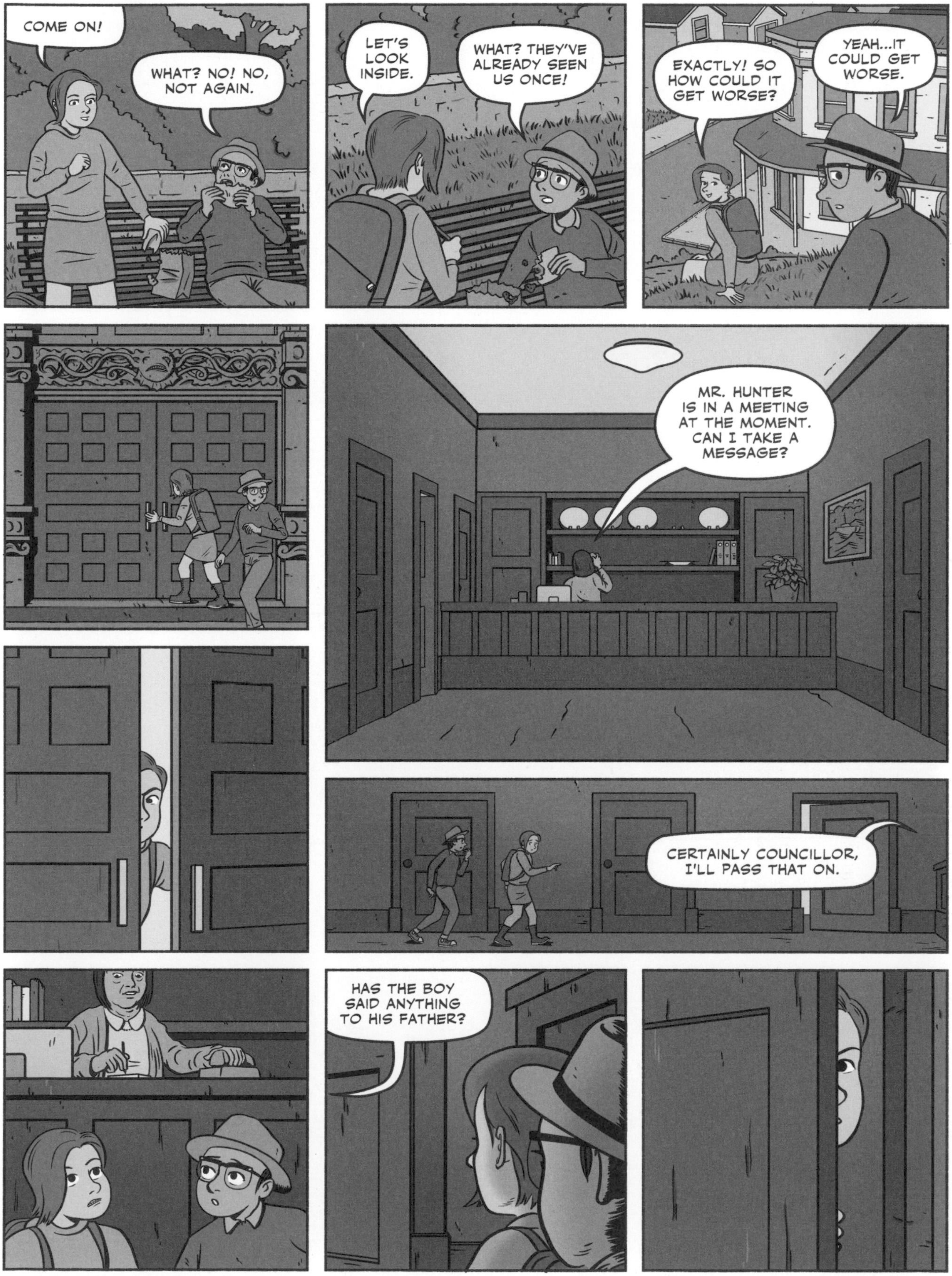
COME ON!
WHAT? NO! NO, NOT AGAIN.
LET'S LOOK INSIDE.
WHAT? THEY'VE ALREADY SEEN US ONCE!
EXACTLY! SO HOW COULD IT GET WORSE?
YEAH...IT COULD GET WORSE.
MR. HUNTER IS IN A MEETING AT THE MOMENT. CAN I TAKE A MESSAGE?
CERTAINLY COUNCILLOR, I'LL PASS THAT ON.
HAS THE BOY SAID ANYTHING TO HIS FATHER?

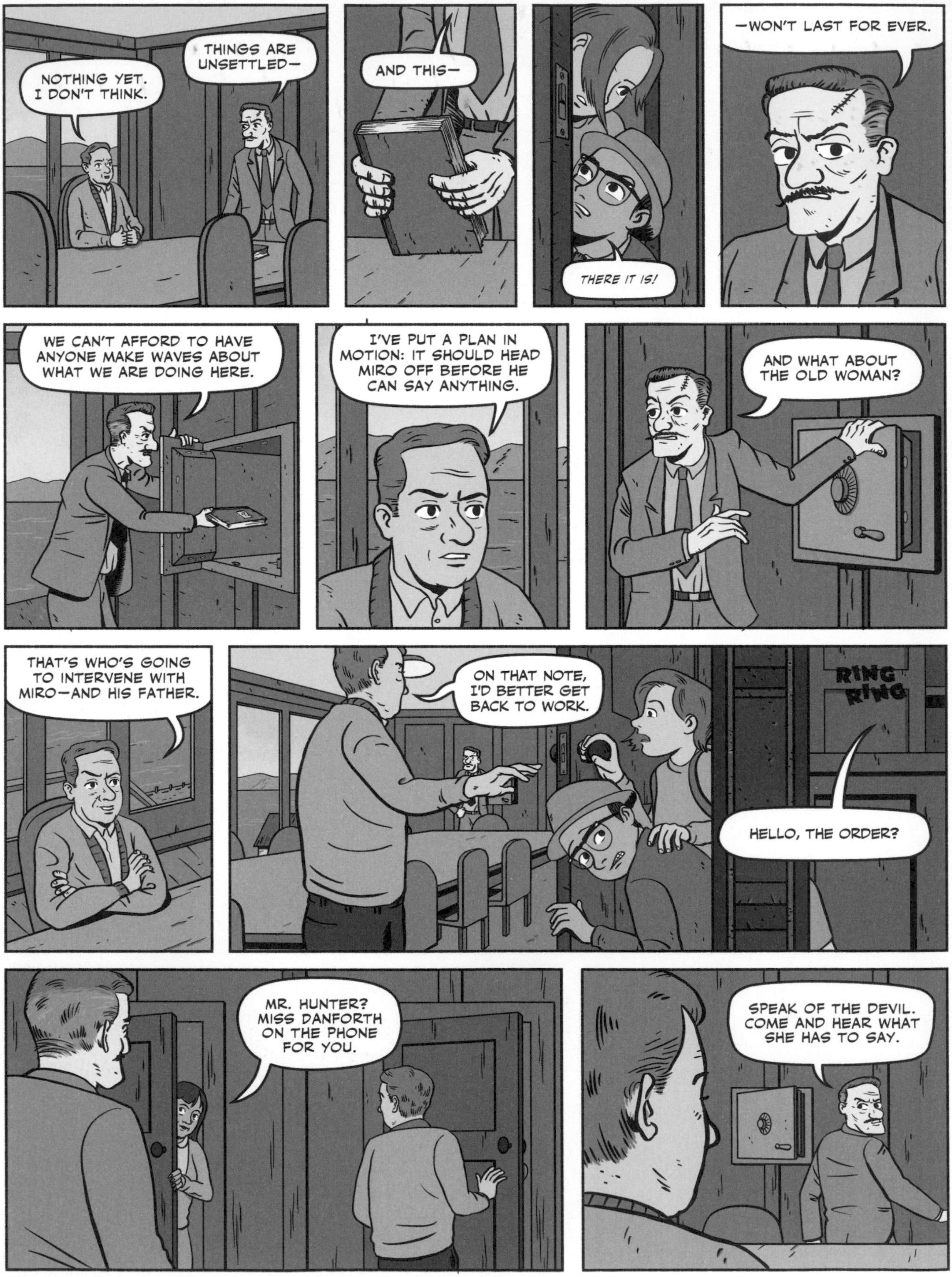
NOTHING YET. I DON'T THINK.
THINGS ARE UNSETTLED—
AND THIS—
THERE IT IS!
—WON'T LAST FOR EVER.
WE CAN'T AFFORD TO HAVE ANYONE MAKE WAVES ABOUT WHAT WE ARE DOING HERE.
I'VE PUT A PLAN IN MOTION: IT SHOULD HEAD MIRO OFF BEFORE HE CAN SAY ANYTHING.
AND WHAT ABOUT THE OLD WOMAN?
THAT'S WHO'S GOING TO INTERVENE WITH MIRO—AND HIS FATHER.
ON THAT NOTE, I'D BETTER GET BACK TO WORK.
RING RING
HELLO, THE ORDER?
MR. HUNTER? MISS DANFORTH ON THE PHONE FOR YOU.
SPEAK OF THE DEVIL. COME AND HEAR WHAT SHE HAS TO SAY.

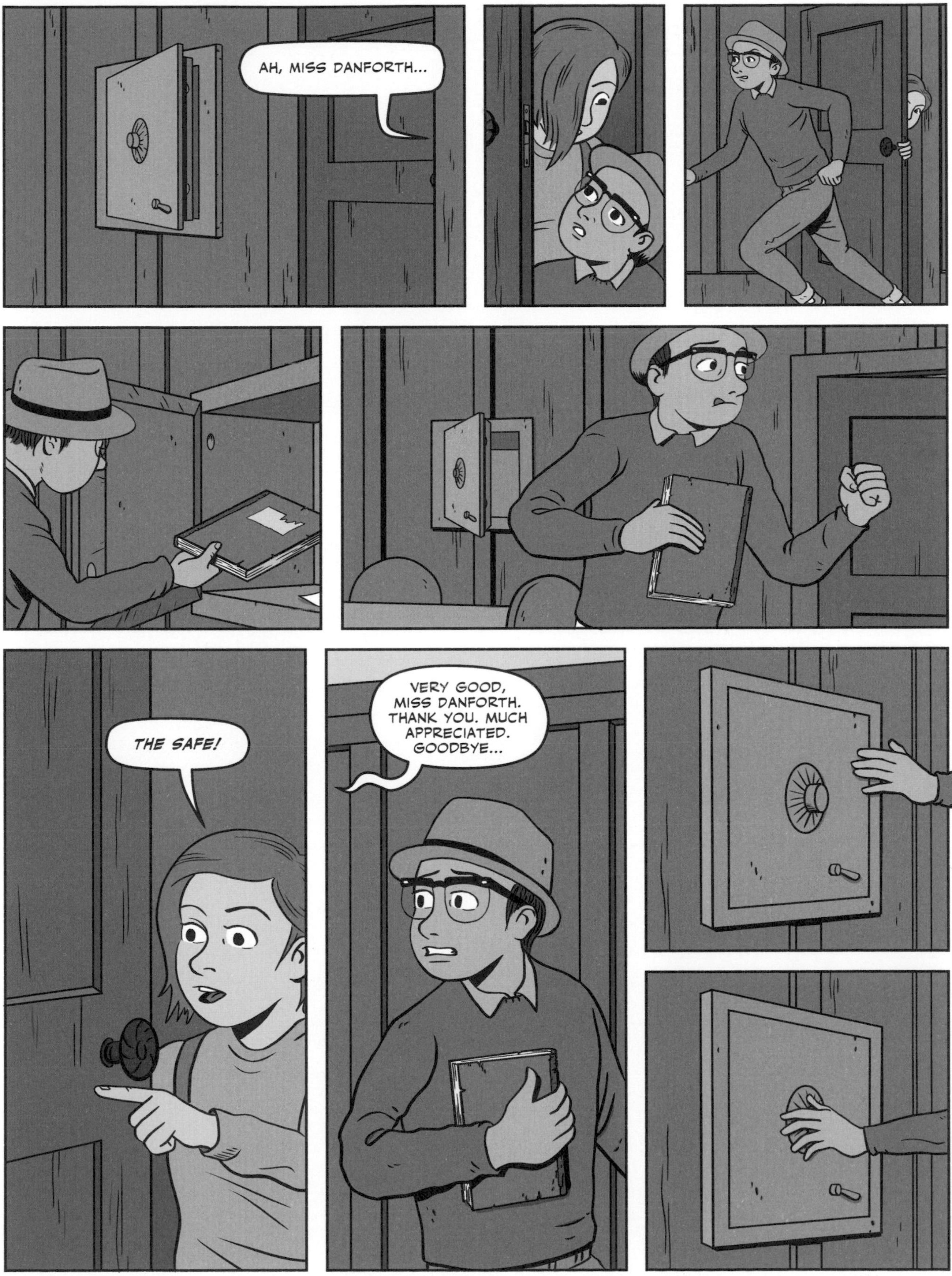
AH, MISS DANFORTH...
THE SAFE!
VERY GOOD, MISS DANFORTH. THANK YOU. MUCH APPRECIATED. GOODBYE...

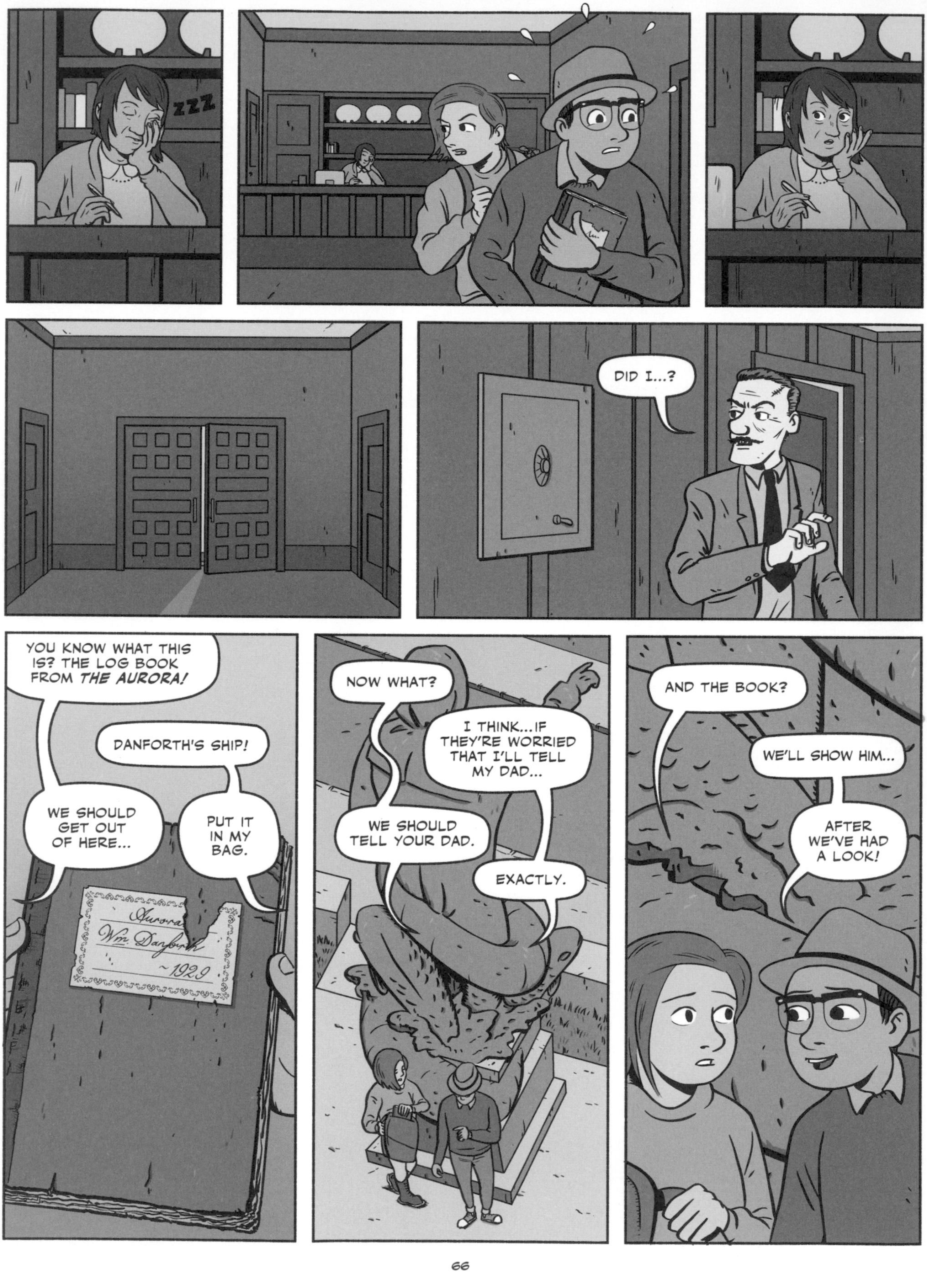
ZZZ
DID I...?
YOU KNOW WHAT THIS IS? THE LOG BOOK FROM *THE AURORA!*
DANFORTH'S SHIP!
WE SHOULD GET OUT OF HERE...
PUT IT IN MY BAG.
Aurora
Wm. Danforth
~1929
NOW WHAT?
WE SHOULD TELL YOUR DAD.
I THINK...IF THEY'RE WORRIED THAT I'LL TELL MY DAD...
EXACTLY.
AND THE BOOK?
WE'LL SHOW HIM...
AFTER WE'VE HAD A LOOK!

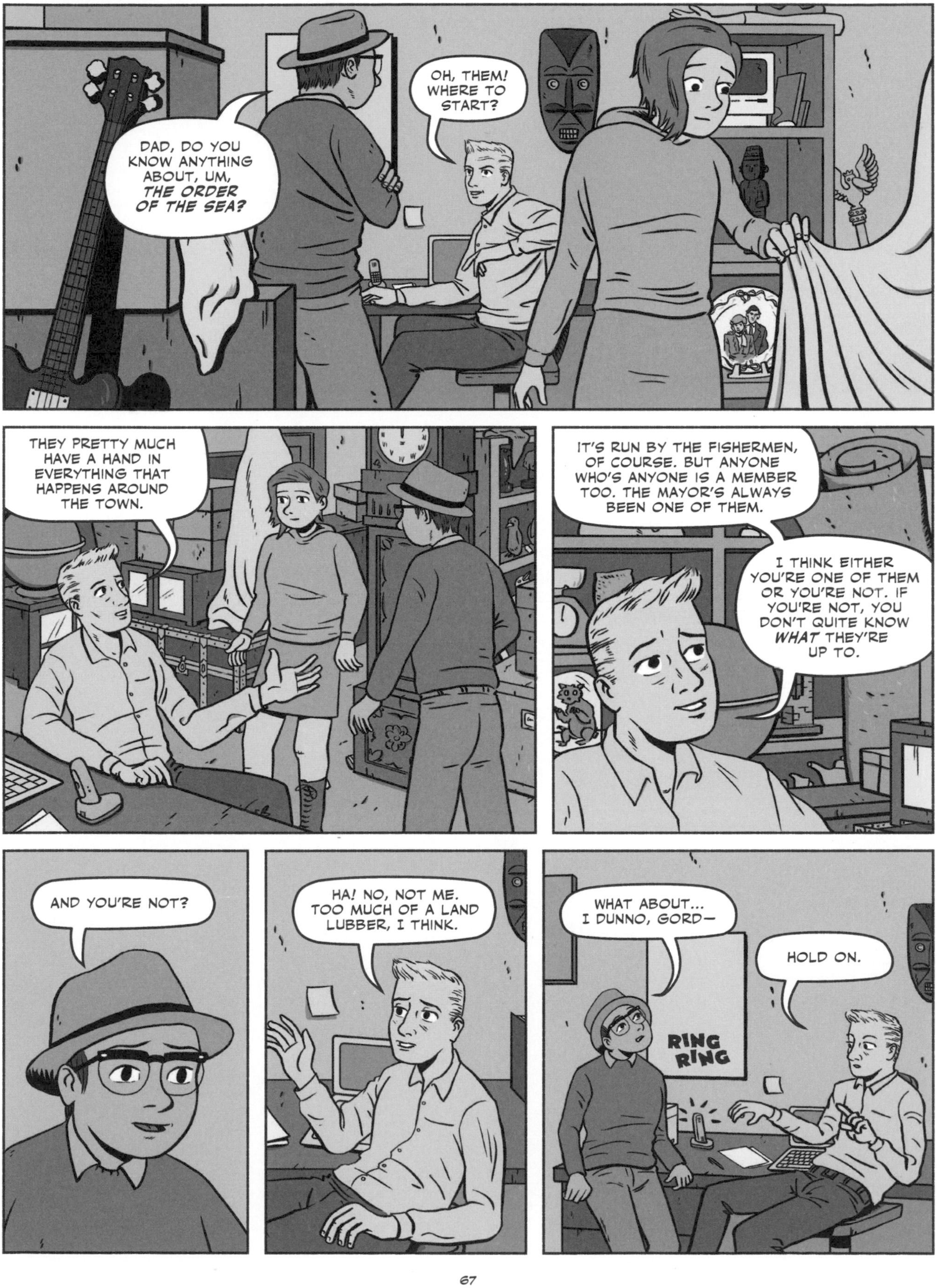
DAD, DO YOU KNOW ANYTHING ABOUT, UM, *THE ORDER OF THE SEA?*
OH, THEM! WHERE TO START?
THEY PRETTY MUCH HAVE A HAND IN EVERYTHING THAT HAPPENS AROUND THE TOWN.
IT'S RUN BY THE FISHERMEN, OF COURSE. BUT ANYONE WHO'S ANYONE IS A MEMBER TOO. THE MAYOR'S ALWAYS BEEN ONE OF THEM.
I THINK EITHER YOU'RE ONE OF THEM OR YOU'RE NOT. IF YOU'RE NOT, YOU DON'T QUITE KNOW *WHAT* THEY'RE UP TO.
AND YOU'RE NOT?
HA! NO, NOT ME. TOO MUCH OF A LAND LUBBER, I THINK.
WHAT ABOUT... I DUNNO, GORD—
RING RING
HOLD ON.

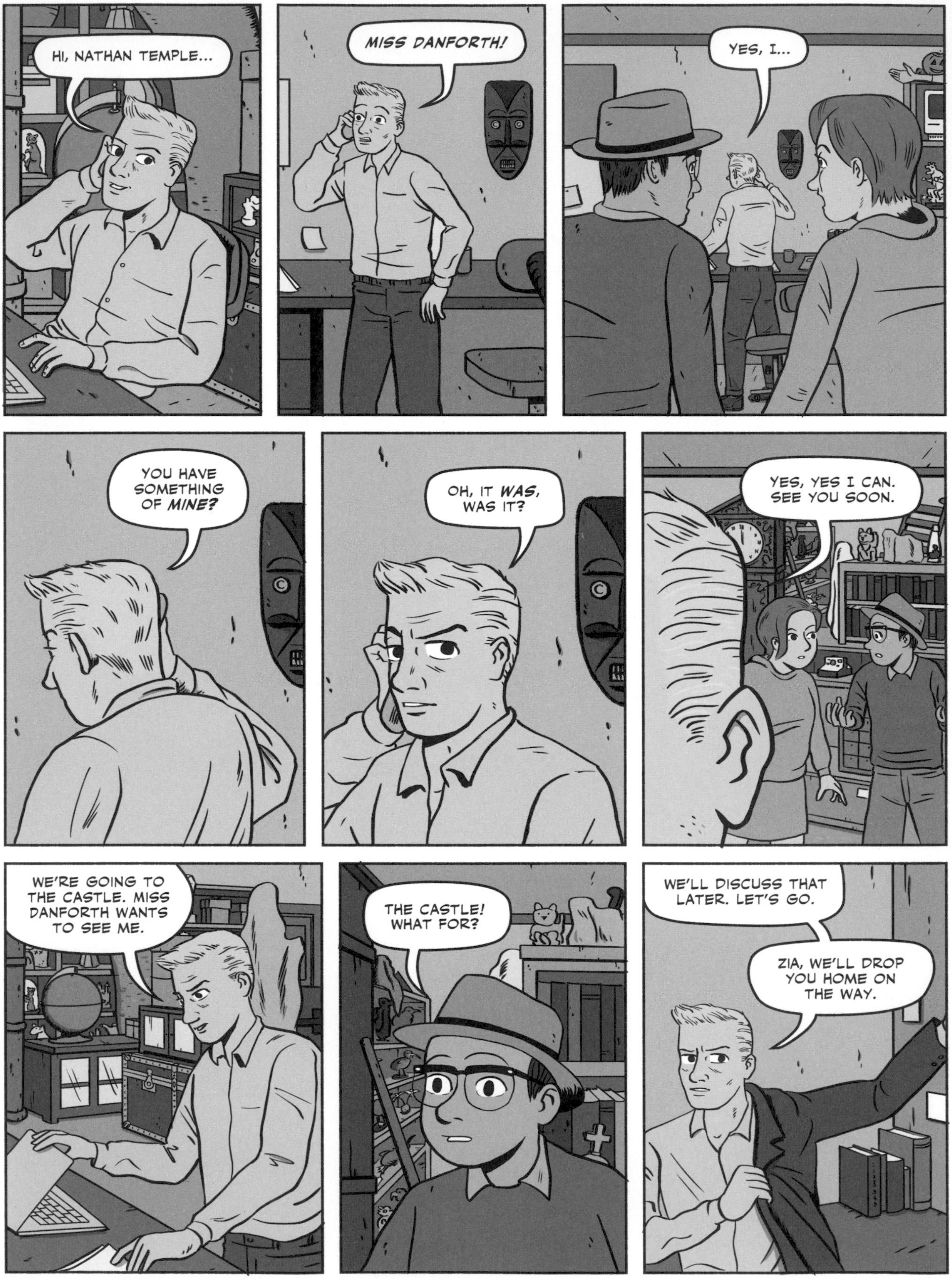
HI, NATHAN TEMPLE...
MISS DANFORTH!
YES, I...
YOU HAVE SOMETHING OF MINE?
OH, IT WAS, WAS IT?
YES, YES I CAN. SEE YOU SOON.
WE'RE GOING TO THE CASTLE. MISS DANFORTH WANTS TO SEE ME.
THE CASTLE! WHAT FOR?
WE'LL DISCUSS THAT LATER. LET'S GO.
ZIA, WE'LL DROP YOU HOME ON THE WAY.

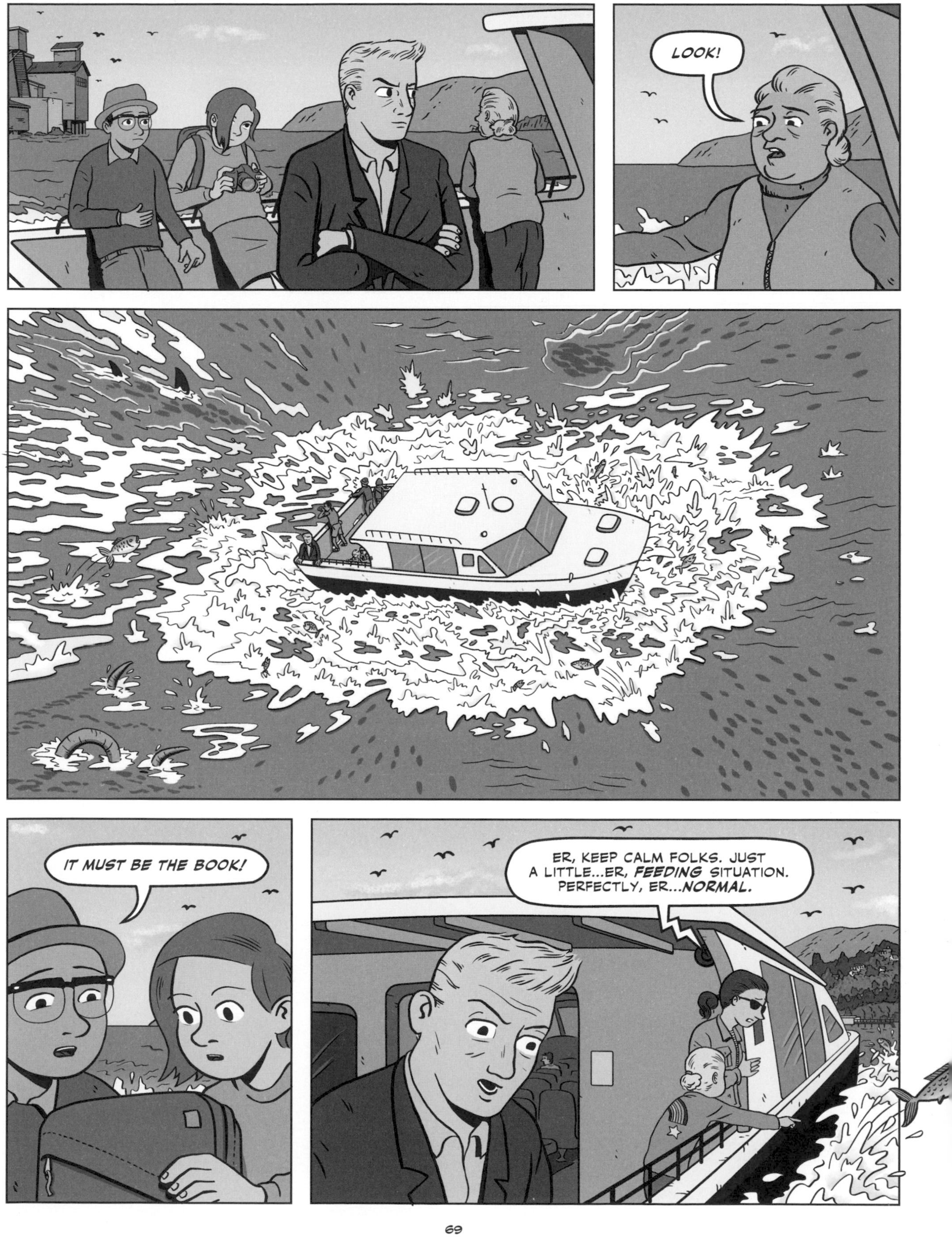
LOOK!
IT MUST BE THE BOOK!
ER, KEEP CALM FOLKS. JUST A LITTLE...ER, FEEDING SITUATION. PERFECTLY, ER...NORMAL.

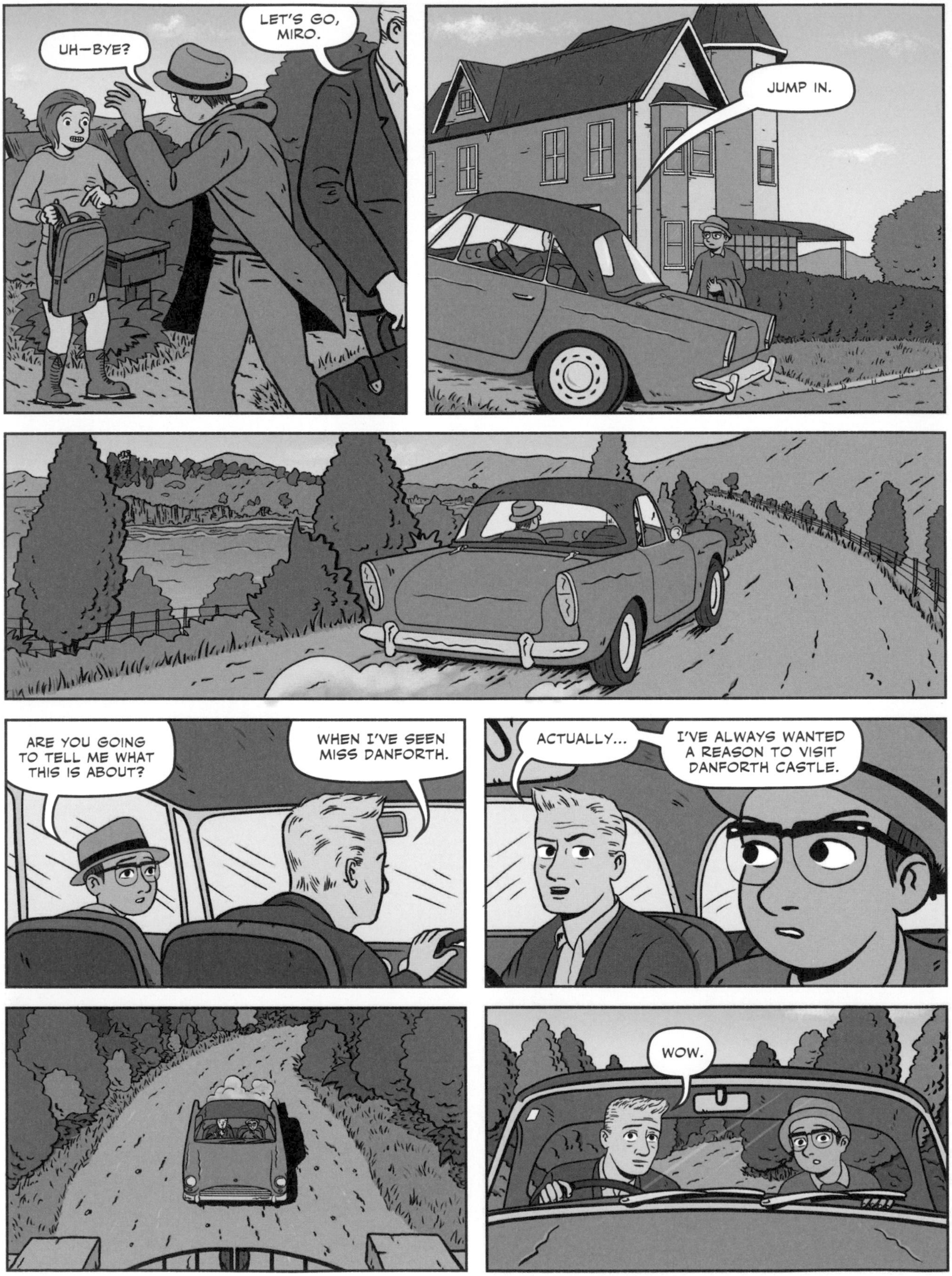
UH—BYE?
LET'S GO, MIRO.
JUMP IN.
ARE YOU GOING TO TELL ME WHAT THIS IS ABOUT?
WHEN I'VE SEEN MISS DANFORTH.
ACTUALLY...
I'VE ALWAYS WANTED A REASON TO VISIT DANFORTH CASTLE.
WOW.

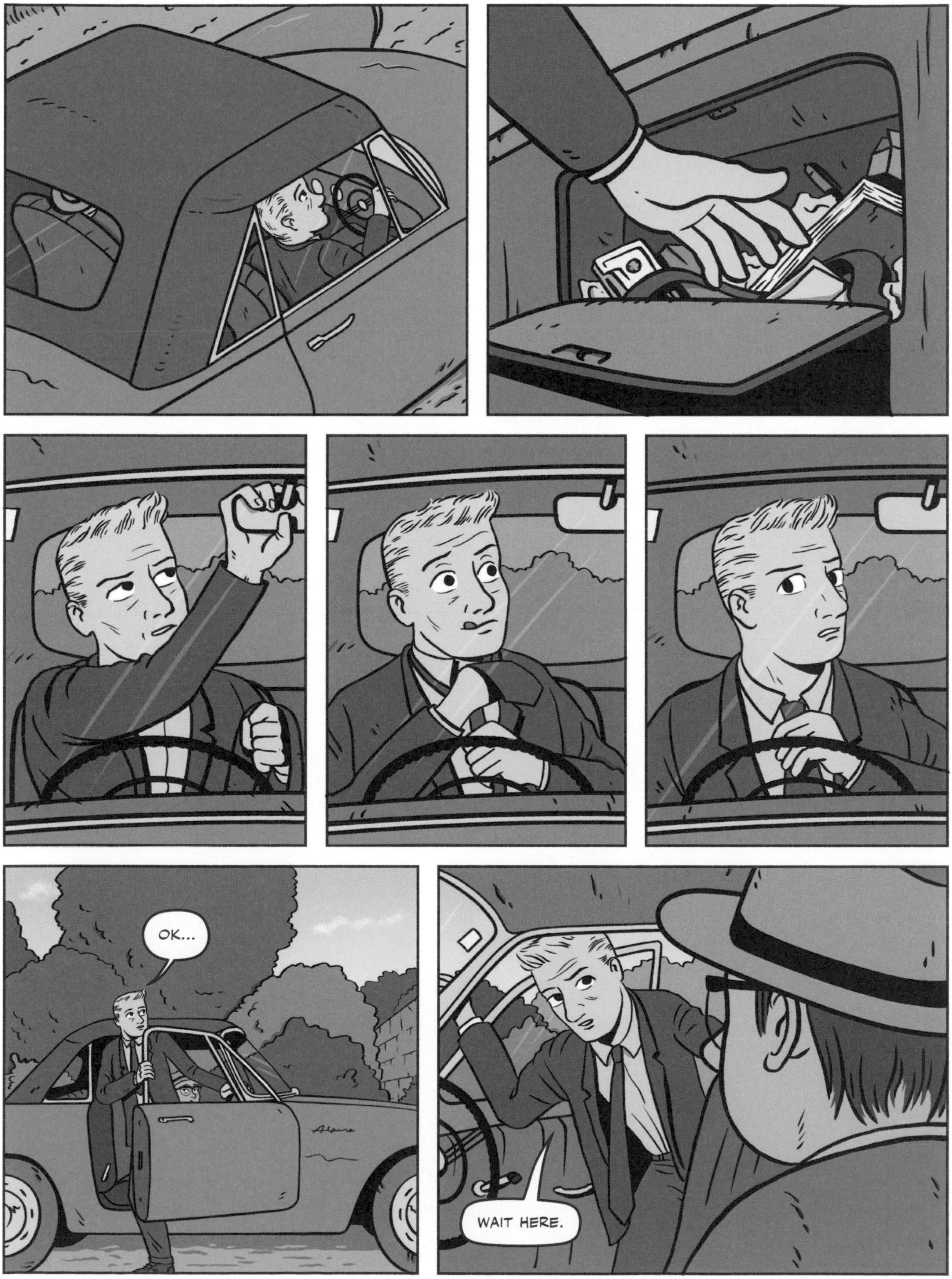
OK...
WAIT HERE.
Alpine

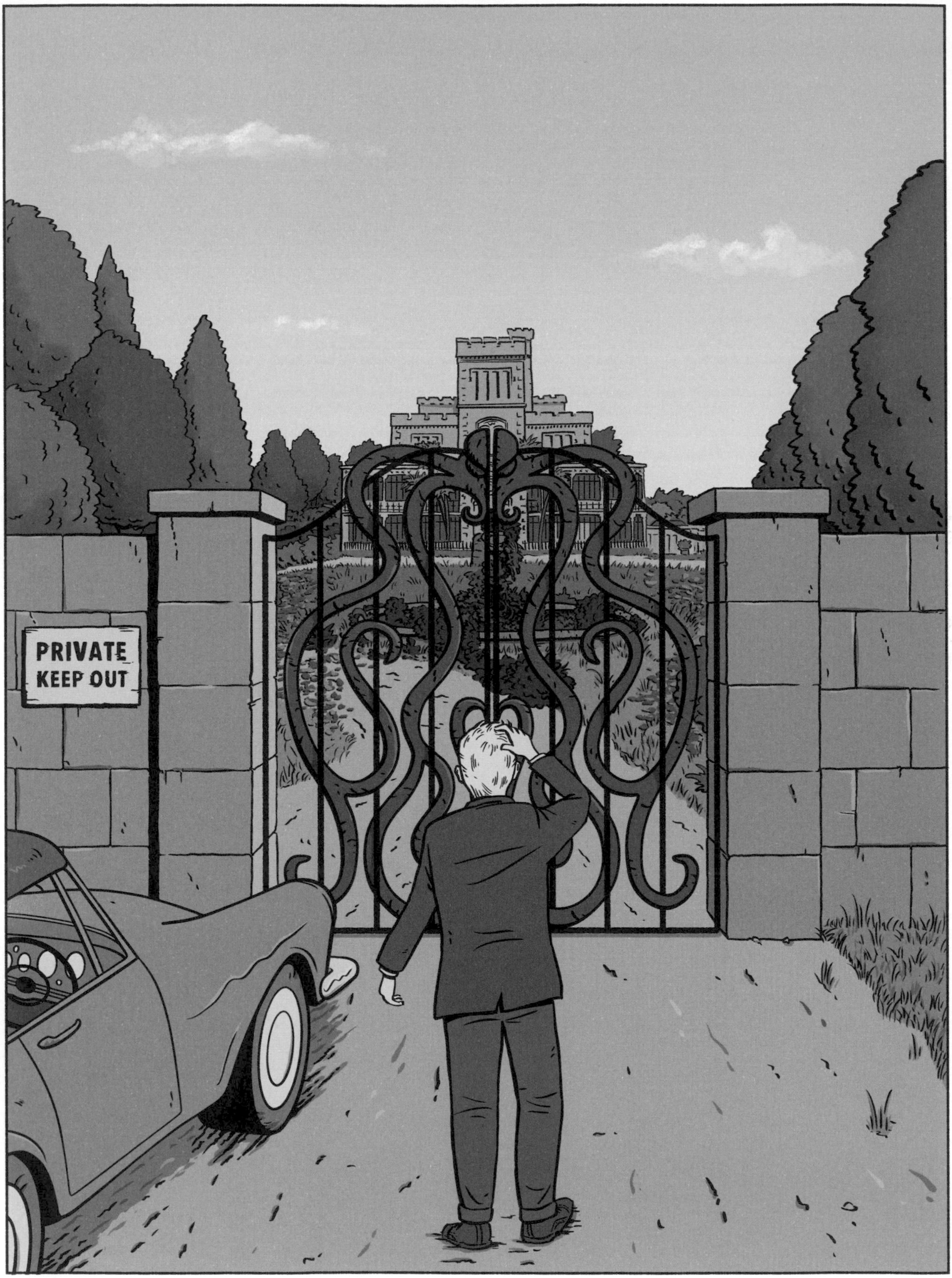
PRIVATE
KEEP OUT

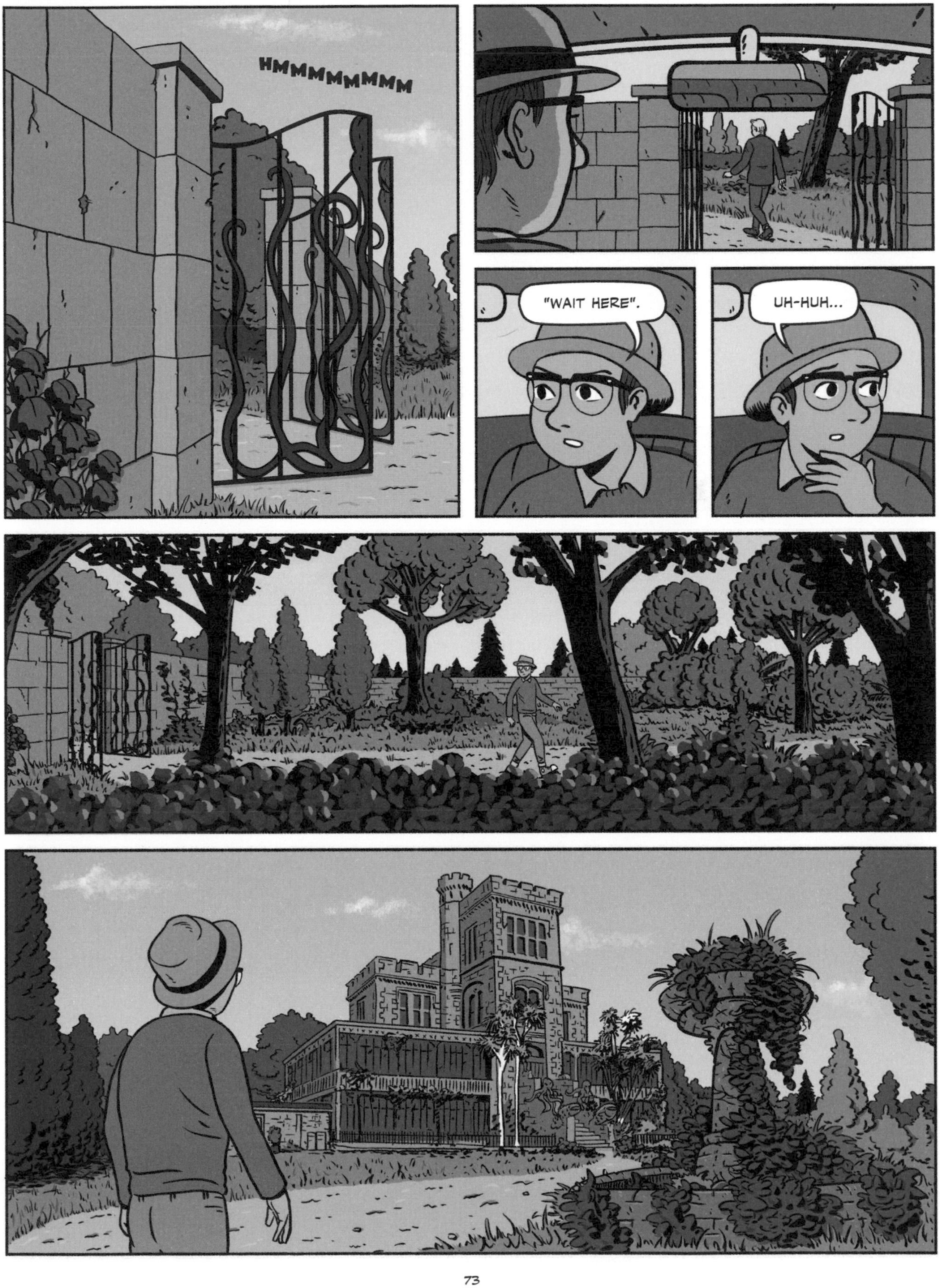
HMMMMMMMMM
"WAIT HERE".
UH-HUH...

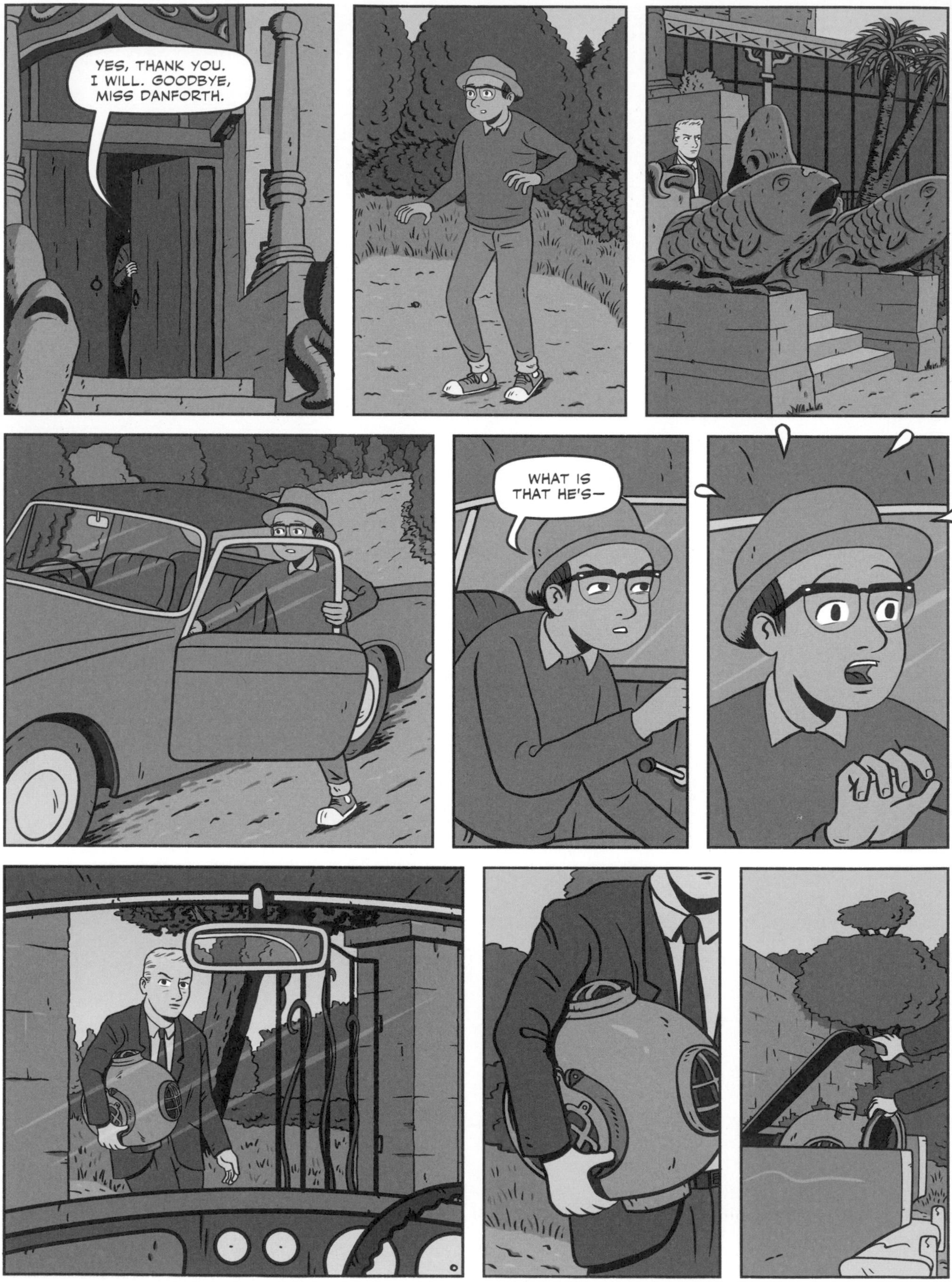
YES, THANK YOU. I WILL. GOODBYE, MISS DANFORTH.
WHAT IS THAT HE'S—

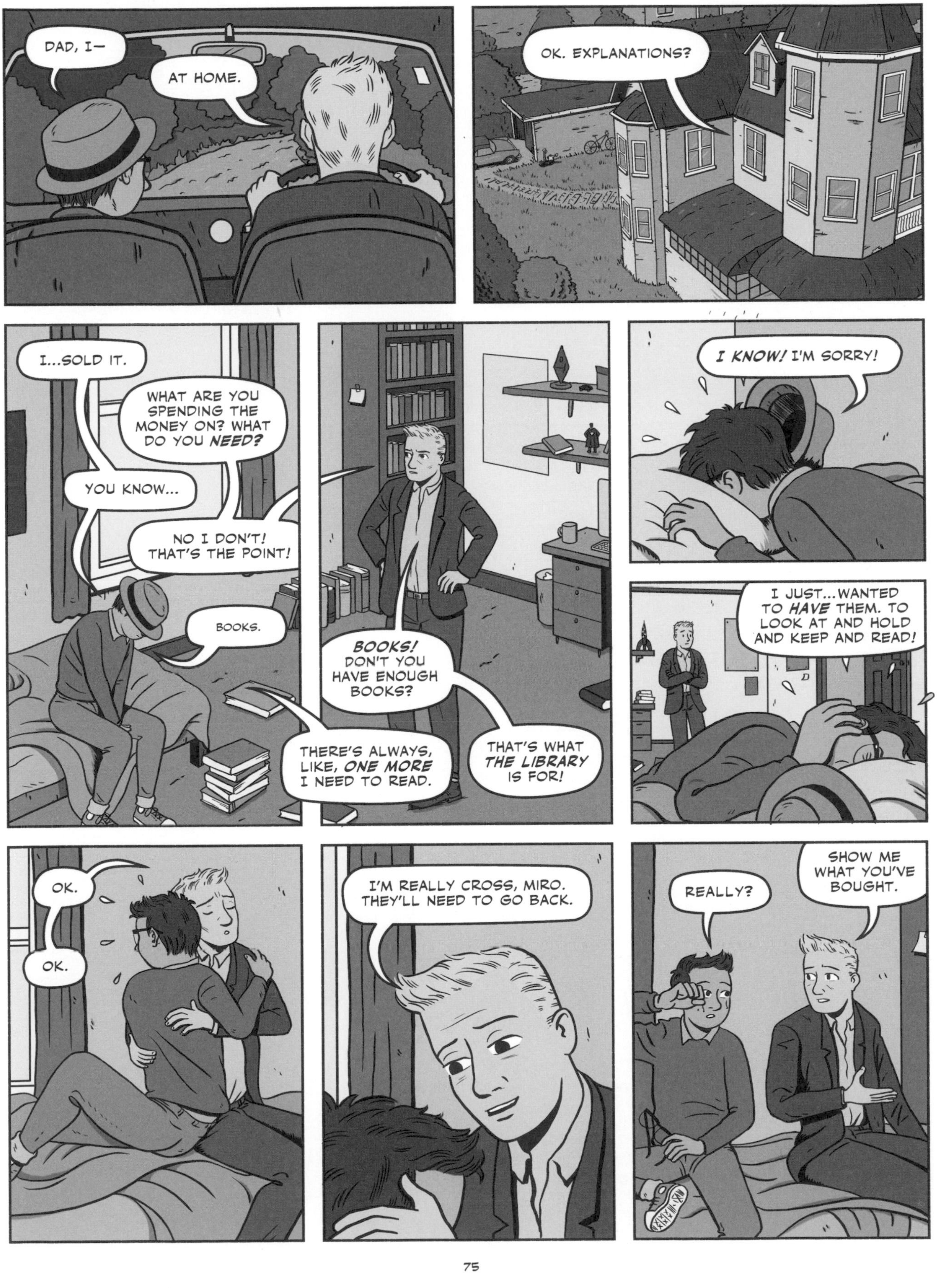
DAD, I—
AT HOME.
OK. EXPLANATIONS?
I...SOLD IT.
WHAT ARE YOU SPENDING THE MONEY ON? WHAT DO YOU *NEED?*
YOU KNOW...
NO I DON'T! THAT'S THE POINT!
BOOKS.
BOOKS! DON'T YOU HAVE ENOUGH BOOKS?
THERE'S ALWAYS, LIKE, *ONE MORE* I NEED TO READ.
THAT'S WHAT *THE LIBRARY* IS FOR!
I KNOW! I'M SORRY!
I JUST...WANTED TO *HAVE* THEM. TO LOOK AT AND HOLD AND KEEP AND READ!
OK.
OK.
I'M REALLY CROSS, MIRO. THEY'LL NEED TO GO BACK.
REALLY?
SHOW ME WHAT YOU'VE BOUGHT.

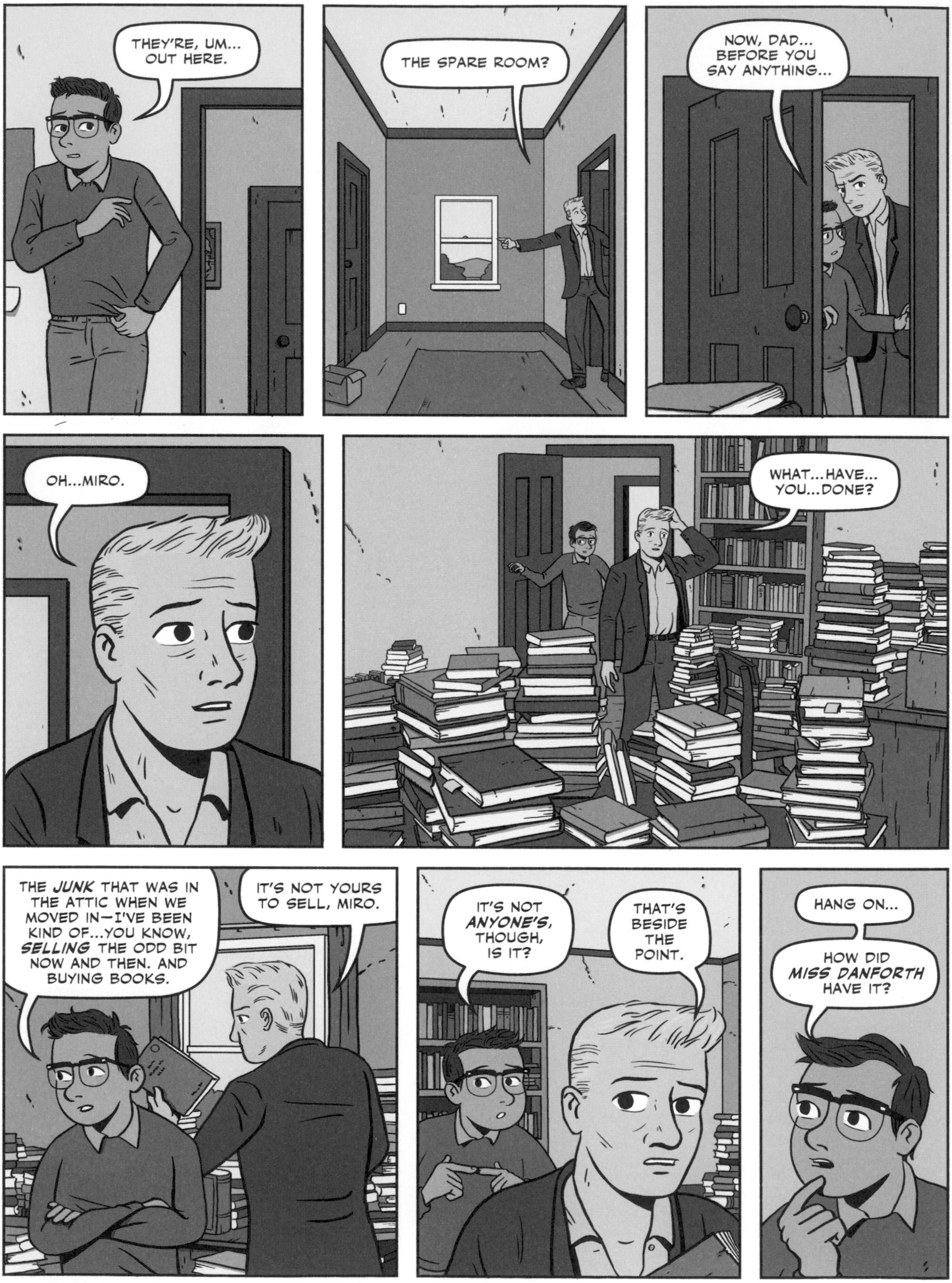
THEY'RE, UM... OUT HERE.
THE SPARE ROOM?
NOW, DAD... BEFORE YOU SAY ANYTHING...
OH...MIRO.
WHAT...HAVE... YOU...DONE?
THE *JUNK* THAT WAS IN THE ATTIC WHEN WE MOVED IN—I'VE BEEN KIND OF...YOU KNOW, *SELLING* THE ODD BIT NOW AND THEN. AND BUYING BOOKS.
IT'S NOT YOURS TO SELL, MIRO.
IT'S NOT *ANYONE'S*, THOUGH, IS IT?
THAT'S BESIDE THE POINT.
HANG ON...
HOW DID *MISS DANFORTH* HAVE IT?

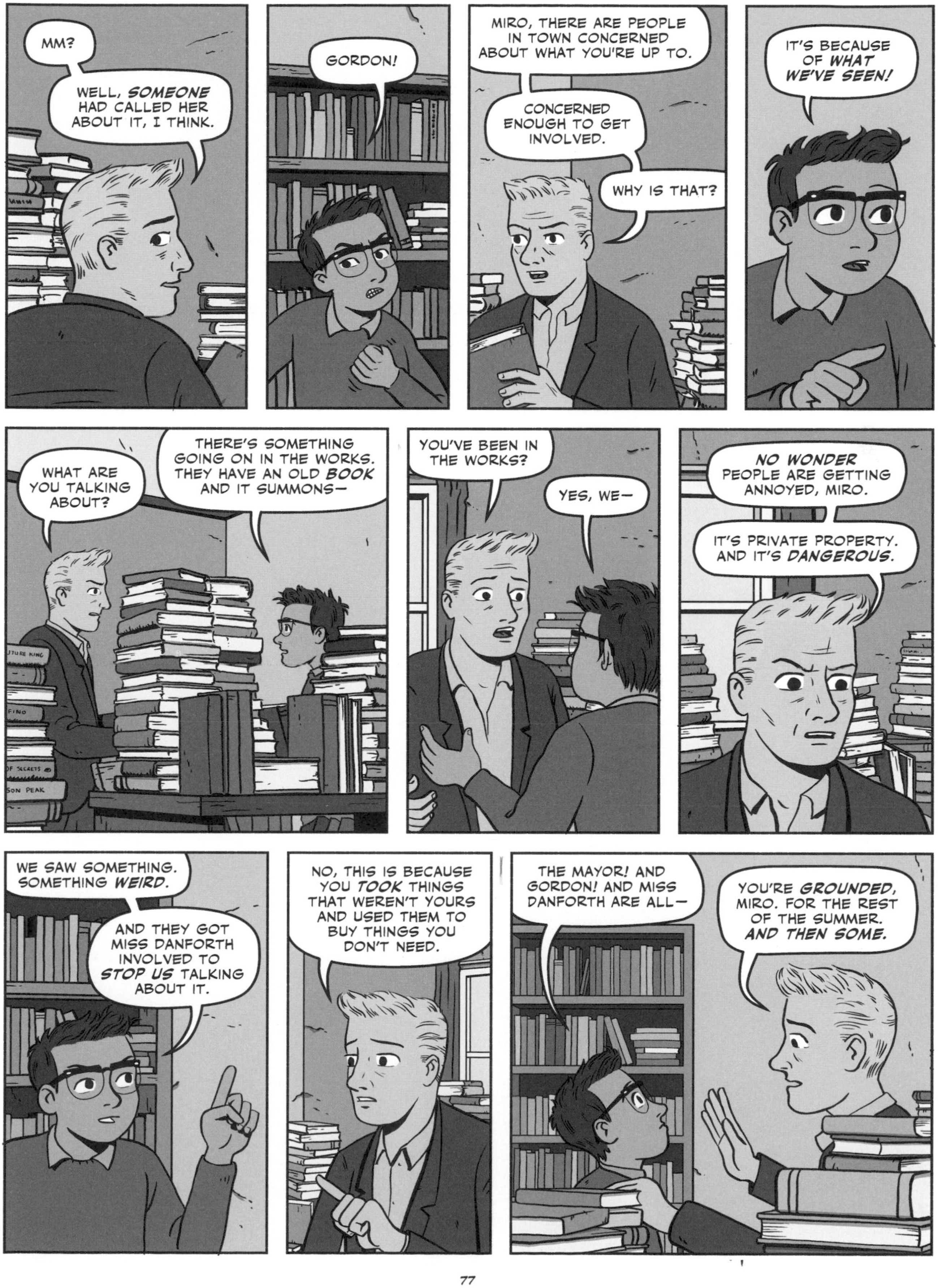
MM?
WELL, SOMEONE HAD CALLED HER ABOUT IT, I THINK.
GORDON!
MIRO, THERE ARE PEOPLE IN TOWN CONCERNED ABOUT WHAT YOU'RE UP TO.
CONCERNED ENOUGH TO GET INVOLVED.
WHY IS THAT?
IT'S BECAUSE OF WHAT WE'VE SEEN!
WHAT ARE YOU TALKING ABOUT?
THERE'S SOMETHING GOING ON IN THE WORKS. THEY HAVE AN OLD BOOK AND IT SUMMONS—
YOU'VE BEEN IN THE WORKS?
YES, WE—
NO WONDER PEOPLE ARE GETTING ANNOYED, MIRO.
IT'S PRIVATE PROPERTY. AND IT'S DANGEROUS.
WE SAW SOMETHING. SOMETHING WEIRD.
AND THEY GOT MISS DANFORTH INVOLVED TO STOP US TALKING ABOUT IT.
NO, THIS IS BECAUSE YOU TOOK THINGS THAT WEREN'T YOURS AND USED THEM TO BUY THINGS YOU DON'T NEED.
THE MAYOR! AND GORDON! AND MISS DANFORTH ARE ALL—
YOU'RE GROUNDED, MIRO. FOR THE REST OF THE SUMMER. AND THEN SOME.

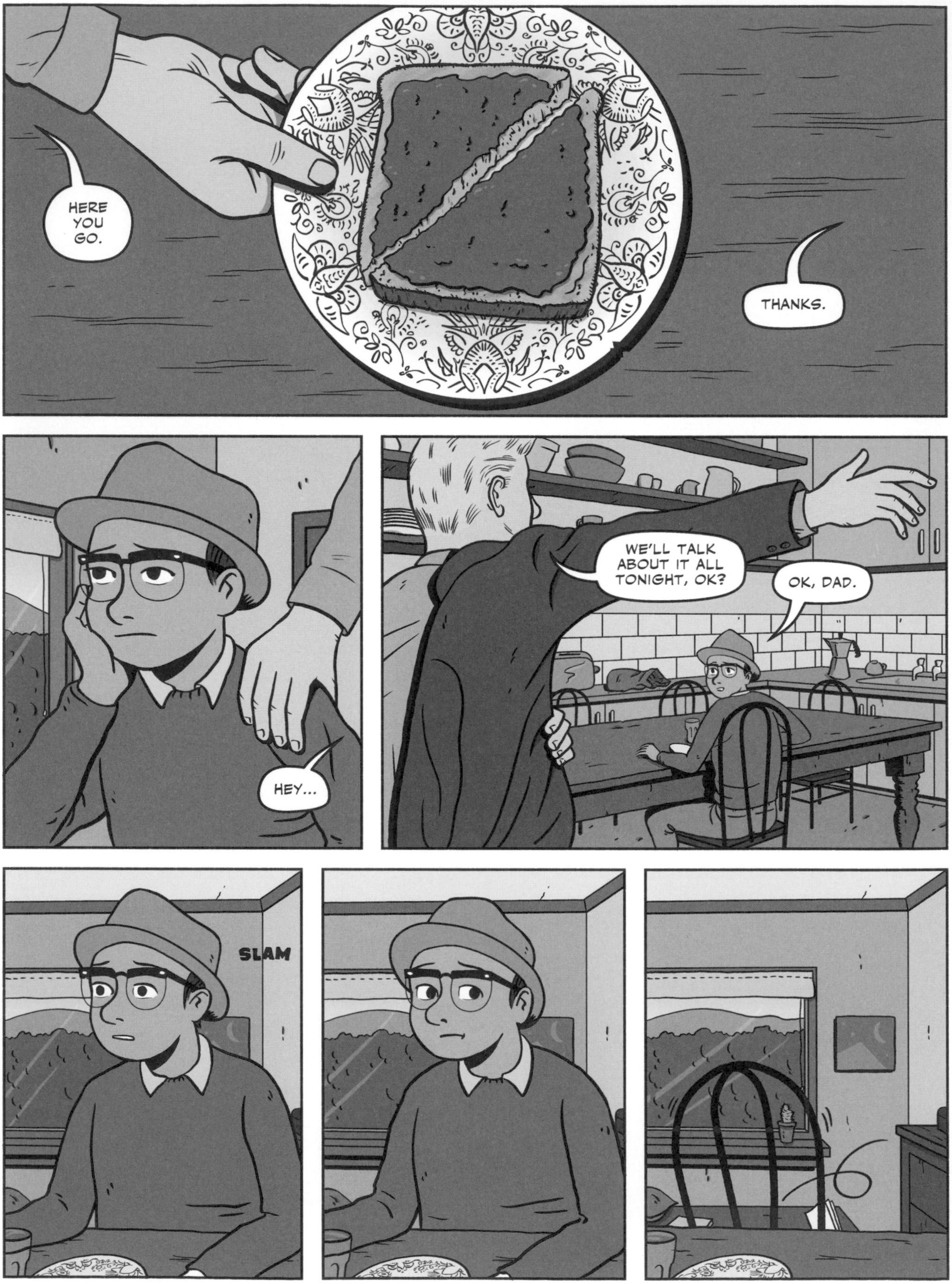
HERE YOU GO.
THANKS.
HEY...
WE'LL TALK ABOUT IT ALL TONIGHT, OK?
OK, DAD.
SLAM

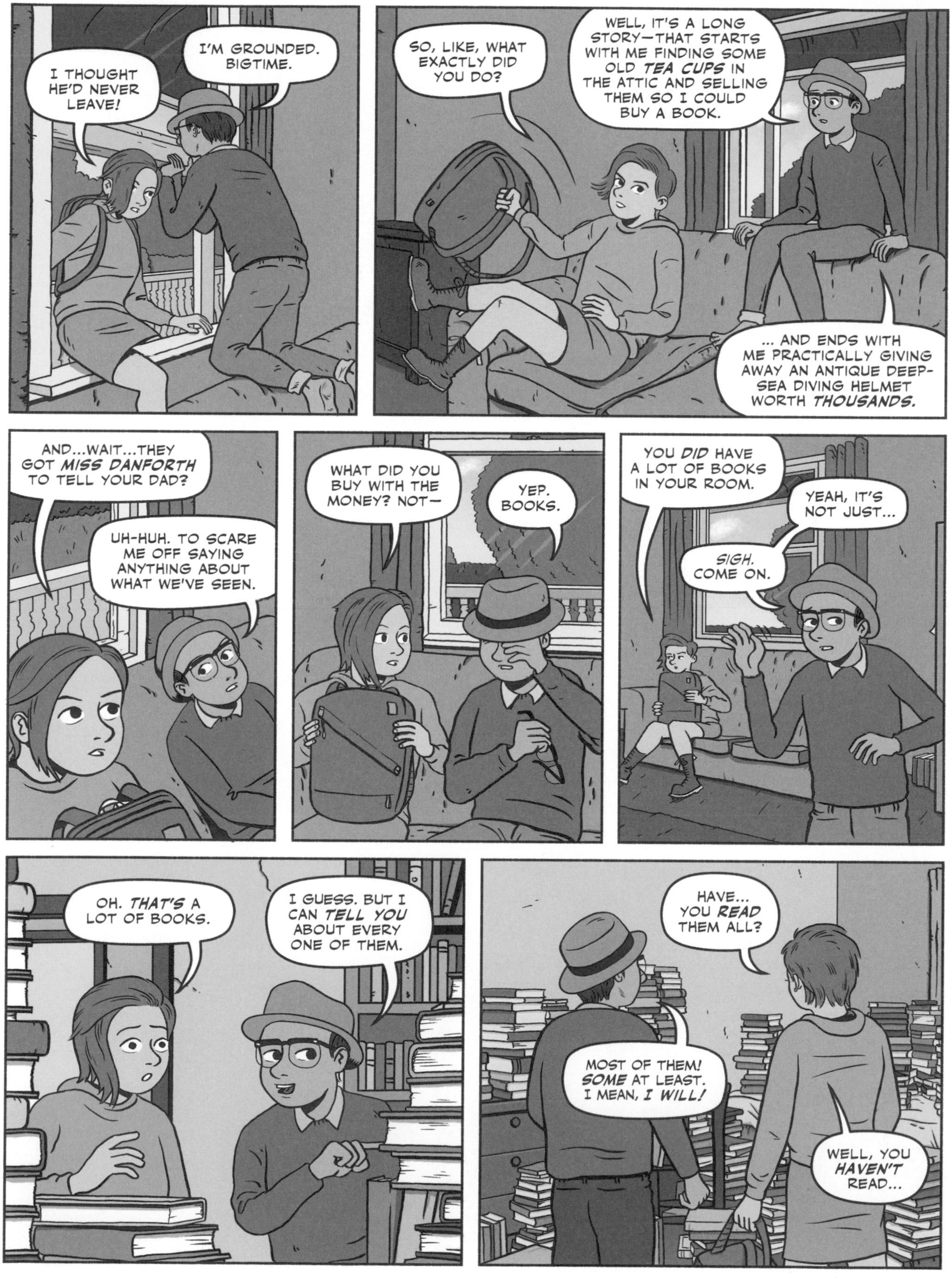
I THOUGHT HE'D NEVER LEAVE!
I'M GROUNDED. BIGTIME.
SO, LIKE, WHAT EXACTLY DID YOU DO?
WELL, IT'S A LONG STORY—THAT STARTS WITH ME FINDING SOME OLD *TEA CUPS* IN THE ATTIC AND SELLING THEM SO I COULD BUY A BOOK.
... AND ENDS WITH ME PRACTICALLY GIVING AWAY AN ANTIQUE DEEP-SEA DIVING HELMET WORTH *THOUSANDS.*
AND...WAIT...THEY GOT *MISS DANFORTH* TO TELL YOUR DAD?
UH-HUH. TO SCARE ME OFF SAYING ANYTHING ABOUT WHAT WE'VE SEEN.
WHAT DID YOU BUY WITH THE MONEY? NOT—
YEP. BOOKS.
YOU *DID* HAVE A LOT OF BOOKS IN YOUR ROOM.
YEAH, IT'S NOT JUST...
SIGH. COME ON.
OH. *THAT'S* A LOT OF BOOKS.
I GUESS. BUT I CAN *TELL YOU* ABOUT EVERY ONE OF THEM.
HAVE... YOU *READ* THEM ALL?
MOST OF THEM! *SOME* AT LEAST. I MEAN, *I WILL!*
WELL, YOU *HAVEN'T* READ...

—*THIS* ONE!

YOU READ IT?

FROM COVER TO COVER. OR, AT LEAST, TILL I GOT TO *RIPPED-OUT PAGES* TOWARDS THE BACK.

AND?

TELL ME!

YOU WON'T BELIEVE IT!

OK. SO...IT'S THE SHIP'S LOG. *AURORA*—HE NAMED IT AFTER THE TOWN HE GREW UP IN.

HERE.

RIGHT. THEY WERE HEADING FOR *ANTARCTICA*— FOLLOWING IN SCOTT'S AND SHACKLETON'S FOOTSTEPS. ON THE WAY THE SHIP WAS *CAUGHT IN THE ICE*—

LIKE SHACKLETON.

EXACTLY.

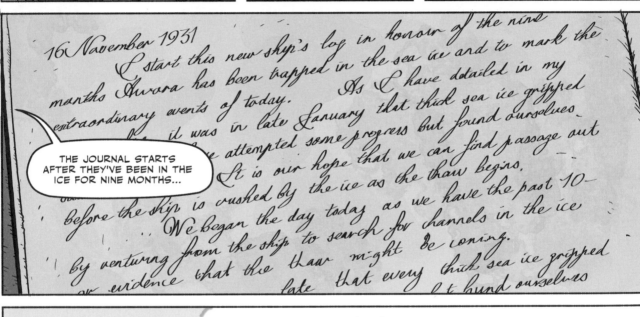

16 November 1931

I start this new ship's log in honour of the nine months *Aurora* has been trapped in the sea ice and to mark the extraordinary events of today. As I have detailed in my [log?] it was in late January that thick sea ice gripped [us.] We attempted some progress but found ourselves [stuck.] It is our hope that we can find passage out before the ship is crushed by the ice as the thaw begins.

We began the day today as we have the past 10— by venturing from the ship to search for channels in the ice or evidence that the thaw might be coming.

THE JOURNAL STARTS AFTER THEY'VE BEEN IN THE ICE FOR NINE MONTHS...

My fear is that if the ice does not release us soon, the ship will be crushed and lost...

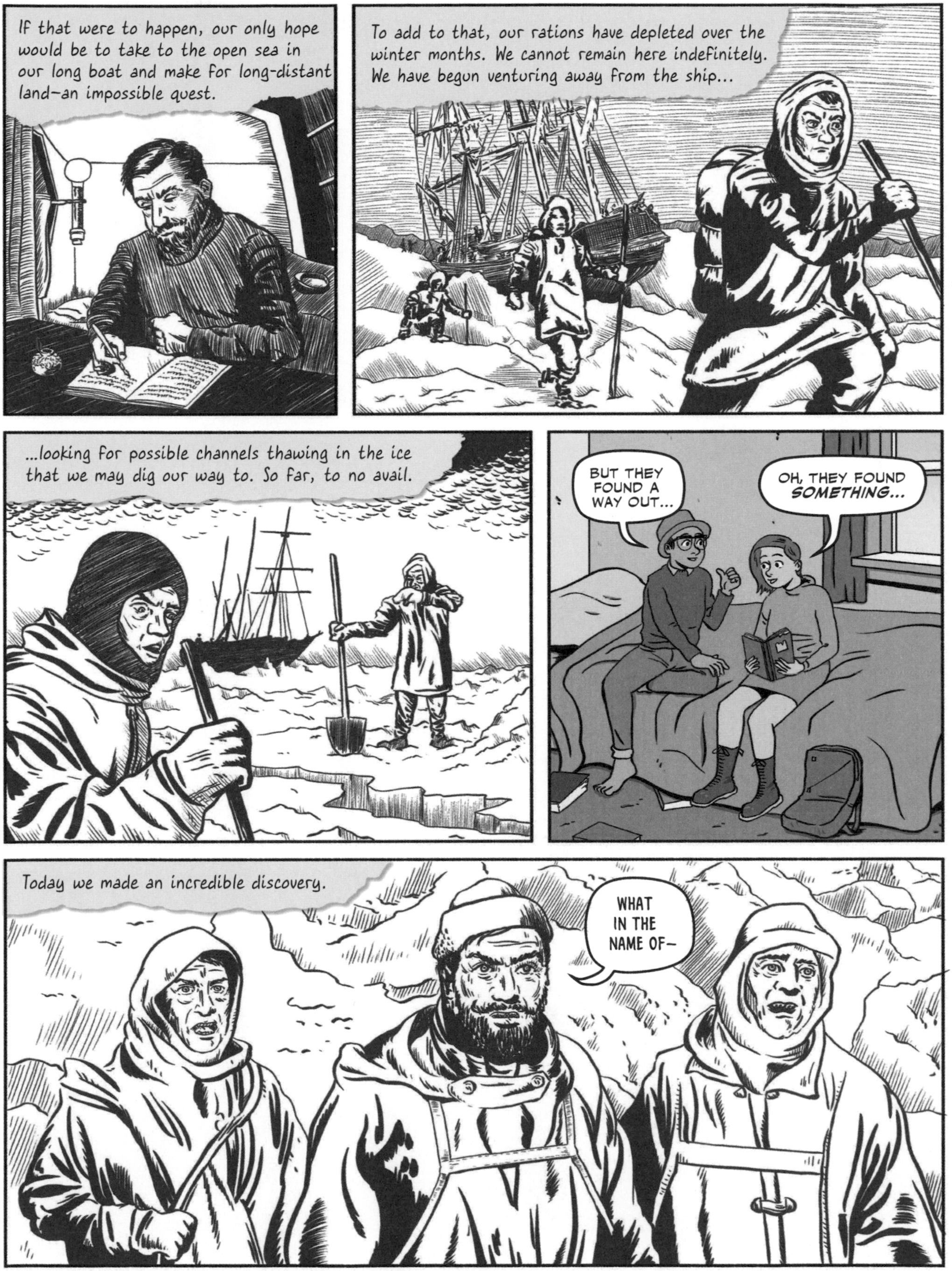
If that were to happen, our only hope would be to take to the open sea in our long boat and make for long-distant land—an impossible quest.
To add to that, our rations have depleted over the winter months. We cannot remain here indefinitely. We have begun venturing away from the ship...
...looking for possible channels thawing in the ice that we may dig our way to. So far, to no avail.
BUT THEY FOUND A WAY OUT...
OH, THEY FOUND *SOMETHING*...
Today we made an incredible discovery.
WHAT IN THE NAME OF—

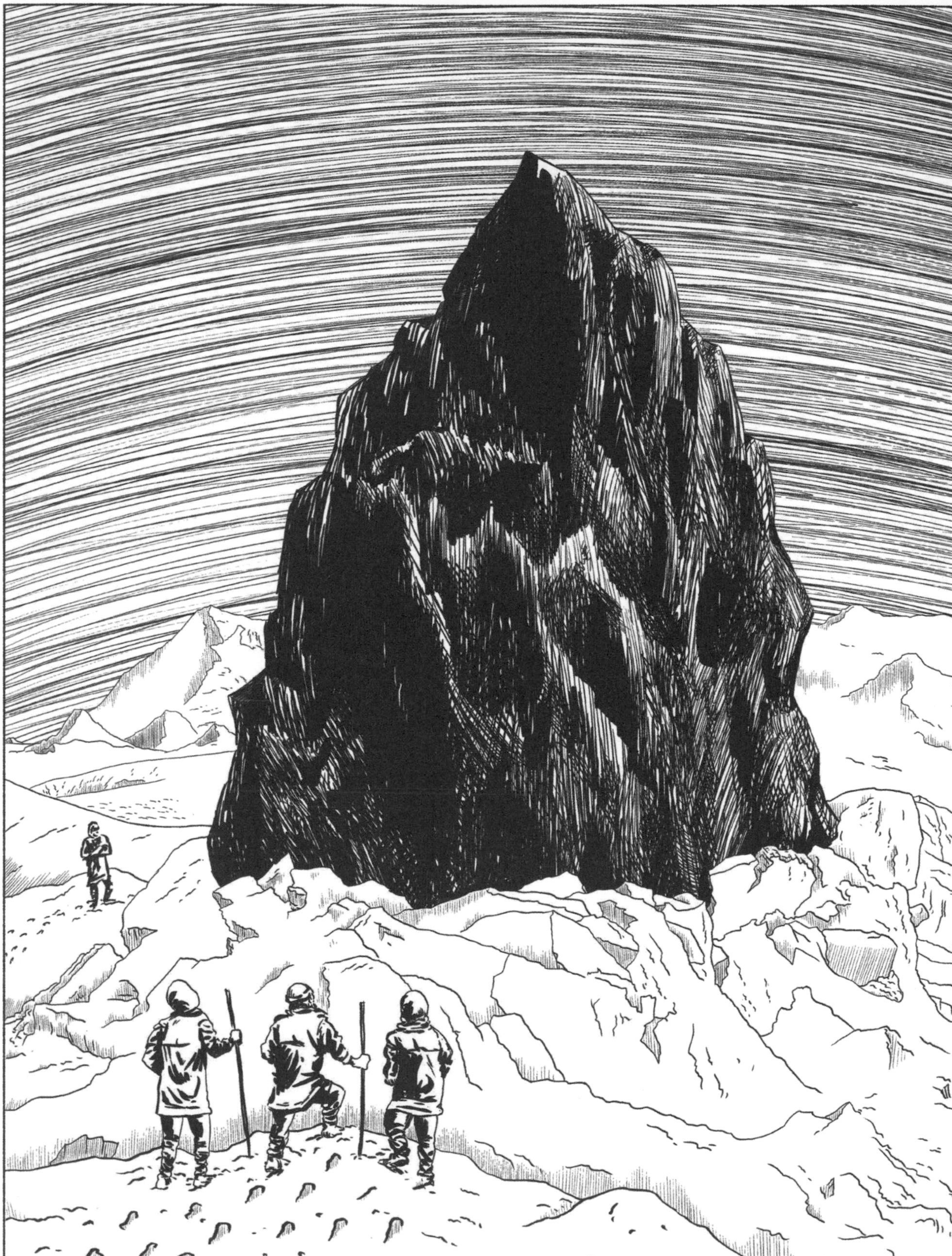

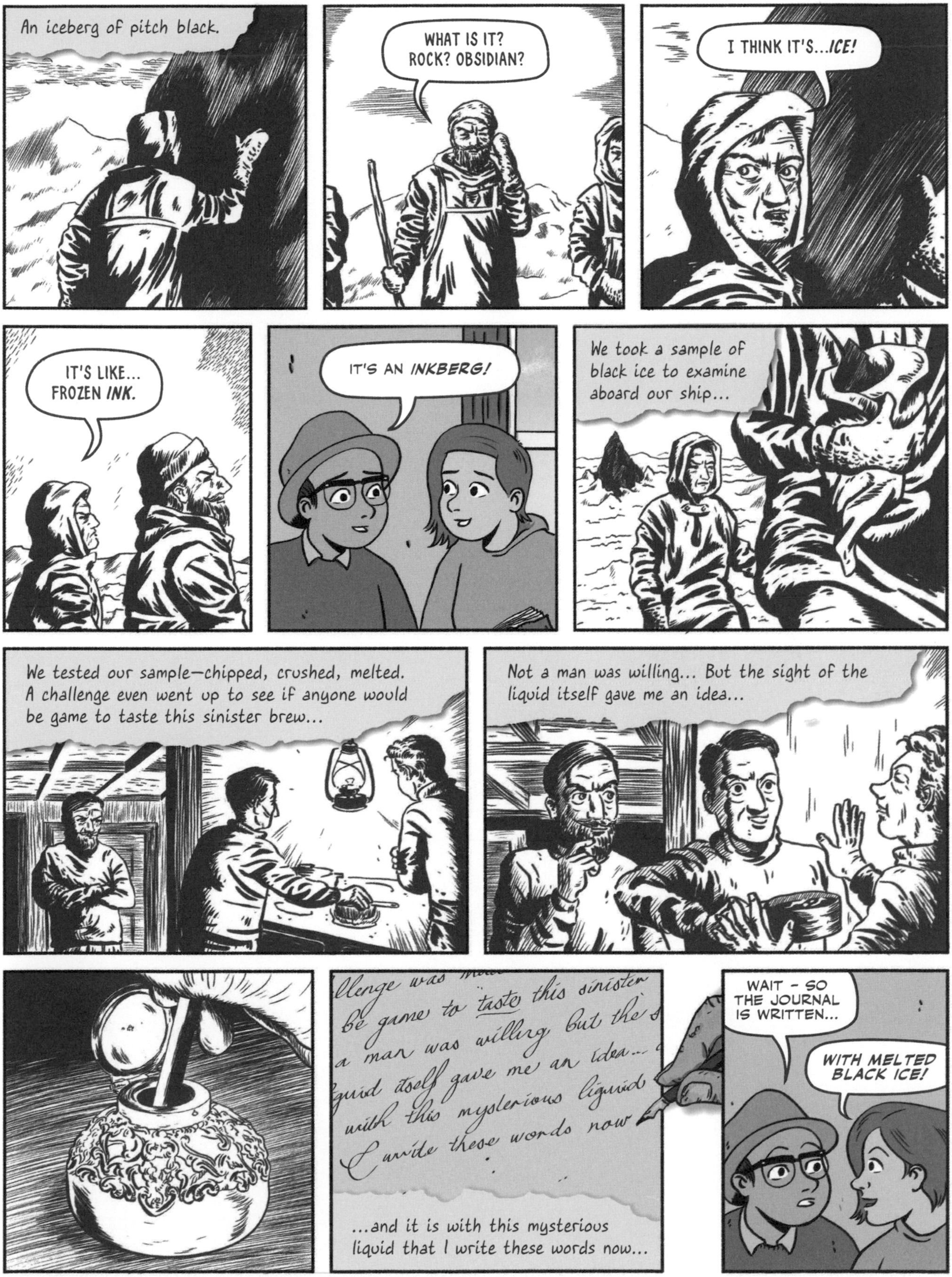

An iceberg of pitch black.
WHAT IS IT? ROCK? OBSIDIAN?
I THINK IT'S...ICE!
IT'S LIKE... FROZEN INK.
IT'S AN INKBERG!
We took a sample of black ice to examine aboard our ship...
We tested our sample—chipped, crushed, melted. A challenge even went up to see if anyone would be game to taste this sinister brew...
Not a man was willing... But the sight of the liquid itself gave me an idea...
...and it is with this mysterious liquid that I write these words now...
WAIT - SO THE JOURNAL IS WRITTEN...
WITH MELTED BLACK ICE!

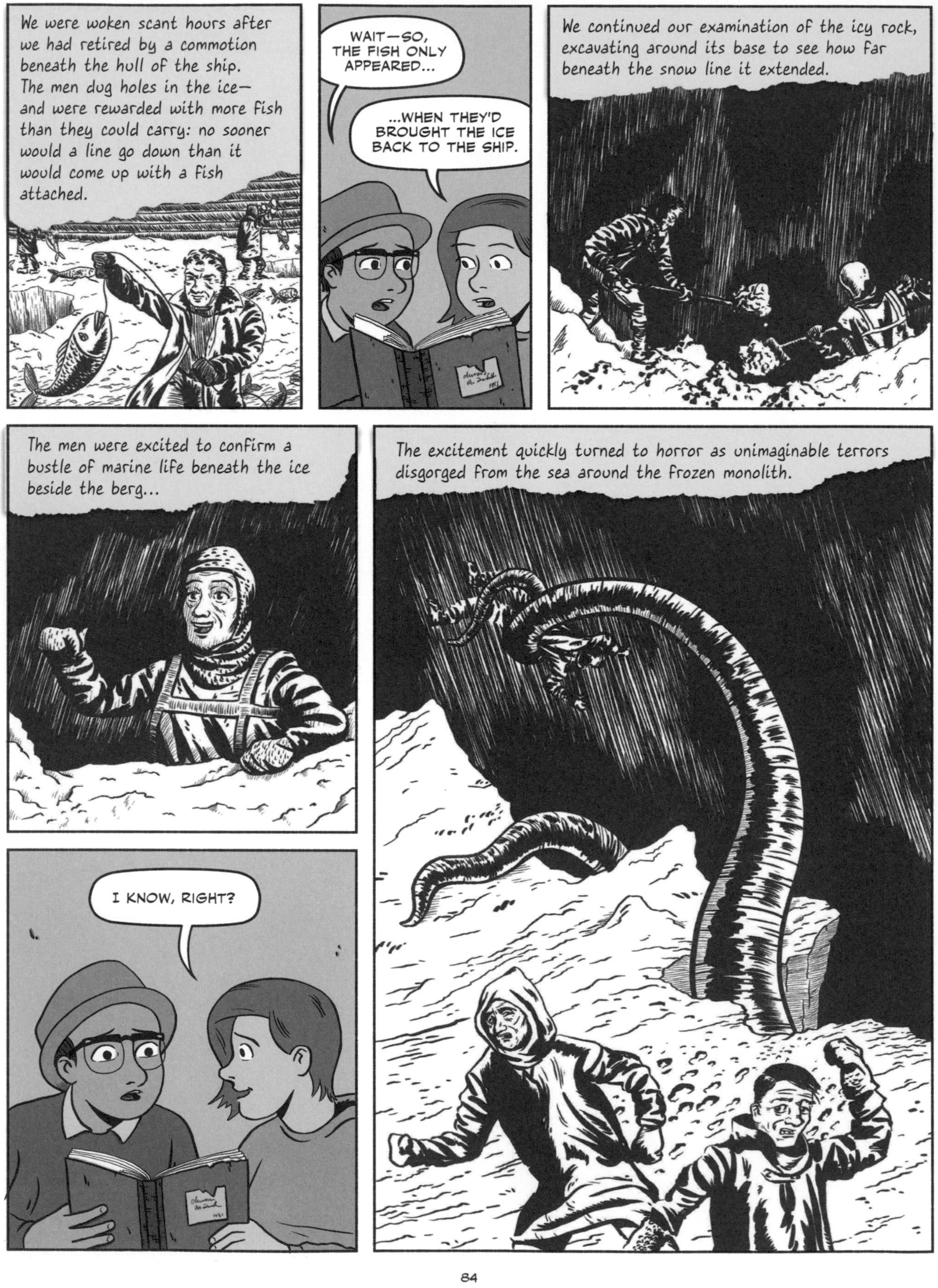
We were woken scant hours after we had retired by a commotion beneath the hull of the ship. The men dug holes in the ice— and were rewarded with more fish than they could carry: no sooner would a line go down than it would come up with a fish attached.
WAIT—SO, THE FISH ONLY APPEARED...
...WHEN THEY'D BROUGHT THE ICE BACK TO THE SHIP.
We continued our examination of the icy rock, excavating around its base to see how far beneath the snow line it extended.
The men were excited to confirm a bustle of marine life beneath the ice beside the berg...
I KNOW, RIGHT?
The excitement quickly turned to horror as unimaginable terrors disgorged from the sea around the frozen monolith.

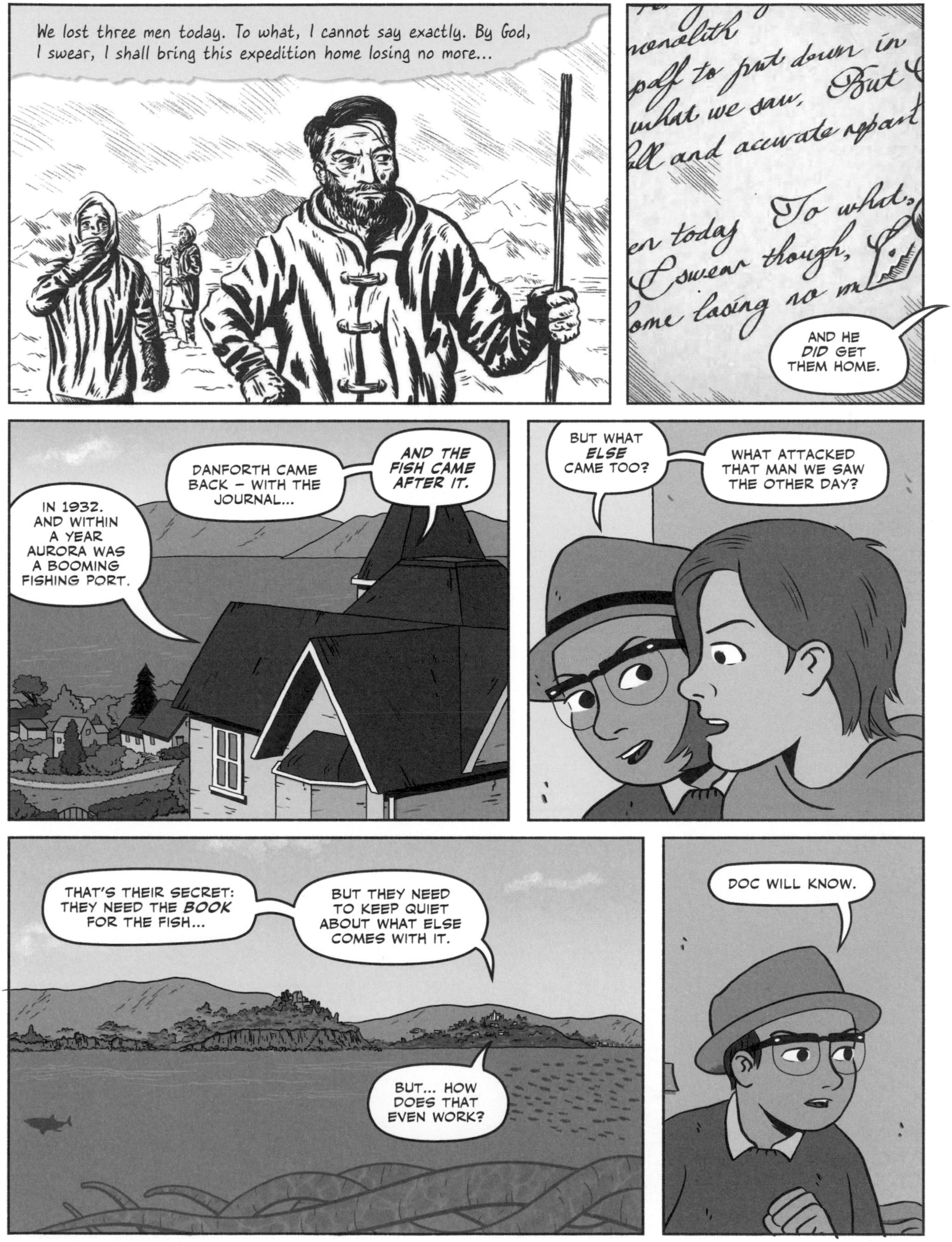

We lost three men today. To what, I cannot say exactly. By God, I swear, I shall bring this expedition home losing no more...
to put down in
what we saw, But
and accurate report
today To what,
swear though,
losing no
AND HE DID GET THEM HOME.
IN 1932. AND WITHIN A YEAR AURORA WAS A BOOMING FISHING PORT.
DANFORTH CAME BACK – WITH THE JOURNAL...
AND THE FISH CAME AFTER IT.
BUT WHAT ELSE CAME TOO?
WHAT ATTACKED THAT MAN WE SAW THE OTHER DAY?
THAT'S THEIR SECRET: THEY NEED THE BOOK FOR THE FISH...
BUT THEY NEED TO KEEP QUIET ABOUT WHAT ELSE COMES WITH IT.
BUT... HOW DOES THAT EVEN WORK?
DOC WILL KNOW.

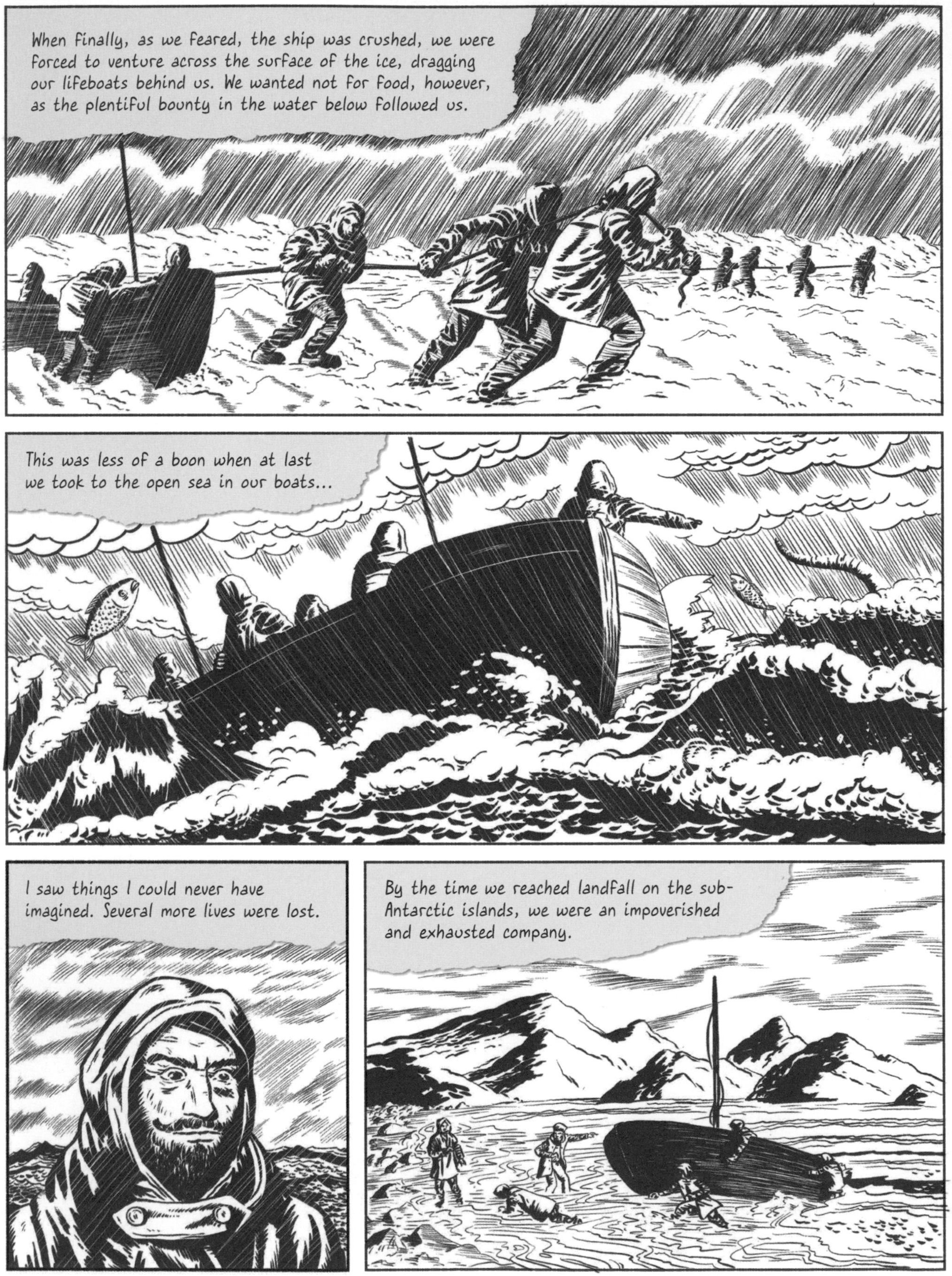
When finally, as we feared, the ship was crushed, we were forced to venture across the surface of the ice, dragging our lifeboats behind us. We wanted not for food, however, as the plentiful bounty in the water below followed us.
This was less of a boon when at last we took to the open sea in our boats...
I saw things I could never have imagined. Several more lives were lost.
By the time we reached landfall on the sub-Antarctic islands, we were an impoverished and exhausted company.

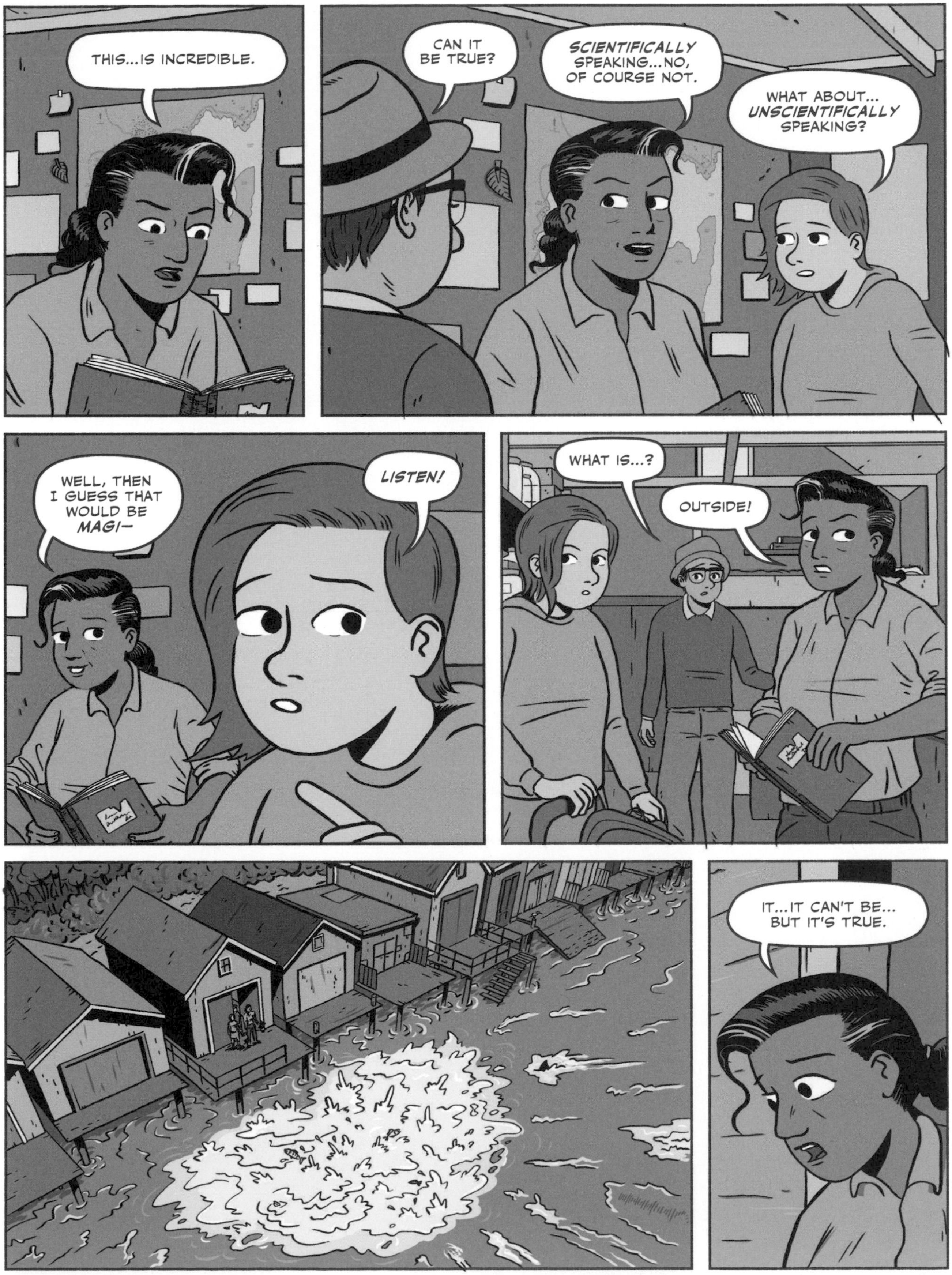
THIS...IS INCREDIBLE.
CAN IT BE TRUE?
SCIENTIFICALLY SPEAKING...NO, OF COURSE NOT.
WHAT ABOUT... UNSCIENTIFICALLY SPEAKING?
WELL, THEN I GUESS THAT WOULD BE MAGI—
LISTEN!
WHAT IS...?
OUTSIDE!
IT...IT CAN'T BE... BUT IT'S TRUE.

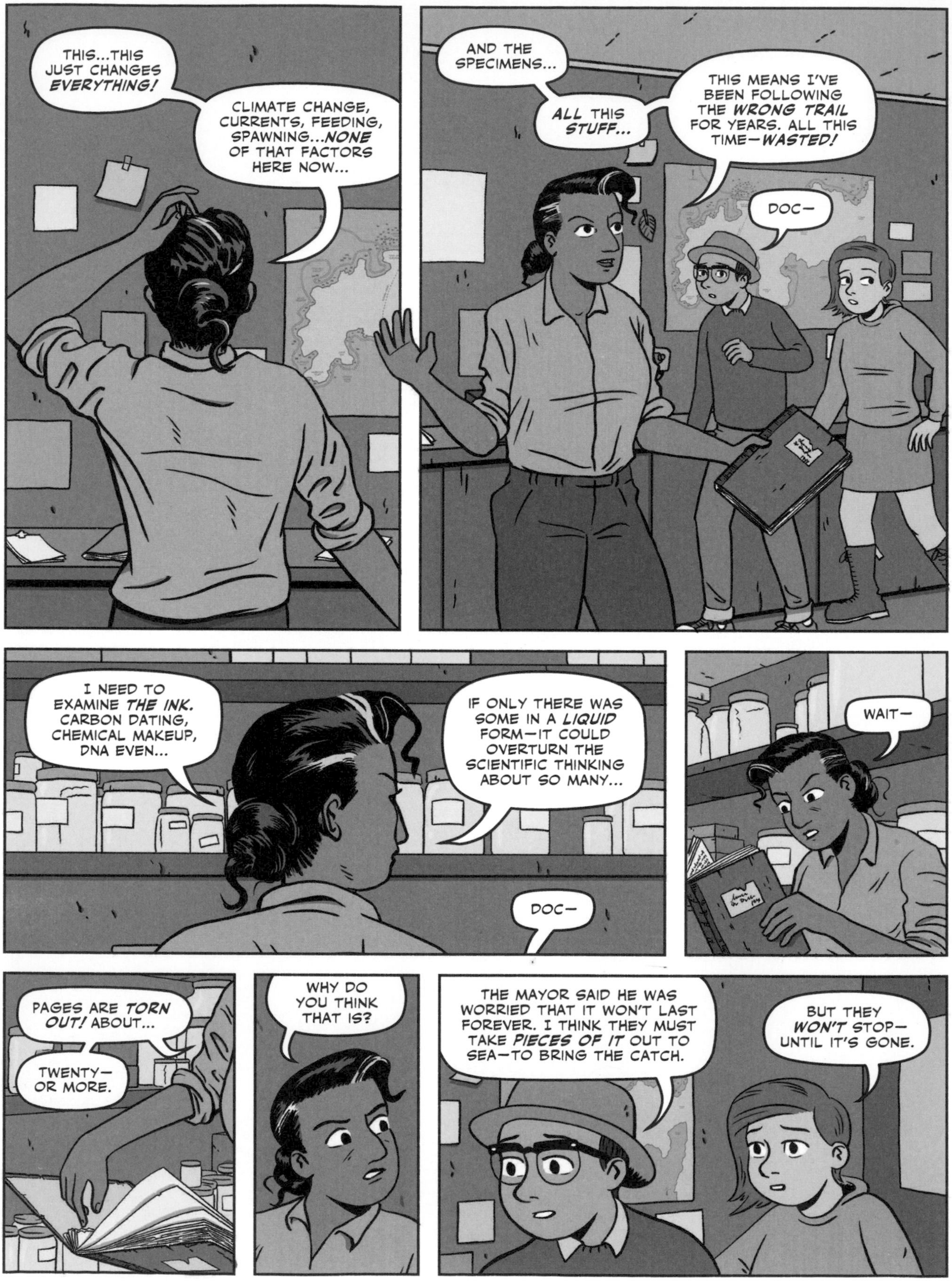
THIS...THIS JUST CHANGES EVERYTHING!
CLIMATE CHANGE, CURRENTS, FEEDING, SPAWNING...NONE OF THAT FACTORS HERE NOW...
AND THE SPECIMENS...
ALL THIS STUFF...
THIS MEANS I'VE BEEN FOLLOWING THE WRONG TRAIL FOR YEARS. ALL THIS TIME—WASTED!
DOC—
I NEED TO EXAMINE THE INK. CARBON DATING, CHEMICAL MAKEUP, DNA EVEN...
IF ONLY THERE WAS SOME IN A LIQUID FORM—IT COULD OVERTURN THE SCIENTIFIC THINKING ABOUT SO MANY...
DOC—
WAIT—
PAGES ARE TORN OUT! ABOUT...
TWENTY—OR MORE.
WHY DO YOU THINK THAT IS?
THE MAYOR SAID HE WAS WORRIED THAT IT WON'T LAST FOREVER. I THINK THEY MUST TAKE PIECES OF IT OUT TO SEA—TO BRING THE CATCH.
BUT THEY WON'T STOP—UNTIL IT'S GONE.

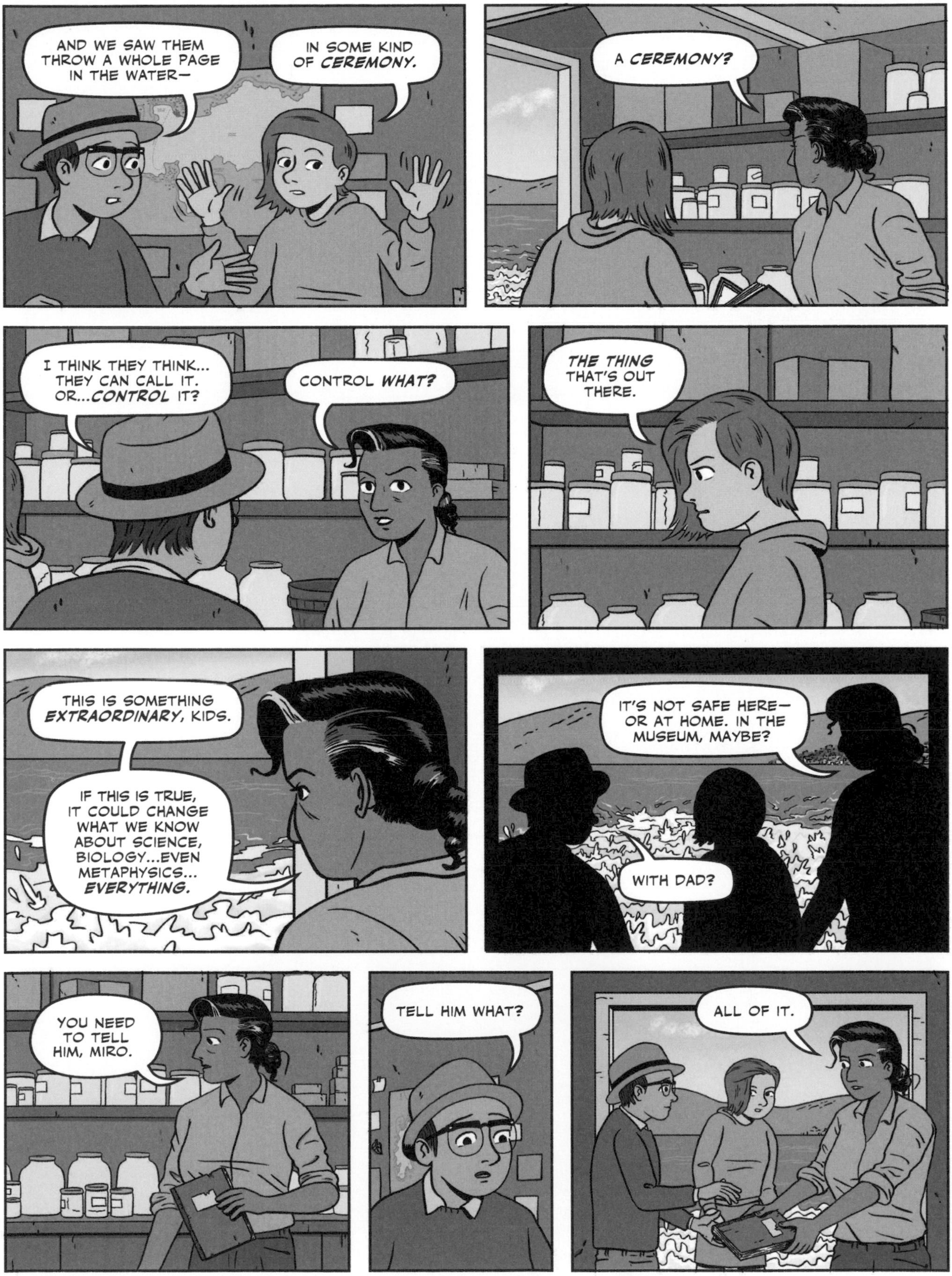
AND WE SAW THEM THROW A WHOLE PAGE IN THE WATER—
IN SOME KIND OF CEREMONY.
A CEREMONY?
I THINK THEY THINK... THEY CAN CALL IT. OR...CONTROL IT?
CONTROL WHAT?
THE THING THAT'S OUT THERE.
THIS IS SOMETHING EXTRAORDINARY, KIDS.
IF THIS IS TRUE, IT COULD CHANGE WHAT WE KNOW ABOUT SCIENCE, BIOLOGY...EVEN METAPHYSICS... EVERYTHING.
IT'S NOT SAFE HERE— OR AT HOME. IN THE MUSEUM, MAYBE?
WITH DAD?
YOU NEED TO TELL HIM, MIRO.
TELL HIM WHAT?
ALL OF IT.

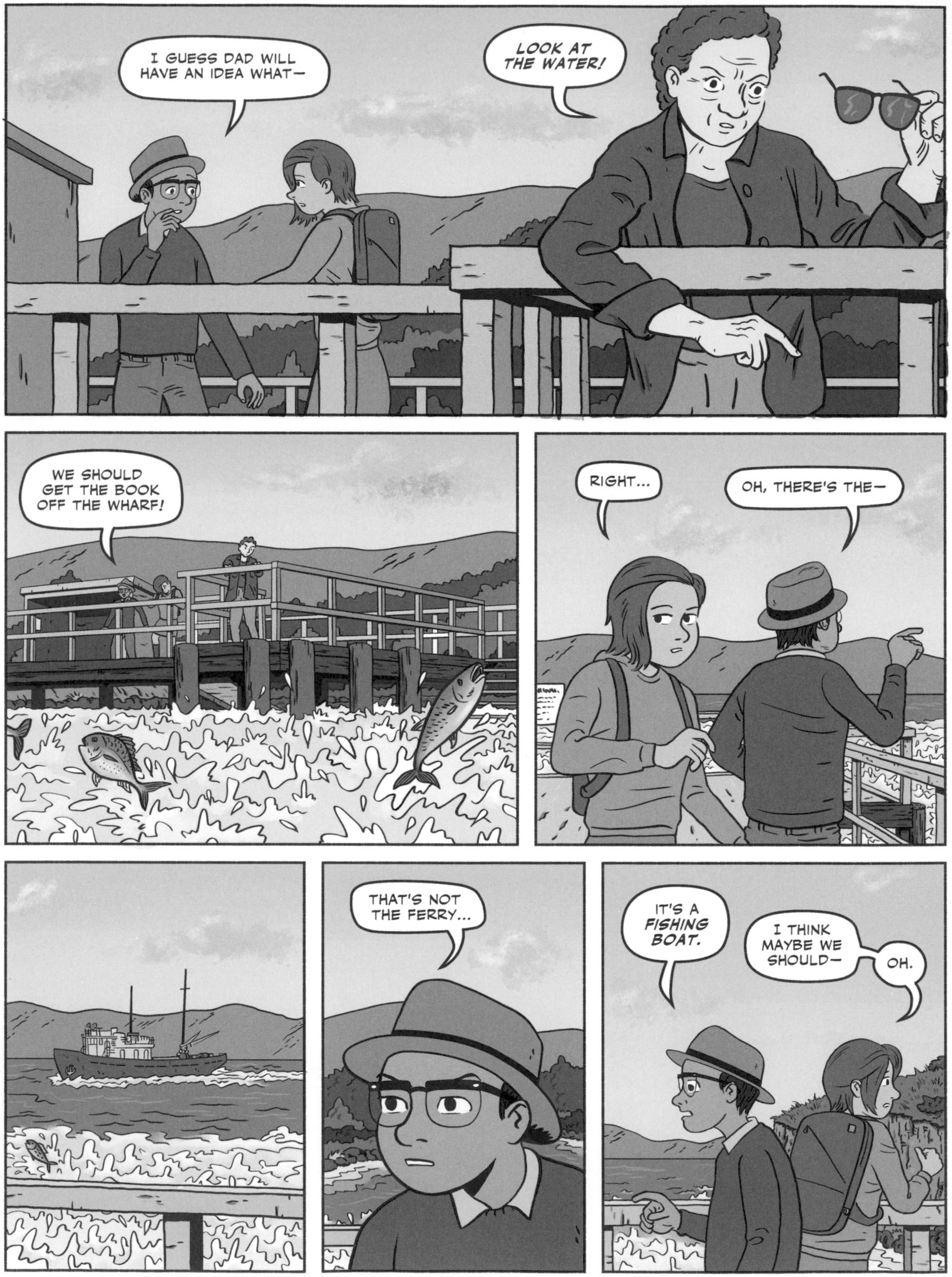
I GUESS DAD WILL HAVE AN IDEA WHAT—
LOOK AT THE WATER!
WE SHOULD GET THE BOOK OFF THE WHARF!
RIGHT...
OH, THERE'S THE—
THAT'S NOT THE FERRY...
IT'S A FISHING BOAT.
I THINK MAYBE WE SHOULD—
OH.

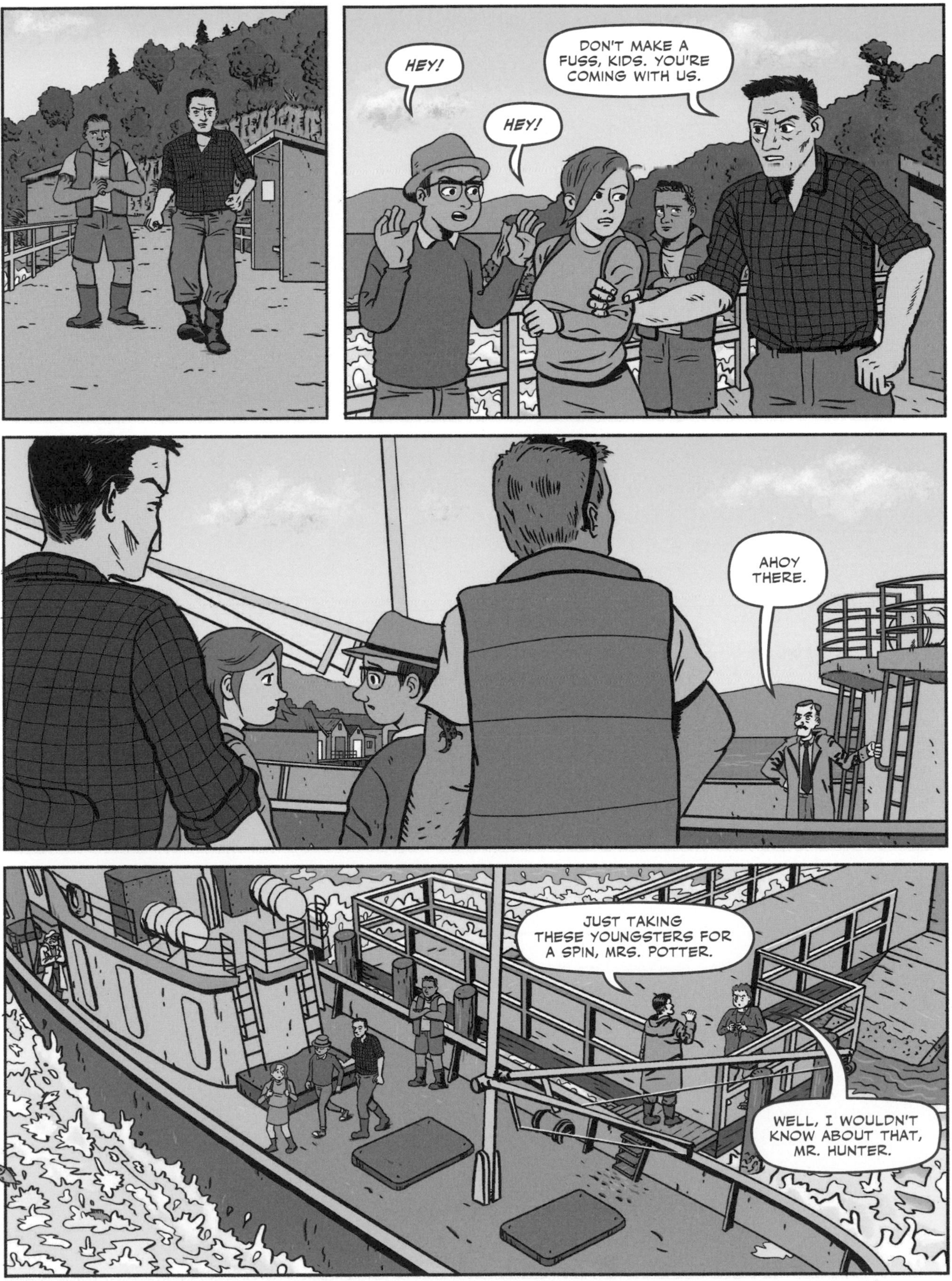
HEY!
HEY!
DON'T MAKE A FUSS, KIDS. YOU'RE COMING WITH US.
AHOY THERE.
JUST TAKING THESE YOUNGSTERS FOR A SPIN, MRS. POTTER.
WELL, I WOULDN'T KNOW ABOUT THAT, MR. HUNTER.

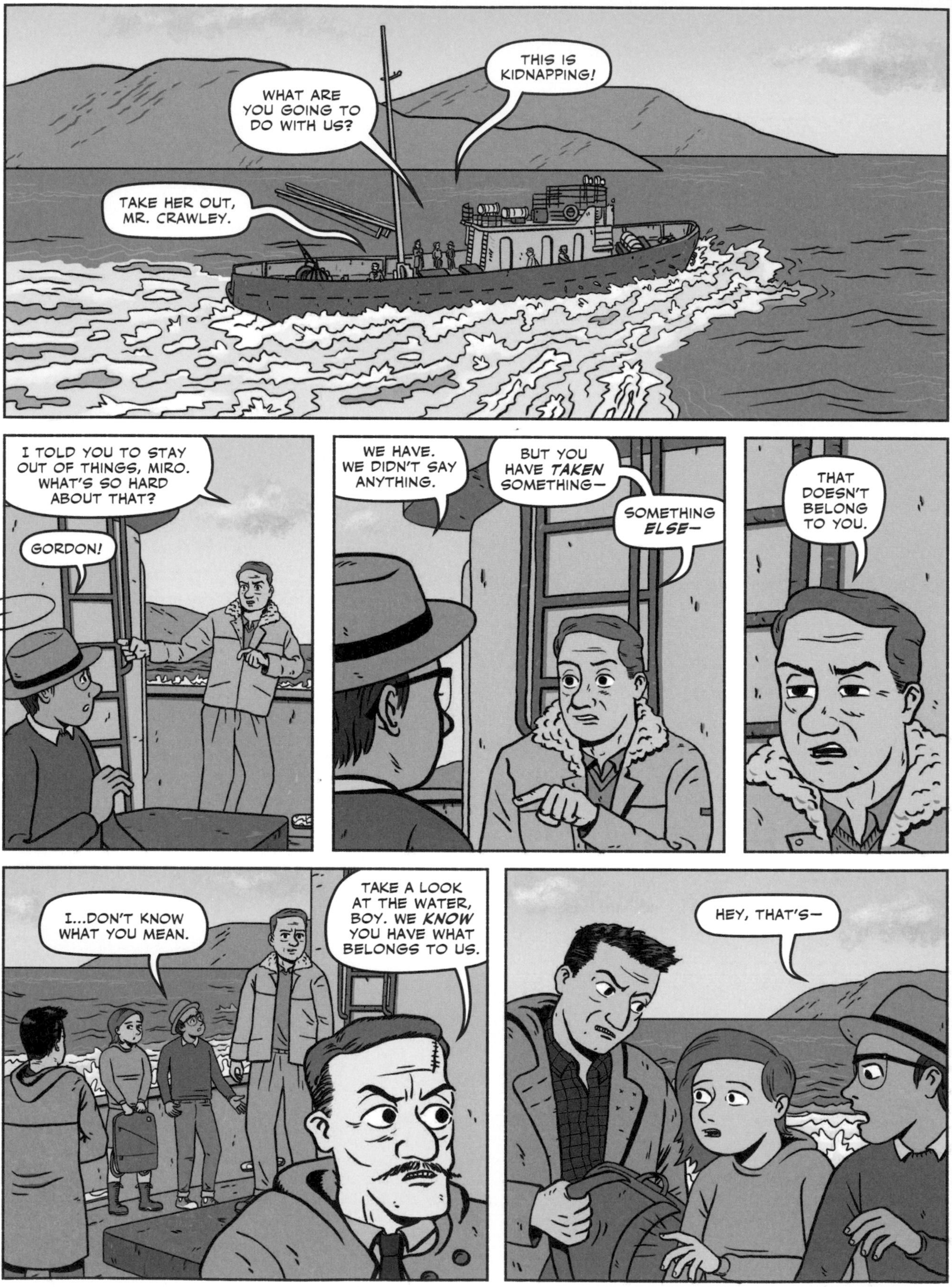
WHAT ARE YOU GOING TO DO WITH US?
THIS IS KIDNAPPING!
TAKE HER OUT, MR. CRAWLEY.
I TOLD YOU TO STAY OUT OF THINGS, MIRO. WHAT'S SO HARD ABOUT THAT?
GORDON!
WE HAVE. WE DIDN'T SAY ANYTHING.
BUT YOU HAVE *TAKEN* SOMETHING—
SOMETHING *ELSE*—
THAT DOESN'T BELONG TO YOU.
I...DON'T KNOW WHAT YOU MEAN.
TAKE A LOOK AT THE WATER, BOY. WE *KNOW* YOU HAVE WHAT BELONGS TO US.
HEY, THAT'S—

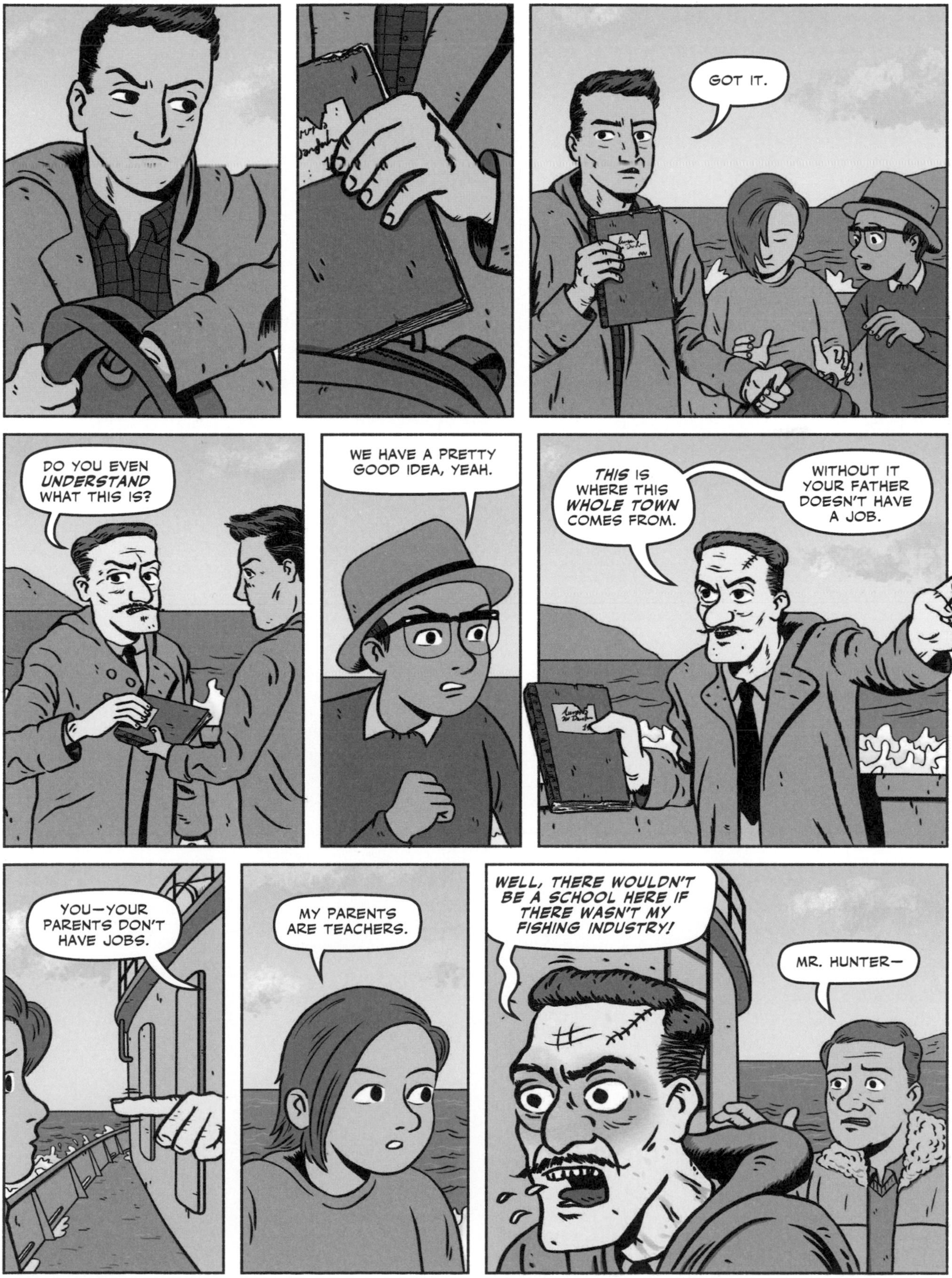
GOT IT.
DO YOU EVEN *UNDERSTAND* WHAT THIS IS?
WE HAVE A PRETTY GOOD IDEA, YEAH.
THIS IS WHERE THIS *WHOLE TOWN* COMES FROM.
WITHOUT IT YOUR FATHER DOESN'T HAVE A JOB.
YOU—YOUR PARENTS DON'T HAVE JOBS.
MY PARENTS ARE TEACHERS.
WELL, THERE WOULDN'T BE A SCHOOL HERE IF THERE WASN'T MY FISHING INDUSTRY!
MR. HUNTER—

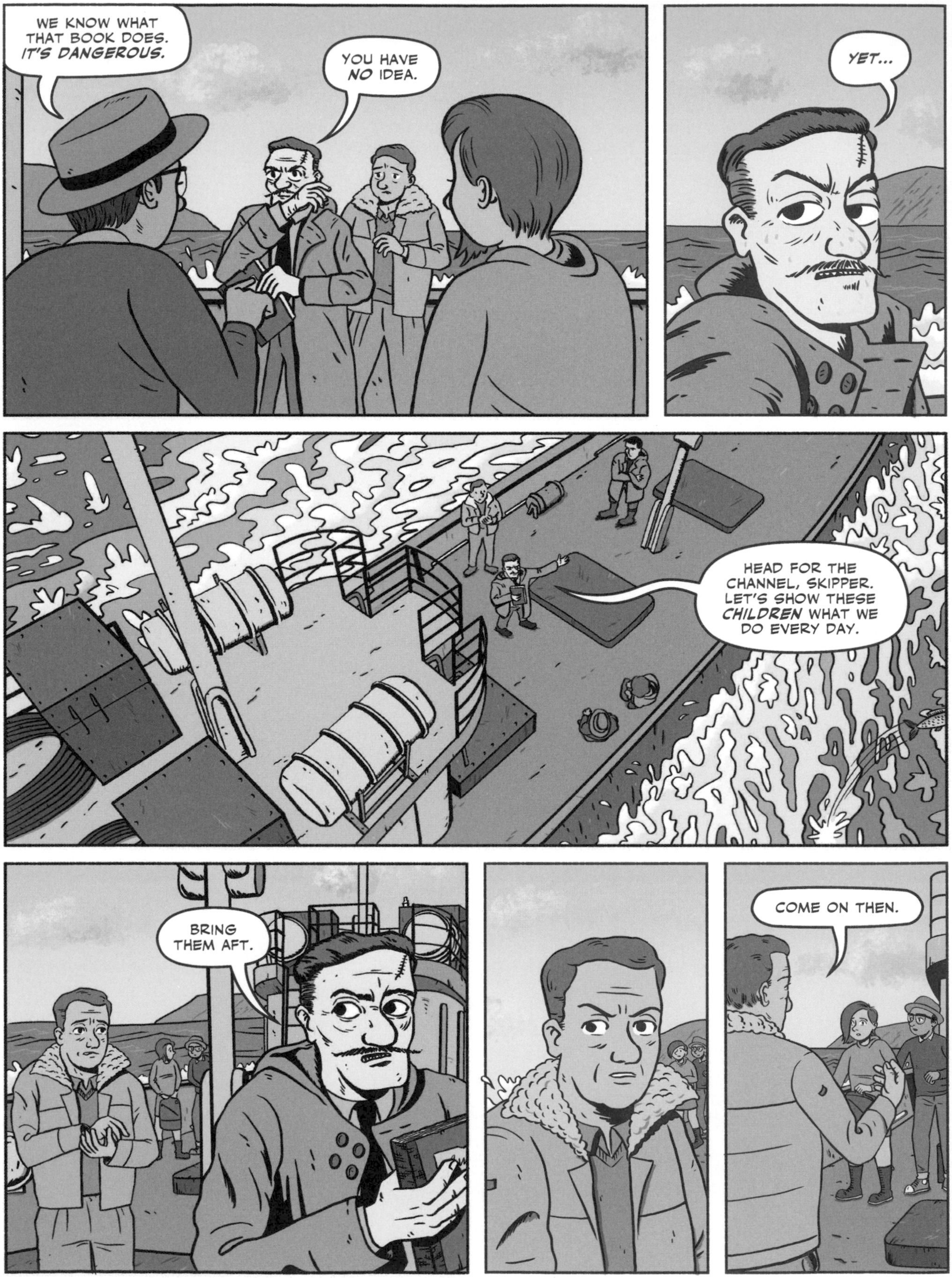
WE KNOW WHAT THAT BOOK DOES. IT'S DANGEROUS.
YOU HAVE NO IDEA.
YET...
HEAD FOR THE CHANNEL, SKIPPER. LET'S SHOW THESE CHILDREN WHAT WE DO EVERY DAY.
BRING THEM AFT.
COME ON THEN.

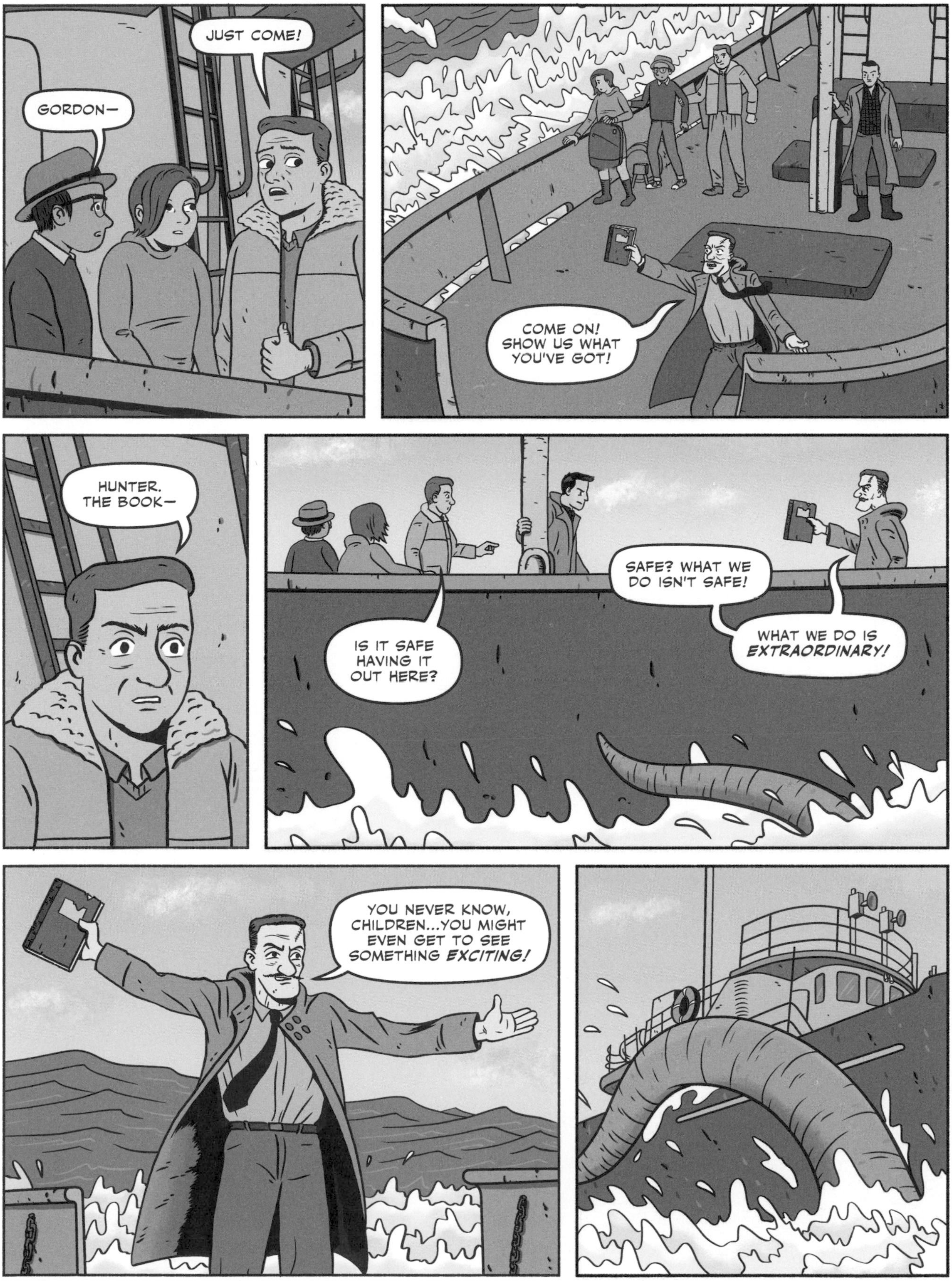
JUST COME!
GORDON—
COME ON! SHOW US WHAT YOU'VE GOT!
HUNTER. THE BOOK—
IS IT SAFE HAVING IT OUT HERE?
SAFE? WHAT WE DO ISN'T SAFE!
WHAT WE DO IS *EXTRAORDINARY!*
YOU NEVER KNOW, CHILDREN...YOU MIGHT EVEN GET TO SEE SOMETHING *EXCITING!*

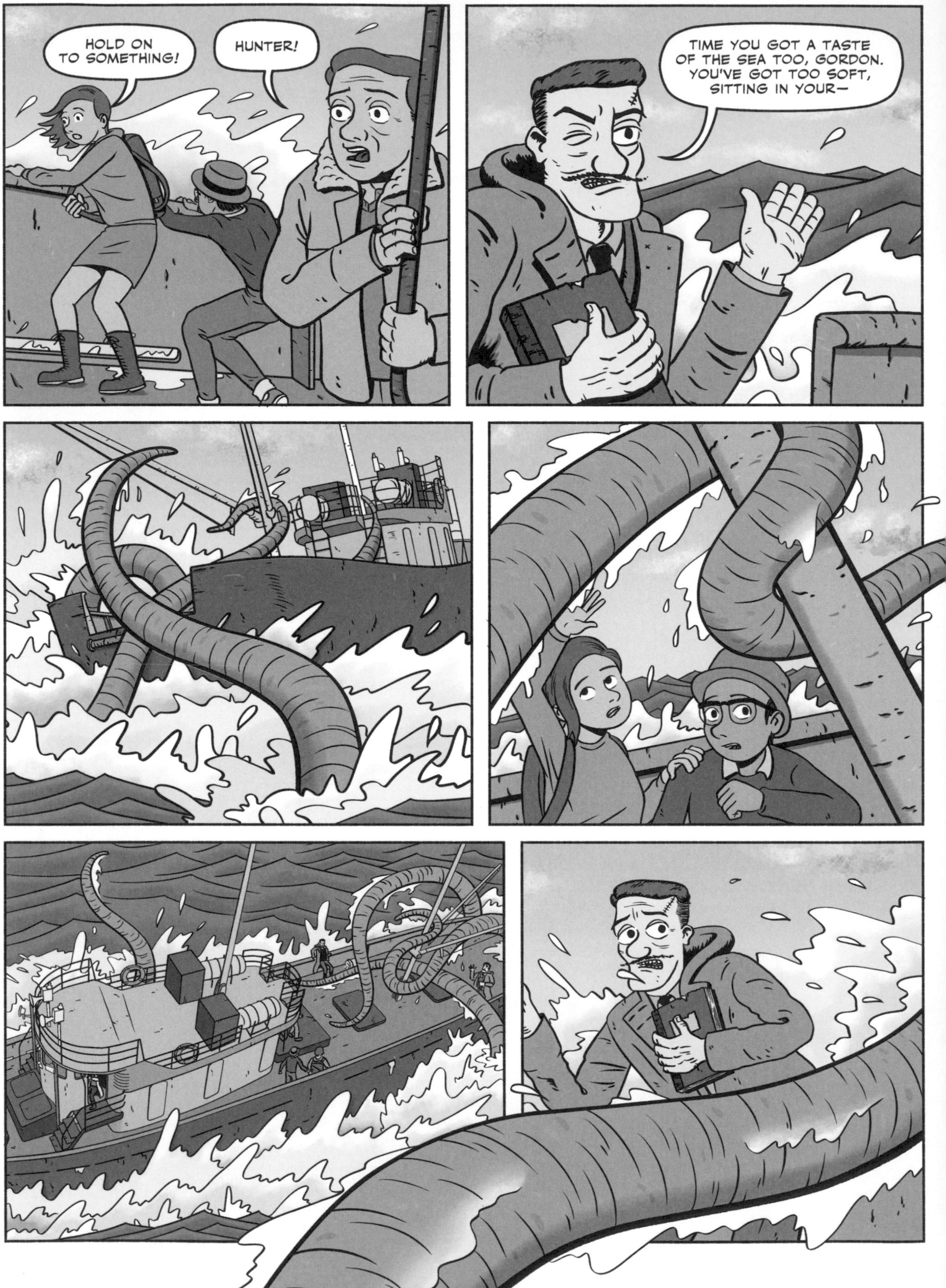
HOLD ON TO SOMETHING!
HUNTER!
TIME YOU GOT A TASTE OF THE SEA TOO, GORDON. YOU'VE GOT TOO SOFT, SITTING IN YOUR—

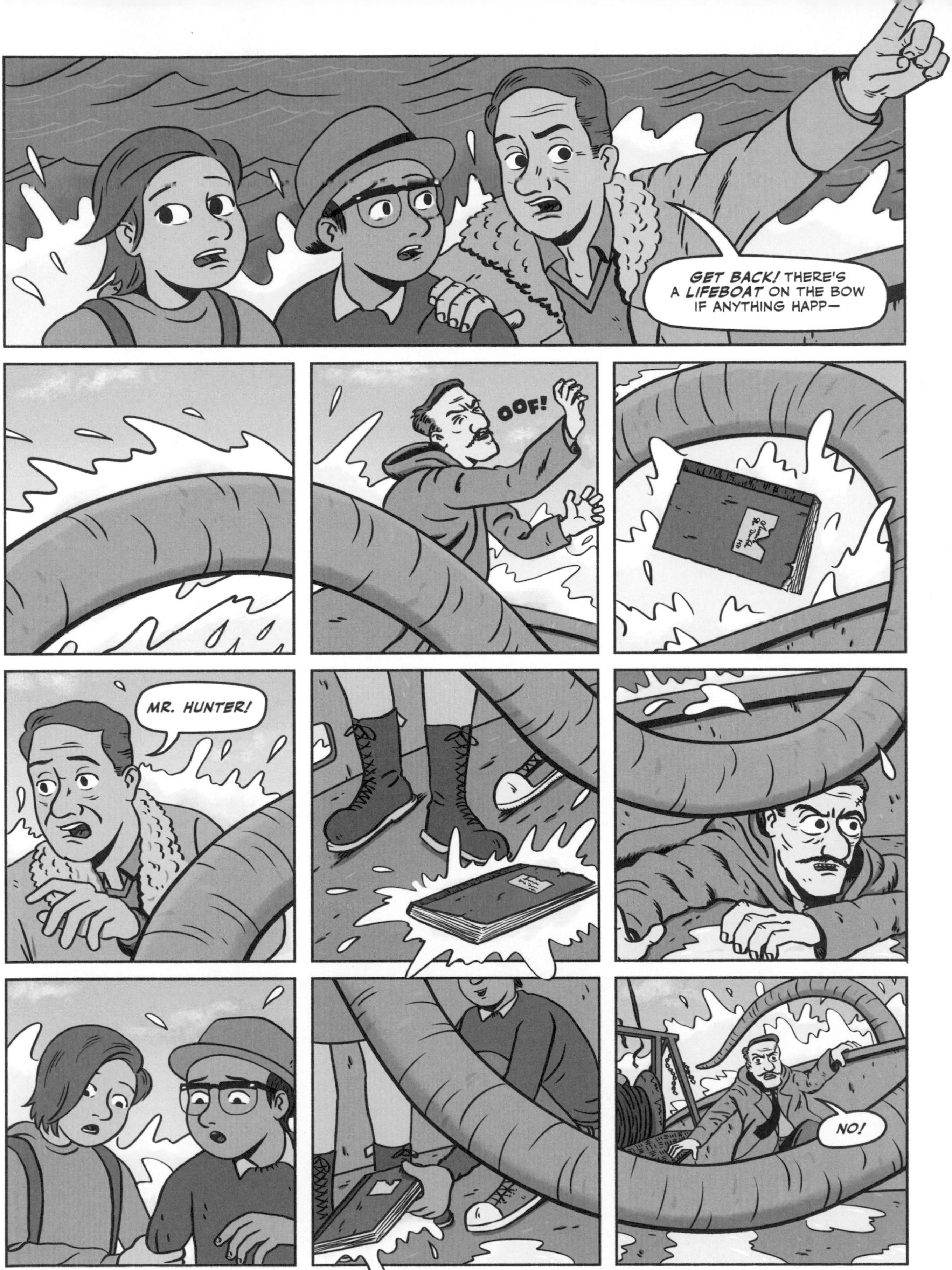
GET BACK! THERE'S A LIFEBOAT ON THE BOW IF ANYTHING HAPP—
OOF!
MR. HUNTER!
NO!

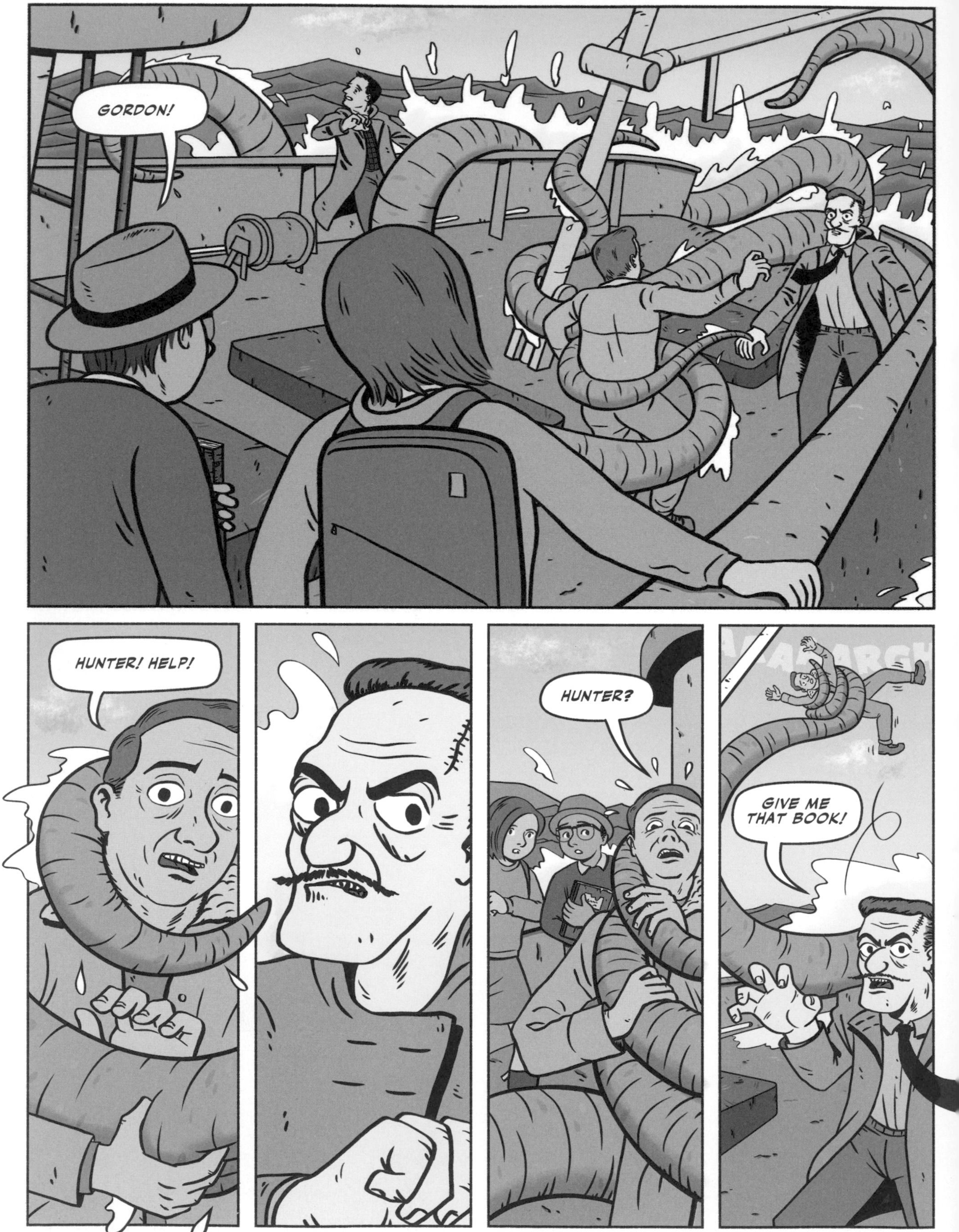
GORDON!
HUNTER! HELP!
HUNTER?
GIVE ME THAT BOOK!

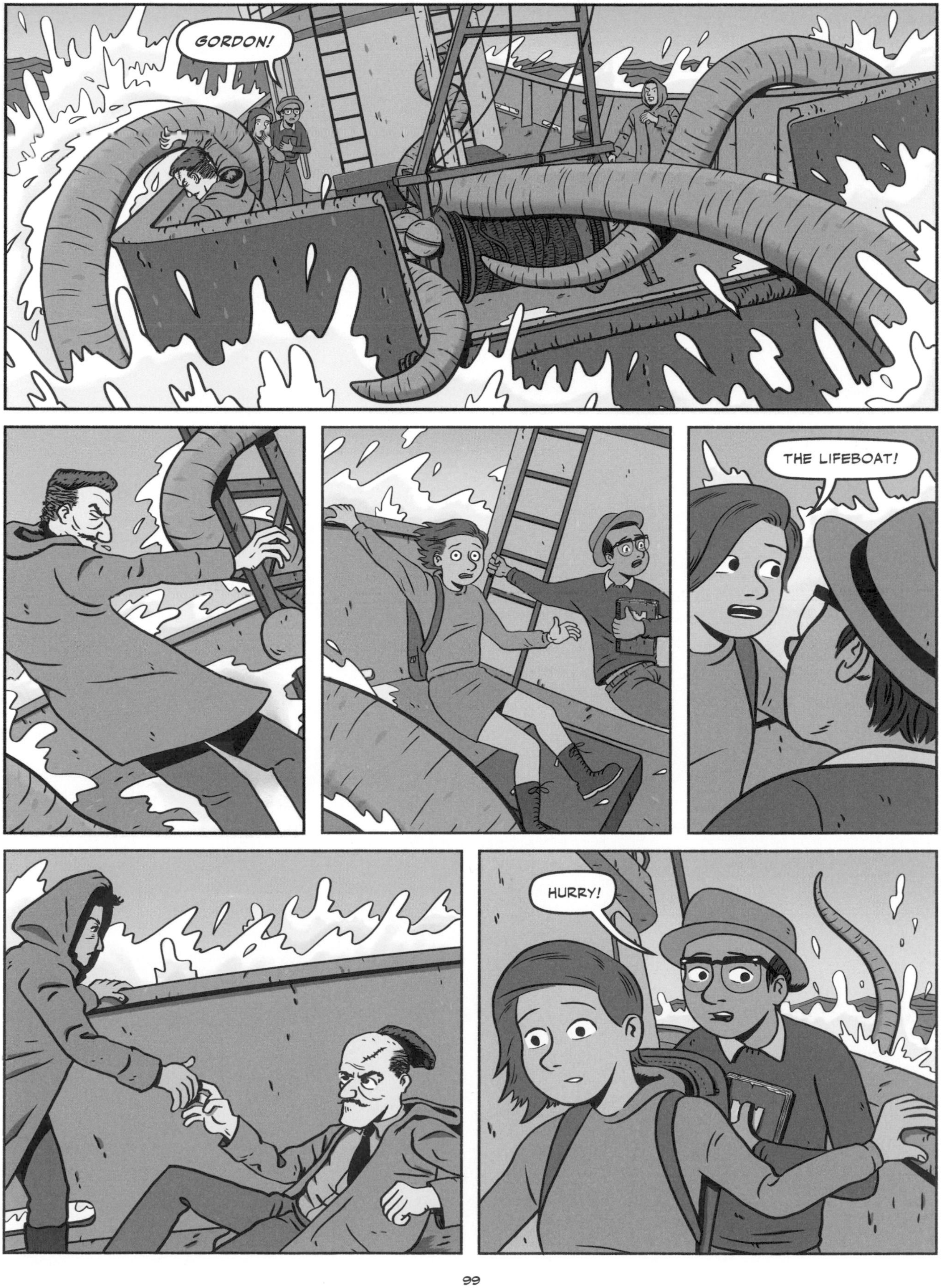
GORDON!
THE LIFEBOAT!
HURRY!

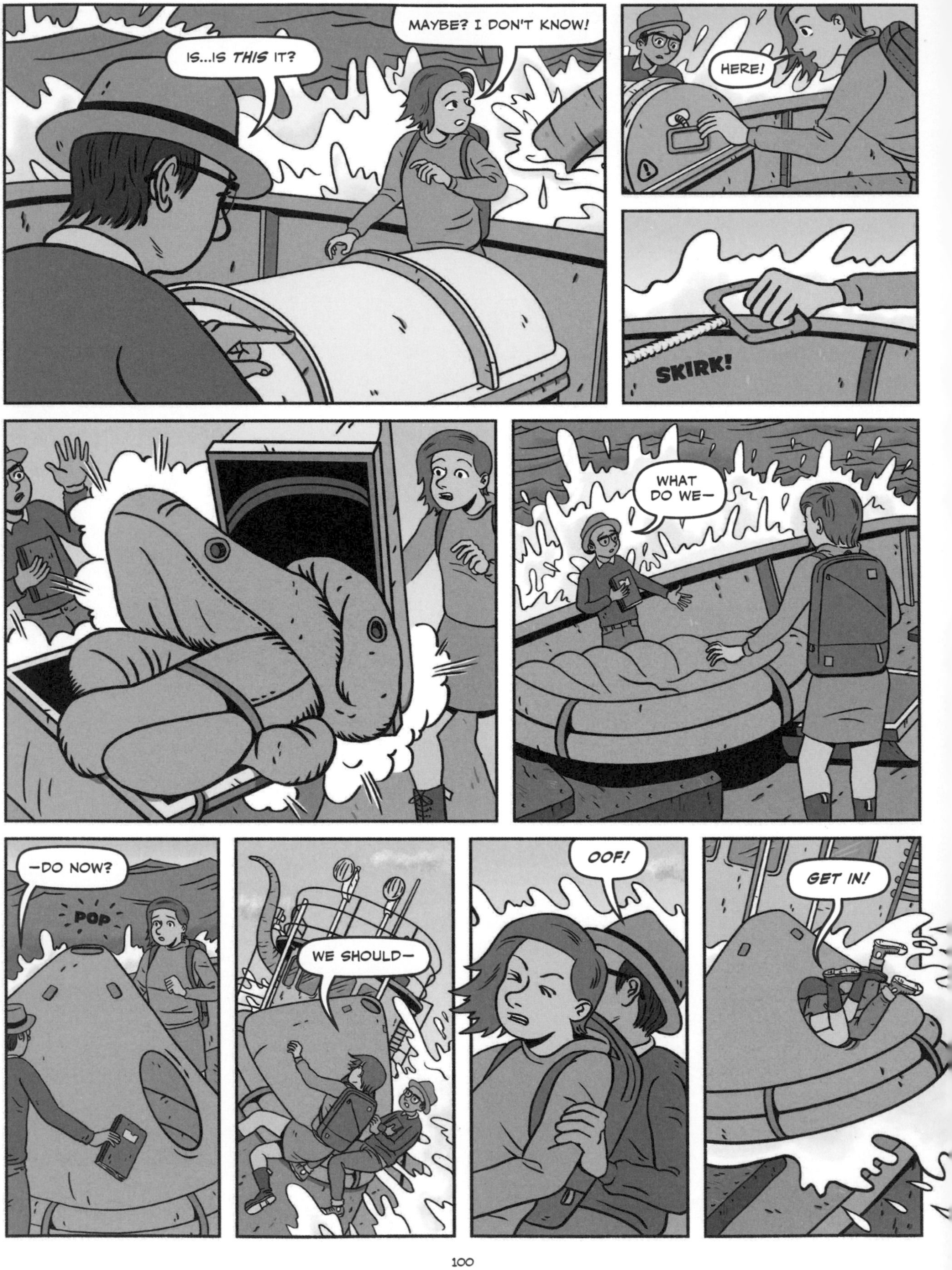
IS...IS THIS IT?
MAYBE? I DON'T KNOW!
HERE!
SKIRK!
WHAT DO WE—
—DO NOW?
POP
WE SHOULD—
OOF!
GET IN!

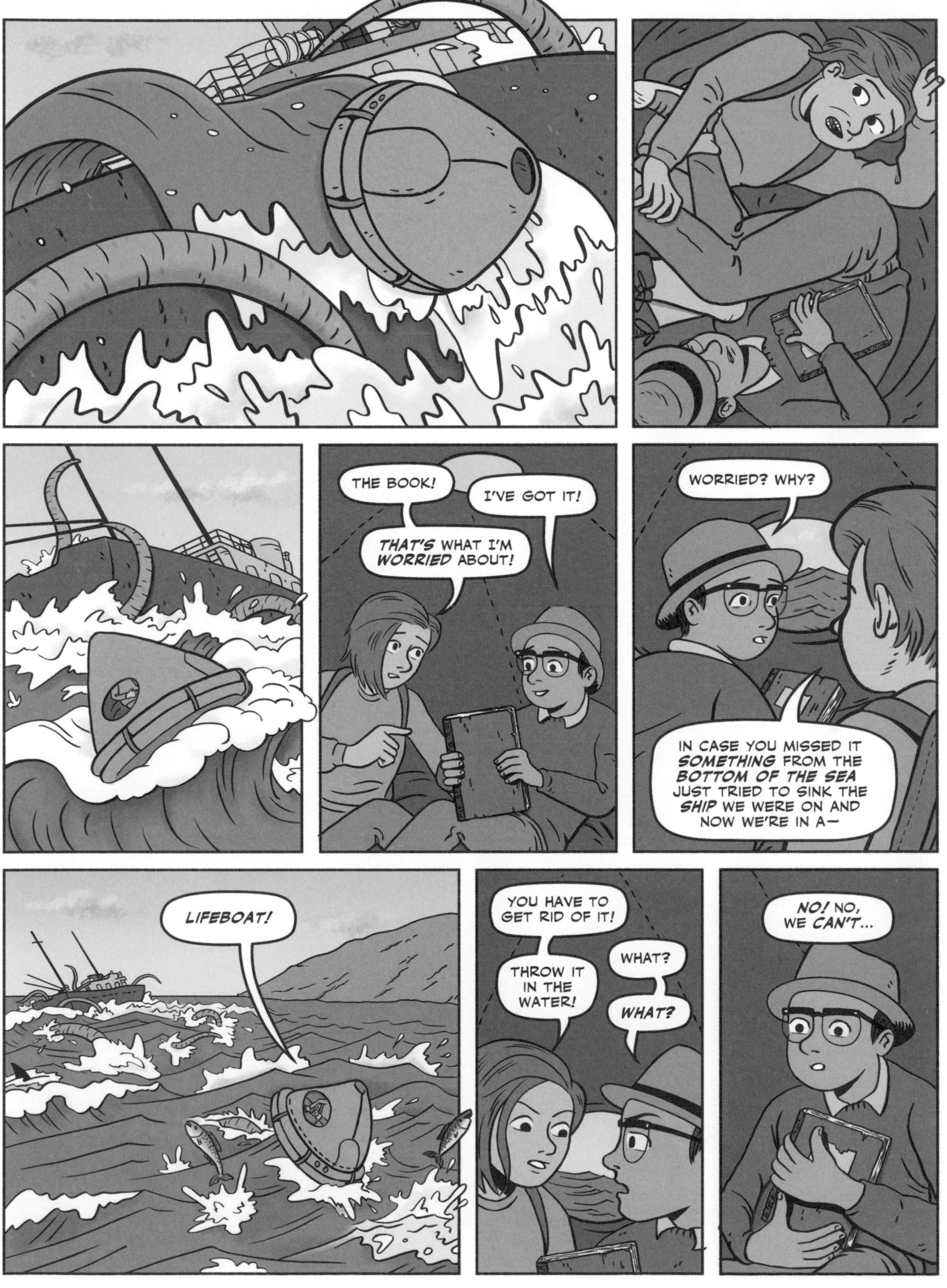

THE BOOK!
I'VE GOT IT!
THAT'S WHAT I'M WORRIED ABOUT!
WORRIED? WHY?
IN CASE YOU MISSED IT SOMETHING FROM THE BOTTOM OF THE SEA JUST TRIED TO SINK THE SHIP WE WERE ON AND NOW WE'RE IN A—
LIFEBOAT!
YOU HAVE TO GET RID OF IT!
THROW IT IN THE WATER!
WHAT?
WHAT?
NO! NO, WE CAN'T...

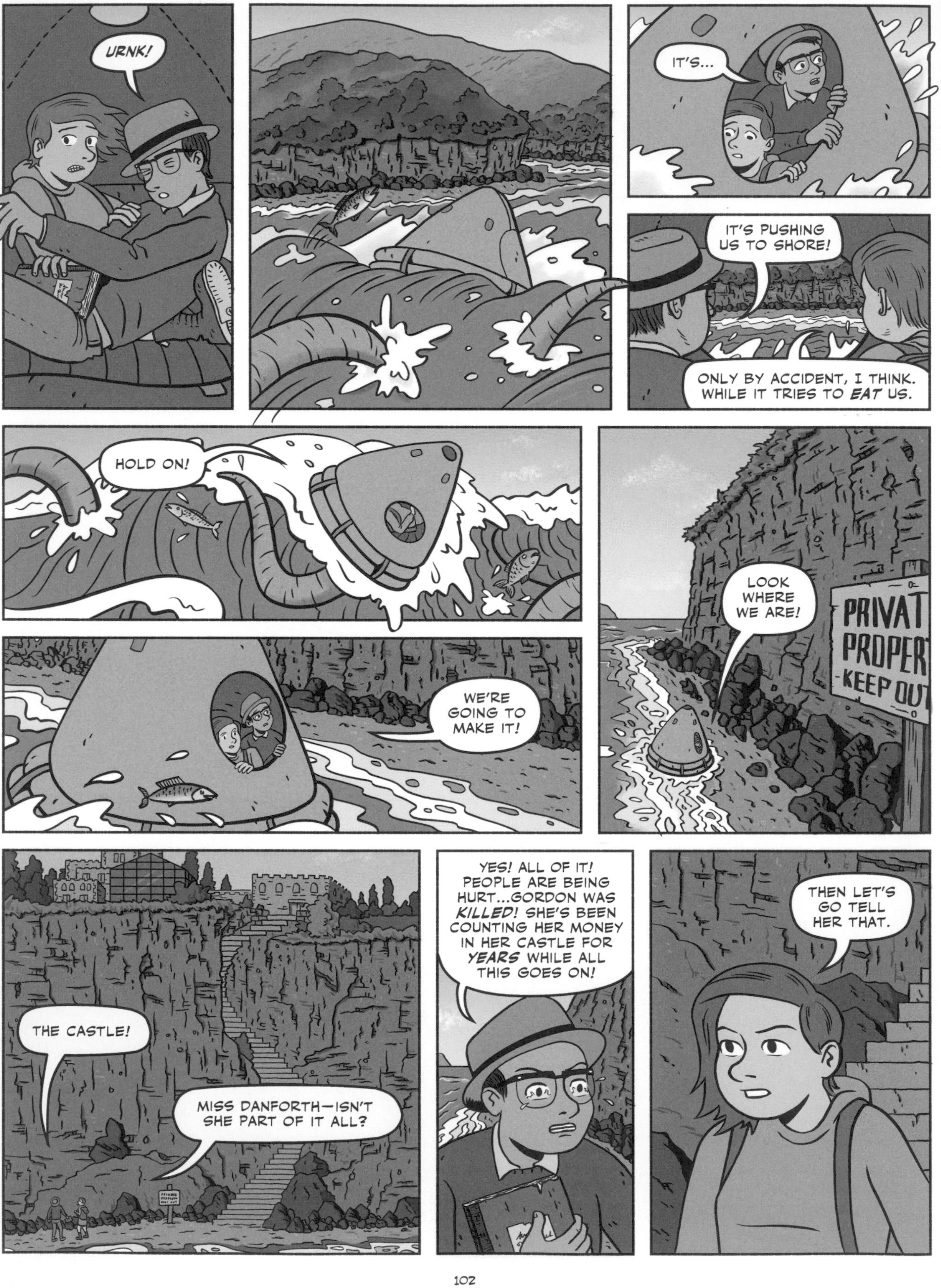
URNK!
IT'S...
IT'S PUSHING US TO SHORE!
ONLY BY ACCIDENT, I THINK. WHILE IT TRIES TO EAT US.
HOLD ON!
LOOK WHERE WE ARE!
PRIVAT PROPERT KEEP OUT
WE'RE GOING TO MAKE IT!
THE CASTLE!
MISS DANFORTH—ISN'T SHE PART OF IT ALL?
YES! ALL OF IT! PEOPLE ARE BEING HURT...GORDON WAS KILLED! SHE'S BEEN COUNTING HER MONEY IN HER CASTLE FOR YEARS WHILE ALL THIS GOES ON!
THEN LET'S GO TELL HER THAT.

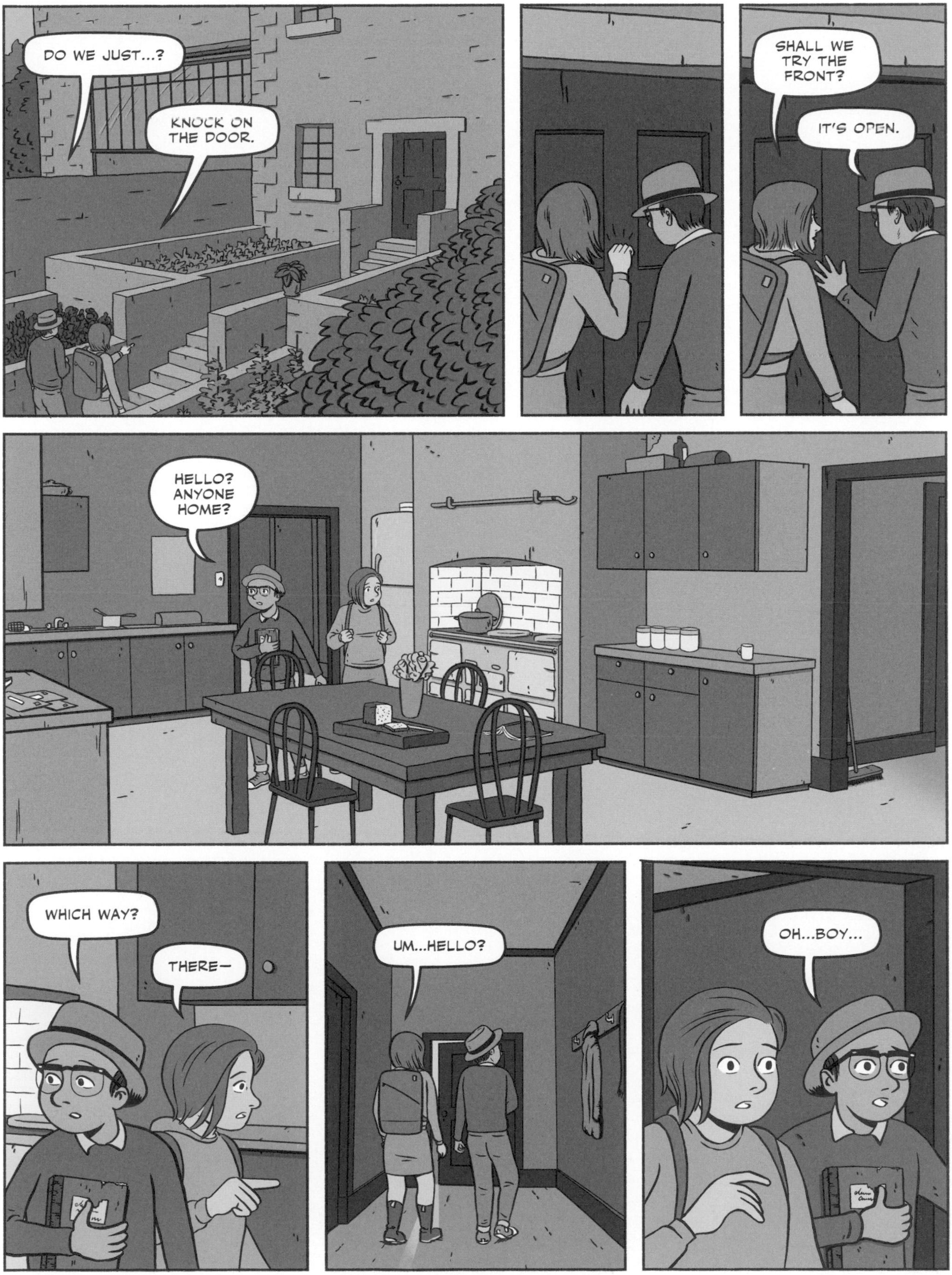
DO WE JUST...?
KNOCK ON THE DOOR.
SHALL WE TRY THE FRONT?
IT'S OPEN.
HELLO? ANYONE HOME?
WHICH WAY?
THERE—
UM...HELLO?
OH...BOY...

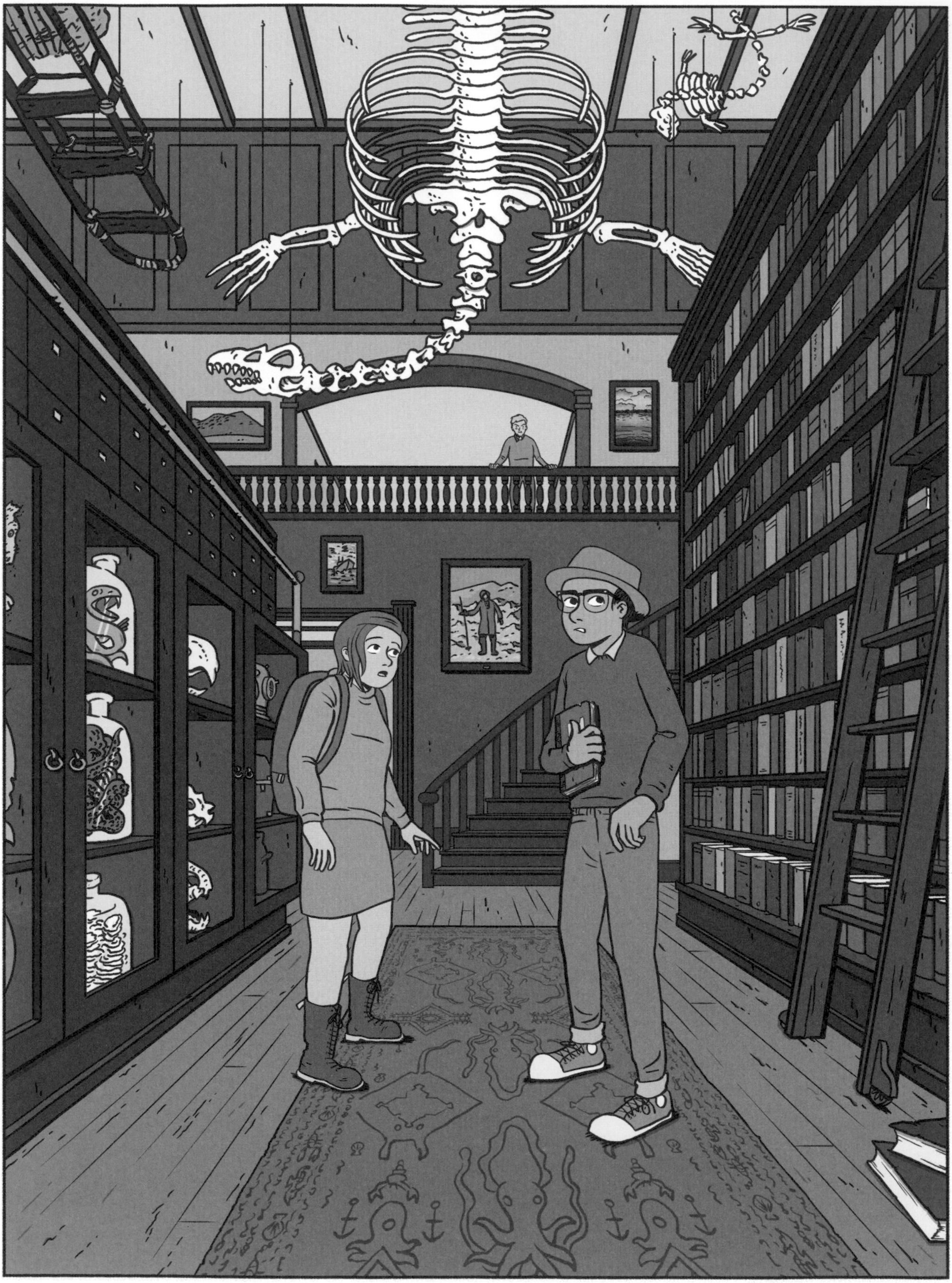

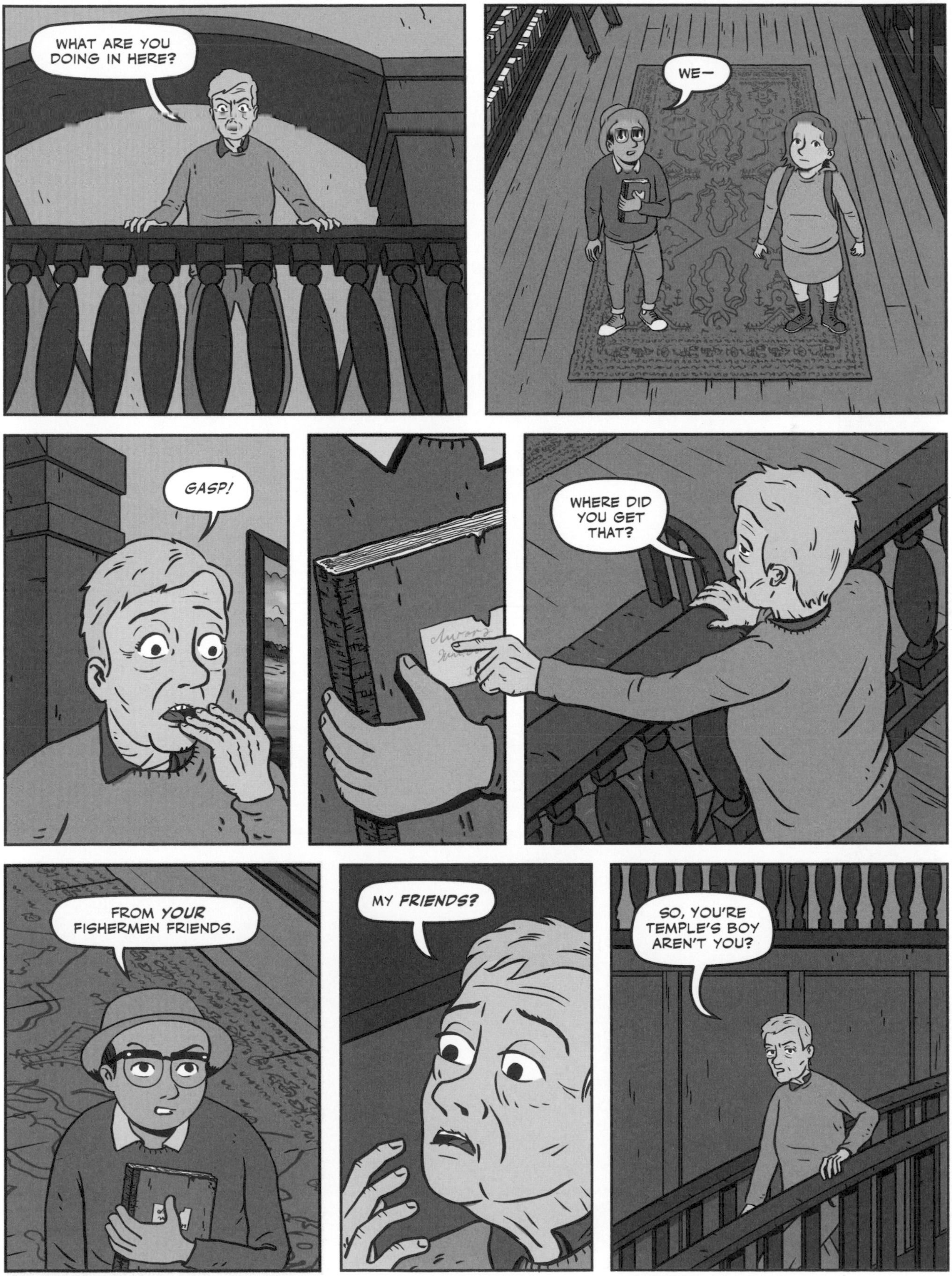
WHAT ARE YOU DOING IN HERE?
WE—
GASP!
WHERE DID YOU GET THAT?
FROM *YOUR* FISHERMEN FRIENDS.
MY *FRIENDS?*
SO, YOU'RE TEMPLE'S BOY AREN'T YOU?

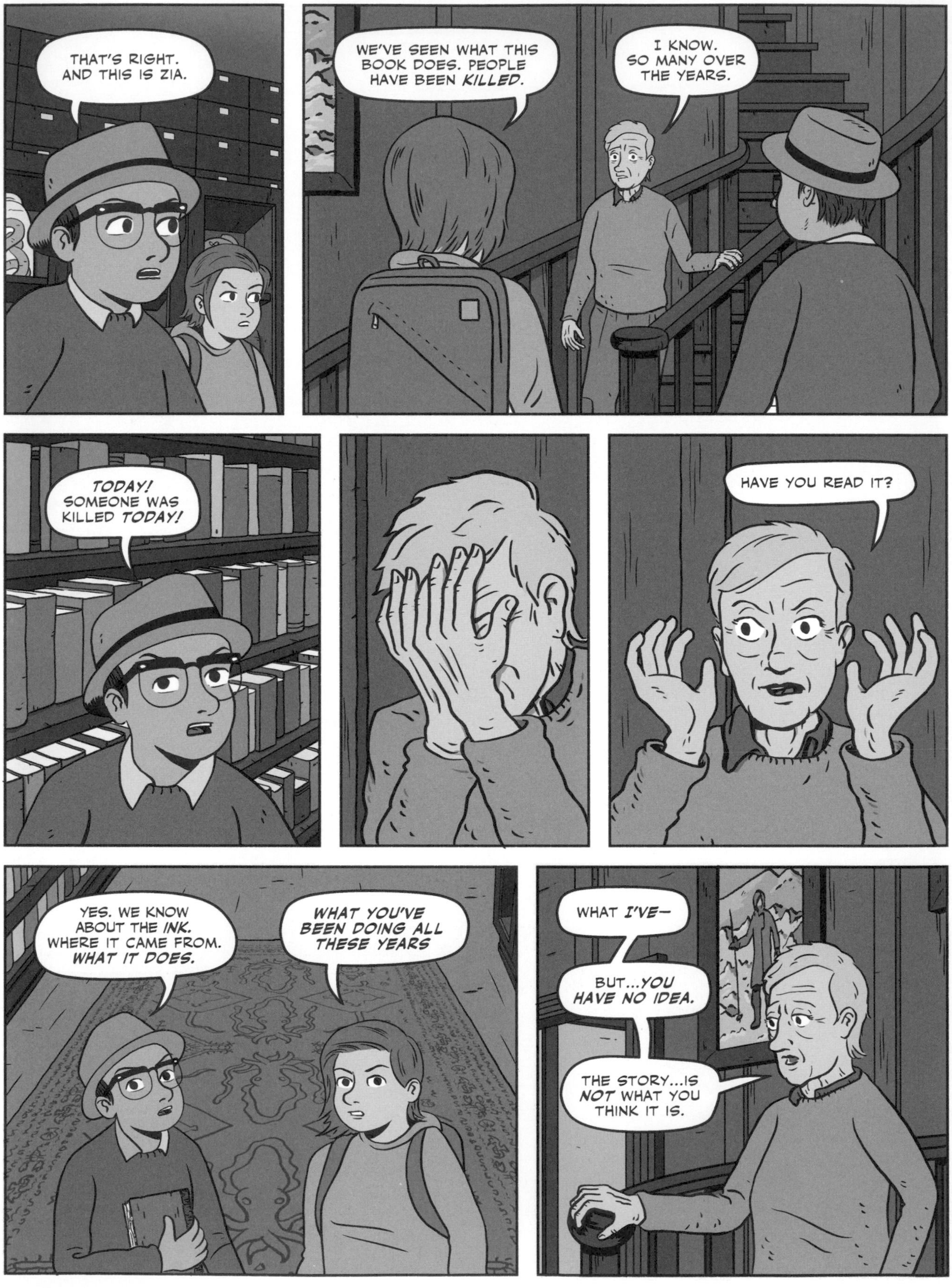
THAT'S RIGHT. AND THIS IS ZIA.
WE'VE SEEN WHAT THIS BOOK DOES. PEOPLE HAVE BEEN *KILLED*.
I KNOW. SO MANY OVER THE YEARS.
TODAY! SOMEONE WAS KILLED *TODAY!*
HAVE YOU READ IT?
YES. WE KNOW ABOUT THE *INK*. WHERE IT CAME FROM. *WHAT IT DOES.*
WHAT YOU'VE BEEN DOING ALL THESE YEARS
WHAT *I'VE*—
BUT...*YOU HAVE NO IDEA.*
THE STORY...IS *NOT* WHAT YOU THINK IT IS.

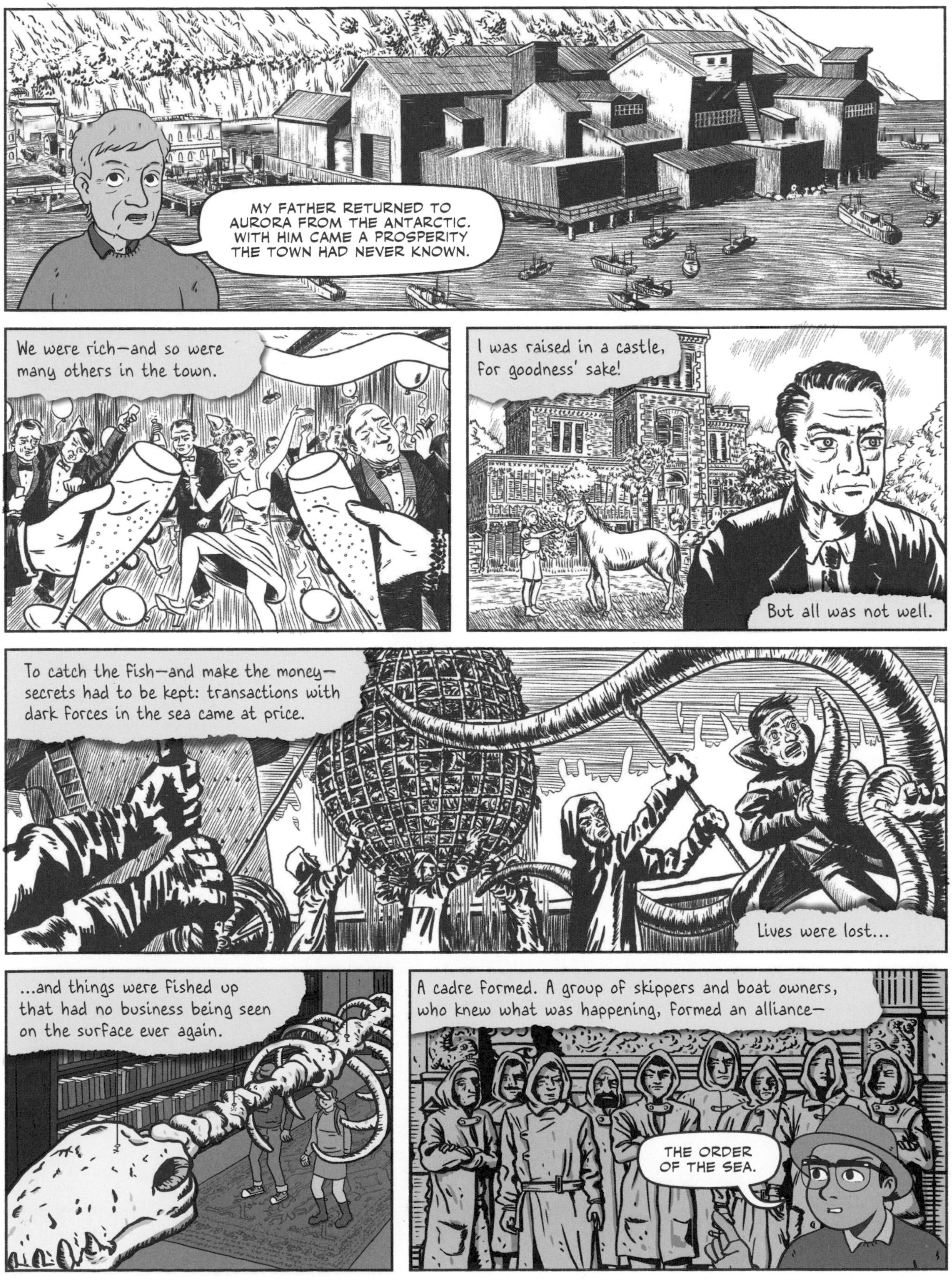
MY FATHER RETURNED TO AURORA FROM THE ANTARCTIC. WITH HIM CAME A PROSPERITY THE TOWN HAD NEVER KNOWN.
We were rich—and so were many others in the town.
I was raised in a castle, for goodness' sake!
But all was not well.
To catch the fish—and make the money—secrets had to be kept: transactions with dark forces in the sea came at price.
Lives were lost...
...and things were fished up that had no business being seen on the surface ever again.
A cadre formed. A group of skippers and boat owners, who knew what was happening, formed an alliance—
THE ORDER OF THE SEA.

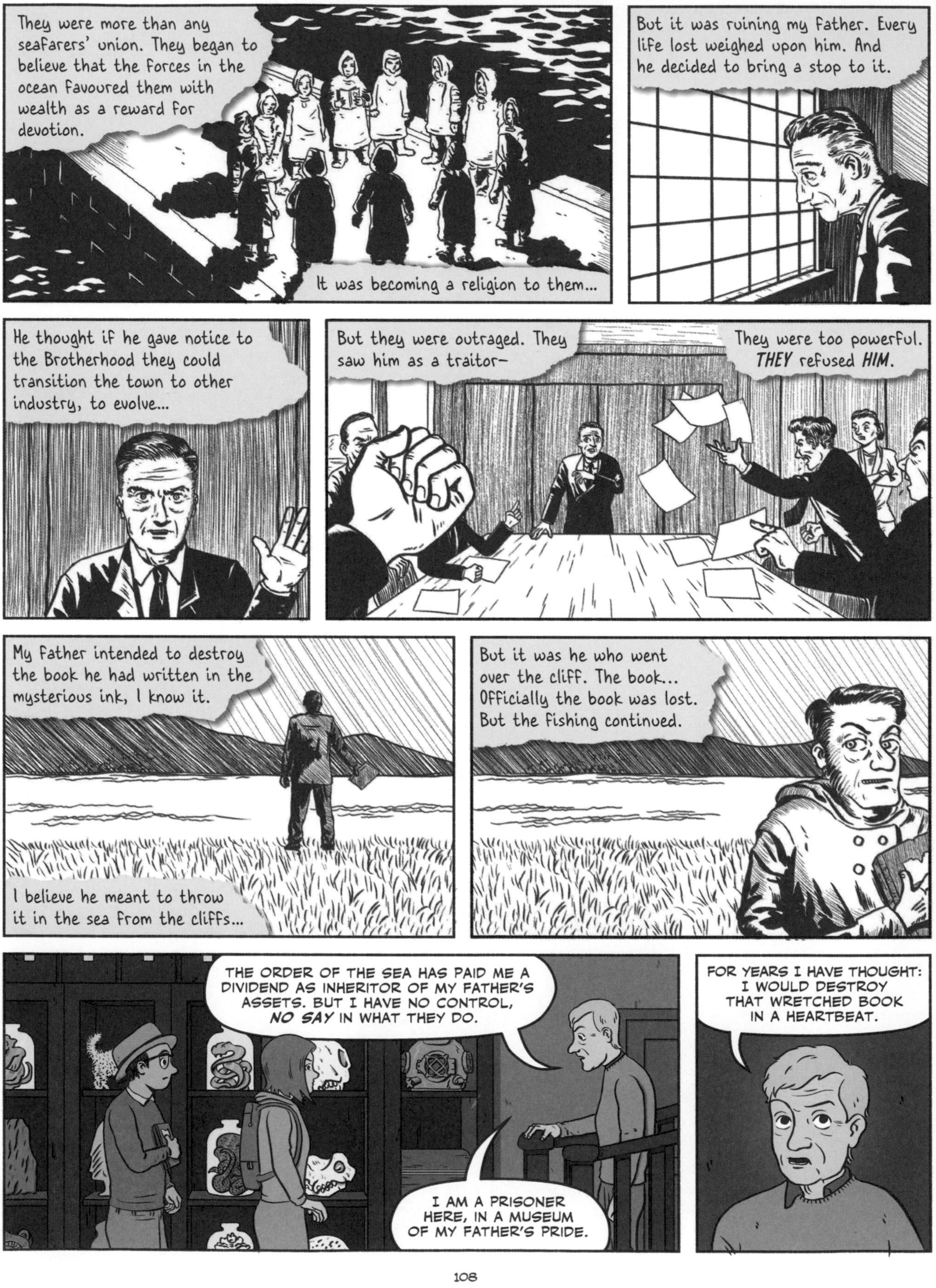
They were more than any seafarers' union. They began to believe that the forces in the ocean favoured them with wealth as a reward for devotion.
It was becoming a religion to them...
But it was ruining my father. Every life lost weighed upon him. And he decided to bring a stop to it.
He thought if he gave notice to the Brotherhood they could transition the town to other industry, to evolve...
But they were outraged. They saw him as a traitor—
They were too powerful. THEY refused HIM.
My father intended to destroy the book he had written in the mysterious ink, I know it.
I believe he meant to throw it in the sea from the cliffs...
But it was he who went over the cliff. The book... Officially the book was lost. But the fishing continued.
THE ORDER OF THE SEA HAS PAID ME A DIVIDEND AS INHERITOR OF MY FATHER'S ASSETS. BUT I HAVE NO CONTROL, NO SAY IN WHAT THEY DO.
I AM A PRISONER HERE, IN A MUSEUM OF MY FATHER'S PRIDE.
FOR YEARS I HAVE THOUGHT: I WOULD DESTROY THAT WRETCHED BOOK IN A HEARTBEAT.

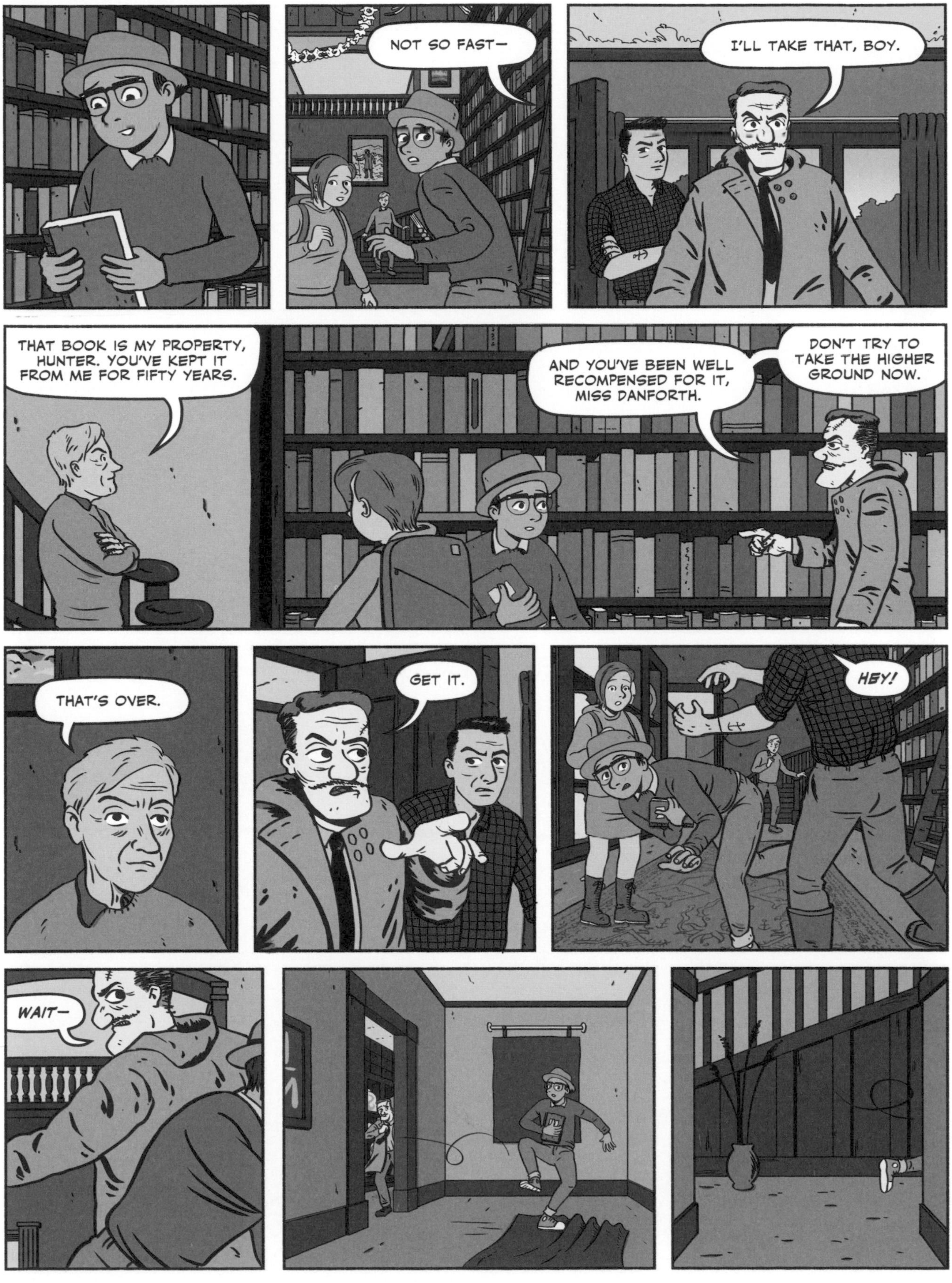
NOT SO FAST—
I'LL TAKE THAT, BOY.
THAT BOOK IS MY PROPERTY, HUNTER. YOU'VE KEPT IT FROM ME FOR FIFTY YEARS.
AND YOU'VE BEEN WELL RECOMPENSED FOR IT, MISS DANFORTH.
DON'T TRY TO TAKE THE HIGHER GROUND NOW.
THAT'S OVER.
GET IT.
HEY!
WAIT—

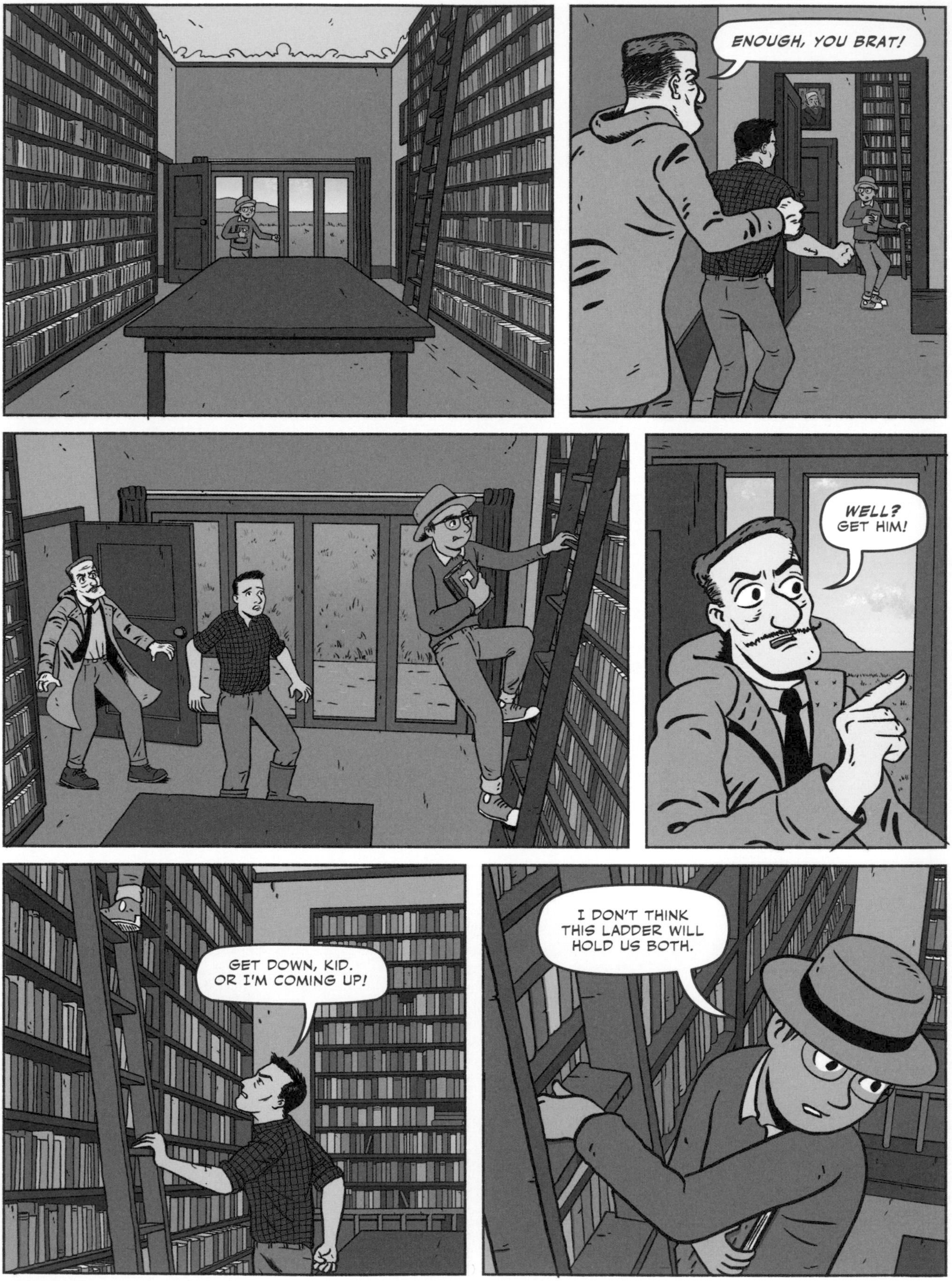
ENOUGH, YOU BRAT!
WELL? GET HIM!
GET DOWN, KID. OR I'M COMING UP!
I DON'T THINK THIS LADDER WILL HOLD US BOTH.

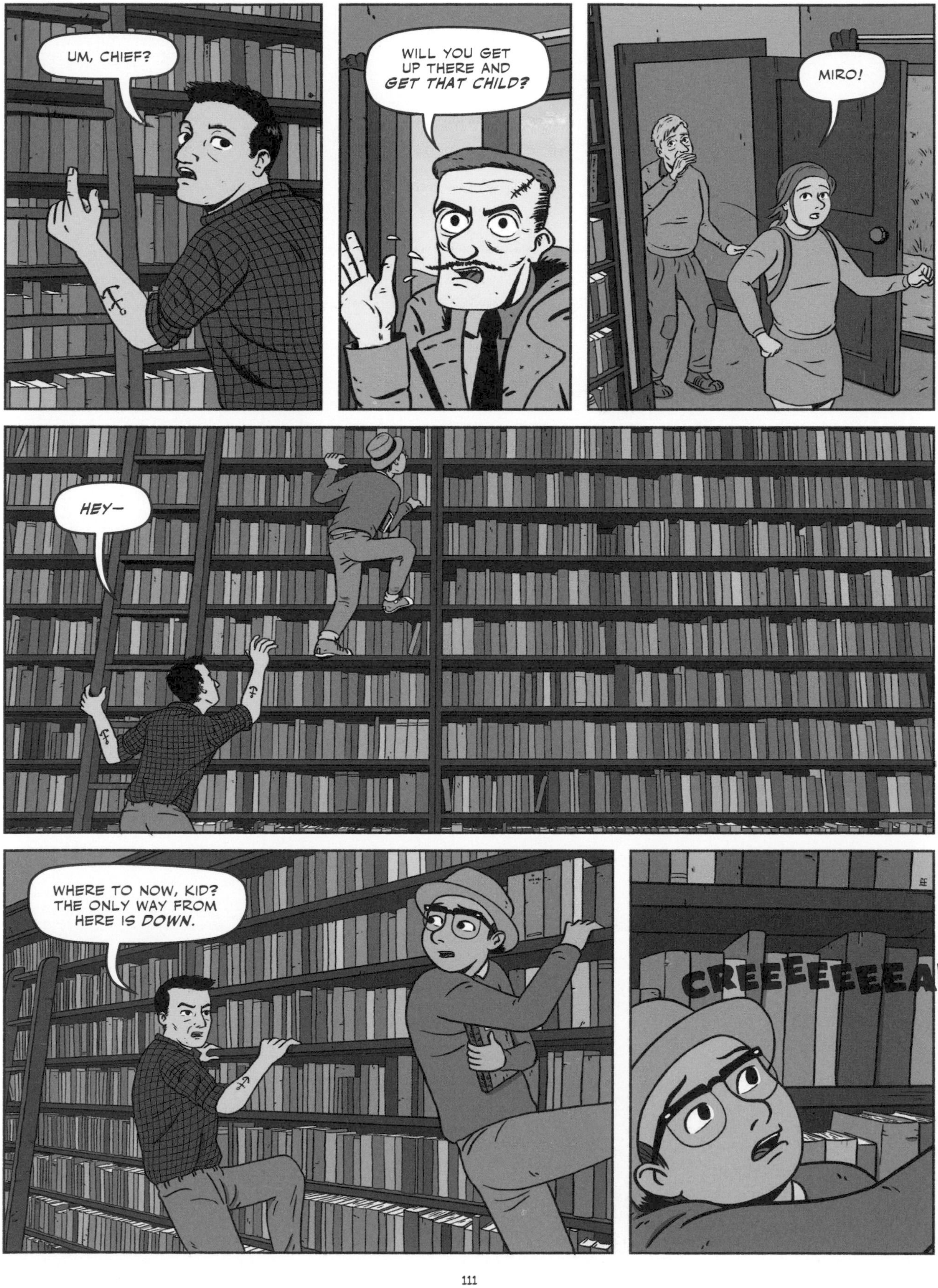
UM, CHIEF?
WILL YOU GET UP THERE AND GET THAT CHILD?
MIRO!
HEY—
WHERE TO NOW, KID? THE ONLY WAY FROM HERE IS DOWN.
CREEEEEEEEAK

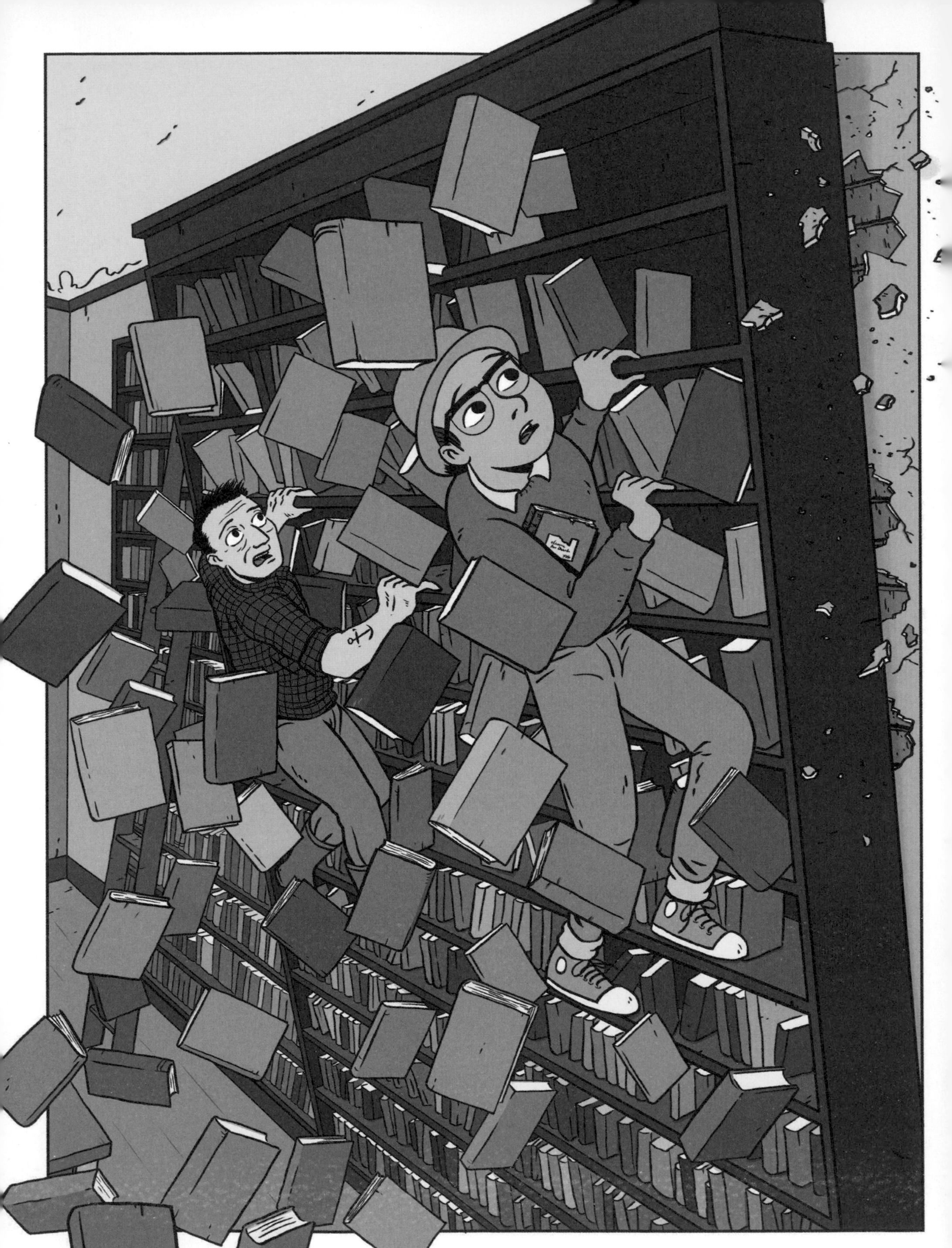

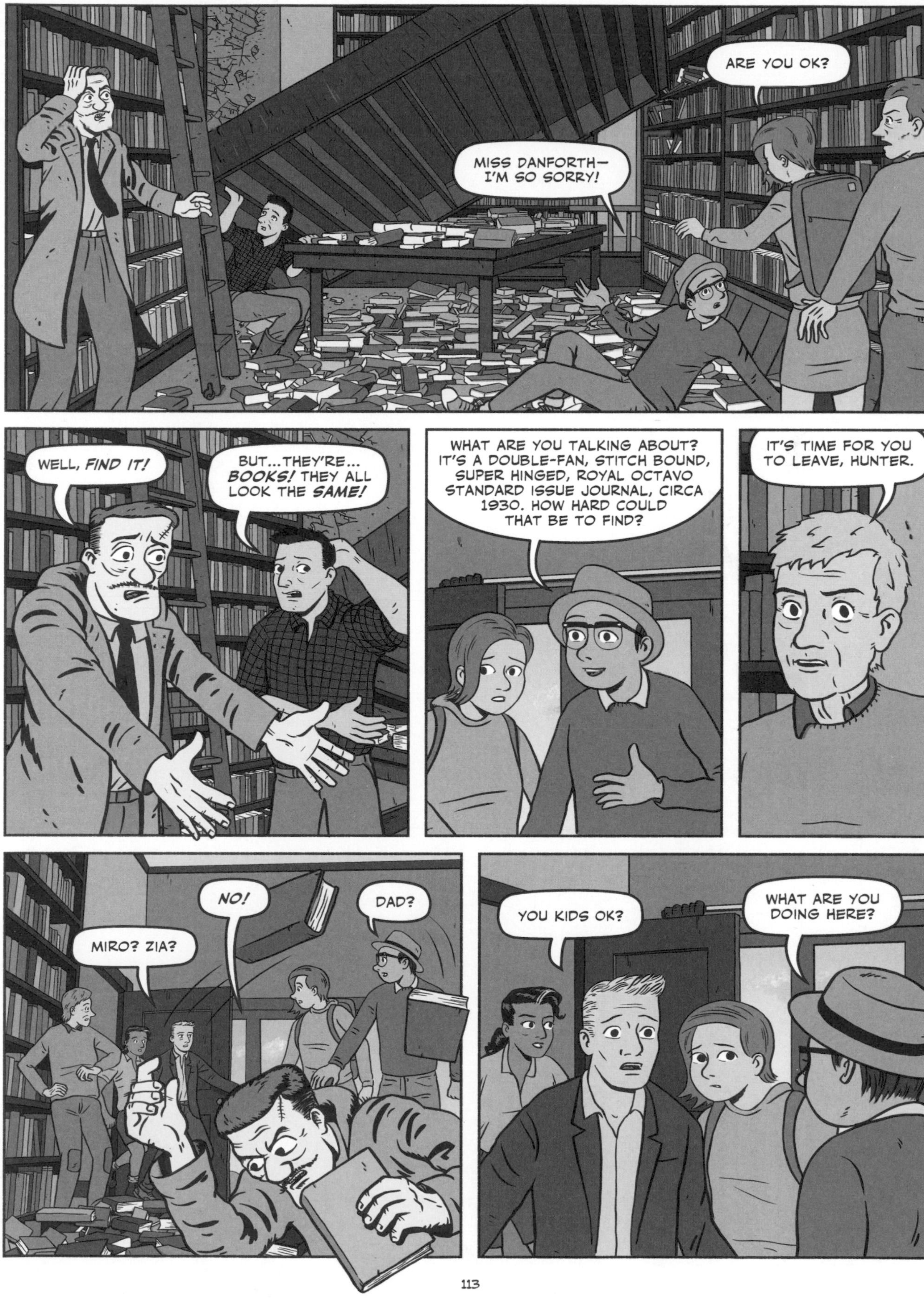
ARE YOU OK?
MISS DANFORTH— I'M SO SORRY!
WELL, *FIND IT!*
BUT...THEY'RE... ***BOOKS!*** THEY ALL LOOK THE ***SAME!***
WHAT ARE YOU TALKING ABOUT? IT'S A DOUBLE-FAN, STITCH BOUND, SUPER HINGED, ROYAL OCTAVO STANDARD ISSUE JOURNAL, CIRCA 1930. HOW HARD COULD THAT BE TO FIND?
IT'S TIME FOR YOU TO LEAVE, HUNTER.
MIRO? ZIA?
NO!
DAD?
YOU KIDS OK?
WHAT ARE YOU DOING HERE?

DOC SAW THE BOAT PICK YOU UP—

THEN WE SAW IT ANCHORED HERE AND—

DR. TEMPLE, YOUR SON HAS—

DONE *THIS?* I'M SO SORRY. WE'LL—

NO—

THESE CHILDREN HAVE *RETURNED* SOMETHING VERY *IMPORTANT* TO ME.

I'M VERY GRATEFUL TO THEM.

THE BOOK. GOOD WORK, YOU TWO.

OK. WOW. WELL DONE, YOU GUYS.

WHERE IS IT?

DAD, CATCH—

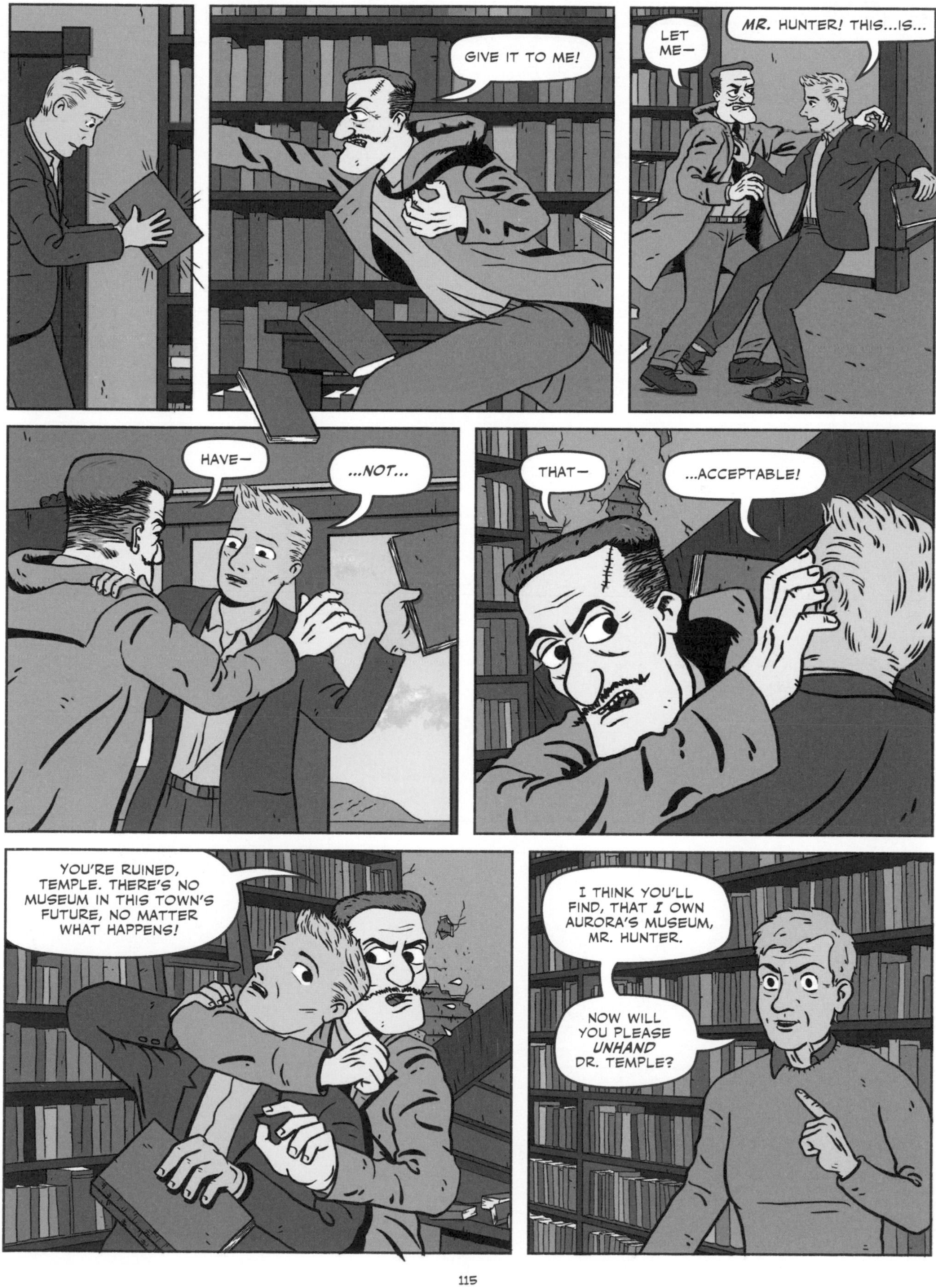
GIVE IT TO ME!
LET ME—
MR. HUNTER! THIS...IS...
HAVE—
...NOT...
THAT—
...ACCEPTABLE!
YOU'RE RUINED, TEMPLE. THERE'S NO MUSEUM IN THIS TOWN'S FUTURE, NO MATTER WHAT HAPPENS!
I THINK YOU'LL FIND, THAT I OWN AURORA'S MUSEUM, MR. HUNTER.
NOW WILL YOU PLEASE UNHAND DR. TEMPLE?

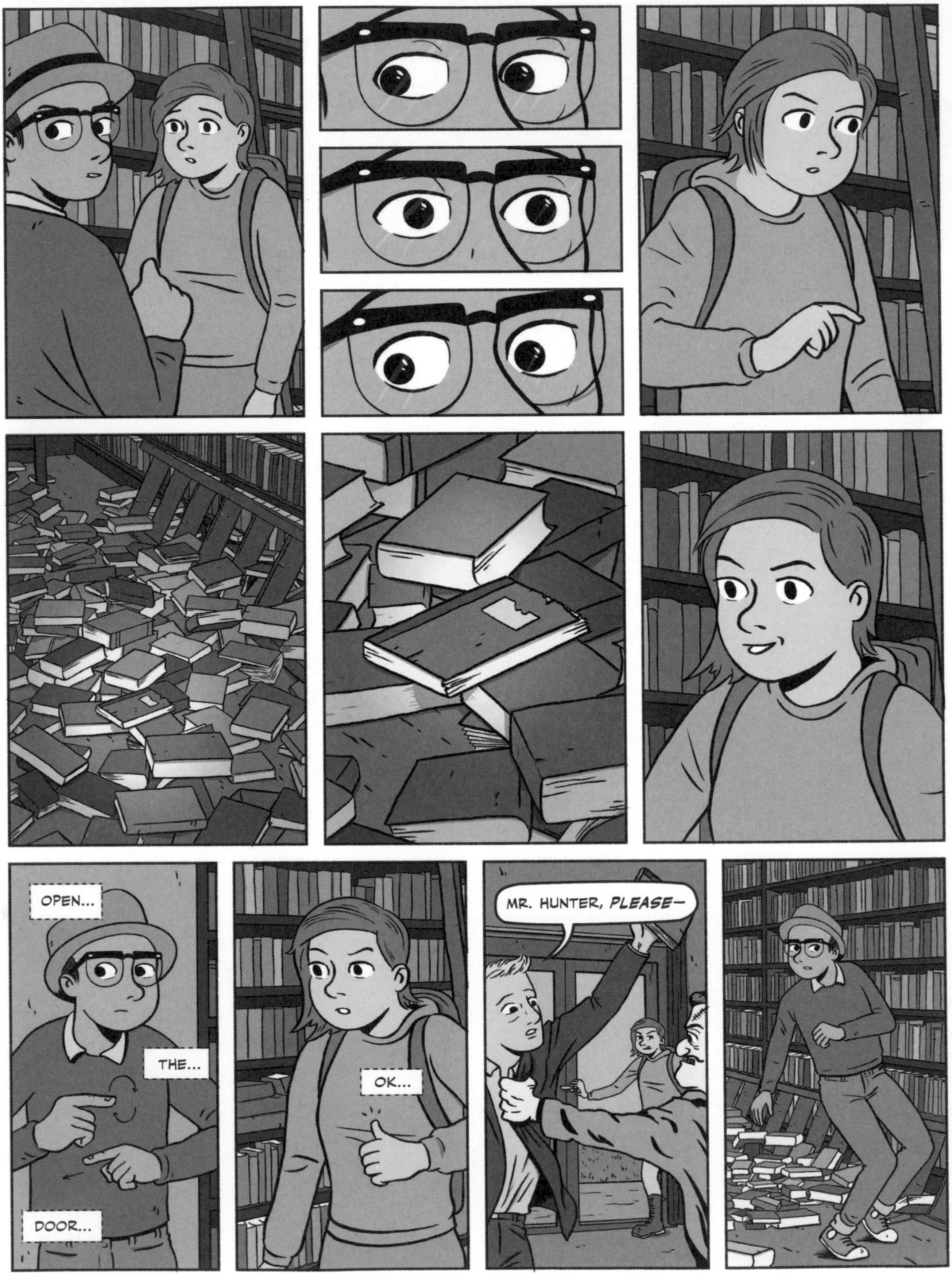
OPEN...
THE...
DOOR...
OK...
MR. HUNTER, *PLEASE*—

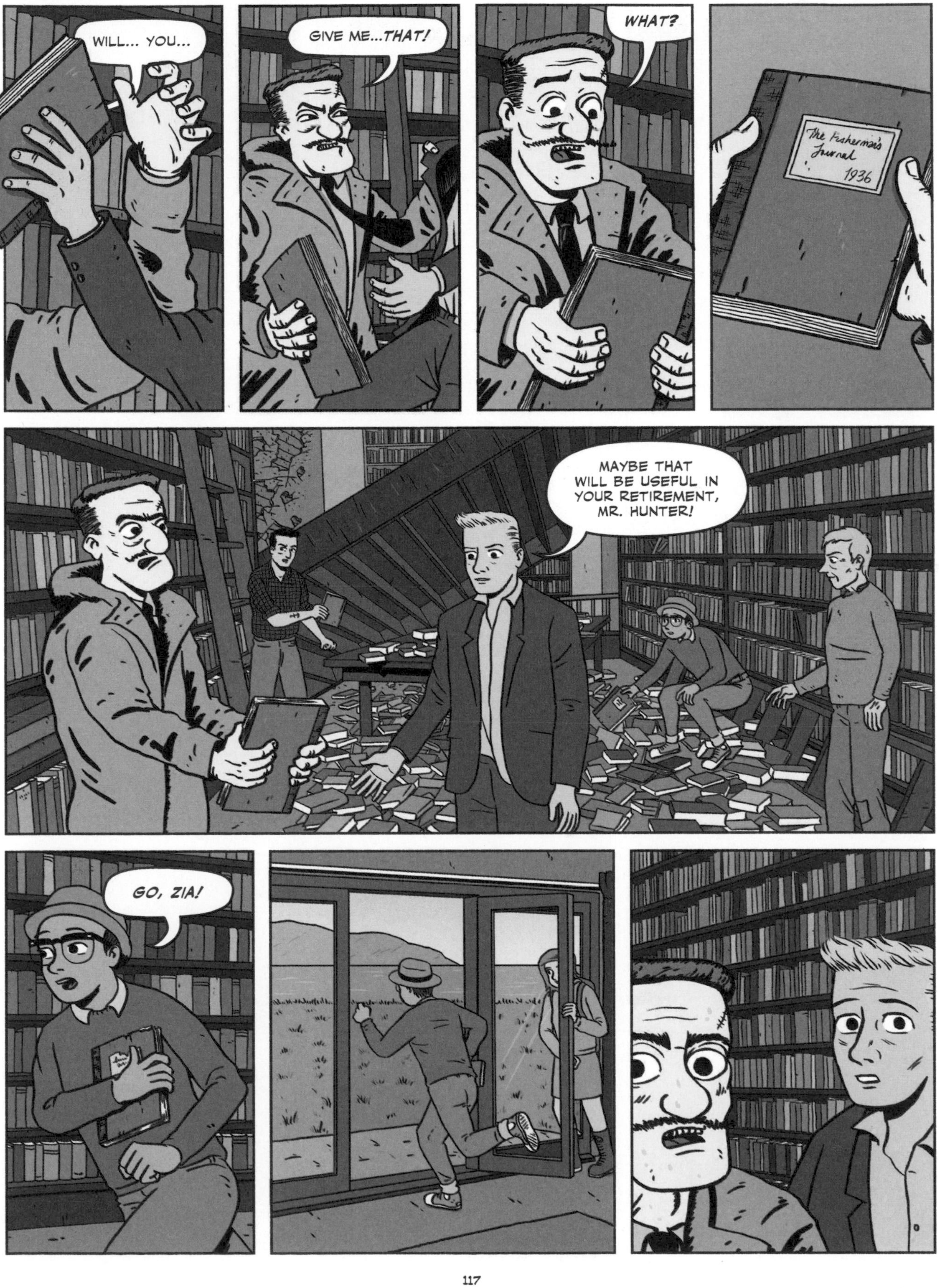
WILL... YOU...
GIVE ME...THAT!
WHAT?
The Fisherman's Journal 1936
MAYBE THAT WILL BE USEFUL IN YOUR RETIREMENT, MR. HUNTER!
GO, ZIA!

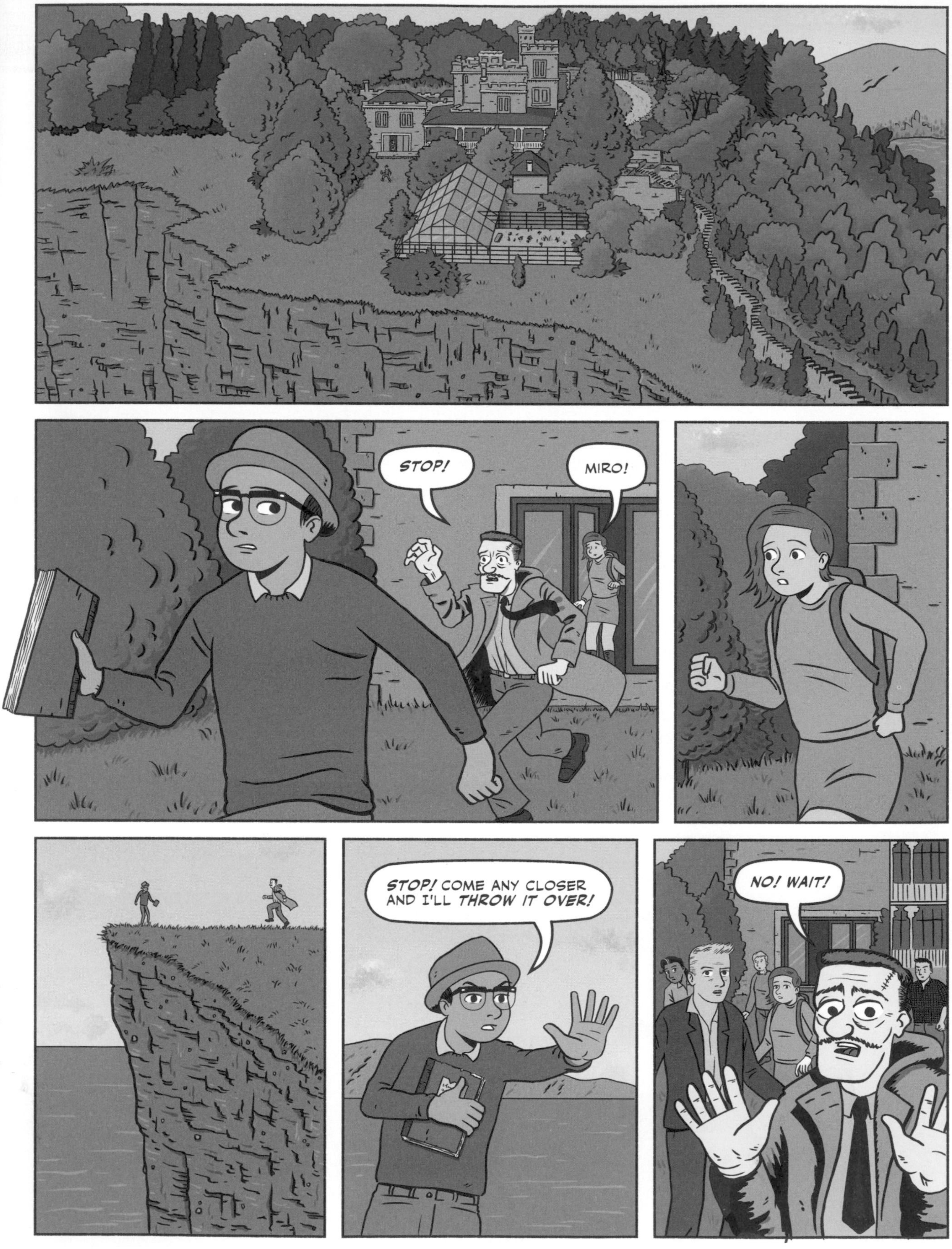
STOP!
MIRO!
STOP! COME ANY CLOSER AND I'LL THROW IT OVER!
NO! WAIT!

MIRO—BE CAREFUL! COME BACK, PLEASE.

YOU WON'T DO IT, BOY. I KNOW YOU: BOOKS ARE *YOUR THING*, AREN'T THEY? YOUR HOBBY? NOW STEP THIS WAY AND GIVE ME WHAT IS RIGHTFULLY *MINE.*

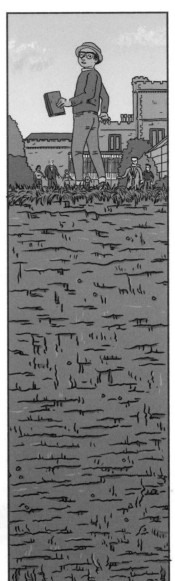

NOD

THIS BOOK BELONGS... *TO THE SEA.*

NOOOOOOOOOOOO

119

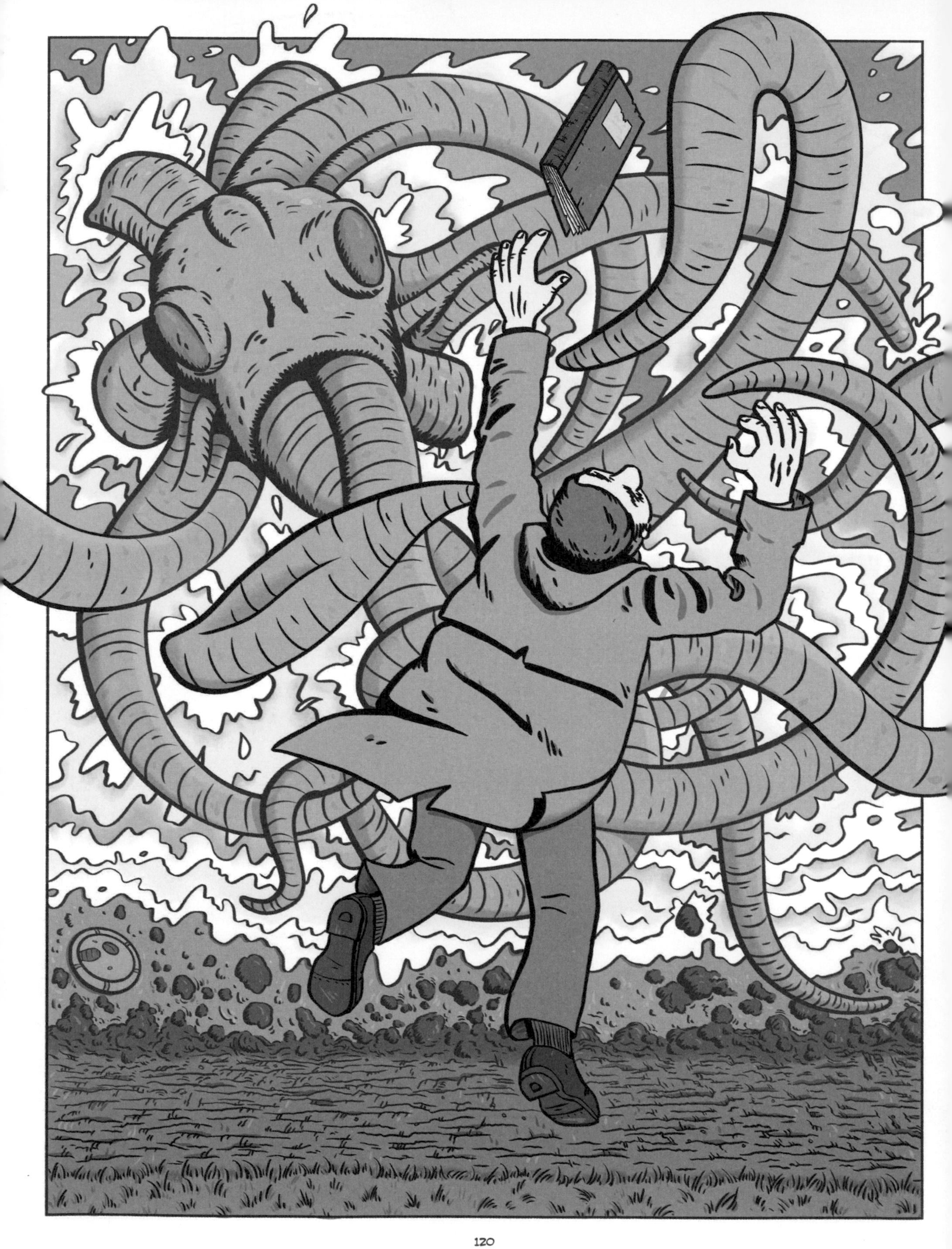

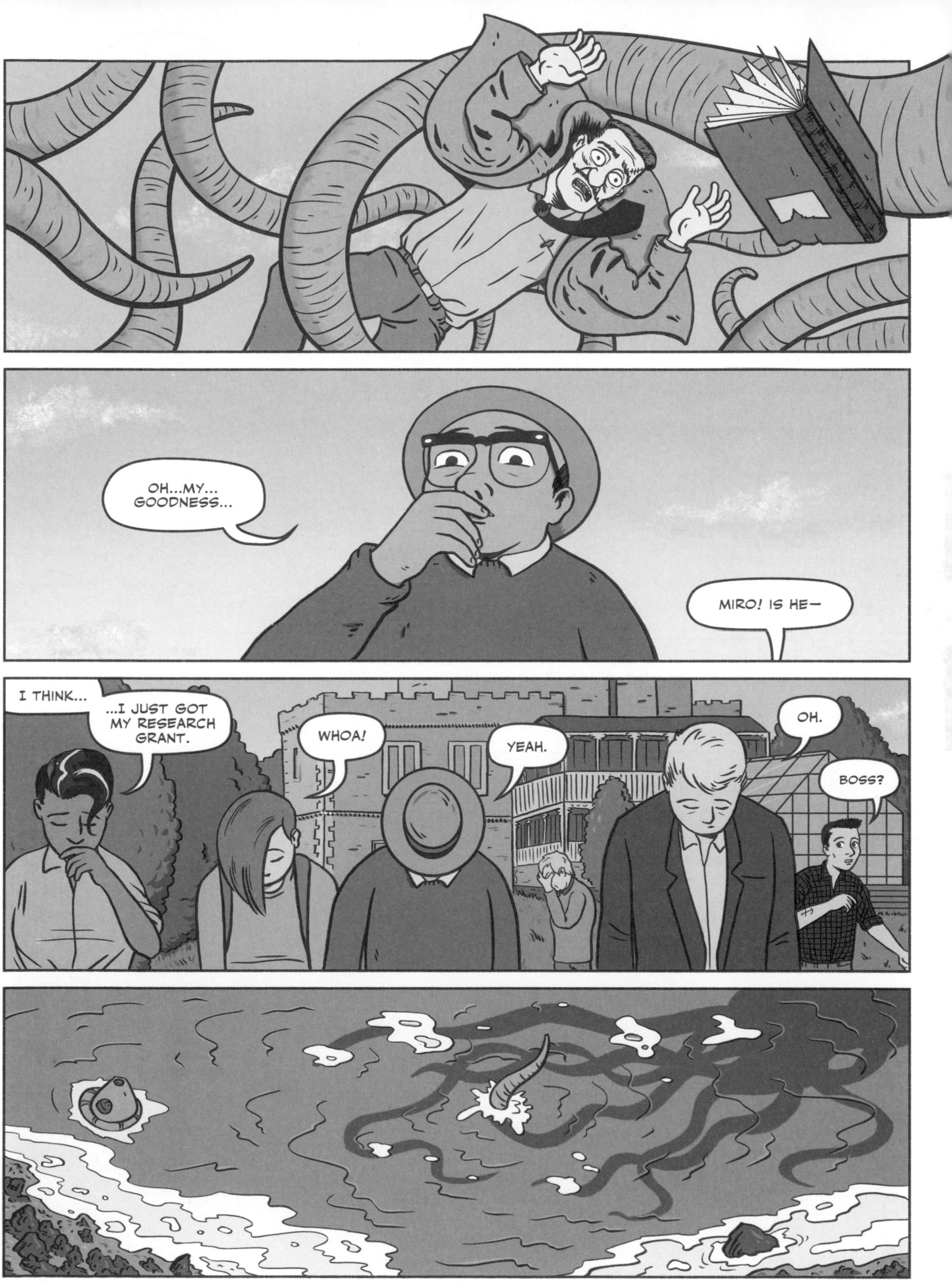
OH...MY... GOODNESS...
MIRO! IS HE—
I THINK...
...I JUST GOT MY RESEARCH GRANT.
WHOA!
YEAH.
OH.
BOSS?

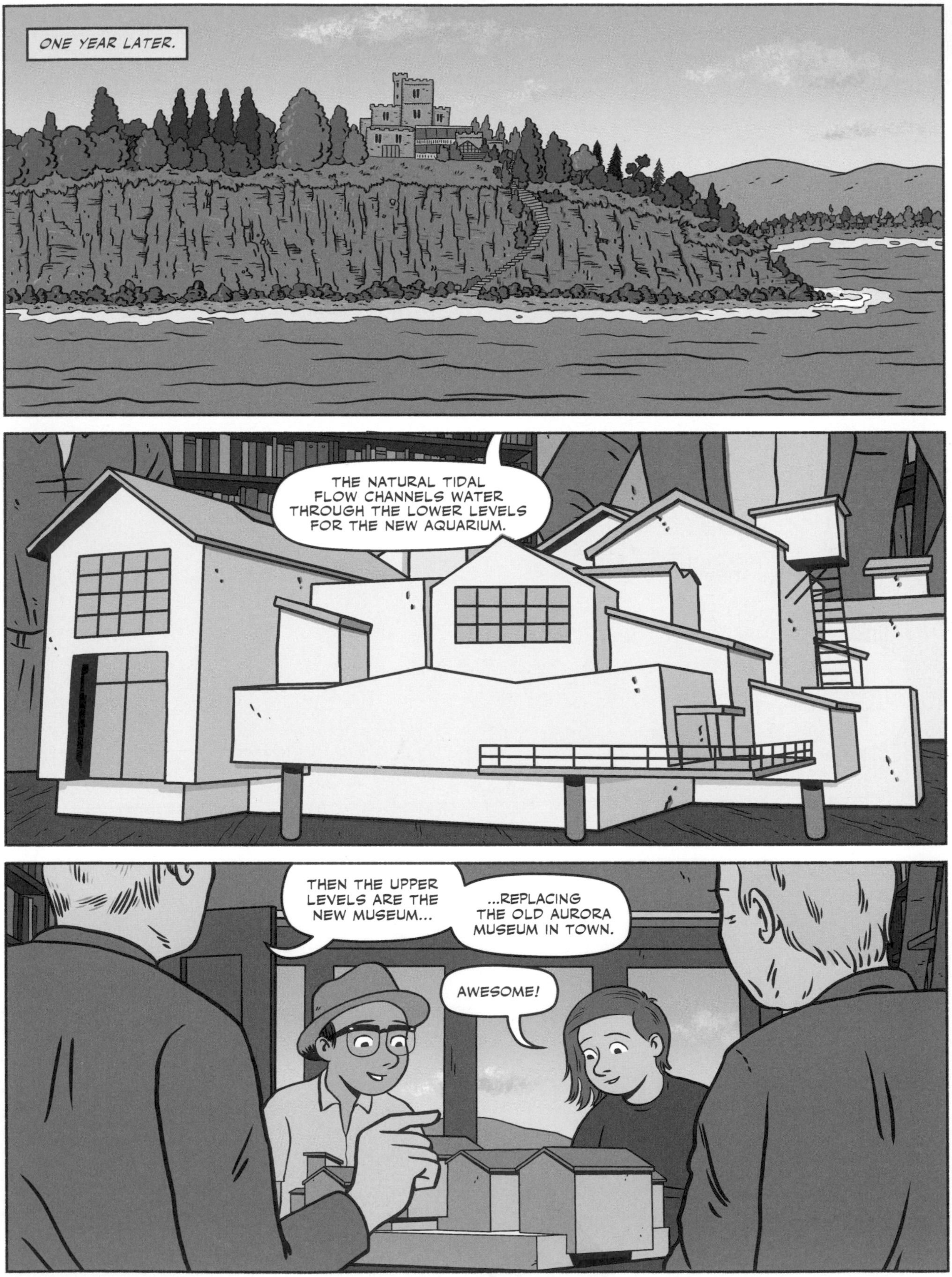
ONE YEAR LATER.
THE NATURAL TIDAL FLOW CHANNELS WATER THROUGH THE LOWER LEVELS FOR THE NEW AQUARIUM.
THEN THE UPPER LEVELS ARE THE NEW MUSEUM...
...REPLACING THE OLD AURORA MUSEUM IN TOWN.
AWESOME!

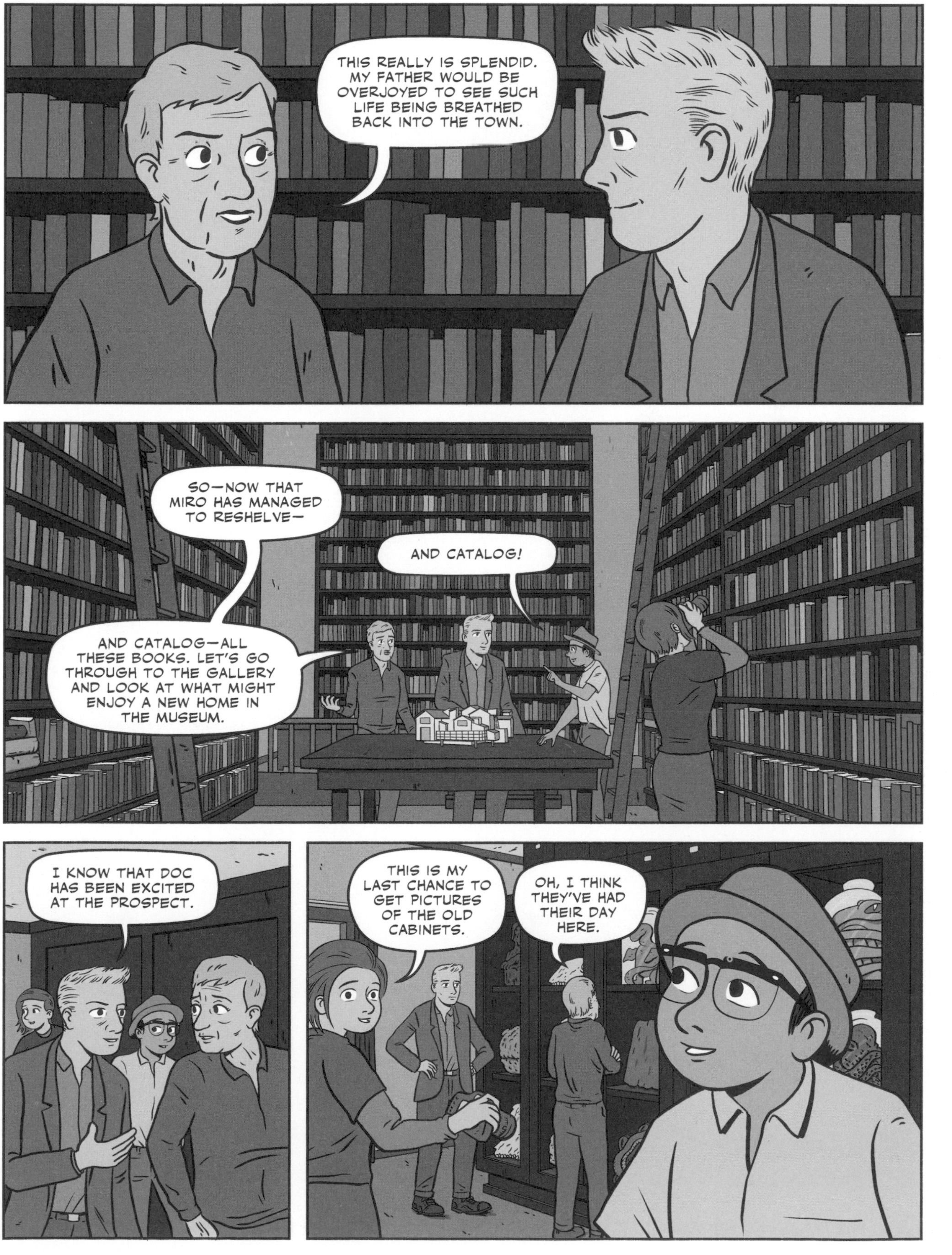
THIS REALLY IS SPLENDID. MY FATHER WOULD BE OVERJOYED TO SEE SUCH LIFE BEING BREATHED BACK INTO THE TOWN.
SO—NOW THAT MIRO HAS MANAGED TO RESHELVE—
AND CATALOG!
AND CATALOG—ALL THESE BOOKS. LET'S GO THROUGH TO THE GALLERY AND LOOK AT WHAT MIGHT ENJOY A NEW HOME IN THE MUSEUM.
I KNOW THAT DOC HAS BEEN EXCITED AT THE PROSPECT.
THIS IS MY LAST CHANCE TO GET PICTURES OF THE OLD CABINETS.
OH, I THINK THEY'VE HAD THEIR DAY HERE.

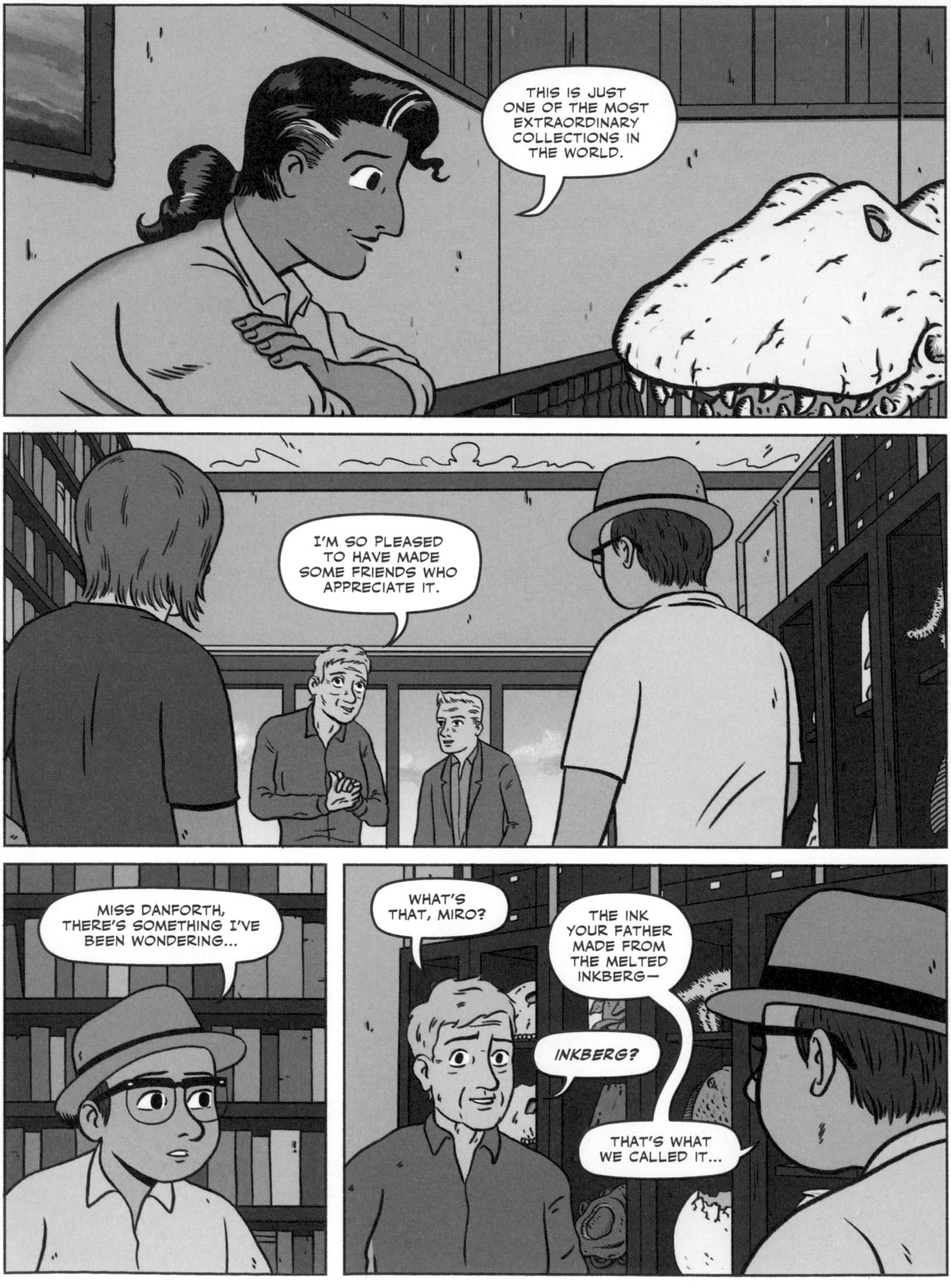
THIS IS JUST ONE OF THE MOST EXTRAORDINARY COLLECTIONS IN THE WORLD.
I'M SO PLEASED TO HAVE MADE SOME FRIENDS WHO APPRECIATE IT.
MISS DANFORTH, THERE'S SOMETHING I'VE BEEN WONDERING...
WHAT'S THAT, MIRO?
THE INK YOUR FATHER MADE FROM THE MELTED INKBERG—
INKBERG?
THAT'S WHAT WE CALLED IT...

WAS THERE ANY OF THE *INK* LEFT WHEN HE RETURNED?

WELL...YES.

THERE WAS— JUST A LITTLE.

AND WHEN I THOUGHT I'D LOST THE BOOK I WANTED TO *KEEP IT CLOSE.*

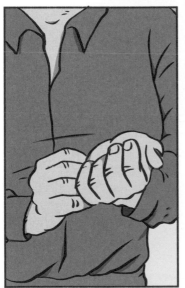

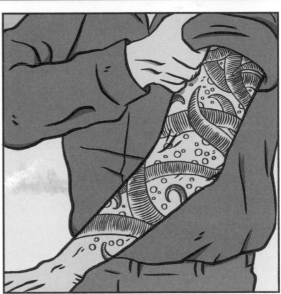

BUT LET'S JUST KEEP THAT BETWEEN US, SHALL WE?

THANKS TO

MY FAMILY, FOR THEIR FORBEARANCE
AS I COMPLETED THIS BOOK.

JULIA MARSHALL AND RACHEL LAWSON AT
GECKO PRESS—FOR THEIR KIND INVITATION
TO COME IN AND TALK ABOUT A BOOK AND
FOR THEIR SUPPORT AND PATIENCE AS IT
CAME, FINALLY, TO FRUITION.

DYLAN HORROCKS—FOR HIS SUPPORT
AND ENCOURAGEMENT, AND THOUGHTFUL
EARLY READING AND ADVICE.

MATTHEW GRAINGER FOR, AS ALWAYS,
PERCEPTIVE READING AND ESSENTIAL ADVICE.

JAN PRIESTLEY FOR THE MUCH NEEDED
SPELL IN 'THE SANITORIUM'.

MIKE DICKISON FOR SHOWING US BEHIND THE
SCENES AT THE WHANGANUI MUSEUM.

CREATIVE NEW ZEALAND FOR THEIR SUPPORT.

KATE DE GOLDI & SUSAN PARIS, ADRIAN KINNAIRD,
AND DAMON KEEN & AMIE MAXWELL FOR
PUBLISHING MY COMICS ALONG THE WAY TO HERE.

THE INKBERG ENIGMA WAS DRAWN BY HAND
IN CLIP STUDIO ON AN IPAD PRO,
WITH CUSTOM BRUSHES BY @FRENDEN.

THIS TYPEFACE IS *HUSH HUSH* BY COMICRAFT.

SEE MORE COMICS AND CONTACT THE AUTHOR AT

WWW.JKING.NZ

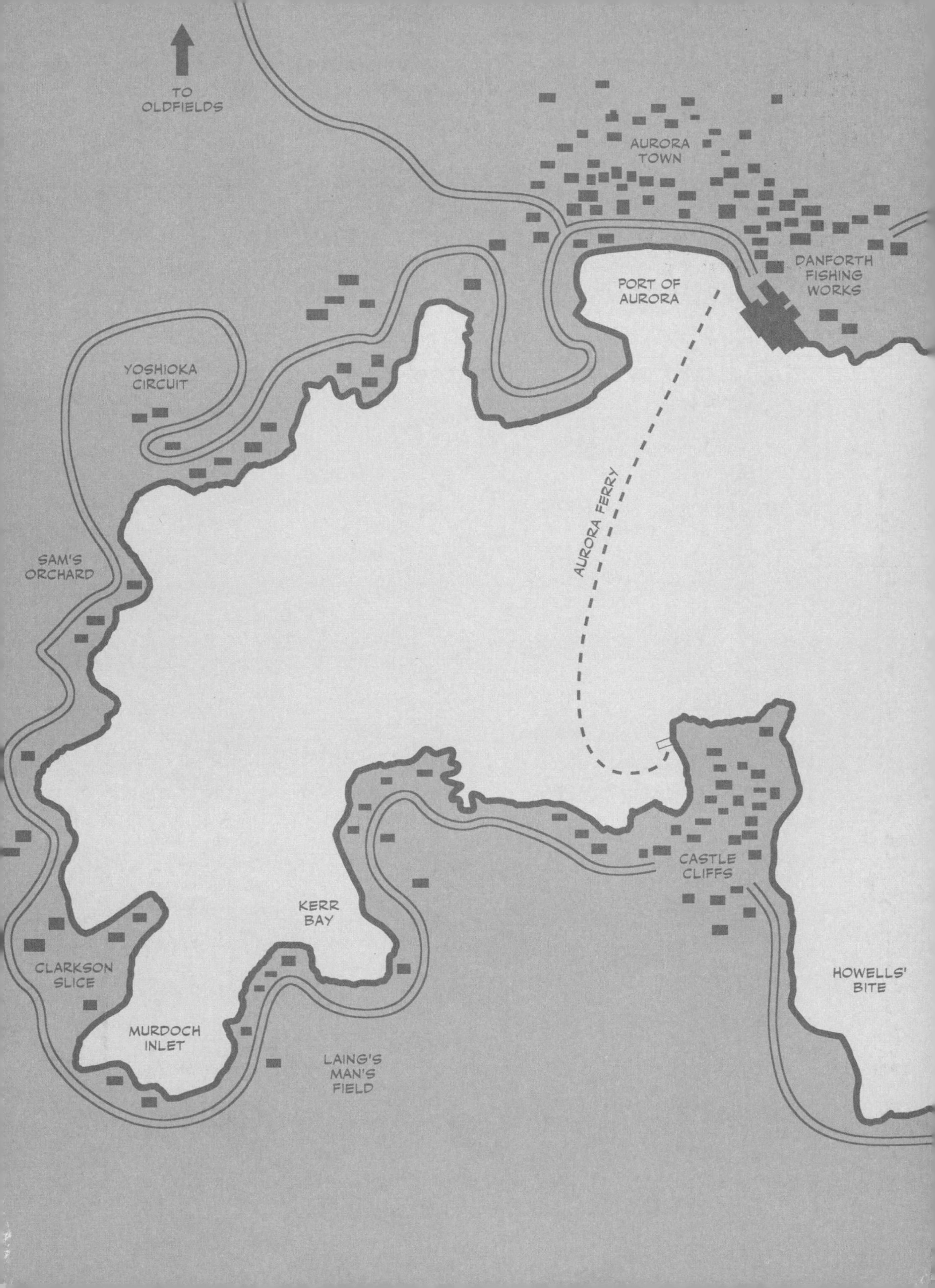
TO OLDFIELDS
AURORA TOWN
DANFORTH FISHING WORKS
PORT OF AURORA
YOSHIOKA CIRCUIT
AURORA FERRY
SAM'S ORCHARD
KERR BAY
CASTLE CLIFFS
CLARKSON SLICE
HOWELLS' BITE
MURDOCH INLET
LAING'S MAN'S FIELD